DOOM CASTL

NEIL. MUNRO was born in 1863, the illegitimate son of an Inveraray kitchen-maid. After leaving school, he worked for a time in a lawyer's office, before leaving the Highlands for a career in journalism, eventually editing the *Glasgow Evening News*. However, it was his work as a poet and novelist that established Munro as one of Scotland's finest writers. His historical novels, such as *Doom Castle*, were acknowledged as masterpieces of the genre; but he also achieved great success with the *Para Handy* tales and other light-hearted stories he wrote under the pseudonym Hugh Foulis. *Doom Castle* was Munro's second novel. Neil Munro died in 1930.

Other B&W titles by Neil Munro

THE NEW ROAD
JOHN SPLENDID

DOOM CASTLE

NEIL MUNRO

Introduced by Brian D Osborne

EDINBURGH
B&W PUBLISHING
1996

First published 1901
This edition © 1996
B&W Publishing Ltd
Edinburgh
Introduction © Brian D Osborne 1996
ISBN 1 873631 51 0

The publisher acknowledges subsidy
from the Scottish Arts Council towards
the publication of this volume.

British Library Cataloguing in Publication Data:
A catalogue record for this book is available
from the British Library.

Cover illustration:
Detail from *John Long Bateman, Esq.*
by Stephen Slaughter (1697-1765)
reproduced by kind permission
of The Bridgeman Art Library.

Printed by Werner Söderström

CONTENTS

INTRODUCTION

Brian D Osborne

When *Doom Castle* was published by the Edinburgh publishing house of William Blackwood & Sons in May 1901, after earlier serialisation in *Blackwood's Magazine*, it received extremely favourable notices. The *Glasgow Herald* critic felt that it added greatly to Munro's "reputation as a writer of romance" and praised its "compactness and dramatic interest". The Edinburgh-based *British Weekly* had few reservations about the standards which should be applied in judging the book: "In *Doom Castle* we have the first essential of a great work of fiction—a plot of great interest. Since *Kidnapped* and *Catriona* there has been no Scottish novel of more unmistakable genius." This comparison with the works of Robert Louis Stevenson, then just six years dead, was one which many other critics would make, particularly in connection with Munro's later, and perhaps greatest, novel *The New Road*.

Doom Castle also attracted lavish praise from English critics—the journal *Literature* had no reservations: "The best and most sincere Highland historical romance that has ever been published", while the *Morning Post* considered that "*Doom Castle* as a story is the best that Mr Munro has yet written, as he alone of modern novelists can write, with an atmosphere and poetry all of his own". The *Pall Mall Gazette* clearly placed the author in the top flight of contemporaries: "Mr Munro may now be ranked with absolute confidence among the small company of novelists whose work really counts as literature." A slightly discordant note came from the prestigious literary weekly *The Athenaeum*, whose reviewer suggested that "The author of *John Splendid* has not entirely maintained the level of that excellent romance in his present story, which is slighter in texture, although the fabric is still

vii

tartan of the genuine dye". The *Spectator*, on the other hand, felt that *Doom Castle* "Maintains the repute of the author of *John Splendid* as an ingenious and vivid romancer, with a just sense of the pageantry of words and a singular appreciation of the peculiar qualities of the Highlander."

The modern reader, coming fresh to Munro's novels, might well wonder why works which once won such high praise have for so long been out of print, and might well harbour the suspicion that the market place has been, in the long run, a better judge of them than the literary establishment of 1901. It is undoubtedly true that Munro's historical novels, like *John Splendid*, *The New Road* and *Doom Castle*, have suffered an undeserved eclipse but they are, most certainly, still well worth the attention of readers almost a century after their first appearance. They are in fact works of historical fiction of the first rank. What may well strike a new reader of *Doom Castle* are just those qualities that so impressed the *Spectator's* reviewer: "the pageantry of words and a singular appreciation of the peculiar qualities of the Highlander."

With *Doom Castle* Munro returned to his beloved Argyll-shire and to Inveraray and Loch Fyne which are at the heart of most of his writing. His hero, for once, is not a Scot. Count Victor Jean de Montaiglon is a Frenchman come to Argyllshire in search of revenge upon a mysterious Scotsman— Drimdarroch—who had moved among the Scots Jacobite exiles in France, and had betrayed both them and Victor's love, Cécile. When Victor arrives on Loch Fyne-side he is attacked by a band of broken men and seeks refuge in Doom Castle, the last remnant of the estate of Baron Lamond, a Jacobite sympa-thiser, to whom Victor had been recommended by one of the Scots émigré community in France.

Victor's mission to Scotland takes place in the autumn of 1752, the year in which James Stewart of the Glen was tried in Inveraray for the murder of Colin Campbell of Glenure—the Appin Murder. Indeed Victor sees the military escort taking Stewart to his trial—an assize which Stevenson had so memorably described in *Kidnapped*:

"... it'll be tried in Inverara, the Campbell's head place; with fifteen Campbells in the jury-box, and the biggest Campbell of all (and that's the Duke*) sitting cocking on the bench."

However, with Munro's rather cavalier disregard for accurate chronology he has, in Chapter 13, the Duke of Argyll chiding his Chamberlain, Simon MacTaggart: "Wake up, Sim! wake up! this is '55 . . ." Oddly enough, Stevenson, in *Kidnapped*, also changed the date of the Appin Murder. There is no reason, though, to suppose that Munro's story needs a later setting, and the reference to 1755 seems simply to be a slip.

Doom Castle's inhabitants show Munro's strengths and weaknesses as a portrayer of character, with the male characters being somewhat more interesting and developed than the female. Lamond is a sympathetically drawn character, although somewhat pathetic in his misfortune. We see him in a private room in the castle dressing himself in the tartan made illegal by the post-Culloden Disarming Act of 1746, and buckling on the forbidden accoutrements of his nation and rank—the bonnet with eagle plumes, the knife, pistols, dirk, and sword: ". . . with every item of the discarded and degraded costume of his race he seemed to put on a grace not there before, a manliness, a spirit that had lain in abeyance with the clothes in that mothy chest."

Lamond is a man out of his proper age, a man finding great difficulty in adjusting to the changing times: "I have been robbed of credit, and even of my name: I have seen king and country foully done by, and black affront brought on our people . . ."

His daughter Olivia, who it emerges is in love with MacTaggart, the Duke's Chamberlain, is a less convincing character, but one who quickly enough wins Montaiglon's

---

* Archibald Campbell, the 3rd Duke of Argyll (1682-1761), was at once the head of Clan Campbell and as such a supporter of the House of Hanover against the Jacobite cause, the head of the Scottish judiciary as Lord Justice General and also one of the Government's principal political managers in Scotland.

ix

heart. The other female occupant of Doom Castle, the Highland servant with the second sight, Annapla, is only remarkable for her name.

Doom Castle may be in the Highlands, but its steward, general factotum and man of all work, Mungo Boyd, is a pawky son of the Kingdom of Fife. His colourful speech and idiomatic humour show Munro's ability to depict Lowland characters as well as Highland. The militarily inclined Boyd boasts to Montaiglon about Scottish fighting men: "Scots regiments, sir, a' the warld ower, hae had the best o't for fechtin', marchin', or glory." Unfortunately, when the Frenchman asks the servant if he had served himself, the bold Mungo is forced to admit: ". . . no jist a'thegether what ye micht call i' the wars—though in a mainner o' speakin', gey near't. . . . If it hadnae been for the want o' a half inch or thereby in the height o' my heels I wad hae been in the airmy mysel'."

However, the irrepressible Mungo succeeds in delivering a characteristically Scottish put-down to Doom Castle's aristocratic French visitor: "Ye were daunderin' aboot the lobby wi' thae fine French manners I hae heard o'—frae the French theirsels . . ." In Mungo Boyd, Munro has created a servant figure worthy to be mentioned alongside such characters from Walter Scott as Andrew Fairservice in *Rob Roy* and Caleb Balderstone in *The Bride of Lammermuir*.

Montaiglon, who has listened to the Scots Jacobite exiles boasting of their ancestral castles, is less than impressed by the austerity and poverty of Doom Castle—a fictionalised version of Dunderave Castle, a stronghold of the Clan MacNachtan—some six miles from Inveraray, on Loch Fyneside. He eventually gets to Inveraray Castle, and is suitably impressed by the seat of the all-powerful Duke of Argyll. The building Montaiglon would have seen, and attended a Ducal Ball in, was the old castle. Construction of the present home of the Dukes of Argyll was started under Duke Archibald—the Duke of this novel—but it was not a habitable residence until after 1758. Nevertheless, Munro's description owes more to the new castle than to the old tower house it replaced. Munro also contrives to give Duke Archibald a wife, Jean, with whom he is "a very boy in love". Indeed it is in the Duchess Jean's honour that the Ball is held. However, when one considers that the historical record shows that the Duke had been unhappily married to Anne Whitfield for just ten years, had been a widower since 1723, and incidentally was a widower with a mistress by whom he had at least three illegitimate children, one may conclude that *Doom Castle*, for all its merits as fiction, is not to be relied on as architectural or family history. A further point here is that the Duke is said to be 66 years old, which would make the period of the novel's action 1748 rather than 1752. Munro blithely ignores such minutiae of history in his search for the bigger picture and the underlying truths about the effects of historical change on his native land and people.

Doom Castle is in the grand tradition of Munro's novels. His finest work is set in and around Argyllshire at a variety of critical moments when the process of change and the advent of new ways was affecting the old settled order of the Highlands. In *John Splendid*, set in the period of the Wars of the Covenant, we find a new type of chief for Clan Campbell—a man quite unlike the generations of warriors who had previously ruled Argyll with the sword; a complex man of policy, of plans and self-doubt. *The New Road*, set in the period between the two Jacobite Risings, has the new military road built by General Wade as the instrument of change. *Doom Castle* is set at a time when the Government's attack on the clan system—signalled by the abolition of the ancient heritable jurisdiction of the clan chiefs, and the ban on carrying arms and the wearing of tartan—was starting to work its effects on Highland society. We see the old order, represented by the Baron of Doom, in full retreat. The Baron remarks near the end of the novel: "We builded with the sword, and fell upon the sheepskin", a reference to the legal documents, inscribed on vellum or sheepskin, which now regulated life and which, by the Baron's various legal misfortunes, had resulted in the loss of most of his lands. Even the two castles of the novel can be seen as potent symbols of this change— Doom Castle, with its foreboding inscription: "Doom. Man,

Behauld the End of All. Be Nocht Wiser than the Hiest. Hope in God!" is a plain, stark, chieftain's tower, fallen on hard times, with scarce even a crust to spare for the beggar at the door. Duke Archibald's new Castle of Inveraray is a Gothic fantasy, a palace for *MacCailein Mór*, set in a new planned town, part of a remarkable assembly of buildings which impressed Dr Samuel Johnson when he visited Inveraray some twenty years later: "What I admire here is the total defiance of expence."

In 1909 Neil Munro, at the height of his fame as a novelist, was made a Freeman of Inveraray. Referring to his home town in his speech of thanks to the Town Council, Munro was quoted as saying that ever since he had begun to write seriously he had never written anything that came within reasonable distance of pleasing him about any place else. He never apparently could keep Inveraray and the romantic district of Argyll out of any story of his, and possibly he never would. It might be said, by those who understood the scope and principles of art, to be a very small field to till, but he was certain that if he wrote about the scenes and characters of his native county for fifty years he could not exhaust the possibilities, however much he might misapply his opportunities. For the things they loved intensely were the only things worth writing about in poetry or romance, and the parish was a miniature of the world.

Munro undoubtedly loved his native town in spite of all the difficulties that must surely have surrounded his early life there. He was born in 1863, the illegitimate son of Ann Munro, a kitchen maid; and rumour persistently identifies his father as a member of the family of the Dukes of Argyll. This connection is perhaps lent additional credence by his finding employment, on leaving the local school, in the office of the Sheriff-Clerk of Argyllshire. This appointment is described in Munro's own words: "When I was fourteen or fifteen years of age, I was insinuated, without any regard for my own desires, into a country lawyer's office . . ." Like many Highlanders, before and since, Munro had to leave his home to follow his chosen career, first as a journalist and then as a novelist. He left Inveraray but, as his 1909 remarks suggest, Inveraray never left him, and many lyrically descriptive passages in *Doom Castle* testify to this. Even the light-hearted newspaper stories about Para Handy and the crew of the puffer "Vital Spark", the works for which he is now best known, are mostly set in Loch Fyne; and characteristically he named his last home, in Helensburgh, "Cromalt", after a stream in Inveraray.

In 1935, five years after his death, a monument was erected to the memory of Munro in a remote spot in Glen Aray. Significantly, perhaps, a site did not seem to be available nearer to Inveraray, on the Duke of Argyll's extensive lands. At the dedication of the monument the Scottish traveller, writer, politician, aristocrat and revolutionary, Robert Bontine Cunningham-Graham, said of Munro that he was "the apostolic successor of Sir Walter Scott", and went on to remark that his characters ". . . were real men, with blood in their veins, who knew how to wield the sword gloriously and had the gift of oratory, which were the natural gifts of the Gael."

Doom Castle certainly reveals all the romantic characteristics to which Cunningham-Graham refers. It is full of the excitement of ambush, midnight raid, romance and duel, and real men are certainly present—for example in the well-drawn portrait of the heroic Montaiglon, who learns to reject the backward-looking, and essentially sterile, idea of vengeance that had brought him to Scotland. However, *Doom Castle* does much more than this—it also reveals Munro's very considerable insight into the complexities of Highland character, and moreover into those of Highland history. He is indeed in the tradition of Sir Walter Scott in his use of history, not simply as a colourful background setting for a story, but as a potent force that shapes his character's lives. Munro's response to the changes he records always seems ambivalent— at once regretting the passing of the old ways while recognising their moral defects and the historical inevitability of their disappearance. This contradictory nature, and the accompanying sense of detachment, runs through all his work—it was surely no accident that Munro chose the pen-name of "The Looker-On" for his regular column in the *Evening News*.

I

Count Victor Comes to a Strange Country

It was an afternoon in autumn, with a sound of wintry breakers on the shore, the tall woods copper-colour, the thickets dishevelled, and the nuts, in the corries of Ardkinglas, the braes of Ardno, dropping upon bracken burned to gold. Until he was out of the glen and into the open land, the traveller could scarcely conceive that what by his chart was no more than an arm of the ocean could make so much ado; but when he found the incoming tide fretted here and there by black rocks, and elsewhere, in little bays, the beaches strewn with massive boulders, the high rumour of the sea-breakers in that breezy weather seemed more explicable. And still, for him, it was above all a country of appalling silence in spite of the tide thundering. Fresh from the pleasant rabble of Paris, the tumult of the streets, the unending gossip of the faubourgs that were at once his vexation and his joy, and from the eager ride that had brought him through Normandy when its orchards were busy from morning till night with cheerful peasants plucking fruit, his ear had not grown accustomed to the still of the valleys, the terrific hush of the mountains, in whose mist or sunshine he had ridden for two days. The woods, with leaves that fell continually about him, seemed in some swoon of nature, with no birds carolling on the boughs; the cloisters were monastic in their silence. A season of most dolorous influences, a land of sombre shadows and ravines, a day of sinister solitude; the sun slid through scudding clouds, high over a world blown upon by salt airs brisk and tonic, but man was wanting in those weary valleys, and the heart of Victor Jean, Comte de Montaiglon, was almost sick for very loneliness.

Thus it came as a relief to his ear, the removal of an oppression little longer to be endured, when he heard behind him what were

1

apparently the voices of the odd-looking uncouth natives he had seen a quarter of an hour ago lurking, silent but alert and peering, phantoms of old story rather than humans, in the fir-wood near a defile made by a brawling cataract. They had wakened no suspicions in his mind. It was true they were savage-looking rogues in a ragged plaid-cloth of a dull device, and they carried arms he had thought forbidden there by law. To a foreigner fresh from gentle lands there might well be a menace in their ambuscade, but he had known men of their race, if not of so savage an aspect, in the retinues of the Scots exiles who hung about the side-doors of Saint Germains, passed mysterious days between that domicile of tragic comedy and Avignon or Rome, or ruffled it on empty pockets at the gaming-tables, so he had no apprehension. Besides, he was in the country of the Argyll, at least on the verge of it; a territory accounted law-abiding even to dulness by every Scot he had known since he was a child at Cammercy, and snuff-strewn conspirators, come to meet his uncles, took him on their knees when a lull in the cards or wine permitted, and recounted their adventures for his entertainment in a villainous French: he could not guess that the gentry in the wood behind him had taken a fancy to his horse, that they were broken men (as the phrase of the country put it), and that when he had passed them at the cataract—a haughty, well-set-up *duine uasail* all alone with a fortune of silk and silver lace on his apparel and the fob of a watch dangling at his groin most temptingly—they had promptly put a valuation upon himself and his possessions, and decided that the same were sent by Providence for their enrichment.

Ten of them ran after him clamouring loudly to give the impression of larger numbers; he heard them with relief when oppressed by the inhuman solemnity of the scenery that was too deep in its swoon to give back even an echo to the breaker on the shore, and he drew up his horse, turned his head a little and listened, flushing with annoyance when the rude calls of his pursuers became, even in their unknown jargon, too plainly peremptory and meant for him.

"Dogs!" said he, "I wish I had a chance to open school here

and teach manners," and without more deliberation he set his horse to an amble, designed to betray neither complacency nor a poltroon's terrors.

"*Stad! stad!*" cried a voice closer than any of the rest behind him; he knew what was ordered by its accent, but no Montaiglon stopped to an insolent summons. He put the short rowels to the flanks of the sturdy lowland pony he bestrode, and conceded not so little as a look behind.

There was the explosion of a bell-mouthed musket and something smote the horse and spattered behind the rider's left boot. The beast swerved, gave a scream of pain, fell clumsily on its side. With an effort, Count Victor saved himself from the falling body and clutched his pistols. For a moment he stood bewildered at the head of the suffering animal. The pursuing shouts had ceased. Behind him, short hazel-trees clustering thick with nuts, reddening bramble, and rusty bracken, tangled together in a coarse rank curtain of vegetation, quite still and motionless (but for the breeze among the upper leaves), and the sombre distance, dark with pine, had the mystery of a vault. It was difficult to believe his pursuers harboured there, perhaps reloading the weapon that had put so doleful a conclusion to his travels with the gallant little horse he had bought on the coast of Fife. That silence, that prevailing mystery, seemed to be the essence and the mood of this land, so different from his own, where laughter was ringing in the orchards and a myriad towns and clamant cities brimmed with life.

II

The Pursuit

Nobody who had acquaintance with Victor de Montaiglon would call him coward. He had fought with De Grammont, and brought a wound from Dettingen under circumstances to set him up for life in a repute for valour, and half a score of duels were at his credit or discredit in the chronicles of Paris society.

And yet, somehow, standing there in an unknown country beside a brute companion wantonly struck down by a robber's shot, and the wood so still around, and the thundering sea so unfamiliar, he felt vastly uncomfortable, with a touch of more than physical apprehension. If the enemy would only manifest themselves to the eye and ear as well as to the unclassed senses that inform the instinct, it would be much more comfortable. Why did they not appear? Why did they not follow up their assault upon his horse? Why were they lurking in the silence of the thicket, so many of them, and he alone and so obviously at their mercy? The pistols he held provided the answer.

"What a rare delicacy!" said Count Victor, applying himself to the release of his mail from the saddle whereto it was strapped. "They would not interrupt my regretful tears. But for the true *élan* of the trade of robbery, give me old Cartouche picking pockets on the Pont Neuf."

While he loosened his mails with one hand, with the other he directed at the thicket one of the pistols that seemed of such wholesome influence. Then he slung the bags upon his shoulder and encouraged the animal to get upon its legs, but vainly, for the shot was fatal.

"Ah!" said he regretfully, "I must sacrifice my bridge and my good comrade. This is an affair!"

Twice—three times, he placed the pistol at the horse's head

and as often withdrew it, reluctant, a man, as all who knew him wondered at, gentle to womanliness with a brute, though in a cause against men the most bitter and sometimes cruel of opponents.

A rustle in the brake at last compelled him. "*Allons!*" said he impatiently with himself, "I do no more than I should have done with myself in the like case," and he pulled the trigger.

Then having deliberately charged the weapon anew, he moved off in the direction he had been taking when the attack was made.

It was still, he knew, some distance to the castle. Half an hour before his rencontre with those broken gentry, now stealing in his rear with the cunning and the bloodthirstiness of their once native wolves (and always, remember, with the possibility of the blunderbuss for aught that he could tell), he had, for the twentieth time since he left the port of Dysart, taken out the rude itinerary, written in ludicrous Scoto-English by Hugh Bethune, one time secretary to the Lord Marischal in exile, and read:

> . . . and so on to the Water of Leven (the brewster-wife at the howff near Loch Lomond mouth keeps a good glass of *aqua*), then by Luss (with an eye on the Gregarach), thereafter a bittock to Glencroe and down upon the House of Ardkinglas, a Hanoverian rat whom 'ware. Round the loch head and three miles further the Castle o' the Baron. Give him my devoirs and hopes to challenge him to a Bowl when Yon comes off which God kens there seems no hurry.

By that showing the castle of Baron Lamond must be within half an hour's walk of where he now moved without show of eagerness, yet quickly none the less, from a danger the more alarming because the extent of it could not be computed.

In a little the rough path he followed bent parallel with the sea. A tide at the making licked ardently upon sand-spits strewn with ware, and at the forelands, overhung by harsh and stunted seaside shrubs, the breakers rose tumultuous. On the sea there was utter vacancy; only a few screaming birds slanted above the wave, and the coast, curving far before him, gave his eye no sign at first of the castle to which he had got the route from M. Hugh Bethune.

Then his vision, that had been set for something more imposing, for the towers and embrasures of a stately domicile, if not for a Chantilly, at least for the equal of the paternal chateau in the Meuse valley, with multitudinous chimneys and the incense of kind luxuriant hearths, suave parks, gardens, and gravelled walks, contracted with dubiety and amazement upon a dismal tower perched upon a promontory.

Revealed against the brown hills and the sombre woods of the farther coast, it was scarcely a wonder that his eye had failed at first to find it. Here were no pomps of lord or baron; little luxuriance could prevail behind those eyeless gables; there could be no suave pleasance about those walls hanging over the noisy and inhospitable wave. No pomp, no pleasant amenities; the place seemed to jut into the sea, defying man's oldest and most bitter enemy, its gable ends and one crenellated bastion or turret betraying its sinister relation to its age, its whole aspect arrogant and unfriendly, essential of war. Caught suddenly by the vision that swept the fretted curve of the coast, it seemed blackly to perpetuate the spirit of the land, its silence, its solitude and terrors.

These reflections darted through the mind of Count Victor as he sped, monstrously uncomfortable with the burden of the bags that bobbed on his back, not to speak of the indignity of the office. It was not the kind of castle he had looked for; but a castle, in the narrow and squalid meaning of a penniless refugee like Bethune, it doubtless was, the only one apparent on the landscape, and therefore too obviously the one he sought.

"Very well, God is good!" said Count Victor, who, to tell all and leave no shred of misunderstanding, was in some regards the frankest of pagans, and he must be jogging on for its security.

But as he hurried, the ten broken men who had been fascinated by his too ostentatious fob and the extravagance of his

6

embroidery, and inspired furthermore by a natural detestation of any foreign *duine uasail* apparently bound for the seat of MacCailein Mor, gathered boldness, and soon he heard the thicket break again behind him.

He paused, turned sharply with the pistols in his hands. Instantly the wood enveloped his phantom foes; a bracken or two nodded, a hazel sapling swung back and forward more freely than the wind accounted for. And at the same time there rose on the afternoon the wail of a wildfowl high up on the hill, answered in a sharp and querulous too-responsive note of the same character in the wood before.

The gentleman who had twice fought *à la barrière* felt a nameless new thrill, a shudder of the being, born of antique terrors generations before his arms were quartered with those of Rochefoucauld and Modene.

It was becoming all too awkward, this affair. He broke into a more rapid walk, then into a run, with his eyes intent upon the rude dark keep that held the promontory, now the one object in all the landscape that had to his senses some aspect of human fellowship and sympathy.

The caterans were assured; *Dieu du ciel*, how they ran too! Those in advance broke into an appalling halloo, the shout of hunters on the heels of quarry. High above the voice of the breakers it sounded savage and alarming in the ears of Count Victor, and he fairly took to flight, the bags bobbing more ludicrously than ever on his back.

It was like the man, that, in spite of dreads not to be concealed from himself, he should be seized as he sped with a notion of the grotesque figure he must present, carrying that improper burden. He must even laugh when he thought of his austere punctilious maternal aunt, the Baronne de Chenier, and fancied her horror and disgust could she behold her nephew disgracing the De Chenier blood by carrying his own baggage and outraging several centuries of devilishly fine history by running—positively running—from ill-armed footpads who had never worn breeches. She would frown, her bosom would swell till her bodice would appear to crackle at the armpits, the seven hairs on her upper lip would bristle all the worse against her purpling face as she cried it was the little Lyons shopkeeper in his mother's grandfather that was in his craven legs. Doubt it who will, an imminent danger will not wholly dispel the sense of humour, and Montaiglon, as he ran before the footpads, laughed softly at the Baronne.

But a short knife with a black hilt hissed past his right ear and buried three-fourths of its length in the grass, and so abruptly spoiled the comedy. This was ridiculous. He stopped suddenly, turned him round about in a passion, and fired one of the pistols at an unfortunate robber too late to duck among the bracken. And the marvel was that the bullet found its home, for the aim was uncertain, and the shot meant more for an emphatic protest than for attack.

The gled's cry rose once more, rose higher on the hill, echoed far off, and was twice repeated nearer hand with a dropping melancholy cadence. Gaunt forms grew up straight among the undergrowth of trees, indifferent to the other pistol, and ran back or over to where the wounded comrade lay.

"Heaven's thunder!" cried Count Victor, "I wish I had aimed more carefully." He was appalled at the apparent tragedy of his act. A suicidal regret and curiosity kept him standing where he fired, with the pistol still smoking in his hand, till there came from the men clustered round the body in the brake a loud simultaneous wail unfamiliar to his ear, but unmistakable in its import. He turned and ran wildly for the tower that had no aspect of sanctuary in it; his heart drummed noisily at his breast; his mouth parched and gaped. In upon his lips in a little dropped water; he tasted the salt of his perspiration. And then he knew weariness, great weariness, that plucked at the sinews behind his knees, and felt sore along the hips and back—the result of his days of hard riding come suddenly to the surface. Truly he was not happy.

But if he ran wearily he ran well, better at least than his pursuers, who had their own reasons for taking it more leisurely, and in a while there was neither sight nor sound of the enemy.

He was beginning to get some satisfaction from this, when, turning a bend of the path within two hundred yards of the castle, behold an unmistakable enemy barred his way! An ugly, hoggish, obese man, with bare legs most grotesquely like pillars of granite and a protuberant paunch; but the devil must have been in his legs to carry him more swiftly than thoroughbred limbs had borne Count Victor. He stood sneering in the path, turning up the right sleeve of a soiled and ragged saffron shirt with his left hand, the right being engaged most ominously with a sword of a fashion that might well convince the Frenchman he had some new methods of fence to encounter in a few minutes.

High and low looked Count Victor as he slacked his pace, seeking for some way out of this sack, releasing as he did so the small sword from the tanglement of his skirts, and feeling the Mechlin deucedly in his way. As he approached closer to the man barring his path he relapsed into a walk and opened a parley in English that except for the slightest of accents had nothing in it of France, where he had long been the comrade of compatriots to this preposterous savage with the manners of mediæval Provence when footpads lived upon Damoiselle Picoree.

"My good fellow," said he airily, as one might open with a lackey, "I protest I am in a hurry, for my presence makes itself much desired elsewhere. I cannot comprehend why in Heaven's name so large a regiment of you should turn out to one unfortunate traveller."

The fat man fondled the brawn of his sword-arm and seemed to gloat upon the situation.

"Come, come!" said Count Victor, affecting a cheerfulness, "my waistcoat would scarcely adorn a man of your inches, and as for my pantaloons"—he looked at the ragged kilt—"as for my pantaloons, now on one's honour, would you care for them? They are so essentially a matter of custom."

He would have bantered on in this strain up to the very nose of the enemy, but the man in his path was utterly unresponsive to his humour. In truth he did not understand a word of the nobleman's pleasantry. He uttered something like a war-cry, threw his bonnet off a head as bald as an egg, and smote out vigorously with his broadsword.

Count Victor fired the pistol *à bout-portant* with deliberation; the flint, in the familiar irony of fate, missed fire, and there was nothing more to do with the treacherous weapon but to throw it in the face of the Highlander. It struck full; the trigger-guard gashed the jaw and the metalled butt spoiled the sight of an eye.

"This accounts for the mace in the De Chenier quartering," thought the Count whimsically. "It is obviously the weapon of the family." And he drew the rapier forth.

A favourite, a familiar arm, as the carriage of his head made clear at any time, he knew to use it with the instinct of the eyelash, but it seemed absurdly inadequate against the broad long weapon of his opponent, who had augmented his attack with a dirk drawn in the left hand, and sought lustily to bring death to his opponent by point as well as edge. A light dress rapier obviously must do its business quickly if it was not to suffer from the flailing blow of the claymore, and yet Count Victor did not wish to increase the evil impression of his first visit to this country by a second homicide, even in self-defence. He measured the paunched rascal with a rapid eye, and with a flick at the left wrist disarmed him of his poignard. Furiously the Gael thrashed with the sword, closing up too near on his opponent. Count Victor broke ground, beat an appeal that confused his adversary, lunged, and skewered him through the thick of the active arm.

The Highlander dropped his weapon and bawled lamentably as he tried to stanch the copious blood; and safe from his further interference, Count Victor took to his heels again.

Where the encounter with the obese and now discomfited Gael took place was within a hundred yards of the castle, whose basement and approach were concealed by a growth of stunted whin. Towards the castle Count Victor rushed, still hearing the shouts in the wood behind, and as he seemed, in spite of his burden, to be gaining ground upon his pursuers, he was elate at the prospect of escape. In his gladness he threw a taunting cry behind, a hunter's greenwood challenge.

And then he came upon the edge of the sea. The sea! *Peste!*
That he should never have thought of that! There was the castle,
truly, beetling against the breakers, very cold, very arrogant upon
its barren promontory. He was not twenty paces from its walls,
and yet it might as well have been a league away, for he was cut
off from it by a natural moat of sea-water that swept about it
in yeasty little waves. It rode like a ship, oddly independent of
aspect, self-contained, inviolable, eternally apart, for ever by
nature indifferent to the mainland, where a Montaiglon was
vulgarly quarrelling with *sans culottes*.

For a moment or two he stood bewildered. There was no
drawbridge to this eccentric moat; there was, on this side of the
rock at least, not so little as a boat; if Lamond ever held inter-
course with the adjacent isle of Scotland he must seemingly swim.
Very well; the Count de Montaiglon, guilty of many outrages
against his ancestry today, must swim too if that were called for.
And it looked as if that were the only alternative. Vainly he called
and whistled; no answer came from the castle, that he might have
thought a deserted ruin if a column of smoke did not arise from
some of its chimneys.

It was his one stroke of good fortune that for some reason the
pursuit was no longer apparent. The dim woods behind seemed
to have swallowed up sight and sound of the broken men, who,
at fault, were following up their quarry to the castle of MacCailein
Mor instead of to that of Baron Lamond. He had therefore time
to prepare himself for his next step. He sat on the shore and took
off his elegant long boots, the quite charming silk stockings so
unlike travel in the wilds; then looked dubiously at his limbs and
at the castle. No! manifestly, an approach so frank was not to
be thought of, and he compromised by unbuttoning the foot of
his pantaloons and turning them over his knees. In any case, if
one had to swim over that yeasty and alarming barrier, his
clothing must get wet. *A porte basse, passant courbé*. He would
wade as far as he could, and if he must, swim the rest.

With the boots and the mails and the stockings and the skirts
of his coats tucked high in his arms, the Count waded into the

11

tide, that chilled deliciously after the heat of his flight.

But it was ridiculous! It was the most condemnable folly! His face burned with shame as he found himself half-way over the channel and the waves no higher than his ankles. It was to walk through a few inches of water that he had nearly stripped to nature!

And a woman was laughing at him, *morbleu!* Decidedly a woman was laughing—a young woman, he could wager, with a monstrously musical laugh, by St Denys! and witnessing (though he could not see her even had he wished) this farce from an upper window of the tower. He stood for a moment irresolute, half inclined to retreat from the ridicule that never failed to affect him more unpleasantly than danger the most dire; his face and neck flamed; he forgot all about the full-bosomed Baronne or remembered her only to agree that nobility demanded some dignity even in fleeing from an enemy. But the shouts of the pursuers that had died away in the distance grew again in the neighbourhood, and he pocketed his diffidence and resumed his boots, then sought the entrance to a dwelling that had no hospitable portal to the shore.

Close at hand the edifice gained in austerity and dignity while it lost the last of its scanty air of hospitality. Its walls were of a rough rubble of granite and whinstone, grown upon at the upper storeys with grasses and weeds wafted upon the ledges by the winds that blow indifferent, bringing the green messages of peace from God. A fortalice dark and square-built, flanked to the southern corner by a round turret, lit by few windows, and these but tiny and suspicious, it was as Scots and arrogant as the thistle that had pricked Count Victor's feet when first he set foot upon the islet.

A low wall surrounded a patch of garden-ground to the rear, one corner of it grotesquely adorned with a bower all bedraggled with rains, yet with the red berry of the dog-rose gleaming in the rusty leafage like grapes of fire. He passed through the little garden and up to the door. Its arch, ponderous, deep-moulded, hung a scowling eyebrow over the black and studded oak, and over all was an escutcheon with a blazon of hands fesswise and castles embattled, and the legend:

"𝔇oom.

Man, Behauld the End of All. Be Nocht
Wiser than the Hiest. Hope in God!"

He stood on tiptoe to read the more easily the time-blurred characters, his baggage at his feet, his fingers pressed against the door. Some of the words he could not decipher nor comprehend, but the first was plain to his understanding.

"Doom!" said he airily and half aloud. "Doom! *Quelle félicité!* It is an omen."

Then he rapped lightly on the oak with the pommel of his sword.

III

Baron of Doom

Deep in some echoing corridor of the stronghold a man's voice rose in the Gaelic language, ringing in a cry for service, but no one came.

Count Victor stepped back and looked again upon the storm-battered front, the neglected garden, the pathetic bower. He saw smoke but at a single chimney, and broken glass in the little windows, and other evidences that suggested meagre soup as common fare in Doom.

"M. Bethune's bowl," he said to himself, "is not likely to be brimming over if he is to drink it here. M. le Baron shouting there is too much of the gentleman to know the way to the back of his own door; Glengarry again for a *louis*!—Glengarry *sans feu ni lieu*, but always the most punctilious when most nearly penniless."

Impatiently he switched with the sword at the weeds about his feet; then reddened at the apprehension that had made him all unconsciously bare the weapon at a door whose hospitality he was seeking, rapped again, and sheathed the steel.

A shuffling step sounded on the stones within, stopped apparently just inside the door, and there fell silence. No bolt moved, no chain clanked. But something informed the Count Victor that he was being observed, and he looked all over the door till he saw that one bolt-boss was missing about the height of his head, and that through the hole an eye was watching him. It was the most absurd thing, an experiment with a hole in a door will not make plain the reason of it; but in that eye, apparently little discomfited by the stranger having observed it, Count Victor saw its owner fully revealed.

A grey eye inquiring, an eye of middle age that had caution

14

as well as humour. A domestic—a menial eye too, but for the life of him Count Victor could not resist smiling back to it.

And then it disappeared and the door opened, showing on the threshold, with a stool in his hand, a very little bow-legged man of fifty years or thereby, having a face all lined, like a chart, with wrinkles, ruddy at the cheeks as a winter apple, and attired in a mulberry-brown. He put his heels together with a mechanical precision and gravely gave a military salute.

"Doom?" inquired Count Victor formally, with a foot inside the door.

"Jist that," answered the servitor a little drily, and yet with a smile puckering his face as he put an opposing toe of a coarse unbuckled brogue under the instep of the stranger. The accent of the reply smacked of Fife; when he heard it, Count Victor at a leap was back in the port of Dysart, where it shrank beneath tall rocks, and he was hearing again for the first time with an amused wonder the native mariners crying to each other on the quays.

"Is your master at home?" he asked.

"At hame, quo' he! It wad depend a'thegether on wha wants to ken," said the servant cautiously. Then in a manner ludicrously composed of natural geniality and burlesque importance, "It's the auld styles aboot Doom, sir, though there's few o' us left to keep them up, and whether the Baron's oot or in is a thing that has to be studied maist scrupulously before the like o' me could say."

"My name is De Montaiglon; I am newly from France; I—"

"Step your ways in, Monsher de Montaiglon," cried the little man with a salute more profound than before. "We're prood to see you, and hoo are they a' in France?"

"Tolerably well, I thank you," said Count Victor, amused at this grotesque combination of military form and familiarity.

Mungo Boyd set down the stool on which he had apparently been standing to look through the spyhole in the door, and seized the stranger's mails. With three rapid movements of the feet, executed in the mechanical time of a soldier, he turned to the right-about, paused a second, squared his shoulders, and led

15

the way into a most barren and chilly interior.

"This way, your honour," said he. "Ye'll paurdon my discreetion, for it's a pernikity hoose this for a' the auld, bauld, gallant forms and ceremonies. I jalouse ye cam roond in a wherry frae the toon, and it's droll I never saw ye land. There was never mony got into Doom withoot the kennin' o' the garrison. It happened aince in Black Hugh's time wi' a corps o' Campbells frae Ardkinglas, and they found themselves in a wasps' byke."

The Count stumbled in the dusk of the interior, for the door had shut of itself behind them, and the corridor was unlit except by what it borrowed from an open door at the far end, leading into a room. An odour of burning peats filled the place; the sound of the sea-breakers was to be heard in a murmur as one hears far-off and magic seas in a shell that is held to the ear. And Count Victor, finding all his pleasant anticipations of the character of this baronial dwelling utterly erroneous, mentally condemned Bethune to perdition as he stumbled behind the little grotesque aping the soldier's pompous manner.

The door that lent what illumination there was to his entrance was held half open by a man who cast at the visitor a glance wherein were surprise and curiosity.

"The Monsher de Montaiglon frae France," announced Mungo, stepping aside, still with the soldier's mechanical precision, and standing by the door to give dignity to the introduction and the entrance.

The Baron may have flushed for the overdone formality of his servant when he saw the style of his visitor, standing with a Kevenhuller cocked hat in one hand and fondling the up-turned moustache with the other; something of annoyance at least was in his tone as he curtly dismissed the man and gave admission to the stranger, on whom he turned a questioning and slightly embarrassed countenance, handing him one of the few chairs in the most sparsely furnished of rooms.

"You are welcome, sir," he said simply in a literal rendering of his native Gaelic phrase; "take your breath. And you will have refreshment?"

16

Count Victor protested no, but his host paid no heed. "It is the custom of the country," said he, making for a cupboard and fumbling among glasses, giving, as by a good host's design, the stranger an opportunity of settling down to his new surroundings. A room ill-furnished as a monk's cell, lit by narrow windows, two of them looking to the sea and one along the coast, though not directly on it, windows sunk deep in massive walls built for a more bickering age than this—Count Victor took all in at a glance, and found revealed to him in a flash the colossal mendacity of all the Camerons, Macgregors, and Macdonalds, who had implied, if they had not deliberately stated, over many games of piquet or lansquenet at Cammercy, the magnificence of the typical Highland stronghold.

The Baron had been reading; at least beside the chair drawn up to a fire of peat that perfumed the apartment lay a book upon a table, and it was characteristic of the Count, who loved books as he loved sport, and Villon above all, that he should strain his eyes a little and tilt his head slightly to see what manner of literature prevailed in these wilds. And the book gave him great cheer, for it was an old French folio of arms, 'Les Arts de L'homme d'Epée; ou, Le Dictionnaire du Gentilhomme,' by one Sieur de Guille. Doom Castle was a curious place, but apparently Hugh Bethune was in the right when he described its master as "ane o' the auld gentry, wi' a tattie and herrin' to his dejeune, but a scholar's book open against the ale-jug." A poor Baron (of a vastly different state from the Baron of France), English spoken too, with not much of the tang of the heather in his utterance though droll of his idiom, hospitable (to judge from the proffered glass still being fumbled for in the cupboard), a man who had been in France on the right side, a reader of the *beau langage*, and a student of the lore of *arme blanche*—come, here was luck!

And the man himself? He brought forward his spirits in a bottle of quaint Dutch cut, with hollow pillars at each of its four corners, and two glasses extravagantly tall of stem, and he filled out the drams upon the table, removing with some embarrassment before he did so the book of arms. It surprised Count Victor

17

that he should not be in the native tartan of the Scots Highlander. Instead he wore a demure coat and breeches of some dark fabric, and a wig conferred on him all the more of the look of a lowland merchant than of a chief of clan. He was a man at least twenty years the senior of his visitor—a handsome man of his kind, dark, deliberate of his movements, bred in the courtesies, but seemingly, to the acuter intuitions of Montaiglon, possessed of one unpardonable weakness in a gentleman—a shame of his obvious penury.

"I have permitted myself, M. le Baron, to interrupt you on the counsel of a common friend," said Count Victor, anxious to put an end to a situation somewhat droll.

"After the goblet, after the goblet," said Lamond softly, himself but sipping at the rim of his glass. "It is the custom of the country—one of the few that's like to be left to us before long."

"*À la santé de la bonne cause!*" said the Count politely, choking upon the fiery liquor, and putting down the glass with an apology.

"I am come from France—from Saint Germains," he said. "You may have heard of my uncle; I am the Count de Montaiglon."

The Baron betrayed a moment's confusion.

"Do you tell me, now?" said he. "Then you are the more welcome. I wish I could say so in your own language—that is, so far as ease goes, known to me only in letters. From Saint Germains . . ." making a step or two up and down the room, with a shrewd glance upon his visitor in the bygoing—"H'm, I've been there on a short turn myself; there are several of the Highland gentry about the place."

"There is one Bethune—Hugh Bethune of Ballimeanach, Baron," replied Count Victor meaningly. "Knowing that I was coming to this part of the world, and that a person of my tongue and politics might be awkwardly circumstanced in the province of Argyll, he took the liberty to give me your direction as one in whose fidelity I might repose myself. I came across the sleeve to Albion and skirted your noisy eastern coast with but one

18

name of a friend, *pardieu*, to make the strange cliffs cheerful."

"You are very good," said the Baron simply, with half a bow. "And Hugh Bethune, now—well, well! I am proud that he should mind of his old friend in the tame Highlands. Good Hugh!"—a strange wistfulness came to the Baron's utterance— "Good Hugh! he'll wear tartan when he has the notion, I'm supposing, though, after all, he was no Gael, or a very far-out one, for all that he was in the Marischal's tail."

"I have never seen him in the tartan, beyond perhaps a waistcoat of it at a *bal masque*."

"So? And yet he was a man generally full of Highland spirit." Count Victor smiled.

"It is perhaps his only weakness that nowadays he carries it with less dignity than he used to do. A good deal too much of the Highland spirit, M. le Baron, wears hoops, and comes into France in Leith frigates."

"Ay, man!" said the Baron, heedless of the irony, "and Hugh wears the tartan?"

"Only in the waistcoat," repeated Count Victor, complacently looking at his own scallops.

"Even that!" said the Baron, with the odd wistfulness in his voice. And then he added hurriedly, "Not that the tartan's anything wonderful. It cost the people of this country a bonny penny one way or another. There's nothing honest men will take to more readily than the breeks, say I—the douce, honest breeks. . . ."

"Unless it be the petticoats," murmured the Count, smiling, and his fingers went to the pointing of his moustache.

"Nothing like the breeks; the philabeg was aye telling your parentage in every line, so that you could not go over the moor to Lennox there but any drover by the roadside kent you for a small clan or a family of caterans. Some people will be grumbling that the old dress should be proscribed, but what does it matter?"

"The tartan is forbidden?" guessed Count Victor, somewhat puzzled.

Doom flushed; a curious gleam came into his eyes; he turned

to fumble noisily with the glasses as he replaced them in the cupboard.

"I thought that was widely enough known," said he. "Put down by the law, and perhaps a good business too. *Diaouil!*" He came back to the table with this muttered objurgation, sat and stared into the grey film of the peat-fire. "There was a story in every line," said he, "a history in every check, and we are odd creatures in the glens, Count, that we could never see the rags without minding what they told. Now the tartan's in the dye-pot, and you'll see about here but *crotal*-colour—the old stuff stained with lichen from the rock."

"Ah, what damage!" said Count Victor with sympathetic tone. "But there are some who wear it yet?"

The Baron started slightly. "Sir?" he questioned, without taking his eyes from the embers.

"The precipitancy of my demands upon your gate and your hospitality must have something of an air of an impertinence," said Count Victor briskly, unbuckling his sword and laying it before him on the table; "but the cause of it lay with several zealous gentlemen, who were apparently not affected by any law against tartan, for tartan they wore, and *sans culottes* too, though the dirt of them made it difficult to be certain of either fact. In the East it is customary, I believe, for the infidel to take off his boots when he intrudes on sacred ground; nothing is said about stockings, but I had to divest myself of both boots and stockings. I waded into Doom a few minutes ago, for all the world like an oyster-man with my bag on my back."

"Good God!" cried the Baron. "I forgot the tide. Could you not have whistled?"

"Whole operas, my dear M. le Baron, but the audience behind me would have made the performance so necessarily allegretto as to be ineffective. It was wade at once or pipe and perish. *Mon Dieu!* but I believe you are right; as an honest man I cannot approve of my first introduction to your tartan among its own mountains."

"It must have been one of the corps of watches; it must have been some of the king's soldiers," suggested the Baron.

Count Victor shrugged his shoulders. "I think I know a red-coat when I see one," said he. "These were quite unlicensed hawks, with the hawk's call for signal too."

"Are you sure?" cried the Baron, standing up, and still with an unbelieving tone.

"My dear M. le Baron, I killed one of the birds to look at the feathers. That is the confounded thing too! So unceremonious a manner of introducing myself to a country where I desire me above all to be circumspect; is it not so?"

As he spoke he revealed the agitation that his flippant words had tried to cloak—by a scarcely perceptible tremor of the hand that drummed the table, a harder note in his voice, and the biting of his moustache. He saw that Doom guessed his perturbation, and he compelled himself to a careless laugh, got lazily to his feet, twisted his moustache points, drew forth his rapier with a flourish, and somewhat theatrically saluted and lunged in space as if the action gave his tension ease.

The Baron for a moment forgot the importance of what he had been told as he watched the graceful beauty of the movement, that revealed not only some eccentricity but personal vanity of a harmless kind and wholesome tastes and talents.

"Still I'm a little in the dark," he said when the point dropped and Count Victor recovered.

"Pardon," said his guest. "I am vexed at what you may perhaps look on as a trifle. The ruffians attacked me a mile or two farther up the coast, shot my horse below me, and chased me to the very edge of your moat. I made a feint to shoot one with my pistol, and came closer on the gold than I had intended."

"The Macfarlanes!" cried Doom, with every sign of uneasiness. "It's a pity, it's a pity; not that a man more or less of that crew makes any difference, but the affair might call for more attention to this place and your presence here than might be altogether wholesome for you or me."

He heard the story in more detail, and when Count Victor had finished, ran into an adjoining room to survey the coast from a window there. He came back with a less troubled vision.

"At least they're gone now," said he in a voice that still had some perplexity. "I wish I knew who it was you struck. Would it be Black Andy of Arroquhar now? If it's Andy, the gang will be crying 'Loch Sloy!' about the house in a couple of nights; if it was a common man of the tribe, there might be no more about it, for we're too close on the Duke's gallows to be meddled with noisily; that's the first advantage I ever found in my neighbourhood."

"He was a man of a long habit of body," said Count Victor, "and he fell with a grunt."

"Then it was not Andy. Andy is like a hogshead—a blob of creesh with a turnip on the top—and he would fall with a curse."

"Name of a pipe! I know him; he debated the last few yards of the way with me, and I gave him De Chenier's mace in the jaw."

"Sir?"

"I put him slightly out of countenance with the butt and trigger-guard of my pistol. Again I must apologise, dear Baron, for so unceremonious and ill-tempered an approach to your hospitality. You will confess it is a sort of country the foibles of whose people one has to grow accustomed to, and Bethune gave me no guidance for such an emergency as banditti on the fringe of Argyll's notoriously humdrum Court."

"Odd!" repeated Doom. "Will you step this way?" He led Count Victor to the window that commanded the coast, and their heads together filled the narrow space as they looked out. It was a wondrous afternoon. The sun swung low in a majestic sky, whose clouds of gold and purple seemed to the gaze of Montaiglon a continuation of the actual hills of wood and heather whereof they were the culmination. He saw, it seemed to him, the myriad peaks, the vast cavernous mountain clefts of a magic land, the abode of seraphim and the sun's eternal smile.

"God is good!" said he again, no way reverently, but with some emotion. "I thought I had left for ever the place of hope, and here's paradise with open doors." Then he looked upon the nearer country, upon the wooded hills, the strenuous shoulders of the bens upholding all that glory of sinking sunshine, and on one he saw upstanding, a vulgar blotch upon the landscape, a gaunt long spar with an overhanging arm.

"Ah!" he said airily, "there is civilisation in the land after all."

"Plenty of law at least," said the Baron. "Law of its kind— MacCailein law. His Grace, till the other day, as it might be, was Justiciary of the shire, Sheriff of the same, Regality Lord, with rights of pit and gallows. My place goes up to the knowe beside his gallows; but his Grace's regality comes beyond this, and what does he do but put up his dule-tree there that I may see it from my window and mind the fact. It's a fine country this; man, I love it! I'm bound to be loving it, as the saying goes, waking and sleeping, and it brought me back from France, that I had no ill-will to, and kept me indoors in the 'Forty-five,' though my heart was in the rising, as Bethune would tell you. A grand country out and in, wet and dry, winter and summer, and only that tree there and what it meant to mar the look and comfort of it. But here I'm at my sentiments and you starving, I am sure, for something to eat."

He moved from the window out at which he had been gazing with a fondness that surprised and amused his visitor, and called loudly for Mungo.

In a moment the little retainer was at the door jauntily saluting in his military manner.

"Hae ye been foraging the day, Mungo?" asked the master indulgently.

"Na, na, there was nae need wi' a commissariat weel provided for voluntary. Auld Dugald brought in his twa kain hens yesterday; ane's on the bauk, and the cauld corp o' the ither o' them's in the pantry. There's the end o' a hench o' venison frae Strathlachlan, and twa oors syne, when the tide was oot, there was beef padovies and stoved howtowdies, but I gied them to twa gaun-aboot bodies."

They both looked inquiringly at Count Victor.

"I regret the what-do-you-call-it?—the stoved howtowdy,"

said he, laughing, "more for the sound of it than for any sense its name conveys to me."

"There's meat as weel as music in it, as the fox said when he ate the bagpipes," said Mungo. "There's waur nor howtowdy. And oh! I forgot the het victual, there's jugged hare."

"Is the hare ready?" asked the Baron suspiciously.

"It's no jist a'thegether what ye micht ca' ready," answered Mungo without hesitation; "but it can be here het in nae time, and micht agree wi' the Count better nor the cauld fowl."

"Tell Annapla to do the best she can," broke in the Baron on his servant's cheerful garrulity; and Mungo with another salute disappeared.

"How do your women-folk like the seclusion of Doom?" asked Count Victor, to make conversation while the refection was in preparation. "With the sea about you so, and the gang of my marauding obese friend in the wood behind, I should think you had little difficulty in keeping them under your eye."

The Baron was obviously confused. "Mungo's quite enough to keep his eye on Annapla," said he. "He has the heart and fancy to command a garrison; there's a drum for ever beating in his head, a whistle aye fifing in his lug, and he will amuse you with his conceits of soldiering ancient and modern, a trade he thinks the more of because Heaven made him so unfit to become prentice to it. Good Mungo! there have been worse men; indeed what need I grudge admitting there have been few better? He has seen this place more bien than it is today in my father's time, and in my own too before the law-pleas ate us up; you will excuse his Scots freedom of speech, Count, he—"

A shot rang outside in some shrubbery upon the mainland, suddenly putting an end to the Baron's confidence. Count Victor, sure that the Macfarlanes were there again, ran to the window and looked out, while his host in the rear bit his lip with every sign of annoyance. As Montaiglon looked he saw Mungo emerge from the shrubbery with a rabbit in his hand and push off hurriedly in a little boat, which apparently was in use for communication with the shore under such circumstances.

24

"And now," said the Count, without comment upon what he had seen, "I think, with your kind permission, I shall change my boots before eating."

"There's plenty of time for that, I jalouse," said Doom, smiling somewhat guiltily, and he showed his guest to a room in the turret.

It was up a flight of corkscrew stairs, and lit with singular poverty by an orifice more of the nature of a port-hole for a piece than a window, and this port or window, well out in the angle of the turret, commanded a view of the southward wall or curtain of the castle.

Montaiglon, left to himself, opened the mails that Mungo had placed in readiness for him in what was evidently the guest-room of the castle, transformed the travelling half of himself into something that was more in conformity with the gay nature of his upper costume, complacently surveyed the result when finished, and hummed a *chanson* of Pierre Gringoire's, altogether unremembering the encounter in the wood, the dead robber, and the stern nature of his embassy here so far from France.

He bent to close the valise, and with a start abruptly concluded his song at the sight of a miniature with the portrait of a woman looking at him from the bottom of the bag.

"*Mort de ma vie!* what a fool I am, what a forgetful *vengeur*, to be chanting Gringoire in the house of Doom and my quarry still to hunt!" His voice had of a sudden gained a sterner accent; the pleasantness of his aspect—that came almost wholly from his eyes—became clouded by a frown. Looking round the contracted room, and realising how like a prison-cell it was compared with what he had expected, he felt oppressed as with the want of air. He sought vainly about the window for latch or hinge to open it, and as he did so glanced along the castle wall painted yellow by the declining sun. He noticed idly that someone was putting out upon the sill of a window on a lower stage what might have been a green kerchief had not the richness of its fabric and design suggested more a pennon or banneret. It was carefully placed by a woman's hands—the woman herself

25

unseen. The incident recalled an old exploit of his own in Marney, and a flood of humorous memories of amorous intrigue.

"Mademoiselle Annapla," said he whimsically, "has a lover, and here's his signal. The Baron's daughter? the Baron's niece? the Baron's ward? or merely the Baron's domestic? M. Bethune's document suffers infernally from the fault of being too curt. He might at least have indicated the fair recluse."

IV

Seeking a Spy

The wail of a mountain pipe, poorly played, as any one accustomed to its strains would have admitted, even if the instrument were one he loved, and altogether execrable in the ears of Montaiglon, called him to the *salle*, where Doom joined him in a meal whereof good Mungo's jugged hare formed no part. Mungo, who had upheld ancient ceremony by his crude performance on the *piob mhor*, was the attendant upon the table,—an office he undertook with his bonnet on his head, "in token," as his master whisperingly explained to Count Victor, "of his sometimes ill-informed purpose of conducting every formal task in Doom upon the strict letter of military codes as pertained in camps, garrisons, and strongholds." It was amusing to witness the poor fellow's pompous precision of movement as he stood behind his master's chair or helped the guest to his humble meal; the rigidity of his inactive moments, or the ridiculous jerkiness with which he passed a platter as 'twere to the time of a drill-sergeant's baton. More amusing still for one able, like Count Victor, to enter into the humour of the experience, was it to have his garrulity get the better of him in spite of the military restraint.

"The Baron was telling me aboot your exploit wi' the Loch Sloy pairty. Man! did I no' think ye had come by boat," he whispered over a tendered ale-glass. "It was jist my luck to miss sic a grand ploy. I wad hae backed ye to haud the water against Black Andy and all his clan, and they're no' slack at a tulzie."

"Ye may be grand in a fight, Mungo, but only a middling man at forage," interrupted his master. "I think ye said jugged hare?"

"It wasna my faut," explained the domestic, "that ye havena what was steepulated; ye wadna bide till the beast was cooked."

Doom laughed. "Come, come, Mungo," said he, "the Count

27

could scarcely be expected to wait for the cooking of an animal running wild in the bracken twenty minutes ago."

"Oh, it disna tak' sae terrible lang to cook a hare," said the unabashed retainer.

"But was it a hare after a', Mungo?" asked his master. "Are ye sure it wasna a rabbit?"

"A rabbit!" cried he in astonishment; then more cautiously, "Weel, if it was a rabbit, it was a gey big ane, that's a' I can say," and he covered his perturbation by a retreat from the room to resume his office of musician, which, it appeared, demanded a tune after dinner as well as before it.

What had seemed to Montaiglon a harsh, discordant torturing of reeds when heard on the stair outside his chamber, seemed somehow more mellowed and appropriate—pleasing even—when it came from the garden outside the castle, on whose grass-grown walk the little lowlander strutted as he played the evening melody of the house of Doom—a pibroch all imbued with passion and with melancholy. The distance lulled it into something more than human music, into a harmony with the monotone of the wave that thundered on the rock; it seemed the voice of choiring mermen; it had the bitterness, the agonised remembrance, of the sea's profound; it was full of hints of stormy nights and old wars. For a little Doom and his visitor sat silent listening to it, the former with a strain upon his countenance, tapping nervously with his fingers upon the arm of his chair.

"An old custom in the Highlands," he explained. "I set, perhaps, too little store by it myself, but Mungo likes to maintain it, though he plays the pipe but indifferently, and at this distance you might think the performance not altogether without merit."

"I love all music," replied Count Victor with polite ambiguity, and he marvelled at the signs of some deep feeling in his host.

Till a late hour they sat together while Count Victor explained his mission to the Highlands. He told much, but, to be sure, he did not at first tell all. He recounted the evidences of the spy's guilt as a correspondent with the British Government, whose pay he drew while sharing the poor fortunes and the secrets of the

28

exiled Jacobites. "Iscariot, my dear Baron," he protested, "was a Bayard compared with this wretch. His presence in your locality should pollute the air; have you not felt a malaise?"

"It's dooms hard," admitted the Baron, throwing up distressed hands, "but, man, I'm feared he's not the only one. Do you know, I could mention well-kent names far ben in the Cause—men not of hereabouts at all, but of Lochaber no less, though you may perhaps not guess all that means—and they're in Paris up to the elbow now in the same trade. It's well known to some of yourselves, or should be, and it puzzles me that you should come to the shire of Argyll on account of one, as I take it, no worse than three or four you might have found by stepping across the road to Roisin's coffee-house in the Rue Vaugirard. The commoners in the late troubles have been leal enough, I'll give them that credit, but some of the gentry wag their tongues for Prince Tearlach and ply their pens for Geordie's pay."

The servant came in with two candles, placed them on the table, and renewed the fire. He had on a great woollen night-cowl of gaudy hue with a superb tassel that bobbed grotesquely over his beady eyes.

"I'll awa' to my bed, if it's your will, Baron," said he with the customary salute. "I was thinkin' it might be needful for me to bide up a while later in case ony o' the Coont's freends cam' the way; but the tide'll keep them aff till mornin' anyway, and I'm sure we'll meet them a' the baulder then if we hae a guid sleep." He got permission to retire, and passed into the inky darkness of the corridor, and crept to that part of the vacant dwelling in which he had his bed.

"There might be another reason for my coming here," said Montaiglon, resuming the conversation where Mungo's entrance had broken it off. "In this affair there was a lady. I knew her once." He paused with a manner showing discomposure.

"And there was liking; I can comprehend," said Doom with sympathy.

"Liking is but love without wings," said Montaiglon. "My regard soared above the clay; I loved her, and I think she was

29

not indifferent to me till this man came in her way. He had, they say, the devil's tongue; at least he had the devil's heart, and she died six months ago with her head on my arm. I could tell you the story, M. le Baron, but it is in all the books, and you can fancy it easily. She died forgiving her betrayer, and sending a message to that effect by me. I come to deliver it, and, by God! to push it to his heart."

"It is a dangerous errand in this country and at this time," said Doom, looking into the fire.

"Ah! but you did not know Cécile," replied Montaiglon, simply.

"But I know the human heart. I know it in any man under the sober age of thirty. Better to let it rest, this. Excuse my interference. It does not matter much to me that it should be out of my house you should go seeking for your vengeance, but I'm an older man than you, and have learned how quickly the worst misfortunes and wrongs may be forgotten. In your place I would leave this man to the punishment of his own conscience."

Montaiglon laughed bitterly. "That," said he, "is to assume a mechanism that in his case never existed. Pardon me, I pray you, but I prefer the old reckoning, which will be all the fairer because he has the reputation of being a good swordsman, and I am not without some practice."

"And the man's name? you have not mentioned it."

"But there you puzzle me. He was eight months in France, six of these in a lodging beside the Baigneurs on the Estrapade, Rue Dauphine. He came with no credentials but from Glengarry, and now Glengarry can give no account of him except that he had spoken familiarly to him of common friends in the Highlands."

"Oh, Glengarry—Alasdair Rhuadh!" exclaimed the Baron, drily.

"And presumed to be burdened with a dangerous name, he passed with the name of Drimdarroch."

"Drimdarroch!" repeated the Baron with some apparent astonishment.

"I have never seen the man so far as I know, for I was at

Cammercy when he hung about the lady."

"Drimdarroch!" repeated Doom reflectively, "a mere land title."

"And some words he dropped in the ear of the lady made me fancy he might be found about the Court of Argyll."

"Drimdarroch! Drimdarroch! I ken no one of the name, though the name itself, for very good reasons, is well known to me. Have you any description of the man?"

"Not much. A man older than myself, dark, well-bred. I should say a man something like yourself, if you will pardon the comparison, with a less easy mind, if he remembers his friends and his past."

Doom pushed back his chair a little from the fire, but without taking his eyes from the peats, and made a curious suggestion.

"You would not take it to be me, would you?" he asked. Count Victor laughed, with a gesture of his hands that made denial all unnecessary.

"Oh! but you do not know," went on the Baron. "Some months of caballing with our friends—even our Hielan' friends—in the France, left me with an unwholesome heart that would almost doubt my father in his grave. You mentioned the name Drimdarroch—is it not the odd thing that you should speak it to the only man in the shire that ever had the right to use it? Do you see this?" and rising he stepped to a recess in the wall, only half curtained, so that its contents overflowed into the chamber, and by a jerk of the hand revealed a strange accumulation of dusty documents in paper and in parchment. He looked at them with an aspect of disgust, and stirred them with a contemptuous toe as if he meddled with the litter of a stye.

"That's Drimdarroch!" said he, intensely bitter; "that's Drimdarroch, and Duntorvil, that's the Isles, the bonny Isles of Lochow; that's damn like to be Doom too! That and this ruckle of stones we sit in are all that's left of what was my father's and my grandfather's and their forebears, back till the dark of time. And how is it, ye may ask? Let us pretermit the question till another occasion; anyway here's Drimdarroch wi' the lave, at

31

any rate the weight of it in processes, records, caveats, multiple-poindings, actions of suspension and declarator, interim decrees, fugie warrants, compts and reckonings—God! I have the cackle of the law in my head like a ballant, and what's the wonder at that wi' all my practice?"

He stooped and picked up from the confused heap of legal scrivenings by fingertips that seemed to fear infection a parchment fouled with its passage through the courts and law offices. "You're in luck indeed," said he; "for there's Drimdarroch—all that's left of it to me: the land itself is in the hands of my own doer, Petullo the writer down-by, and scab seize his bestial!"

Back he threw the relic of his patrimony; he dropped the curtain; he turned on his guest a face that tried to smile. "Come, let us sit down again," he said, "and never heed my havers. Am I not thankful to have Doom itself left me, and the company of the hills and sea? After all, there are more Drimdarrochs than one in the Highlands, for the name means just 'the place at the back of the oak-wood or the oaken shaw,' and oaks are as plentiful hereabout as the lawyers are in the burgh down-by. I but mentioned it to show you the delicacy of your search, for you do not know but what I'm the very man you want, though I'm sitting here looking as if acting trusty for the Hanoverian cause did not fill my pouches."

"*Tenez!* M. Bethune was scarcely like to send me to Doom in that case," said the Count laughing.

"But Bethune, like yourself, may never have seen the man."

"But yes, it is true, he did not see him any more than I did. Drimdarroch, by all accounts, was a spendthrift, a player, a *bavard*, his great friends, Glengarry and another Scot, Balhaldie—"

"Oh, Balhaldie! blethering Balhaldie!" cried Doom, contempt upon his countenance. "And Balhaldie would sell him, I'll warrant. He seems, this Drimdarroch, to have been dooms unlucky in his friends. I say all I've said to you, Count, because you're bound to find it out for yourself some day if you prosecute your search here, and you might be coming round to me at last with your ower-ready pistol when I was ill-prepared to argue out my identity. Furthermore, I do not know the man you want. About the castle down-by his Grace has a corps of all kinds that you might pick from nine times out of ten without striking an honest man. Some of them are cadets of his own family, always blunt opponents of mine and of our cause here and elsewhere; some are incomers, as we call them; a few of them from clans apparently friendly to us when in other quarters, but traitors and renegades at the heart; some are spies habit and repute. There's not a friend of mine among them, not in all the fat and prosperous rabble of them; but I wish you were here on another errand, though to Doom, my poor place, you are welcome. I am a widower, a lonely man, with my own flesh and blood rebel against me"—he checked his untimeous confidence—"and yet I have been chastened by years and some unco experiences from a truculent man to one preferring peace except at the last ditch."

"*Eh bien!* monsieur; *this* is the last ditch!" said Montaiglon. "Spy and murderer, M. le Baron, and remember I propose to give him more than the murderer's chance when I agree to meet him on a fair field with a sword in his hand."

"I have seen you lunge, sir," said Doom meaningly; "I ken the carriage of a fencer's head; your eye's fast, your step's light; with the sword I take it Drimdarroch is condemned, and your practice with the pistol, judging from the affair with the Macfarlanes, seems pretty enough. You propose, or I'm mistaken, to make yourself the executioner. It is a step for great deliberation, and for the sake of a wanton woman—"

"Sir!" cried Montaiglon, half rising in his chair.

Doom's eyes gleamed, a quiver ran over his brow, and a furrow came to the jaw; his hand went to his side, where in other days there might have been a dagger. It was the flash of a moment, and died again almost before Montaiglon had seen and understood.

"*Mille pardons!*" said Doom with uncouth French. "I used the word in its most innocent sense, with its kindliest meaning; but I was a fool to use it at all, and I withdraw it."

Count Victor bowed his head. "So," said he. "Perhaps I am

33

too much Quixote for I saw her but a few times, and that briefly. She was like a—like a fine air once heard, not all to be remembered, never wholly to be forgot. She had a failing, perhaps— the error of undue affection to qualify her for a sinful world. As it was, she seemed among other women some rarity out of place—Venus at a lantern feast."

"And ye would send this man to hell that he may find his punishment in remembering her? If I thought so much of vengeance I would leave him on the earth forgetting."

"M. le Baron, I make you my compliments of your complacence," said Count Victor, rising to his feet and desirous to end the discussion. "I am only Victor de Montaiglon, poorly educated in the forgiveness of treachery, and lamentably incapable of the nobility of the heart that you profess. But I can be grateful; and if you give me the hospitality of your house for a day or two, I shall take care that neither it nor its owner will be implicated in my little affair. Touching retirement"—he went on with a smile—"I regret exceedingly an overpowering weariness. I have travelled since long before dawn, and burning the candle *par les deux bouts* is not, as Master Mungo hints, conducive to a vigorous reception of the Macfarlanes if they feel like retaliating tomorrow, and making your domicile the victim of my impetuosity and poor marksmanship."

Doom sighed, took up a candle, and led the way into the passage. A chill air was in the corridor, that smelled like a cellar underground, and as their footsteps sounded reverberant upon the flags uncarpeted, Doom Castle gave the stranger the impression of a vault. Fantastic shadows danced macabre in the light of the candles; they were the only furniture of that part of the rough dwelling that the owner shuffled through as quickly as he could to save his guest from spying too closely the barrenness of the land. He went first to the outer door with the candle before he said good night, drew back great bars, and opened the oak. The sky was studded with pale golden stars; the open air was dense with the perfume of the wood, the saline indication of the seaware. On the rocky edge of the islet at one part showed the

34

white fringe of the waves now more peaceful; to the north brooded enormous hills, seen dimly by the stars, couchant terrors, vague vast shapes of dolours and alarms. Doom stood long looking at them with the flame of the candle blowing inward and held above his head—a mysterious man beyond Montaiglon's comprehension. He stood behind him a pace or two, shivering in the evening air.

"You'll be seeing little there, I'll warrant, Count, but a cold night and inhospitable vacancy, hard hills and the robber haunting them. For me, that prospect is my evening prayer. I cannot go to sleep without it, for fear I wake in Paradise and find it's all by with Doom and the native hills for me."

And by that he seemed to Montaiglon more explicable: it was the lover he was; the sentimentalist, the poet, knowing the ancient secret of the animate earth, taking his hills and valleys passionately to his heart. The Frenchman bowed his sympathy and understanding.

"It's a wonder Mungo kept his word and went to bed," said the Baron, recovering his ordinary manner, "for it would just suit his whim to bide up and act sentry here, very well pleased at the chance your coming gave him of play-acting the man of war."

He bolted the door again with its great bars, then gravely preceded his guest to the foot of the turret stair, where he handed him the candle.

"You're in a dreary airt of the house," he said apologetically, "but I hope you may find it not uncomfortable. Doom is more than two-thirds but empty shell, and the bats have the old chapel above you. *Oidhche mhath!* Good night!" He turned upon his heel and was gone into the farther end of the passage.

As Montaiglon went up to his room, the guttering candle-flame, puffed at by hidden and mischievous enemies from broken ports and gun-slits, showed upon the landing lower than his own a long corridor he had not observed upon his first ascent. With the candle held high above his head he glanced into the passage, that seemed to have several doors on either hand. In a castle so sparsely occupied the very knowledge of this long and empty corridor in the neighbourhood of his sleeping apartment conferred a sense of chill and mystery. He thought he could perceive the odour of damp, decayed wood, crumbled lime, hanging rotten in stagnant airs and covered upon with the dust of years. "*Dieu!*" he exclaimed involuntarily, "this is no Cammercy." He longed for some relief from the air of mystery and dread that hung about the place. A laugh would have been a revelation, a strain of song a miracle of healing. And all at once he reflected upon the Annapla as yet unseen.

"These might be her quarters," he reflected, finding a solace in the thought. The chill was at once less apparent, a pleasant glow of companionship came over him. Higher up he held the light to see the farther into the long passage, and as he did so the flame was puffed out. It seemed so human a caprice that he drew himself sharply against the wall, ready by instinct to evade any rush or thrust that was to follow. And then he smiled at his own alarm at a trick of the wind through some of Lamond's ill-patched walls, and found his consolation in the sense of companionship confirmed by sight of a thin line of light below a door midway up the curious passage.

"Annapla, for a *louis*!" he thought cheerfully. "Thank Heaven for one petticoat in Doom—though that, in truth, is to concede the lady but a scanty wardrobe." And he hummed softly as he entered his own room.

Wearied exceedingly by the toils of the day, he had no sooner thrown himself upon the bed than he slept, with no need for the lullaby aid of the sea that rumoured light and soothingly round the rock of Doom.

V

The Flageolet

He woke from a dream of pressing danger and impotent flight
to marvel where he was in darkness; fancied himself at first in
some wayside inn midway over Scotland, and sat up suddenly
with an exclamation of assurance that he was awake to the
supposititious landlord who had called, for the sense of some
sound but stilled on the second of his waking was strong within
him. He fastened upon the vague starlit space of the little window
to give him a clue to his situation. Then he remembered Doom,
and, with the window for his key, built up the puzzle of his room,
and wondered at the cause of his alarm.

The wind had risen and sent a loud murmur through the trees
along the coast; the sea, in breakers again, beat on the rock till
Doom throbbed. But there was nothing in that to waken a man
who had ridden two days on coarse roads and encountered and
fought with banditti. Decidedly there was some menace in the
night; danger on hard fields had given him blood alert and
unsleeping; the alarum was drumming at his breast. Stealthily he
put out his hand, and it fell as by a fiddler's instinct upon the
spot desired—the hilt of his sword. There he kept it with his
breath subdued, and the alarum severely quelled.

An owl's call sounded on the shore, extremely pensive in its
note, and natural, but unusual in the rhythm of its repetition. It
might have passed for the veritable call of the woods to an
unsuspicious ear, but Montaiglon knew it for a human signal.
As if to prove it so, it was followed by the grating of the outer
door upon its hinge, and the sound of a foot stumbling among
stones.

He reflected that the tide was out in all probability, and at
once the notion followed that here were his searchers, the

Macfarlanes, back in force to revenge his impetuous injury to their comrades. But then—a second thought almost as promptly told him—in that case there should be no door opened.

A sound of subdued voices came from the foot of the tower and died in the garden behind or was swept elsewhere by the wind; then, through the voice of the wave, the moan of the wind, and its whistle in vent and cranny, came a strain of music,—not the harsh uncultured pipe of Mungo the servitor, but the more dulcet tone of flute or flageolet. In those dark savage surroundings it seemed a sound inhuman, something unreal, something of remembrance in delirium or dream, charged for this Parisian with a thousand recollections of fond times, gay times, passionate times elsewhere. Doom throbbed to the waves, but the flageolet stirred in him not so much surprise at this incongruous experience as a wave of emotion where all his past of gaillard was crystalled in a second—many nights of dance and song anew experienced in a mellow note or two; an old love reincarnated in a phrase (and the woman in the dust); the evenings of Provence lived again, and Louis's darling flute piping from the chateau over the field and river; moons of harvest vocal with some peasant cheer; in the south the nightingale searching to express his kinship with the mind of man and the creatures of the copse, his rapture at the star.

Somehow the elusive nature of the music gave it more than half its magic. It would die away as the wind declined, or come in passionate crescendo. For long it seemed to Montaiglon—and yet it was too short—the night was rich with these incongruous but delightful strains. Now the player breathed some soft, slow, melancholy measure of the manner Count Victor had often heard the Scottish exiles croon with tears at his father's house, or sing with too much boisterousness at the dinners of the St Andrew's Club, for which the Leith frigates had made special provision of the Scottish wine. Anon the fingers strayed upon an Italian symphony full of languors and of sun, and once at least a dance gave quickness to the execution.

But more haunting than all was one simple strain and brief,

indeed never wholly accomplished, as if the player sought to recollect a song forgot, that was repeated over and over again, as though it were the motive of the others or refrain. Sometimes Montaiglon thought the player had despaired of concluding this bewitching melody when he changed suddenly to another, and he had a very sorrow at his loss; again, when its progress to him was checked by a veering current of the wind, and the flageolet rose once more with a different tune upon it, he dreaded that the conclusion had been found in the lacuna.

He rose at last and went to the window, and tried in the wan illumination of the heavens to detect the mysterious musician in the garden, but that was quite impossible: too dark the night, too huge and profound the shadows over Doom. He went to his door and opened it and looked down the yawning stairway; only the sigh of the wind in the gun-slits occupied the stairway, and the dark was the dark of Genesis. And so again to bed, to lie with his weariness for long forgotten. He found that tantalising fragment return again and again, but fated never to be complete. It seemed, he fancied, something like a symbol of a life—with all the qualities there, the sweetness, the affection, the passion, the divine despair, the longing, even the valours and the faiths to make a great accomplishment, but yet lacking some essential note. And as he waited once again for its recurrence he fell asleep.

VI

Mungo Boyd

It was difficult for Count Victor, when he went abroad in the morning, to revive in memory the dreary and mysterious impressions of his arrival; and the melody he had heard so often half-completed in the dark waste and hollow of the night was completely gone from his recollection, leaving him only the annoying sense of something on the tongue's-tip, as we say, but as unattainable as if it had never been heard. As he walked upon a little knoll that lay between the seaside of the castle and the wave itself, he found an air of the utmost benignity charged with the odours of wet autumn woodlands in a sunshine. And the sea stretched serene; the mists that had gathered in the night about the hills were rising like the smoke of calm hearths into a sky without a cloud. The castle itself, for all its natural arrogance and menace, had something pleasant in its aspect looked at from this small eminence, where the garden did not display its dishevelment and even the bedraggled bower seen from the rear had a look of trim composure.

To add to the morning's cheerfulness Mungo was afoot whistling a ballad air of the low country, with a regard for neither time nor tune in his puckered lips as he sat on a firkin-head at an outhouse door and gutted some fish he had caught with his own hands in a trammel net at the river-mouth before Montaiglon was awake and the bird, as the Gaelic goes, had drunk the water.

"Gude mornin' to your honour," he cried with an elaborately flourished salute as Montaiglon sauntered up to him. "Ye're early on the move, monsher; a fine caller mornin'. I hope ye sleepit weel; it was a gowsty nicht."

In spite of his assumed indifference and the purely casual nature of his comment upon the night, there was a good deal of cunning, thought Montaiglon, in the beady eyes of him, but the stranger only smiled at the ease of those Scots domestic manners.

"I did very well, I thank you," said he. "My riding and all the rest of it yesterday would have made me sleep soundly inside the drum of a marching regiment."

"That's richt, that's richt," said Mungo, ostentatiously handling the fish with the awkward repugnance of one unaccustomed to a task so menial, to prove perhaps that cleansing them was none of his accustomed office. "That's richt. When we were campaignin' wi' Marlborough oor lads had many a time to sleep wi' the cannon dirlin' aboot them. Ye get us'd to't, as Annapla says aboot bein' a weedow woman. And if ye hae noticed it, Coont, there's nae people mair adapted for fechtin' under diffeeculties than oor ain; that's what maks the Scots the finest sogers in the warld. It's the build o' them, Lowlan' or Hielan', the breed o' them; the dour hard character o' their country and their mainner o' leevin'. We gied the English a fleg at the 'Forty-five,' didnae we? That was where the tartan cam' in: man, there's naethin' like us!"

"You do not speak like a Highlander," said Montaiglon, finding some of this gasconade unintelligible.

"No, I'm no' exactly a'thegither a Hielan'man," Mungo admitted, "though I hae freends connekit wi' the auldest clans, and though I'm, in a mainner o' speakin', i' the tail o' Doom, as I was i' the tail o' his faither afore him—peace wi' him, he was the grand soger!—but Hielan' or Lowlan', we gied them their scuds at the 'Forty-five.' Scots regiments, sir, a' the warld ower, hae had the best o't for fechtin', marchin', or glory. See them at the auld grand wars o' Sweden wi' Gustavus, was there ever the like o' them? Or in your ain country, whaur's the bate o' the Gairde Ecossay, as they ca't?"

He spoke with such a zest, he seemed to fire with such a martial glow, that Montaiglon began to fancy that this amusing grotesque, who in stature came no higher than his waist, might have seen some service as sutler or groom in a campaigning regiment.

"*Ma foi!*" he exclaimed, with his surprise restrained from the most delicate considerations for the little man's feelings; "have you been in the wars?"

It was manifestly a home-thrust to Mungo. He had risen, in his moment of braggadocio, and was standing over the fish with a horn-hilted gutting-knife in his hands, that were sanguine with his occupation, and he had, in the excess of his feeling, made a flourish of the knife, as if it were a dagger, when Montaiglon's query checked him. He was a bubble burst, his backbone—that braced him to the tension of a cuirassier of guards—melted into air, into thin air, and a ludicrous limpness came on him, while his eye fell, and confusion showed about his mouth.

"In the wars!" he repeated. "Weel—no jist a'thegether what ye micht call i' the wars—though in a mainner o' speakin', gey near't. I had an uncle oot wi' Balmerino; ye may hae heard tell o'm, a man o' tremendous valour, as was generally alooed—Dugald Boyd, by my faither's side. There's been naethin' but sogers in oor faimily since the beginnin' o' time, and mony ane o' them's deid and dusty in foreign lands. If it hadnae been for the want o' a half inch or thereby in the height o' my heels"—here he stood upon his toes—"I wad hae been in the airmy mysel'. It's the only employ for a man o' spunk, and there's spunk in Mungo Boyd, mind I'm tellin' ye!"

"It is the most obvious thing in the world, good Mungo," said Montaiglon, smiling. "You eviscerate fish with the gusto of a gladiator."

And then an odd thing happened to relieve Mungo's embarrassment and end incontinent his garrulity. Floating on the air round the bulge of the turret came a strain of song in a woman's voice, not powerful but rich and sweet, young in its accent, the words inaudible but the air startling to Count Victor, who heard no more than half a bar before he had realised that it was the unfinished melody of the nocturnal flageolet. Before he could comment upon so unexpected and surprising a phenomenon, Mungo had dropped his gutting-knife, and made with suspicious rapidity for the entrance of the castle, without a word of explanation or leave-taking.

"I become decidedly interested in Annapla," said Montaiglon to himself, witnessing this odd retreat, "and my host gives me no opportunity of paying my homages. Malediction! It cannot be a wife; Bethune said nothing of a wife, and then M. le Baron himself spoke of himself as a widower. A domestic, doubtless; that will more naturally account for the ancient fishmonger's fleet retirement. He goes to chide the erring abigail. Or—or—or the cunning wretch!" continued Montaiglon with new meaning in his eyes, "he is perhaps the essential lover. Let the Baron at breakfast elucidate the mystery."

But the Baron at breakfast said never a word of the domestic economy of his fortalice. As they sat over a frugal meal of oat porridge, the poached fish, and a smoky high-flavoured mutton ham whose history the Count was happy not to know, his host's conversation was either upon Paris, where he had spent some months of sad expatriation, yawning at its gaiety (it seemed) and longing for the woods of Doom; or upon the plan of the search for the spy and double traitor.

Montaiglon's plans were simple to crudeness. He had, though he did not say so, anticipated some assistance from Doom in identifying the object of his search; but now that this was out of the question, he meant, it appeared, to seek the earliest and most plausible excuse for removal into the immediate vicinity of Argyll's castle, and on some pretext to make the acquaintance of as many of the people there as he could, then to select his man from among them, and push his affair to a conclusion.

"A plausible scheme," said Doom when he heard it, "but contrived without any knowledge of the situation. It's not Doom, M. le Count—oh no, it's not Doom down-by there; it's a far more kittle place to learn the outs and ins of. The army and the law are about it, the one about as numerous as the other, and if your Drimdarroch, as I take it, is a traitor on either hand—to Duke Archie as well as to the king across the water, taking the money of both as has happened before now, he'll be no

Drimdarroch, you may wager, and not kent as such down there. Indeed, how could he? for Petullo the writer body is the only Drimdarroch there is to the fore, and he has a grieve in the place. Do you think this by-named Drimdarroch will be going about cocking his bonnet over his French amours and his treasons? Have you any notion that he will be the more or the less likely to do so when he learns that there's a French gentleman of your make in the countryside, and a friend of Doom's, too, which means a Jacobite? A daft errand, if I may say it; seeking a needle in a haystack was bairn's play compared to it."

"If you sit down on the haystack you speedily find the needle, M. le Baron," said Montaiglon playfully. "In other words, trust my sensibility to feel the prick of his presence whenever I get into his society. The fact that he may suspect my object here will make him prick all the quicker and all the harder."

"Even yet you don't comprehend Argyll's court. It's not Doom, mind you, but a place hotching with folk—half a hundred perhaps of whom have travelled as this Drimdarroch has travelled, and in Paris too, and just of his visage perhaps. Unless you challenged them all seriatim, as Petullo would say, I see no great prospect."

"I wish we could coax the fly here! That or something like it was what I half expected to be able to do when Bethune gave me your address as that of a landlord in the neighbourhood."

Doom reddened, perhaps with shame at the altered condition of his state in the house of his fathers. "I've seen the day," said he—"I've seen the day they were throng enough buzzing about Doom, but that was only so long as honey was to rob with a fair face and a nice humming at the robbery. Now that I'm a rooked bird and Doom a herried nest, they never look the road I'm on."

Mungo, standing behind his master's chair, gave a little crackling laugh and checked it suddenly at the angry flare in his master's face.

"You're mighty joco!" said the Baron; "perhaps you'll take my friend and me into your confidence;" and he frowned with more than one meaning at the little-abashed retainer.

"Paurdon! paurdon!" said Mungo, every part of the chart-like face thrilled with some uncontrollable sense of drollery, and he exploded in laughter more violent than ever.

"Mungo!" cried his master in the accent of authority.

The domestic drew himself swiftly to attention.

"Mungo!" said his master, "you're a damned fool! In the army ye would have got the triangle for a good deal less. Right about face."

Mungo saluted and made the required retreat with a great deal less than his usual formality.

"There's a bit crack in the creature after all," said the Baron, displaying embarrassment and annoyance, and he quickly changed the conversation, but with a wandering mind, as Count Victor could not fail to notice. The little man, to tell the truth, had somehow laughed at the wrong moment for Count Victor's peace of mind. For why should he be amused at the paucity of the visitors from Argyll's court to the residence of Doom? Across the table at a man unable to conceal his confusion, Montaiglon stole an occasional glance with suspicion growing on him irresistibly.

An inscrutable face was there, as many Highland faces were to him, even among old friends in France, where Balhaldie, with the best possible hand at a game of cards, kept better than any gambler he had ever known before a mask of dull and hopeless resignation. The tongue was soft and fair-spoken; the hand seemed generous enough, but this by all accounts had been so even with Drimdarroch himself, and Drimdarroch was rotten to the core.

"Very curious," thought Montaiglon, making poor play with his braxy ham. "Could Bethune be mistaken in this extraordinary Baron?" And he patched together in his mind Mungo's laughter with the Baron's history as briefly known to him, and the inexplicable signal and alarm of the night.

"Your Mademoiselle Annapla seems to be an entrancing vocalist," said he airily, feeling his way to a revelation.

The Baron, in his abstraction, scarcely half comprehended.

45

"The maid," he said, "just the maid!" and never a word more, but into a new topic.

"I trust so," thought the Count; "but the fair songster who signals from her window and has clandestine meetings at midnight with masculine voices must expect some incredulity on that point. Can it be possible that here I have Blue Beard or Lothario? The laughter of the woman seems to indicate that if here is not Lothario, here at all events is something more than seems upon the surface. *Tonnerre de Dieu!* I become suspicious of the whole breed of mountaineers. And not a word about last night's alarm— that surely, in common courtesy, demands some explanation to the guest whose sleep is marred."

They went out together upon the mainland in the forenoon to make inquiries as to the encounter with the Macfarlanes, of whose presence not a sign remained. They had gone as they had come, without the knowledge of the little community on the south of Doom, and the very place among the bracken where the Count had dropped his bird revealed no feather; the rain of the morning had obliterated every trace. He stood upon the very spot whence he had fired at the luckless robber and restored, with the same thrill of apprehension, the sense of mystery and of dread that had hung round him as he stole the day before through voiceless woods to the sound of noisy breakers on a foreign shore. He saw again the brake nod in a little air of wind as if a form was harboured, and the pagan rose in him—not the sceptic but the child of nature, early and remote, lost in lands of silence and of omen in dim-peopled and fantastic woods upon the verge of clamorous seas.

"*Dieu!*" said he with a shiver, turning to his host. "This is decidedly not Verray's in the Rue Conde. I would give a couple of *louis d'or* for a moment of the bustle of Paris."

"A sad place yon!" said Doom.

And back they went to the castle to play a solemn game of lansquenet.

VII

The Bay of the Boar's Head

A solemn game indeed, for the Baron was a man of a sobriety
unaccountable to Montaiglon, who, from what he knew of
Macdonnel of Barisdel, Macleod, Balhaldie, and the others of the
Gaelic gang in Paris, had looked for a roysterer in Doom. It was
a man with strange melancholies he found there, with a ludicrous
decorum for a person of his condition, rising regularly on the
hour, it seemed, and retiring early to his chamber like a peasant,
keeping no company with the neighbouring lairds because he
could not even pretend to emulate their state, passing his days
among a score of books in English, some (as the Sieur de Guille)
in French, and a Bedel Bible in the Irish letter, and as often
walking aimlessly about the shore looking ardently at the hills,
and rehearsing to himself native rhymes that ever account native
women the dearest and the same hills the most beautiful in God's
creation. He was the last man to look to for aid in an enterprise
like Montaiglon's: if he had an interest in the exploit it seemed
it was only to discourage the same, and an hour or two of his
company taught the Count he must hunt his spy unaided.

But the hunting of the spy, in the odd irrelevance or incon-
sistency of nature, was that day at least an enterprise altogether
absent from his thoughts. He had been diverted from the object
of his journey to Scotland by just such a hint at romance as never
failed to fascinate a Montaiglon, and he must be puzzling himself
about the dulcet singer and her share in the clandestine midnight
meeting. When he had finished his game with his host, and the
latter had pleaded business in the burgh as an excuse for his
absence in the afternoon, Count Victor went round Doom on
every side trying to read its mystery. While it was a house
whose very mortar must be drenched with tradition, whose

every window had looked upon histories innumerable worth retelling, nothing was revealed of the matter in hand.

Many rooms of it were obviously unoccupied, for in the domestic routine of the Baron and of Mungo and the lady of song there were two storeys utterly unoccupied, and even in the flats habited there were seemingly chambers vacant, at least ever unopened and forlorn. Count Victor realised, as he looked at the frowning and taciturn walls, that he might be in Doom a twelvemonth and have no chance to learn from that abstracted scholar, its owner, one-half of its interior economy.

From the ground he could get no clear view of the woman's window: that he discovered early, for it was in the woman he sought the key to all Doom's little mystery. He must, to command the window, climb to his own chamber in the tower, and even then it was not a full front view he had but a foreshortened glance at the side of it and the signal, if any more signalling there might be. He never entered that room without a glance along the sunlit walls; he never passed the mouth of that corridor on the half landing where his candle had blown out without as curious a scrutiny as good-breeding might permit. And nothing was disclosed.

Mungo pervaded the place—Mungo toiling in the outhouses at tasks the most menial, feeding the half-dozen moulting poultry, digging potatoes in the patch of garden or plucking colewort there, climbing the stairs with backets of peat or wood, shaking a table-cloth to the breeze; and in the *salle* the dark and ruminating master indulging his melancholy by rebuilding the past in the red ash of the fire, or looking with pensive satisfaction from his window upon the coast, a book upon his knee—that was Doom as Count Victor was permitted to know it.

He began at last to doubt his senses, and half believe that what he had heard on the night of his arrival had been some chimera— a dream of a wearied and imperilled man in unaccustomed surroundings.

Mungo saw him walk with poorly concealed curiosity about the outside of the stronghold, and smiled to himself as one who knows the reason for a gentleman's prying. Montaiglon caught that smile once: his chagrin at its irony was blended with a pleasing delusion that the frank and genial domestic might proffer a solution without indelicate questioning. But he was soon undeceived: the discreet retainer knew but three things in this world—the grandeur of war, the ancient splendour of the house of Doom, and the excellent art of absent-mindedness. When it came to the contents of Doom, Mungo Boyd was an oyster.

"It must have been a place of some importance in its day," said Count Victor, gazing up at the towering walls and the broken embrasures.

"And what is't yet?" demanded Mungo, jealously, with no recollection that a moment ago he had been mourning its decline.

"*Eh bien!* It is quite charming, such of it as I have had the honour to see; still, when the upper stages were habitable . . ." and Count Victor mentally cursed his luck that he must fence with a blunt-witted scullion.

"Oh ay! I'll allo' I've seen it no' sae empty, if that's what ye mean; but if it's no' jist Dumbarton or Dunedin, it's still auld bauld Doom, and an ill deevil to crack, as the laddie said that found the nutmeg."

"But surely," conceded Montaiglon, "and yet, and yet—have you ever heard of Jericho, M. Boyd? Its capitulation was due to so simple a thing as the playing of a trumpet or two."

"I ken naething aboot trumpets," said Mungo curtly, distinguishing some *arrière pensée* in the interrogator.

"*Fi donc!* and you so much the old *sabreur*! Perhaps your people marched to the flageolet—a seductive instrument, I assure you."

The little man betrayed confusion. "Annapla thrieps there's a ghaistly flageolet aboot Doom," said he, "but it'll hae to play awa' lang or the wa's o' oor Jericho fa',—they're seeven feet thick."

"He plays divinely this ghostly flageoleteer, and knows his Handel to a demi-semi-quaver," said Count Victor, coolly.

49

"O Lord! lugs! I told them that!" muttered Mungo.

"Pardon!"

"Naething; we're a' idiots noo and then, and—and I maun awa' in."

So incontinently he parted from Count Victor, who, to pass the afternoon, went walking on the mainland highway. He walked to the south through the little hamlet he and Doom had visited earlier in the day; and as the beauty of the scenery allured him increasingly the farther he went, he found himself at last on a horn of the great bay where the Duke's seat lay sheltered below its hilly ramparts. As he had walked to this place he had noticed that where yesterday had been an empty sea was now a fleet of fishing-boats scurrying in a breeze off land, setting out upon their evening travail—a heartening spectacle; and that on either side of him once the squalid huts of Doom were behind—was a more dainty country with cultivated fields well fenced, and so he was not wholly unprepared for the noble view revealed when he turned the point of land that hid the policies of MacCailein Mor.

But yet the sight somewhat stunned. In all his notions of Drimdarroch's habitation, since he had seen the poverty of Doom, he had taken his idea from the Baron's faded splendour, and had ludicrously underestimated the importance of Argyll's court and the diffculty of finding his man. Instead of a bleak bare countryside, with the ducal seat a mean tower in the midst of it, he saw a wide expanse of thickly wooded and inhabitable country speckled for miles with comfortable dwellings, the castle itself a high embattled structure, clustered round by a town of some dimensions, and at its foot a harbour, where masts were numerous and smoke rose up in clouds.

Here was, plainly, a different society from Doom; here was something of what the exiled chiefs had bragged of in their cups. The Baron had suggested no more than a dozen of cadets about the place. *Grand Dieu!* there must be a regiment in and about this haughty palace with its black and yellow banner streaming in the wind, and to seek Drimdarroch there and round that busy neighbourhood seemed a task quite hopeless.

For long he stood on the nose of land, gazing with a thousand speculations at where probably lay his prey, and when he returned to the castle of Doom it looked all the more savage and inhospitable in contrast with the lordly domicile he had seen. What befell him there on his return was so odd and unexpected that it clean swept his mind again of every interest in the spy.

VIII

An Apparition

The tide in his absence had come in around the rock of Doom, and he must signal for Mungo's ferry. Long and loud he piped but there was at first no answer; and when at last the little servitor appeared, it was to look who called, and then run back with a haste no way restrained by any sense of garrison punctilio. He was not long gone, but when he came down again to the boat his preparations for crossing took up an unconscionable time. First the boat must be baled, it seemed, and then a thole-pin was to find; when launched the craft must tangle her bow unaccountably and awkwardly in the weeds. And a curt man was Mungo, though his salute for Count Victor had lost none of its formality. He seemed to be the family's friend resenting, as far as politeness might, some inconvenience to which it was being subjected without having the power to prevent the same.

Before they had gained the rock, dusk was on the country, brought the sooner for a frost-fog that had been falling all afternoon. It wrapped the woods upon the shore, made dim the yeasty water-way, and gave Doom itself the look of a phantom edifice. It would be ill to find a place less hospitable and cheerful in its outer aspect; not for domestic peace it seemed, but for dark exploits. The gloomy silhouette against the drab sky rose inconceivably tall, a flat plane like a cardboard castle giving little of an impression of actuality, but as a picture dimly seen, flooding an impressionable mind like Count Victor's with a myriad sensations, tragic and unaccustomed. From the shore side no light illumined the sombre masonry; but to the south there was a glow in what he fancied now must be the woman's window, and higher up, doubtless in the chapel above the flat he occupied himself, there was a radiance on which Mungo at

52

the oars turned round now and then to look.

Whistling a careless melody, and with no particularly acute observation of anything beyond the woman's window, which now monopolised his keenest interest in Doom, Count Victor leaped out of the boat as soon as it reached the rock, and entered the castle by the door which Mungo had left open.

What had been a crêpe-like fog outside was utter gloom within. The corridor was pitch-black, the stair, as he climbed to his room, was like a wolf's throat, as the saying goes; but as he felt his way up, a door somewhere above him suddenly opened and shut, lending for a moment a gleam of reflected light to his progress. It was followed immediately by a hurried step coming down the stair.

At first he thought he was at length to see the mysterious Annapla, but the masculine nature of the footfall told him he was in error.

"M. le Baron," he concluded, "and home before me by another route," and he stepped closely into the right side of the wall to give passage. But the darkness made identity impossible, and he waited the recognition of himself. It never came. He was brushed past as by a somnambulist, without greeting or question, though to accomplish it the other in the narrow stairway had to rub clothes with him. Something utterly unexpected in the apparition smote him with surprise and apprehension. It was as if he had encountered something groping in a mausoleum— something startling to the superstitious instinct, though not terrific in a material way. When it passed he stood speechless on the stair, looking down into the profound black, troubled with amazement, full of speculation. All the suspicions that he had felt last night, when the signal-calls rose below the turret and the door had opened and the flageolet had disturbed his slumbers came back to him more sinister, more compelling than before. He listened to the declining footfall of that silent mystery; a whisper floated upwards, a door creaked, no more than that, and yet the effect was wildly disturbing, even to a person of the *sang froid* of Montaiglon.

At a bound he went up to his chamber and lit a candle, and stood a space on the floor, lost in thought. When he looked at his face, half unconscious that he did so, in a little mirror on a table he saw revealed there no coward terrors, but assuredly alarm. He smiled at his pallid image, tugged in Gascon manner at his moustache, and threw out his chest; then his sense of humour came to him, and he laughed at the folly of his perturbation. But he did not keep the mood long.

"My *sans culottes* surely do not share the hospitality of Doom with me in its owner's absence," he reflected. "And yet, and yet—! I owe Bethune something for the thrill of the experiences he has introduced me to. Now I comprehend the affection of those weeping exiles for the very plain and commonplace life of France they profess to think so indifferent a country compared with this they have left behind. A week of these ghosts would drive me to despair. Tomorrow—tomorrow—M. de Montaiglon,— tomorrow you make your reluctant adieux to Doom and its inexplicable owner, whose surprise and innuendo are altogether too exciting."

So he promised himself as he walked up and down the floor of his chamber, feeling himself in a cage, yet unable to think how he was to better his condition without the aid of the host whose mysteries disturbed so much by the suspicions they aroused. Bethune had told him Lamond, in spite of his politics and his comparative poverty, was on neighbourly terms with Argyll, and would thus be in a position to put him in touch with the castle of the Duke and the retinue there without creating any suspicion as to the nature of his mission. It was that he had depended on, and to no other quarter could he turn with a hope of being put into communication with the person he sought. But Doom was apparently quite unqualified to be an aid to him. He was, it seemed, at variance with his Grace on account of one of those interminable lawsuits with which the Gaelic chiefs, debarred from fighting in the wholesome old manner with the sword, indulged their contestful passions, and he presented first of all a difficulty that Count Victor in his most hopeless moments had never allowed for—he did not know the identity of the man sought for, and he questioned if it could easily be established. All these considerations determined Count Victor upon an immediate removal from this starven castle and this suspicious host. But when he joined Doom in the *salle* he constrained his features to a calm reserve, showing none of his emotions.

He found the Baron seated by the fire, and ready to take a suspiciously loud but abstracted interest in his ramble.

"Well, Count," said he, "ye've seen the castle o' the King o' the Hielan's, as we call him, have you? And what think ye of MacCailein's quarters?"

Montaiglon lounged to a chair, threw a careless glance at his interrogator, pulled the ever upright moustache, and calmly confessed them charming.

A bitter smile came on the face of his host. "They might well be that," said he. "There's many a picking there." And then he became garrulous upon the tale of his house and family, that seemed to have been dogged by misfortune for a century and a half; that had owned once many of these lush glens, the shoulders of these steep bens, the shores of that curving coast. Bit by bit that ancient patrimony had sloughed off in successive generations, lost to lust, to the gambler's folly, the spendthrift's weakness.

"Hard, is it not?" questioned his host. "I'm the man that should have Doom at its very best, for I could bide among my people here, and like them, and make them like me, without a thought of rambling about the world. 'Mildewing with a ditch between you and life,' my grandfather used to call it when old age took him back from his gaieties abroad. Faith! I wish I had the chance to do it better than I may. All's here I ever wanted of life, and I have tasted it elsewhere too. Give me my own acres and my own people about me, and it would be a short day indeed from the rise of the sun till bedtime—a short day and a happy. My father used, after a week or two at home, to walk round the point of Strone where you were today and look at the skiffs and gabberts in the port down-by, and the sight never failed to put

frolic in the blood of him. If he saw a light out there at sea—
the lamp of a ship outbound, he would stand for hours in his
nightsark at the window gloating on it. As for me, no shiplight
gave me half the satisfaction of the evening star coming up above
the hill Ardno."

"Tomorrow," said Montaiglon—"tomorrow is another day;
that's my consolation in every trial."

"At something on the happy side of thirty it may be that,"
admitted Doom; "at forty-five there's not so muckle satisfaction
in it."

Through all this Count Victor, in spite of the sympathy that
sometimes swept him away into his host's narrative, felt his
doubts come back and back at intervals. With an eye intent
upon the marvel before him, he asked often what this gentleman
was concealing. Was he plotting something? And with whom?
What was the secret of that wind-blown castle, its unseen occupants, its midnight music, the ironic laughter of the domestic
Mungo, the annoyance of its master at his mirth? Could he
possibly be unaware of the strange happenings in his house, of
what signalled by day and crept on stairs at night? To look at
him yearning there, he was the last man in the world to associate
with the thrilling moment of an hour ago when Montaiglon met
the marvel on the stairway; but recollections of Drimdarroch's
treachery, and the admission of Doom himself that it was not
uncommon among the chiefs, made him hopeless of reading that
inscrutable face, and he turned to look about the room for some
clue to what he found nowhere else.

A chamber plain to meanness—there seemed nothing here to
help him to a solution. The few antlered stag-heads upon the
walls were mangy and dusty; the strip of arras that swayed softly
in the draught of a window only sufficed to accentuate the sordid
nature of that once pretentious interior. And the half-curtained
recess, with the soiled and dog-eared documents of the law, was
the evidence of how all this tragedy of a downfallen house had
come about.

Doom's eyes saw his fall upon the squalid pile.

"Ay!" he said, "that's the ashes of Doom, all that's left of what we burned in fiery living and hot law-pleas. We have the ash and the others have warm hands."

Count Victor, who had been warming his chilled fingers at the fire, moved to the curtain and drew it back, the better again to see that doleful cinerary urn.

His host rose hurriedly from his chair.

"Trash! Trash! Only trash, and dear bought at that," said he, seeing his guest's boot-toe push the papers in with a dainty man's fastidiousness.

But the deed was done before the implied protest was attended. The Count's movements revealed a Highland dagger concealed beneath one of the parchments! It was a discovery of no importance in a Highland castle, where, in spite of the proscription of weapons, there might innocently be something so common as a dagger left; but a half-checked cry from the Baron stirred up again all Count Victor's worst suspicions.

He looked at Doom, and saw his face was hot with some confusion, and that his tongue stammered upon an excuse his wits were not alert enough to make.

He stooped and picked up the weapon—an elegant instrument well adorned with silver on the hilt and sheath; caught it at the point, and, leaning the hilt upon his left wrist in the manner of the courtier slightly exaggerated, and true to the delicacies of the *salle-d'armes*, proffered it to the owner.

Doom laughed in some confusion. "Ah!" said he lamely, "Mungo's been at his dusting again," and he tried to restore the easiness of the conversation that the incident had so strangely marred.

But Montaiglon could not so speedily restore his equanimity. For the unknown who had so unceremoniously brushed against him on the dark stair had been attired in Highland clothes. It had been a bare knee that had touched him on the leg; it had been a plaid-fringe that had brushed across his face; and his knuckles had been rapped lightly by the protuberances upon the sheath and hilt of a mountain dagger. M. le Baron's proscription of arms seemed to have some strange exceptions, he told himself. They were not only treated with contempt by the Macfarlanes, but even in Doom Castle, whose owner affected to look upon the garb of his ancestors as something well got rid of. For the life of him, Count Victor could not disassociate the thought of that mysterious figure on the stair, full clad in all Highland panoply against the law, and the men—the broken men—who had shot his pony in the wood and attempted to rob him. All the eccentricities of his host mustered before him—his narrow state here with but one servant apparent, a mysterious room tenanted by an invisible woman, and his coldness—surely far from the Highland temper—to the Count's scheme of revenge upon the fictitious Drimdarroch.

There was an awkward pause even the diplomacy of the Frenchman could not render less uncomfortable, and the Baron fumbled with the weapon ere he laid it down again on the table.

"By the way," said Count Victor, now with his mind made up, "I see no prospect of pushing my discoveries from here, and it is also unfair that I should involve you in my adventure that had much better be conducted from the plain base of an inn, if such there happens to be in the town down there."

A look of unmistakable relief, quelled as soon as it breathed across his face, came to the Baron. "Your will is my pleasure," he said quickly; "but there is at this moment no man in the world who could be more welcome to share my humble domicile."

"Yet I think I could work with more certainty of a quick success from a common lodging in the town than from here. I have heard that now and then French fish dealers and merchants sometimes come for barter to this coast and—"

The ghost of a smile came over Doom's face. "They could scarcely take you for a fish merchant, M. le Count," said he.

"At all events common fairness demands that I should adopt any means that will obviate getting your name into the thing, and I think I shall try the inn. Is there one?"

"There is the best in all the West Country there," said Doom, "kept by a gentleman of family and attainments. But it will not do for you to go down there without some introduction. I shall have to speak of your coming to some folk and see if it is a good time."

"*Eh bien!* Remember at all events that I am in affairs," said Montaiglon, and the thing was settled.

IX

Trapped

It was only at the dawn, or the gloaming, or in night itself—and above all in the night—that the castle of Doom had its tragic aspect. In the sun of midday, as Count Victor convinced himself on the morrow of a night with no alarms, it could be almost cheerful, and from the garden there was sometimes something to be seen with interest of a human kind upon the highway on the shore.

A solitary land, but in the happy hours people were passing to and fro between the entrances to the ducal seat and the north. Now and then bands of vagrants from the heights of Glencroe and the high Rest where Wade's road bent among the clouds would pass with little or no appeal to the hospitality of Doom, whose poverty they knew; now and then rustics in red hoods, their feet bare upon the gravel, made for the town market, sometimes singing as they went till their womanly voices, even in airs unfamiliar and a language strange and guttural, gave to Count Victor an echo of old mirth in another and a warmer land. Men passed on rough short ponies; once a chariot with a great caleche roof swung on the rutted road, once a company of redcoat soldiery shot like a gleam of glory across the afternoon, moving to the melody of a fife and drum.

For the latter Mungo had a sour explanation. They were come, it seemed, to attend a trial for murder. A clansman of the Duke's and a far-out cousin (in the Highland manner of speaking) had been shot dead in the country of Appin; the suspected assassin, a Stewart of course, was on trial; the blood of families and factions was hot over the business, and the Government was sending its soldiery to convoy James Stewart of the Glen, after his conviction, back to the place of execution.

"But, *mon Dieu!* he is yet to try, is he not?" cried Count Victor.

"Oh ay!" Mungo acquiesced, "but that doesna' maitter; the puir cratur is as guid as scragged. The tow's aboot his thrapple and kittlin' him already, I'll warrant, for his name's Stewart, and in this place I would sooner be ca'd Beelzebub; I'd hae a better chance o' my life if I found mysel' in trouble wi' a Campbell jury to try me."

Montaiglon watched this little body of military march along the road, with longing in his heart for the brave and busy outside world they represented. He watched them wistfully till they had disappeared round the horn of land he had stood on yesterday, and their fife and drum had altogether died upon the air of the afternoon. And turning, he found the Baron of Doom silent at his elbow, looking under his hat-brim at the road.

"More trouble for the fesse checkey, Baron," said he, indicating the point whereto the troops had gone.

"The unluckiest blazon on a coat," replied the castellan of Doom; "trouble seems to be the part of everyone who wears it. It's in a very unwholesome quarter when it comes into the boar's den. . . ."

"Boar's den?" repeated Montaiglon interrogatively.

"The head of the pig is his Grace's cognisance. Clan Diarmaid must have got it first by raiding in some Appin stye, as Petullo my doer down-by says. He is like most men of his trade, Petullo; he is ready to make his treasonable joke even against the people who pay him wages, and I know he gets the wages of the Duke as well as my fees. I'm going down to transact some of the weary old business with him just now, and I'll hint at your coming. A Bordeaux wine merchant—it will seem more like the thing than the fish dealer."

"And I know a good deal more about wine than about fish," laughed Count Victor, "so it will be safer."

"I think you would be best to have been coming to the town when the Macfarlanes attacked you, killed your horse, and chased you into my place. That's the most plausible story we

61

can tell, and it has the virtue of being true in every particular, without betraying that Bethune or friendship for myself was in any part of it."

"I can leave it all to your astuteness," said Montaiglon.

The Baron was absent, as he had suggested was possible, all day. The afternoon was spent by Count Victor in a dull enough fashion, for even Mungo seemed morose in his master's absence, perhaps overweighted by the mysteries now left to his charge, disinclined to talk of anything except the vast wars in which his ancestors had shone with blinding splendour, and of the world beyond the confines of Doom. But even his store of reminiscence became exhausted, and Count Victor was left to his own resources. Back again to his seat on the rock he went, and again to the survey of the mainland that seemed so strangely different a clime from this where nothing dwelt but secrecy and decay.

In the afternoon the traffic on the highway had ceased, for the burgh now held all of that wide neighbourhood that had leisure, or any excuse of business to transact in the place where a great event was happening. The few that moved in the sun of the day were, with but one exception, bound for the streets; the exception naturally created some wonder on the part of Count Victor.

For it was a man in the dress (to judge at a distance) of a gentleman, and his action was singular. He was riding a jet-black horse of larger stature than any that the rustics and farmers who had passed earlier in the day bestrode, and he stood for a time half-hidden among trees opposite the place where Count Victor reclined on a patch of grass among whin-bushes. Obviously he did not see Montaiglon, to judge from the calmness of his scrutiny, and assuredly it was not to the Frenchman that, after a little, he waved a hand. Count Victor turned suddenly and saw a responsive hand withdrawn from the window that had so far monopolised all his interest in Doom's exterior. Annapla had decidedly an industrious wooer, more constant than the sun itself, for he seemed to shine in her heavens night and day.

There was, in a sense, but little in the incident, which was open to a score of innocent or prosaic explanations, and the cavalier

62

was spurring back a few minutes later to the south, but it confirmed Count Victor's determination to have done with Doom at the earliest, and off to where the happenings of the day were more lucid.

At supper-time the Baron had not returned. Mungo came up to discover Count Victor dozing over a stupid English book and wakened him to tell him so, and that supper was on the table. He toyed with the food, having no appetite, turned to his book again, and fell asleep in his chair. Mungo again came in and removed the dishes silently, and looked curiously at him—so much the foreigner in that place, so perjink in his attire, so incongruous in his lace with this solitary keep of the mountains. It was a strange face the servant turned upon him there at the door as he retired to his kitchen quarters. And he was not gone long when he came back with a woman who walked tiptoe into the doorway.

"That's the puir cratur," said he; "seekin' for whit he'll never find, like the man with the lantern playin' ki-hoi wi' honesty."

She looked with interest at the stranger, said no word, but disappeared.

The peats sunk upon the hearth, crumbling in hearts of fire: on the outer edges the ashes grew grey. The candles of coarse mould, stuck in a rude sconce upon the wall above the mantelshelf, guttered to their end, set aslant by wafts of errant wind that came in through the half-open door and crevices of the window. It grew cold, and Montaiglon shook himself into wakefulness. He sat up in his chair and looked about him with some sense of apprehension, with the undescribable instinct of a man who feels himself observed by eyes unseen, who has slept through an imminently dangerous moment.

He heard a voice outside.

"M. le Baron," he concluded. "Late, but still in time to say good night to the guest he rather cavalierly treats." And he rose and went downstairs to meet his host. The great door was ajar. He went into the open air. The garden was utterly dark, for clouds obscured the stars, and the air was laden with the saline odour of the wrack below high-water mark. The tide was out. What he had expected was to see Mungo and his master, but behind the castle where they should have been there was no one, and the voices he heard had come from the side next the shore. He listened a little and took alarm, for it was not one voice but the voices of several people he heard, and in the muffled whispers of men upon some dishonest adventure. At once he recalled the Macfarlanes and the surmise of Baron Doom that in two nights they might be crying their slogan round the walls that harboured their enemy. He ran hastily back to the house, quickly resumed the sword that had proved of some little use to him before, took up the more business-like pistol that had spoiled the features of the robber with the bladder-like head, and rushed downstairs again.

"*Qui est là?*" he demanded as he passed round the end of the house and saw dimly on the rock a group of men who had crossed upon the ebb. His appearance was apparently unexpected, for he seemed to cause surprise and a momentary confusion. Then a voice cried "Loch Sloy!" and the company made a rush to bear him down.

He withdrew hastily behind the wall of the garden, where he had them at advantage. As he faced round, the assailants, by common consent, left one man to do his business. He was a large well-built man, so far as might be judged in the gloom of the night, and he was attired in Highland clothes. The first of his acts was to throw off a plaid that muffled his shoulders; then he snapped a futile pistol, and fell back upon his sword, with which he laid out lustily.

In the dark it was impossible to make pretty fighting of the encounter. The Frenchman saw the odds too much against him, and realised the weakness of his flank; he lunged hurriedly through a poor guard of his opponent's, and pierced the fleshiness of the sword-arm. The man growled an oath, and Count Victor retreated.

Mungo, with a blanched face, was trembling in the entrance, and a woman was shrieking upstairs. The hall, lit by a flambeau that Mungo held in one hand, while the other held a huge horse-pistol, looked like the entrance to a dungeon,—something altogether sinister and ugly to the foreigner, who had the uneasy notion that he fought for his life in a prison. And the shrieks aloft rang wildly through the night like something in a story he had once read, with a mad woman incarcerated, and only to manifest herself when danger and mystery threatened.

"In ye come! in ye come!" cried the servant, trembling excessively till the flambeau shook in his hand and his teeth rattled together. "In ye come, and I'll bar the door."

It was time, indeed, to be in; for the enemy leaped at the oak as Count Victor threw it back upon its hinges rather dubious of the bars that were to withstand the weight without.

The sight of them reassured, however: they were no light bars Mungo drew forth from their channels in the masonry, but huge black iron-bound blocks a foot thick that ran in no staples, but could themselves secure the ponderous portals against anything less than an assault with cannon.

It was obvious that the gentry outside knew the nature of this obstruction, for, finding the bars out, they made no attempt to force the door.

Within, the Count and servant looked at each other's faces—the latter with astonishment and fear, the former with dumb questioning, and his ear to the stair whence came the woman's alarms.

"The Baron tell't us there wad be trouble," stammered the retainer, fumbling with the pistol so awkwardly that he endangered the body of his fellow in distress. "Black Andy was never kent to forget an injury, and I aye feared that the low tides wad bring him and his gang aboot the castle. Good God! do you hear them? It's a gey wanchancy thing this!" he cried in terror, as the shout "Loch Sloy!" arose again outside, and the sound of voices was all about the castle.

The woman within heard it too, for her cries became more hysterical than ever.

"D—n ye, ye skirlin' auld bitch!" said the retainer, turning in exasperation, "can ye no steek your jaw, and let them dae the howlin' outside?" But it was in a tone of more respect he shouted up the stair some words of assurance.

Yet there was no abatement of the cries, and Montaiglon, less—to do him justice—to serve his curiosity as to Annapla than from a natural instinct to help a distressed woman, put a foot on the stair to mount.

"Na, na! ye mauna leave me here!" cried Mungo, plucking at his sleeve.

There was something besides fear in the appeal, there was alarm of another sort that made Montaiglon pause and look the servitor in the eyes. He found confusion there as well as alarm at the furore outside and the imminent danger of the castle.

"I wish to God he was here himsel'," said Mungo helplessly, but still he did not relinquish his hold of Count Victor's sleeve.

"That need not prevent us comforting the lady," said Count Victor, releasing himself from the grasp.

"Let her alane; let her alane!" cried the servant distractedly, following the Frenchman upstairs.

Count Victor paid no heed: he was now determined to unveil a mystery that for all he knew might menace himself in this household of strange midnight happenings. The cries of the woman came from the corridor he had guessed her chamber to occupy, and to this he hastened. But he had scarcely reached the corridor when the flambeau Mungo held was suddenly blown out, and this effectively checked his progress. He turned for an explanation.

"D—n that draught!" said Mungo testily, "it's blawn oot my licht."

"We'll have to do without it, then," said the Count, "but you must show me the way to this shrieking woman."

"A' richt," said Mungo, "mind yer feet!" He passed before the Count and cautiously led him up to the passage where the woman's cries, a little less vehement, were still to be heard.

"There ye are! and muckle gude may it dae ye," he said, stopping at a door and pushing it open.

66

Count Victor stepped into darkness, thrust lightly as he went by the servant's hand, and the door closed with a click behind him. He was a prisoner! He had the humour to laugh softly at the conventionality of the deception as he vainly felt in an empty room for a non-existing door-handle, and realised that Mungo had had his own way after all. The servant's steps declined along the corridor and down the stair, with a woman's to keep them company and a woman's sobs, all of which convinced the Count that his acquaintance with Annapla was not desired by the residents of Doom.

X

Sim MacTaggart, Chamberlain

On the roof of a high old church with as little architectural elegance as a dry-stone barn, a bell jerked by a rope from the churchyard indicated the close association of law and the kirk by ringing a sort of triumphal peal to the procession of the judges between the court-room and the inn. Contesting with its not too dulcet music blared forth the fanfare of two gorgeous trumpeters in scarlet and gold lace, tie wigs, silk stockings, and huge cocked hats, who filled the street with a brassy melody that suggested Gabriel's stern and awful judgment-summons rather than gave lightness and rhythm to the feet of those who made up the procession. The procession itself had some dreadful aspects and elements as well as others incongruous and comical. The humorous fancy might see something to smile at in the two grey-wigged bent old men in long scarlet coats who went in front of the trumpeters, prepared to clear the way if necessary (though a gust of shrewd wind would have blown them off their feet), by means of the long-poled halberts they carried; but this impression of the farcical was modified by the nature of the body whereof they were the pioneers or advance guard. Sleek magistrates and councillors in unaccustomed black suits and silver-buckled shoes, the provost ermined at their head, showed the way to the more actual, the more dignified embodiment of stern Scots law. At least a score of wigs were there from the Parliament House of Edinburgh, a score of dusty gowns, accustomed to sweep the lobbies of the Courts of Session, gathered the sand of the burgh street, and in their midst walked the representatives of that old feudal law at long-last ostensibly abandoned, and of the common law of the land. Argyll was in a demure equivalent for some Court costume, with a dark velvet coat, a ribbon of the Thistle upon his shoulder, a sword upon his haunch, and for all his sixty-six years he carried himself less like the lawyer made at Utrecht—like Justice-General and Extraordinary Lord of Session—than like the old soldier who had served with Marlborough and took the field for the House of Hanover in 1715. My Lords Elchies and Kilkerran walked on either side of him—Kilkerran with the lack-lustre eye of the passionate mathematician, the studious moralist devoted to midnight oil, a ruddy, tall, sturdy man, well filling the crimson and white silk gown; Elchies, a shrivelled atomy with a hirpling walk, leaning heavily upon a rattan, both with the sinister black tricorne hats in their hands, and flanked by a company of musketeers.

A great band of children lent the ludicrous element again to the company by following close upon its heels, chanting a doggerel song to the tune of the trumpets; the populace stood at the close-mouths or leaned over their windows looking at the spectacle, wondering at the pomp given to the punishment of a Stewart who a few years ago would have been sent to the gallows by his Grace with no more formality than might have attended the sentence of a kipper salmon-poacher to whipping at the hands of Long Davie the dempster.

His Grace was entertaining the Lords, the Counsel (all but the convict's lawyers—a lot of disaffected Jacobites, who took their food by themselves at the inn, and brusquely refused his Grace's hospitality), the magistracy, and some county friends, to a late dinner at the castle that night, and an hour after saw them round the ducal board.

If Count Victor was astonished at the squalid condition of things in the castle of the poor Baron of Doom, he would have been surprised to find here, within an hour or two's walk of it, so imposing and luxuriant a domesticity. Many lands, many hands, great wealth won by law, battle, and the shrewdness of generations, enabled Argyll to give his castle grandeur and his table the opulence of any southern palace. And it was a bright company that sat about his board, with several ladies in it, for his duchess loved to have her sojourn in her Highland home made gay by the company of young women who might by their beauty and light hearts recall her own lost youth.

A bagpipe stilled in the hall, a lute breathed a melody from a neighbouring room, the servants in claret and yellow livery noiselessly served wine.

Elchies sourly pursed his lips over his liquor, to the mingled amusement and vexation of his Grace, who knew his lordship's cellar, or even the Justiciary Vault in the town (for the first act of the Court had been to send down wine from Edinburgh for their use on circuit), contained no vintage half so good, and "Your Grace made reference on the way up to someone killed in the neighbourhood," he said, as one resuming a topic begun elsewhere.

"Not six miles from where we sit," replied the Duke, his cultivated English accent in a strong contrast with the broad burr of the Edinburgh justiciar, "and scarcely a day before you drove past. The man shot, so far as we have yet learned, was a Macfarlane, one of a small but ancient and extremely dishonest clan whose country used to be near the head of Loch Lomond. Scarcely more than half a hundred of them survive, but they give us considerable trouble, for they survive at the cost of their neighbours' gear and cattle. They are robbers and footpads, and it looks as if the fatality to one of their number near Doom has been incurred during a raid. We still have our raids, Lord Elchies, in spite of what you were saying on the bench as to the good example this part of the country sets the rest of the Highlands— not the raids of old fashion, perhaps, but more prosaic, simply thefts indeed. That is why I have had these troops brought here. It is reported to me pretty circumstantially that some of the Appin people are in the key to attempt a rescue of James Stewart on his way to the place of execution at Lettermore. They would think nothing of attempting it once he was brought the length of Benderloch, if only a law officer or two had him in charge."

"I would have thought the duty of keeping down a ploy of that kind would have been congenial to your own folk," said Elchies, drenching his nostrils vulgarly with macabaw.

70

Argyll smiled. "You may give us credit for willingness to take our share of the responsibility of keeping Appin in order," said he. "I should not wonder if there are half a hundred claymores with hands in them somewhere about our old barracks in Maltland. Eh! Simon?" and he smiled down the table to his Chamberlain.

"Five-and-forty, to be strict," said the gentleman appealed to, and never a word more but a sudden stop, for his half-eaten plum had miraculously gone from his plate in the moment he had looked up at the Duke.

"Was't in your lands?" asked Elchies, indifferent, but willing to help on a good topic in a company where a variety of classes made the conversation anything but brisk.

"No," said Argyll, "it was in Doom, the place of a small landowner, Lamond, whose castle—it is but a ramshackle old bigging now—you may have noticed on your left as you rode round. Lamond himself is a man I have a sort of softness for, though, to tell the truth, he has forced me into more litigation than he had money to pay for and I had patience to take any lasting interest in."

"The Baron of Doom, is that the man?" cried Elchies, drily. "Faith, I ken him well. Some years syne he was living months at a time in the Court of Session, and eating and sleeping in John's Coffee-house, and his tale—it's a gey old one—was that the litigation was always from the other side. I mind the man weel; Baron he called himself, though, if I mind right, his title had never been confirmed by the king *in liberam baroniam*. He had no civil nor criminal jurisdiction. A black-avised man; the last time he came before me—Mr Petullo, ye were there—it was in a long-standing case o' multiple-poinding, and if I'm no' mistaken, a place ca'd Drimadry or Drimdarry, or something like that, changed hands ower the head o't."

Petullo the writer, shrinking near the foot of the table in an adequate sense of his insignificance, almost choked himself by gulping the whole glass of wine at his lips in his confusion, and broke into a perspiration at the attention of the company thus drawn to him. He squeaked back an unintelligible acquiescence;

and completed his own torture by upsetting a compote of fruit upon his black knee-breeches.

Opposite the unhappy lawyer sat a lady of extraordinary beauty—a haughty, cold, supercilious sort of beauty, remarkable mainly from the consciousness of its display. Her profile might have been cut from marble by a Greek; her neck and bust were perfect, but her shoulders, more angular than was common in that time of bottle-shape, were carried somewhat too grandly for a gentle nature. The cruelty of her character betrayed itself in a faint irrestrainable smile at Petullo's discomfiture, all the more cruel because his eyes were entreatingly on hers as he mopped up awkwardly the consequences of his gaucherie. She smiled, but that was not the strangest part of her conduct, for at the same time she nudged with her knee the Chamberlain who sat next to her, and who had brought her into the room. To cap the marvel, he showed no surprise, but took her hint with a conspirator's enforced composure. He looked at the little, dried-up, squeaking creature opposite, and—refused the lady the gratification of a single sign of the amusement she had apparently expected. She reddened, bit her nether lip, and "Your poor man of business is in a sore plight," she whispered, using the name Sim with significant freedom.

"My dear Kate," said he quietly, "as God's my judge, I can find nothing to laugh at in the misery of a poor wretch like yon."

"That's the second time!" she whispered with well-concealed ill-humour, a smile compelled upon her face but a serpent in her voice.

"The second time?" he repeated, lifting his eyebrows questioning, and always keeping a shoulder to her—a most chilly exterior. "Your ladyship is in the humour to give guesses."

She gave a swift reply to some only half-heard remark by her next-hand neighbour, then whispered to him, "It's the second time you have been cruel to me today. You seem bent on making me unhappy, and it is not what you promised. Am I not looking nice?"

"My dear girl," said he calmly, "do you know I am not in the

72

mood for making sport of an old fool to prove my kindness of heart to you."

"To me, Sim!" she whispered, the serpent all gone from her voice, and a warm, dulcet, caressing accent in it, while her eyes were melting with discreetly veiled love. "And I plotted so much to get beside you."

"That is the damned thing," he replied between his teeth, and smiling the while to some comment of his other neighbour, "you plot too much, my dear. I do not want to be unkind, but a little less plotting would become you more. I have no great liking for your husband, as you may guess; but there he's covered with compote and confusion, and for the look of the thing, if for no more, it would suit his wife to pretend some sympathy. In any case, for God's sake do not look at me as if I shared your amusement at his trouble. And I'm sure that Elchies by his glowering saw you eat my plum."

Mrs Petullo cast a glance of disdain at the poor object she was bound to by a marriage for position and money, and for a moment or two gave no attention to the society of his Grace's Chamberlain, who was so suspiciously in her confidence.

Simon MacTaggart played idly with the stem of his glass. He was odd in that bibulous age, in as much as he never permitted wine to tempt his palate to the detriment of his brains, and he listened gravely to the conversation that was being monopolised at the head of the table round the Duke.

Women liked him. Indeed women loved this Chamberlain of Argyll readily, more for his eyes and for his voice and for some odd air of mystery and romance in his presence than for what generally pass for good looks. He had just the history and the career and reputation that to men and women, except the very wisest and the somewhat elderly, have an attraction all unreasonable; for his youth had been stormy; he had known great dangers, tremendous misfortunes, overcoming both by a natural—sometimes spendthrift—courage; he was credited with more than one amorous intrigue, that being in high quarters was considered rather in his favour than otherwise; he was high in the esteem of families in the social scale considerably above his own (that had greatly declined since his people could first boast a coat impaled with the galley of Lorne); he was alert, mind and body, polite to punctilio, a far traveller, a good talker, and above all a lover of his kind, so that he went about with a smile (just touched a little by a poetic melancholy) for all. To the women at Argyll's table he was the most interesting man there, and though materially among the least eminent and successful, had it been his humour to start a topic of his own in opposition to his patron's, he could have captured the interest of the gathering in a sentence.

But Simon MacTaggart was for once not in the mood for the small change of conversation. Some weighty thought possessed him that gave his eye a remote quality even when he seemed to be sharing the general attention in the conversation, and it was as much resentment at the summons from his abstraction and his mood as a general disinclination to laugh at a wretch's misery on the bidding of the wretch's wife, that made him so curt to Mrs Petullo's advances. To him the dinner seemed preposterously unending. More than once his hand went to his fob with an unconscious response to his interest in the passage of the time; with difficulty he clenched his teeth upon the yawns that followed his forced smiles at the murmured pleasantries of the humble bailies and town councillors, who dared only venture on a joke of their own, and that discreetly muffled, when there was a pause in the conversation of the Duke and the Judges. And to the woman at his shoulder (the one on his left—the wife of the Provost, a little fair-haired doll with a giggling appreciation of the importance of her situation in such grand company, and a half-frightened gladness at being so near MacTaggart) he seemed more mysterious and wonderful than ever. Mrs Petullo, without looking at his half-averted face, knew by the mere magnetic current from his cold shoulder that of her he was just now weary, that with his company as a whole he was bored, and that some interest beyond that noisy hall engaged his abstracted thought.

"No," the Duke was saying; "the murderer has not been

74

discovered, nor indeed have we the most important evidence that there was a murder at all—for the body itself is as yet a mere matter of rumour, though of its existence there is no reasonable ground for doubt. It was carried off, as I am informed, by the Macfarlanes, whose anxiety to hush the affair is our main proof that they were on no honest expedition when this happened. But an affair like that gets bruited abroad: it came to us from Cairndhu that the corpse of a Macfarlane was carried past in the gloaming by some of his friends, anxious to get it smuggled through Ardkinglas with as little public notice as possible."

"*Acta exteriora indicant interiora secreta*, to somewhat misapply a well-kent maxim. The *res gestæ* show, I think, that it was a murder on the part of the robbers themselves." It was Elchies who spoke, cracking filberts the while with his great yellow teeth that gave him so cruel a look upon the bench.

"As a matter of fact," said the Chamberlain suddenly, "the man was shot by a French pistol," and a hush fell on the table in expectation of further details, but they were not forthcoming.

"Well, I'm astonished to hear it, and I hope you know where to lay hands on the homicide," said the Duke.

"It's none of our affair—nowadays," said the Chamberlain. "And, forbye, I'm only telling a carried tale after all. There may be no more in it than the fancy of the Glen Fyne folk who told me of it."

The Duke looked at his Chamberlain, saw that the topic, so far as he was concerned, was ended, and signalled to the Duchess. It was not the custom of the time, but her Grace had introduced into her Highland court the practice of withdrawing the ladies for some time after dinner, and leaving the men to their birling of the wine, as they phrased it. Out she swept at her husband's signal with her company—Lady Strachur, Lady Charlotte, Mrs Petullo, the Provost's wife, and three or four of no greater importance to our story—and of all that were left behind, perhaps there was none but her husband, who, oddly enough (as people thought) for a duke, loved her as if he were a boy courting still, to reflect that the room was colder and less human wanting the presence of her and her bright company. His Grace, who cared for the bottle even less than did his Chamberlain, slid round the wine sun-wise for a Highlander's notion of luck; the young advocates, who bleared somewhat at the eyes when they forgot themselves, felt the menacing sleepiness and glowing content of potations carried to the verge of indiscretion; Kilkerran hummed, Petullo hawed, the Provost humbly ventured a sculduddery tale, the Duke politely listening the while to some argument of Elchies upon the right of any one who had been attacked by the Macfarlanes to use arms against them.

"It's a well-allowed principle, your Grace," he maintained. "*Arma in armatos sumere jura sinunt*—the possessor may use violence to maintain his possession, but not to recover that of which he has been deprived." He looked like a Barbary ape as his shrunk jaws masticated the kernels he fed to his mouth with shaking claws: something deep and cunning peered forth below his bristling red eyebrows. The Duke could not but look at his protruding ears and experience an old sensation of his in the company of the more animal of his fellows, that, after all, man with a little practice might easily swing among trees or burrow in the earth.

An ill-trained servant removing empty bottles left the door open behind his Grace's chair, and through it came the strains of a duet in women's voices, accompanied by the strumming of a harp. They sang an English air touching upon groves and moonlit waterfalls, Lady Charlotte lending a dulcet second to the air of the Duchess, who accompanied them upon her instrument in sweeping chords and witching faint arpeggios. Into the room that fumed with tobacco and wine (and the Provost at the second of his tales in the ear of the advocate) the harmony floated like the praise of cherubim, and stilled at once the noisy disquisition round the board.

"Leave the door open," said the Duke to his servants, and they did so. When the song was done he felt his Jean was calling to him irresistibly, and he suggested that they had better join the ladies. They rose—some of them reluctantly—from the bottles,

76

Elchies strewing his front again with snuff to check his hiccoughs. MacTaggart, in an aside to the Duke, pleaded to be excused for his withdrawal immediately, as he felt indisposed.

"I noticed that you were gey glum tonight," said Argyll with a kind and even fraternal tone, for they were cousins and confidants as well as in a purely business relation to each other. "I'm thinking we both want some of the stimulant Elchies and the Provost and the advocate lads take so copiously."

"Bah!" said the Chamberlain; "but Sassenachs, Argyll, but Sassenachs, and they need it all. As for us, we're born with a flagon of heather ale within us, and we may be doing without the drug they must have, poor bodies, to make them sparkle."

Argyll laughed. "Good night, then," said he, "and a riddance to your vapours before the morning's morning."

Mrs Petullo had begun a song before the Duke entered, a melody of the Scots mode, wedded to words that at that period hummed round the country. It was the one triumphant moment of her life—her musically vocal—when she seemed, even to the discriminating who dive for character below the mere skin, to be a perfect angel. Pathos, regret, faith, hope, and love, she could simulate marvellously: the last was all that was really hers, and even that was lawless. She had not half-finished the air when the Duke came into the room softly on his tiptoes, humming her refrain. A keen ear might have perceived the slightest of alterations in the tone of her next stanza; a quick eye might have noticed a shade of disappointment come to her face when her intent but momentary glance at the door revealed that someone she sought was not entering. The only ear that heard, the only eye that saw, was Kilkerran's. He was a moralist by repute, and he would have suspected without reasons. When Mrs Petullo broke down miserably in her third verse, he smiled to himself pawkily, went up to her with a compliment, and confirmed his suspicions by her first question, which was as to the Chamberlain's absence.

As for the Chamberlain, he was by now hurrying with great speed through the castle garden. Only once he slacked his pace, and that was when the garden path joined the more open policies of the Duke, and another step or two would place a thicket of laburnums and hawthorns between him and the sight of the litten windows. He hung on his heel and looked back for a minute or two at the castle, looming blackly in the darkness against the background of Dunchuach; he could hear the broken stanza of Mrs Petullo's ballad.

"Amn't I the damned fool?" said he, half-aloud to himself, with bitter certainty in the utterance. "There's my punishment: by something sham—and I ken it's sham too—I must go through life beguiled from right and content. Here's what was to be the close of my folly, and Sim MacTaggart eager to be a good man if he got anything like a chance, but never the chance for poor Sim MacTaggart!"

He plunged into the darkness of the road that led to the Maltland barracks where the fifty claymores were quartered.

XI

The Woman at the Window

Count Victor heard the woman's lamentation die away in the pit of the stair before he ceased to wonder at the sound and had fully realised the unpleasantness of his own incarceration. It was the cries of the outer assault that roused him from mere amazement to a comprehension of the dangers involved in his being thus penned in a cell and his enemies kept at bay by some wooden bars and a wooden-head. He felt with questioning fingers along the walls, finding no crevice to suggest outer air till he reached the window, and, alas! an escape from a window at that height seemed out of the question without some machinery at hand.

"I suspected the little clown's laughter," said he to himself. "The key of the mystery lies between him and this absurd Baron, and I begin to guess at something of complicity on the part of M. Bethune. A malediction on the whole tribe of mountaineers! The thing's like a play; I've seen far more improbable circumstances in a book. I am shot at in a country reputed to be well-governed even to monotony; a sombre host puzzles, a far too frank domestic perplexes; magic flutes and midnight voices haunt this infernal hold; the conventional lady of the drama is kept in the background with great care, and just when I am on the point of meeting her, the perplexing servitor becomes my jailer. But yes, it is a play; surely it is a play; or else I am in bed in Cammercy suffering from one of old Jeanne's heavy late suppers. It is then that I must waken myself into the little room with the pink hangings."

He raised the point of the sword to prick his finger, more in a humorous mood than with any real belief that it was all a dream, and dropped it fast as he felt a gummy liquor clotting on the blade.

"*Grand Dieu!*" said he softly, "I have perhaps pricked some-one else tonight into his eternal nightmare, and I cannot prick myself out of one."

The noise of the men outside rose louder; a gleam of light waved upon the wall of the chamber, something wan and elusive, bewildering for a moment as if it were a ghost; from the clamour he could distinguish sentences in a guttural tongue. He turned to the window—the counterpart of the one in his own bedroom, but without a pane of glass in its narrow space. Again the wan flag waved across the wall, more plainly the cries of the robbers came up to him. They had set a torch flaring on the scene. It revealed the gloomy gable-end of Doom with a wild, a menacing illumination, deepening the blackness of the night beyond its influence, giving life to shadows that danced upon rock and grass. The light, held high by the man Count Victor had wounded, now wrapped to his eyes in a plaid, rose and fell, touched sometimes on the mainland, showing the bracken and the tree, sometimes upon the sea to show the wave, frothy from its quarrel with the fissured rock, making it plain that Doom was a ship indeed, cast upon troubled waters, cut off from the gentle world.

But little for the sea or for the shore had Count Victor any interest; his eyes were all for the wild band who clamoured about the flambeau. They wore such a costume as he had quarrelled with on his arrival; they cried "Loch Sloy!" with something of theatrical effect, and "Out with the gentleman! out with Black Andy's murderer!" they demanded in English.

He craned his head out at the window and watched the scene. The tall man who had personally assailed him seemed to lead the band in all except their clamour, working eagerly, directing in undertones. They had brought a ladder from the shore, appar-ently provided for such an emergency, and placed it against the wall, with a view to an escalade. A stream of steaming water shot down upon the first who ventured upon the rounds, and he fell back with ludicrous whimperings. Compelled by the leader, another ventured on the ladder, and the better to watch his performance Count Victor leaned farther out at his window, secure from observation in the darkness. As he did so, he saw for the first time that on his right there was a lighted window he could almost touch with his hand as he leaned over. It flashed upon him that here was the woman's room, and that on the deep moulding running underneath the windows he could at some little risk gain it, probably to find its door open, and thus gain the freedom Mungo had so unexpectedly taken from him. He crept out upon the ledge, only then to realise the hazards of such a narrow footing. It seemed as he stood with his hands yet grasping the sides of the window he sought to escape by, that he could never retain his balance sufficiently to reach the other in safety. The greatest of his physical fears—greater even than that of drowning which sometimes whelmed him in dreams and on ships—was the dread of empty space; a touch of vertigo seized him; the enemy gathered round the torch beneath suddenly seemed elves, puny impossible things far off, and he almost slipped into their midst. But he dragged back his senses. "We must all die," he gasped, "but we need not be precipitate about the business," and shut his eyes as he stood up, and with feet upon the moulding stretched to gain grip of the other window. Something fell away below his right foot and almost plunged him into space. With a terrific effort he saved himself from that fate, and his senses, grown of a sudden to miraculous acuteness, heard the crumbled masonry he had released thud upon the patch of grass at the foot of the tower, apprising the enemy of his attempt. A wild commingling of commands and threats came up to him; the night seemed something vast beyond all former estimates, a swinging and giddy horror; the single star that peered through the cloud took to airy dancing, a phantom of the evening heavens; again he might have fallen, but the material, more deadly, world he was accustomed to manifested itself for his relief and his salvation. Through the night rang a pistol-shot, and the ball struck against the wall but an inch or two from his head.

"*Merci beaucoup!*" he said aloud. "There is nothing like a pill," and his grasp upon the sides of the illuminated window was quite strong and confident as he drew himself towards it. He threw himself in upon the floor just in time to escape death from half-a-dozen bullets that rattled behind him.

Safe within, he looked around in wonder. What he had come upon was not what he had expected,—was, indeed, so incongruous with the cell next door and the general poverty of the castle as a whole that it seemed unreal; for here was a trim and tasteful boudoir lit by a silver lamp, warmed by a charcoal fire, and giving some suggestion of dainty womanhood by a palpable though delicate odour of rose-leaves conserved in pot-pourri. Tapestry covered more than three-fourths of the wall, swinging gently in the draught from the open window, a harpsichord stood in a corner, a couch that had apparently been occupied stood between the fireplace and the door, and a score of evidences indicated gentility and taste.

"Annapla becomes more interesting," he reflected, but he spent no time in her boudoir; he made to try the door. It was locked; nor did he wonder at it, though in a cooler moment he might have done so. Hurriedly he glanced about the room for something to aid him to open the door, but there was nothing to suit his purpose. In his search his eye fell on a miniature upon the mantelshelf—the work, as he could tell by its technique and its frame, of a French artist. It was the presentment of a gentleman in the Highland dress, adorned, as was the manner of some years back before the costume itself had become discredited, with fripperies of the mode elsewhere—a long scalloped waistcoat, a deep ruffled collar, the shoes buckled, and the hair *en queue*,— the portrait of a man of dark complexion, distinguished and someways pleasant.

"The essential lover of the story," said Count Victor, putting it down. "Now I know my Annapla is young and lovely. We shall see—we shall see!"

He turned to the door to try its fastenings with his sword, found the task of no great difficulty, for the woodwork round the lock shared the common decay of Doom, and with the silver lamp to light his steps, he made his way along the corridor and down the stair. It was a strange and romantic spectacle he made

82

moving thus through the darkness, the lamp swaying his shadow on the stairway as he descended, and he could have asked for no more astonishment in the face of his jailer than he found in Mungo's when that domestic met him at the stair-foot.

Mungo was carrying hot water in a huge kettle. He put down the vessel with a startled jolt that betrayed his fright.

"God be aboot us! Coont, ye near gied me a stroke there."

"Oh, I demand pardon!" said Count Victor, ironically. "I forgot that a man of your age should not be taken by surprise."

"My age!" repeated Mungo, with a tone of annoyance. "No' sae awfu' auld either. At my age my grandfaither was a sergeant i' the airmy, and married for the fourth time."

"Only half his valour seems to run in the blood," said Count Victor. Then, more sternly, "What did you mean by locking me up there?"

Mungo took up the kettle and placed it to the front of him, with some intuition that a shield must be extemporised against the sword that the Frenchman had menacing in his hand. The action was so droll and futile that, in spite of his indignation, Count Victor had to smile; and this assured the little domestic, though he felt chagrin at the ridicule implied.

"Jist a bit plan o' my ain, Coont, to keep ye oot o' trouble, and I'm shair ye'll excuse the leeberty. A bonny-like thing it wad be if the maister cam' hame and foun' the Macfarlanes were oot on the ran-dan and had picked ye oot o' Doom like a wulk oot o' its shell. It wisna like as if ye were ane o' the ordinar garrison, ye ken; ye were jist a kin' o' veesitor. . . ."

"And it was I they were after," said Count Victor, "which surely gave me some natural interest in the defence."

"Ye were safer to bide whaur ye were; and hoo ye got oot o't 's mair than I can jalouse. We hae scalded aff the rogues wi' het water, and if they're to be keepit aff, I'll hae to be unco gleg wi' the kettle."

As he said these words he saw, apparently for the first time, with a full understanding of its significance, the lamp in Count Victor's hands. His jaw fell; he put down the kettle again helplessly, and, in trembling tones, "Whaur did ye get the lamp?" said he.

"*Ah, mon vieux!*" cried Count Victor, enjoying his bewilderment. "You should have locked the lady's door as well as mine. 'Art a poor warder not to think of the possibilities in two cells so close to each other."

"Cells!" cried Mungo, very much disturbed. " 'Cells!' quo' he," looking chapfallen up the stairway, as if for something there behind his escaped prisoner.

"And now you will give me the opportunity of paying my respects to your no doubt adorable lady."

"Eh!" cried Mungo, incredulous. A glow came to his face. He showed the ghost of a mischievous smile. "Is't that way the lan' lies? Man, ye're a dour birkie!" said he; "but a wilfu' man maun hae his way, and, if naething less'll dae ye, jist gang up to yer ain chaumer, and ye'll find her giein' the Macfarlanes het punch wi' nae sugar till't."

The statement was largely an enigma to Count Victor, but he understood enough to send him up the stairs with an alacrity that drove Mungo, in his rear, into silent laughter. Yet the nearer he came to his door the slower grew his ascent. At first he had thought but of the charming lady, the vocalist, and the recluse. The Baron's share in the dangerous mystery of Doom made him less scrupulous than he might otherwise have been as to the propriety of a domestic's introduction to one apparently kept out of his way for reasons best known to his host; and he advanced to the encounter in the mood of the adventurer, Mungo in his rear beholding it in his jaunty step, in the fingers that pulled and peaked the moustachio, and drew forth a somewhat pleasing curl that looked well across a temple. But a more sober mood overcame him before he had got to the top of the stair. The shouts of the besieging party outside had declined and finally died away; the immediate excitement of the adventure, which with Mungo and the unknown lady he was prepared to share, was gone. He began to realise that there was something ludicrous in the incident that had kept him from making her acquaintance half an hour ago, and reflected that she might well have some doubt of his courage and his chivalry. Even more perturbing was the sudden recollection of the amused laughter that had greeted his barefooted approach to Doom through two or three inches of water, and at the open door he hung back dubious.

"Step in; it's your ain room," cried Mungo, struggling with his kettle; "and for the Lord's sake mind your mainners and gie her a guid impression."

It was the very counsel to make a Montaiglon bold.

He entered; a woman was busy at the open window; he stared in amazement and chagrin.

XII

Omens and Alarms

Beaten back by Annapla's punch-bowl from their escalade, the assailants rallied to a call from their commander, and abandoned, for the time at least, their lawless enterprise. They tossed high their arms, stamped out their torch to blackness, shouted a ribald threat, and were swallowed up by the black mainland. A gentle rain began to fall, and the sea lapsed from a long roll to an oily calm. With no heed for the warnings and protests of Mungo, whose intrepidity was too obviously a merely mental attitude and incapable of facing unknown dangers, Count Victor lit a lantern and went out again into the night that now held no rumour of the band who had so noisily menaced. There was profound silence on the shore and all along the coast—a silence the more sinister because peopled by his enemies. He went round the castle, his lantern making a beam of yellow light before him, showing the rain falling in silvery threads, gathering in silver beads upon his coat and trickling down the channels of his weapon. A wonderful fondness for that shaft of steel possessed him at the moment: it seemed a comrade faithful, his only familiar in that country of marvels and dreads, it was a comfort to have it hand in hand; he spoke to it once in affectionate accents as if it had been a thing of life. The point of it suggested the dark commander, and Count Victor scrutinised the ground beside the dyke-side where he had made the thrust: to his comfort only a single gout of blood revealed itself, for he had begun to fear something too close on a second homicide, which would make his presence in the country the more notorious. A pool of water still smoking showed where Annapla's punch-bowl had done its work; but for the blood and that, the alarms of the night might have seemed to him a

86

dream. Far off to the south a dog barked; nearer, a mountain torrent brawled husky in its chasm. Perfumes of the wet woodland mingled with the odours of the shore. And the light he carried made Doom Castle more dark, more sinister and mysterious than ever, rising strong and silent from his feet to the impenetrable blackness overhead.

He went into the garden; he stood in the bower. There more than anywhere else the desolation was pitiful—the hips glowing crimson on their stems, the eglantine in withering strands, the rustic woodwork green with damp and the base growths of old and mouldering situations, the seat decayed and broken, but propped at its feet as if for recent use. All seemed to express some poignant anguish for lost summers, happy days, for love and laughter ravished and gone for ever. Above all, the rain and sea saddened the moment—the rain dripping through the ragged foliage and oozing on the wood, the cavernous sea lapping monstrous on the rock that some day yet must crumble to its hungry maw.

He held high the lantern, and to a woman at her darkened window her bower seemed to glow like a shell lit in the depths of troubled ocean. He swung the light; a footstep, that he did not hear, was checked in wonder. He came out, and instinct told him someone watched him in the dark beyond the radiance of his lantern.

"*Qui est là?*" he cried, forgetting again the foreign country, thinking himself sentinel in homely camps, and when he spoke a footstep sounded in the darkness.

Someone had crossed from the mainland while he ruminated within. He listened, with the lantern high above his head but to the right of him for fear of a pistol-shot.

One footstep.

He advanced slowly to meet it, his fingers tremulous on his sword, and the Baron came out of the darkness, his hands behind his back, his shoulders bent, his visage a mingling of sadness and wonder.

"M. le Baron?" said Count Victor, questioning, but he got no

87

answer. Doom came up to him and peered at him as if he had been a ghost, a tear upon his cheek, something tense and troubled in his countenance, that showed him for the moment incapable of calm utterance.

"You—you—are late," stammered Count Victor, putting the sword behind him and feeling his words grotesque.

"I took—I took you for a wraith—I took you for a vision," said the Baron plaintively. He put his hand upon his guest's arm. "Oh, man!" said he, "if you were Gaelic, if you were Gaelic, if you could understand! I came through the dark from a place of pomp, from a crowded street, from things new and thriving, and above all the castle of his Grace flaring from foundation to finial like a torch, though murder was done this day in the guise of justice: I came through the rain and the wet full of bitterness to my poor black home, and find no light there where once my father and my father's father and all the race of us knew pleasant hours in the wildest weather. Not a light, not a lowe . . ." he went on, gazing upward to the frowning walls dark glistening in the rain—"and then the bower must out and shine to mind me—to mind me—ah, Montaiglon, my pardons, my regrets! you must be finding me a melancholy host."

"Do not mention it," said Count Victor carelessly, though the conduct of this marvel fairly bewildered him, and his distress seemed poorly accounted for by his explanation. "*Ah, vieux blagueur!*" he thought, "can it be Balhaldie again—a humbug with no heart in his breast but an onion in his handkerchief?" And then he was ashamed of suspicions of which a day or two ago he would have been incapable.

"My dear friends of Monday did me the honour to call in your absence," he said. "They have not gone more than twenty minutes."

"What! the Macfarlanes," cried Doom, every trace of his softer emotion gone, but more disturbed than ever as he saw the sword for the first time. "Well—well—well?" he inquired eagerly. "Well? well? well?" and he gripped Count Victor by the arm and looked him in the eyes.

"Nothing serious happened," replied Count Victor, "except that your domestics suffered some natural alarms."

Doom seemed wondrously relieved. "They did not force an entrance?" said he.

"They did their best, but failed. I pricked one slightly before I fell back on Mungo's barricades; that and some discomfiture from Mistress Annapla's punch-bowl completed the casualties."

"Well? well? well?" cried Lamond, still waiting something. Count Victor only looked at him in wonder, and led the way to the door where Mungo drew back the bars and met his master with a trembling front. A glance of mute inquiry and intelligence passed between the servant and his master: the Frenchman saw it and came to his own conclusions, but nothing was said till the Baron had made a tour of investigation through the house and come at last to join his guest in the *salle*, where the embers of the fire were raked together on the hearth and fed with new peat. The Count and his host sat down together, and when Mungo had gone to prepare some food for his master, Count Victor narrated the night's adventure. He had an excited listener—one more excited, perhaps, than the narrative of itself might account for.

"And there is much that is beyond my poor comprehension," continued Count Victor, looking at him as steadfastly as good breeding would permit.

"Eh?" said Doom, stretching fingers that trembled to the peat-flame that stained his face like wine.

"Your servant Mungo was quite unnecessarily solicitous for my safety, and took the trouble to put me under lock and key."

Doom fingered the bristles of his chin in a manifest perturbation. "He—he did that, did he?" said he, like one seeking to gain time for further reflection. And when Count Victor waited some more sympathetic comment, "It was—it was very stupid, very stupid of Mungo," said he.

"Stupid!" echoed Count Victor ironically. "Ah! so it was. I should not have said stupid myself, but it is so hard, is it not, for a foreigner to find the just word in his poor vocabulary? For a *bêtise* much less unpleasant I have scored a lackey's back with a scabbard. Master Mungo had an explanation, however, though I doubted the truth of it."

"And what was that?"

"That you would be angry if he permitted me to get into danger while I was your guest,—an excuse more courteous than convincing."

"He was right," said Doom, "though I can scarcely defend the manner of executing his trust: I was not to see that he would make a trepanning affair of it. I'm—I'm very much grieved, Count, much grieved, I assure you: I shall have a word or two on the matter the morn's morning with Mungo. A stupid action! a stupid action! but you know the man by this time—an oddity out and out."

"A little too much so, if I may take the liberty, M. le Baron,— a little too much so for a foreigner's peace of mind," said Count Victor softly. "Are you sure, M. le Baron, there are no traitors in Doom?" and he leaned forward with his gaze on the Baron's face.

The Baron started, flushed more crimson than before, and turned an alarmed countenance to his interrogator. "Good God!" he cried, "are you bringing your doubts of the breed of us to my hearthstone?"

"It is absurd, perhaps," said Count Victor, still very softly, and watching his host as closely as he might, "but Mungo—"

"Pshaw! a good lowland heart! For all his clowning, Count, you might trust him with your life."

"The other servant then—the woman?"

Doom looked a trifle uneasy. "Hush!" said he with half a glance behind him to the door. "Not so loud. If she should hear!" he stammered: he stopped, then smiled awkwardly. "Have ye any dread of an Evil Eye?" said he.

"I have no dread of the devil himself, who is something more tangible," replied Count Victor. "You do not suggest that malevolent influence in Mistress Annapla, do you?"

"We are very civil to her in these parts," said Doom, "and I'm not keen to put her powers to the test. I have seen and heard some droll things of her."

"That has been my own experience," said Count Victor. "Are you sure her honesty is on more substantial grounds than her reputation for witchcraft? I demand your pardon for expressing these suspicions, but I have reasons. I cannot imagine that the attack of the Macfarlanes was connived at by your servants, though that was my notion for a little when Mungo locked me up, for they suffered more alarm at the attack than I did, and the reason for the attack seems obvious enough. But are you aware that this woman who commands your confidence is in the practice of signalling to the shore when she wishes to communicate with someone there?"

"I think you must be mistaken," said Doom uneasily.

"I could swear I saw something of the kind," said Count Victor. He described the signal he had seen twice at her window. "Not having met her at the time, I laid it down to some gay gillian's affair with a lover on the mainland, but since I have seen her that idea seems—seems . . ."

"Just so, I should think it did," said the Baron: but though his words were light his aspect was disturbed. He paced once or twice up and down the floor, muttered something to himself in Gaelic, and finally went to the door, which he opened. "Mungo, Mungo!" he cried into the darkness, and the servant appeared with the gaudy nightcap of his slumber already on.

"Tell Annapla to come here," said the Baron.

The servant hesitated, his lip trembled upon some objection that he did not, however, express, and he went on his errand.

In a little the woman entered. It was not surprising that when Count Victor, prepared by all that had gone before to meet a bright young creature when he had gone into his chamber where she was repelling the escalade of the enemy, had been astounded to find what he found there, for Mistress Annapla was in truth not the stuff for amorous intrigues. She had doubtless been handsome enough in her day, but that was long distant; now there were but the relics of her good looks, with only her eyes,

91

dark, lambent, piercing, to tell of passions unconsumed. She had eyes only for her master; Count Victor had no existence for her, and he was all the freer to watch how she received the Baron's examination.

"Do you dry your clothes at the windows in Doom?" asked her master quietly, with none of a master's bluntness, asking the question in English from politeness to his guest.

She replied rapidly in Gaelic.

"For luck," said the Baron dubiously when he had listened to a long guttural explanation that was of course unintelligible to the Frenchman. "That's a new freit. To keep away the witches. Now, who gave ye a notion like that?" he went on, maintaining his English.

Another rapid explanation followed, one that seemed to satisfy the Baron, for when it was finished he gave her permission to go.

"It's as I thought," he explained to Count Victor. "The old body has been troubled with moths and birds beating themselves against her window at night when the light was in it: what must she be doing but taking it for some more sinister visitation, and the green kerchief is supposed to keep them away."

"I should have fancied it might have been a permanency in that case," suggested Count Victor, "unless, indeed, your Highland ghosts have a special preference for Mondays and Wednesdays."

"Permanency!" repeated the Baron thoughtfully. "H'm!" The suggestion had obviously struck him as reasonable, but he baulked at any debate on it.

"There was also the matter of the horseman," went on Count Victor blandly, pointing his moustache.

"Horseman?" queried the Baron.

"A horseman *sans doute*. I noticed most of your people here ride with a preposterously short stirrup; this one rode like a gentleman cavalier. He stopped opposite the castle this forenoon and waved his compliments to the responsive maid."

The effect upon the Baron was amazing. He grew livid with

some feeling repressed. It was only for a moment; the next he was for changing the conversation, but Count Victor had still his quiver to empty.

"Touching flageolets?" said he, but there his arrow missed. Doom only laughed.

"For that," said he, "you must trouble Annapla or Mungo. They have a story that the same's to be heard every night of storm, but my bed's at the other side of the house and I never heard it;" and he brought the conversation back to the Macfarlanes, so that Count Victor had to relinquish his inquisition.

"The doings of tonight," said he, "make it clear I must rid you of my presence *tout à l'heure*. I think I shall transfer me to the town tomorrow."

"You can't, man," protested Doom, though, it almost seemed, with some reluctance. "There could be no worse time for venturing there. In the first place, the Macfarlane's affair is causing a stir; then I've had no chance of speaking to Petullo about you. He was to meet me after the court was over, but his wife dragged him up with her to dinner in the castle. Lord! yon's a wife who would be nane the waur o' a leatherin', as they say in the south. Well, she took the goodman to the castle, though a dumb dog he is among gentrice, and the trip must have been little to his taste. I waited and better waited, and I might have been waiting for his homecoming yet, for it's candle-light to the top flat of MacCailein's tower and the harp in the hall. Your going, Count, will have to be put off a day or two longer."

XIII

A Lawyer's Good Lady

The remainder of the night passed without further alarm, but Count Victor lay only on the frontiers of forgetfulness till morning, his senses all on sentry, and the salt, wind-blown dawn found him abroad before the rest of Doom was well awake. He met the caleche of the Lords going back the way it had come with an outrider in a red jacket from the stable of Argyll: it passed him on the highway so close that he saw Elchies and Kilkerran half sleeping within as they drove away from the scene of their dreadful duties. In a cloak of rough watchet blue he had borrowed from his host and a hat less conspicuous than that he had come in from Stirling, he passed, to such strangers in the locality, for some tacksman of the countryside, or a traveller like themselves. To have ventured into the town, however, where everyone would see he was a stranger and speedily inquire into his business there, was, as he had been carefully apprised by Doom the night before, a risk too great to be run without good reason. Stewart's trial had created in the country a state of mind that made a stranger's presence there somewhat hazardous for himself, and all the more so in the case of a foreigner, for, rightly or wrongly, there was associated with the name of the condemned man as art and part in the murder that of a Highland officer in the service of the French. There had been rumours, too, of an attempted rescue on the part of the Stewarts of Ardshiel, Achnacoin, and Fasnacloich—all that lusty breed of the ancient train: the very numbers of them said to be on the drove-roads with weapons from the thatch were given in the town, and so fervently believed in that the appearance of a stranger without any plausible account to give of himself would have stirred up tumult.

Count Victor eluded the more obvious danger of the town, but in his forenoon ramble stumbled into one almost as great as that he had been instructed to avoid. He had gone through the wood of Strongara and come suddenly upon the cavalcade that bore the doomed man to the scene of his execution thirty or forty miles away.

The wretch had been bound upon a horse—a tall, middle-aged man in coarse home-spun clothing, his eye defiant, but his countenance white with the anxieties of his situation. He was surrounded by a troop of sabres; the horses' hoofs made a great clatter upon the hard road, and Count Victor, walking abstractedly along the riverbank, came on them before he was aware of their proximity. As he stood to let them pass he was touched inexpressibly by the glance the convict gave him, so charged was it with question, hope, dread, and the appetite for some human sympathy. He had seen that look before in men condemned—once in front of his own rapier,—and with the utmost feeling for the unhappy wretch he stood, when the cavalcade had gone, looking after it and conjuring in his fancy the last terrible scene whereof that creature would be the central figure. Thus was he standing when another horseman came upon him suddenly, following wide in the rear of the troop—a civilian who shared the surprise of the unexpected meeting. He had no sooner gazed upon Count Victor than he drew up his horse confusedly and seemed to hesitate between proceeding or retreat. Count Victor passed with a courteous salute no less formally returned. He was struck singularly by some sense of familiarity. He did not know the horseman who so strangely scrutinised him as he passed, but yet the face was one not altogether new to him. It was a face scarce friendly, too, and for his life the Frenchman could not think of any reason for aversion.

He could no more readily have accounted for the action of the horseman had he known that he had ridden behind the soldiers but a few hundred yards after meeting with Count Victor when he turned off at one of the hunting-roads with which the ducal grounds abounded, and galloped furiously back towards the castle of Argyll. Nothing checked him till he reached the entrance, where he flung the reins to a servant and dashed into the turret-room where the Duke sat writing.

"Ah, Sim!" said his Grace, airily, yet with an accent of apprehension, "you have come back sooner than I looked for: nothing wrong with the little excursion, I hope?"

MacTaggart leaned with both hands upon the table where his master wrote. "They're all right, so far as I went with them," said he; "but if your Grace in my position came upon a foreigner in the wood of Strongara—a gentleman by the looks of him and a Frenchman by his moustachio, all alone and looking after Sergeant Donald's company, what would your Grace's inference be?"

Argyll, obviously, did not share much of his Chamberlain's excitement. "There was no more than one there?" he asked, sprinkling sand upon his finished letter. "No! Then there seems no great excuse for your extreme perturbation, my good Sim. I'm lord of Argyll, but I'm not lord of the king's highway, and if an honest stranger cares to take a freeman's privilege and stand between the wind and Simon MacTaggart's dignity—Simon MacTaggart's very touchy dignity it would appear—who am I that I should blame the liberty? You did not ride *ventre à terre* from Strongara (I see a foam-fleck on your breeches) to tell me we had a traveller come to admire our scenery? Come, come, Sim! I'll begin to think these late eccentricities of yours, these glooms, abstractions, errors, and anxieties and indispositions, and above all that pallid face, are due to some affair of the heart." As he spoke Argyll pinched his kinsman playfully on the ear, quite the good companion, with none of the condescension that a duke might naturally display in so doing.

MacTaggart reddened and Argyll laughed. "Ah!" he cried. "Can I have hit it?" he went on, quizzing the Chamberlain. "See that you give me fair warning and I'll practise the accustomed and essential reel. Upon my soul I haven't danced since Lady Mary left, unless you call it so that foolish minuet. You should have seen her Grace at St James's last month. Gad! She footed it like an angel; there's not a better dancer in London town. See that your wife's a dancer whoever she may be, Sim; let her dance and sing and play the harpsichord or the clarsach—they are charms that will last longer than her good looks, and will not weary you so soon as that intellect that's so much in fashion nowadays, when every woman listens to every clever thing you say, that she may say something cleverer or perhaps retail it later as her own."

MacTaggart turned about impatiently, poked with his riding crop at the fire, and plainly indicated that he was not in the mood for badinage.

"All that has nothing to do with my Frenchman, your Grace," said he bluntly.

"Oh, confound your Frenchman!" retorted the Duke, coming over, turning up the skirts of his coat, and warming himself at the fire. "Don't say Frenchman to me, and don't suggest any more abominable crime and intrigue till the memory of that miserable Appin affair is off my mind. I know what they'll say about that: I have a good notion what they're saying already— as if I personally had a scrap of animosity to this poor creature sent to the gibbet on Levenside."

"I think you should have this Frenchman arrested for inquiry: I do not like the look of him."

Argyll laughed. "Heavens!" he cried, "is the man gane wud? Have you any charge against this unfortunate foreigner who has dared to shelter himself in my woods? And if you have, do you fancy it is the old feudal times with us still, and that I can clap him in my dungeon—if I had such a thing—without any consultation with the common law-officers of the land? Wake up, Sim! wake up! this is '55, and there are sundry written laws of the State that unfortunately prevent even the MacCailein Mor snatching a man from the footpath and hanging him because he has not the Gaelic accent and wears his hair in a different fashion from the rest of us. Don't be a fool, cousin, don't be a fool!"

"It's as your Grace likes," said MacTaggart. "But if this man's not in any way concerned in the Appin affair, he may very well be one of the French agents who are bargaining for men for the French service, and the one thing's as unlawful as the other by the Act of '36."

"H'm!" said Argyll, turning more grave, and shrewdly eyeing his Chamberlain—"H'm! Have you any particularly good reason to think that?" He waited for no answer, but went on. "I give it up, MacTaggart," said he, with a gesture of impatience. "Gad! I cannot pretend to know half the plots you are either in yourself or listening on the outside of, though I get credit, I know, for planning them. All I want to know is, have you any reason to think this part of Scotland—and incidentally the Government of this and every well-governed realm as the libels say—would be bettered by the examination of this man? Eh?"

MacTaggart protested the need was clamant. "On the look of the man I would give him the jougs," said he. "It's spy—"

"H'm!" said Argyll, then coughed discreetly over a pinch of snuff.

"Spy or agent," said the Chamberlain, little abashed at the interjection.

"And yet a gentleman by the look of him, said Sim MacTaggart, five minutes syne."

"And what's to prevent that?" asked the Chamberlain almost sharply. "Your Grace will admit it's nothing to the point." said he boldly and smilingly, standing up a fine figure of a man, with his head high and his chest out. "It was the toss of a bawbee whether or not I should apprehend him myself when I saw him, and if I had him here your Grace would be the first to admit my discretion."

"My Grace is a little more judicious than to treat the casual pedestrian like a notour thief," said Argyll; "and yet, after all, I daresay the matter may be left to your good judgment—that is, after you have had a word or two on the matter with Petullo, who will better be able to advise upon the rights to the persons of suspicious characters in our neighbourhood."

With never a word more said MacTaggart clapped on his hat, withdrew in an elation studiously concealed from his master, and fared at a canter to Petullo's office in the town. He fastened the reins to the ring at the door and entered.

The lawyer sat in a den that smelt most wickedly of mildewed vellum, sealing-wax, tape, and all that trash that smothers the soul of man—the appurtenances of his craft. He sat like a sallow mummy among them, like a half-man made of tailor's patches, flanked by piles of docketed letters and Records closed, bastioned by deed-boxes blazoned with the indication of their offices— MacGibbon's Mortification, Dunderave Estate, Coll's Trust, and so on; he sat with a shrieking quill among these things, and MacTaggart entering to him felt like thanking God that he had never been compelled to a life like this in a stinking mortuary, with the sun outside on the windows and the clean sea and the singing wood calling in vain. Perhaps some sense of contrast seized the writer too, as he looked up to see the Chamberlain entering with a pleasant lively air of wind behind him, and health and vigour in his step despite the unwonted wanness of his face. At least, in the glance Petullo gave below his shaggy eyebrows there was a little envy as well as much cunning. He made a ludicrous attempt at smiling.

"Ha!" he cried, "Mr MacTaggart! Glad to see you, Mr MacTaggart. Sit ye down, Mr MacTaggart. I was just thinking about you."

"No ill, I hope," said the Chamberlain, refusing a seat proffered; for anything of the law to him seemed gritty in the touch, and a three-legged stool would, he always felt, be as unpleasant to sit upon as a red-hot griddle.

"Te-he!" squeaked Petullo with an irritating falsetto. "You must have your bit joke, Mr MacTaggart. Did his Grace—did his Grace—I was just wondering if his Grace said anything today about my unfortunate accident with the compote yestreen." He looked more cunningly than ever at the Chamberlain.

"In his Grace's class, Mr Petullo, and incidentally in my own, nothing's said of a guest's gawkiness, though you might hardly believe it for a reason that I never could make plain to you, though I know it by instinct."

99

"Oh! as to gawkiness, an accident of the like might happen to any one," said Petullo irritably.

"And that's true," confessed the Chamberlain. "But, tut! tut! Mr Petullo, a compote's neither here nor there to the Duke. If you had spilt two of them it would have made no difference; there was plenty left. Never mind the dinner, Mr Petullo, just now, I'm in a haste. There's a Frenchman. . . ."

"There's a wheen of Frenchmen seemingly," said the writer oracularly, taking to the trimming of his nails with a piece of pumice-stone he kept for the purpose, and used so constantly that they looked like talons.

"Now, what the devil do you mean?" cried MacTaggart.

"Go on, go on with your business," squeaked Petullo, with an eye upon an inner door that led to his household.

"I have his Grace's instructions to ask you about the advisability of arresting a stranger, seemingly a Frenchman, who is at this moment suspiciously prowling about the policies."

"On whatna charge, Mr MacTaggart, on whatna charge?" asked the writer, taking a confident, even an insolent, tone, now that he was on his own familiar ground. "Rape, arson, forgery, robbery, thigging, sorning, pickery, murder, or high treason?"

"Clap them all together, Mr Petullo, and just call it local inconduciveness," cried MacTaggart. "Simply the Duke may not care for his society. That should be enough for the Fiscal and Long Davie the dempster, shouldn't it?"

"H'm!" said Petullo. "It's a bit vague, Mr MacTaggart, and I don't think it's mentioned in Forbes's 'Institutes.' Fifteen Campbell assessors and the baron bailie might have sent a man to the Plantations on that dittay ten years ago, but we live in different times, Mr MacTaggart—different times, Mr MacTaggart," repeated the writer, tee-heeing till his bent shoulders heaved under his seedy ink-stained surtout coat.

"Do we?" cried the Chamberlain with a laugh. "I'm thinking ye forget a small case we had no further gone than yesterday, when a man with the unlucky name of Stewart . . ." He stopped, meaningly smiled, and made a gesture with his fingers across his neck, at the same time giving an odd sound with his throat.

"Oh! You're an awfu' man," cried Petullo with the accent of a lout. "I wonder if you're on the same track as myself, for I'm like the Hielan' soldier—I have a Frenchman of my own. There's one, I mean, up-by there in Doom, and coming down here tomorrow, or the day after, or as soon as I can order a lodging for him in the town."

"Oh, hell!" cried the secretary, amazingly dumfoundered.

"There's nothing underhand about him, so far as I know, to give even his Grace an excuse for confining him, for it seems he's a wine merchant out of Bordeaux, one Montaiglon, come here on business and stopped at Doom through an attack on his horse by the same Macfarlanes who are of interest to us for another reason, as was spoken of at his Grace's table last night."

"And he's coming here?" asked MacTaggart, incredulous.

"I had a call from the Baron himself today to tell me that."

"Ah, well, there's no more to be said of our suspicions," said MacTaggart. "Not in this form at least." And he was preparing to go.

A skirt rustled within the inner door, and Mrs Petullo, flushed a little to her great becoming in spite of a curl-paper or two, and clad in a lilac-coloured negligee of the charmingest, came into the office with a well-acted start of surprise to find a client there.

"Oh, good morning! Mr MacTaggart," she exclaimed radiantly, while her husband scowled to himself as he relapsed into the chair at his desk and fumbled with his papers. "Good morning; I hope I have not interrupted business?"

"Mr MacTaggart was just going, my dear," said Mr Petullo.

A cracked bell rang within, and the Chamberlain perceived an odour of cooking celery. Inwardly he cursed his forgetfulness, because it was plain that the hour for his call upon the writer was ill-chosen.

"My twelve-hours is unusual sharp today," said Petullo, consulting a dumpy horologe out of his fob. "Would ye—would

101

ye do me the honour of joining me?" with a tone that left, but not too rudely, immediate departure as the Chamberlain's only alternative.

"Thank you, thank you," said MacTaggart. "I rose late today, and my breakfast's little more than done with." He made for the door, Mrs Petullo close in his cry and holding his eye, defying so hurried a departure while she kept up a chattering about the last night's party. Her husband hesitated, but his hunger (he had the voracious appetite of such shrivelled atomies) and a wholesome fear of being accused of jealousy made him withdraw, leaving the office to the pair.

All MacTaggart's anger rose against madame for her machination. "You saw me from the window," said he; "it's a half-cooked dinner for the goodman today, I'll warrant!"

She laughed a most intoxicating laugh, all charged with some sweet velvety charm, put out her hands and caught his. "Oh, Lord! I wish it would choke him, Sim," said she fervently, then lifted up her mouth and dropped a swooning eyelash over her passionate orbs.

"Adorable creature," he thought; "she'll have rat-bane in his broth some day." He kissed her with no more fervour than if she had been a wooden figurehead, but she was not thus to be accepted: she put an arm quickly round his neck and pressed her passionate lips to his. Back he drew wincing. "Oh, damnation!" he cried.

"What's the matter?" she exclaimed in wonder, and turned to assure herself that it was not that someone spied from the inner door, for MacTaggart's face had become exceeding pale.

"Nothing, nothing," he replied; "you are—you are so ferocious."

"Am I, Sim?" said she. "Who taught me? Oh, Sim," she went on pleadingly, "be good to me. I'm sick, I'm *sick* of life, and you don't show you care for me a little bit. Do you love me, Sim?"

"Heavens!" he cried, "you would ask the question fifty times a day if you had the opportunity."

"It would need a hundred times a day to keep up with your

changing moods. Do you love me, Sim!" She was smiling with the most pathetic appeal in her face.

"You look beautiful in that gown, Kate," said he irrelevantly, not looking at it at all but out at the window where showed the gabbarts tossing in the bay and the sides of the hill of Dunchuach all splashed with gold and crimson leafage.

"Never mind my gown, Sim," said she, stamping her foot and pulling at the buttons of his coat. "Once—oh, Sim, do you love me? Tell me, tell me, tell me! Whether you do or not, say it, you used to be such a splendid liar."

"It was no lie," said he curtly; then to himself, "Oh Lord, give me patience with this! and I have brought it on myself."

"It *was* no lie. Oh, Sim!"(And still she was turning wary eyes upon the door that led to her husband's retirement.) "It *was* no lie; you're left neither love nor courtesy. Oh, never mind! say you love me, Sim, whether it's true or not: that's what it's come to with me."

"Of course I do," said he.

"Of course what?"

"Of course I love you." He smiled, but at heart he grimaced.

"I don't believe you," said she, from custom waiting his protestation. But the Duke's Chamberlain was in no mood for protestations. He looked at her high temples made bald by the twisted papilottes, and wondered how he could have thought that bold shoulder beautiful.

"I'm in a great hurry, Kate," said he. "I am sorry to go, but there's my horse at the ring to prove the hurry I'm in!"

"I know, I know; you're always in a hurry now with me: it wasn't always so. Do you hear the brute?" Her husband's squeaky voice querulously shouting on a servant came to them from behind.

The servant immediately after came to the door with an intimation that Mr Petullo desired to know where the spirit-bottle was.

"He knows very well," said Mrs Petullo. "Here is the key— no, I'll take it to him myself."

"It's not the drink he wants, but me, the pig," said she as the servant withdrew. "Kiss me good afternoon, Sim."

"I wish to God it was goodbye!" thought he as he smacked her vulgarly, like a clown at a country fair.

She drew her hand across her mouth, and her eyes flashed indignation.

"There's something between us, Simon," said she in an altered tone; "it used not to be like that."

"Indeed it did not," he thought bitterly, and not for the first time he missed something in her—some spirit of simplicity, freshness, flower-bloom, and purity that he had sought for, seen in many women, and found elusive, as the frost finds the bloom of flowers he would begem.

Her husband shrieked again, and with mute gestures they parted.

The Chamberlain threw himself upon his horse as 'twere a mortal enemy, dug rowel-deep in the shuddering flesh, and the hoof-beats thundered on the causey-stones. The beast whinnied in its pain, reared, and backed to the breast wall of the bay. He lashed it wildly over the eyes with his whip, and they galloped up the roadway. A storm of fury possessed him; he saw nothing, heard nothing.

XIV

Glamour

Count Victor came through the woods from Strongara singularly
disturbed by the inexplicable sense of familiarity which rose from
his meeting with the horseman. It was a dry day and genial, yet
with hints of rain on the horizon and white caps to the waves,
betokening perhaps a storm not far distant. Children were in the
wood of Dunderave—ruddy shy children, gathering nuts and
blackberries, with merriment haunting the landscape as it were
in a picture by Watteau or a tale of the classics, where such
figures happily move for ever and for ever in the right golden
glamour. Little elves they seemed to Count Victor as he came
upon them over an eminence, and saw them for the first time
through the trees under tall oaks and pines, among whose pillars
they moved as if in fairy cloisters, the sea behind them shining
with a vivid and singing blue.

He had come upon them frowning, his mind full of doubts as
to the hazards of his adventure in Argyll, convinced almost that
the Baron of Doom was right, and that the needle in the haystack
was no more hopeless a quest than that he had set out on, and
the spectacle of their innocence in the woodland soothed him like
a psalm in a cathedral as he stood to watch. Unknowing his
presence there, they ran and played upon the grass, their lips
stained with the berry-juice, their pillow-slips of nuts gathered
beneath a bush of whin. They laughed, and chanted merry
rhymes: a gaiety their humble clothing lent them touched the
thickets with romance.

In circumstances other than fate had set about his life, Count
Victor might have been a good man—a good man not in the
common sense that means paying the way, telling the truth,
showing the open hand, respecting the law, going to Mass,

loyalty to the woman and to a friend, but in the rare wide manner that comprehends all these, and has its growth in human affection and religious faith. He loved birds; animals ever found him soft-handed; as for children—the *petites*—God bless them! was he not used to stand at his window at home and glow to see them playing in the street? And as he watched the urchins in the wood of Dunderave, far from the scenes he knew, children babbling in an uncouth language whose smallest word he could not comprehend, he felt an elevation of his spirit that he indulged by sitting on the grass above them, looking at their play and listening to their laughter as if it were an opera.

He forgot his fears, his apprehensions, his ignoble little emprise of revenge; he felt a better man, and he had his reward as one shall ever have who sits a space with childish merriment and woodland innocence. In his case it was something more direct and tangible than the immaterial efflux of the soul, though that too was not wanting: he saw the signal kerchief being placed outside the window, that otherwise, reaching home too early, he had missed.

"It is my last chance if I leave tomorrow," he thought. "I shall satisfy myself as to the nocturnal visitor, the magic flautist, and the bewildering Annapla—and probably find the mystery as simple as the egg in the conjuror's bottle when all's ended!"

That night he yawned behind his hand at supper in the midst of his host's account of his interview with Petullo the Writer, who had promised to secure lodging for Count Victor in a day or two, and the Baron showed no disinclination to conclude their somewhat dull sederunt and consent to an early retirement.

"I have something pressing to do before I go to bed myself," he said, restoring by that simple confession some of Count Victor's first suspicions. They were to be confirmed before an hour was past.

He went up to his room and weighed his duty to himself and to some unshaped rules of courtesy and conduct that he had inherited from a house more renowned for its sense of ceremonial honour, perhaps, than for commoner virtues. His instinct as a stranger in a most remarkable dwelling, creeping with mystery and with numberless evidences of things sinister and perhaps malevolent, told him it was fair to make a reconnnaissance, even if no more was to be discovered than a servant's sordid amours. On the other hand, he could not deny to himself that there was what the Baronne de Chenier would have called the little Lyons shopkeeper in the suspicions he had against his host, and in the steps he proposed to take to satisfy his curiosity. He might have debated the situation with himself till midnight, or as long as Mungo's candles lasted him, had not a shuffling and cautious step upon the stair suggested that someone was climbing to the unused chambers above. Putting punctilio in his pocket, he threw open his door, and had before him a much-perplexed Baron of Doom, wrapped from neck to heel in a great plaid of sombre tartan and carrying a candle!

Doom stammered an inaudible excuse.

"Pardon!" said Count Victor, ironically in spite of himself, as he saw his host's abashed countenance. "I fear I intrude on a masquerade. Pray do not mind me. It was that I thought the upper flat uninhabited and no one awake but myself."

"You have me somewhat at a disadvantage," said Doom coldly, resenting the irony. "I'll explain afterwards."

"Positively there is no necessity," replied Count Victor with a profound bow, and he re-entered and shut the door.

There was no longer any debate between punctilio and pre-caution. He had seen the bulge of the dagger below Lamond's plaid, and the plaid itself had not been drawn too closely round the wearer to conceal wholly the unaccountable fact that he had a Highland dress beneath it. A score of reasons for this eccentric affair came to Montaiglon, but all of them were disquieting, not the least so the notion that his host conspired perhaps with the Macfarlanes, who sought their revenge for their injured clans-man. He armed himself with his sword, blew out his candles, and throwing himself upon his bed lay waiting for the signal he expected. In spite of himself sleep stole on him twice, and he awakened each time to find an hour was gone.

107

It was a night of pouring rain. Great drops beat on the little window, a gargoyle poured a noisy stream of water, and a loud sea cried off the land and broke upon the outer edge of the rock of Doom. A loud sea and ominous, and it was hard for Count Victor in that welter of midnight voices to hear the call of an owl, yet it came to him by-and-by, as he expected, with its repetition. And then the flageolet with its familiar and baffling melody, floating on a current of the wind that piped about the castle vents and sobbed upon the stairs. He opened his door, looked into the depths that fell with mouldering steps into the basement and upwards to the flight where the Baron had been going. Whether he should carry his inquiry further or retire and shut his door again with a forced indifference to these perplexing events was but the toss of a coin. As he listened a slight sound at the foot of the stair—the sound of a door softly closed and a bar run in deep channels—decided him, and he waited to confound the master of Doom.

In the darkness the stern walls about him seemed to weigh upon his heart, and so imbued with vague terrors that he unsheathed his sword. A light revealed itself upon the stair; he drew back into his room, but left the door open, and when the bearer of the light came in front of his door he could have cried out loudly in astonishment, for it was not the Baron but a woman, and no woman that he had seen before, or had any reason to suspect the presence of in Doom Castle. They discovered each other simultaneously,—she, a handsome foreigner fumbling to put a rapier behind him in discreet concealment, much astounded; he, a woman no more than twenty, in her dress and manner all incongruous with this savage domicile.

In his after-years it was Count Victor's most vivid impression that her eyes had first given him the embarrassment that kept him dumb in her presence for a minute after she had come upon him thus strangely ensconced in the dark corridor. It was those eyes— the eyes of the woman born and bred by seas unchanging yet never the same; unfathomable, yet always inviting to the guess,

108

the passionate surmise—that told him first here was a maiden made for love. A figure tremulous with a warm grace, a countenance perfect in its form, full of a natural gravity, yet quick to each emotion, turning from the pallor of sudden alarm to the flush of shyness or vexation. The mountains had stood around to shelter her, and she was like the harebell of the hills. Had she been the average of her sex he would have met her with a front of brass; instead there was confusion in his utterance and his mien. He bowed extremely low.

"Madame; pardon! I—I—was awakened by music, and . . ."

Her silence, unaccompanied even by a smile at the ridiculous nature of the rencontre, and the proud sobriety of her visage, quickened him to a bolder sentiment than he had at first meditated.

"I was awakened by music, and it seems appropriate. With madame's permission I shall return to earth."

His foolish words perhaps did not quite reach her: the wind eddied noisily in the stair, that seemed, in the light from his open door, to gulp the blackness. Perhaps she did not hear, perhaps she did not fully understand, for she hesitated more than a moment as if pondering, not a whit astonished or abashed, with her eyes upon his countenance. Count Victor wished to God that he had lived a cleaner life: somehow he felt that there were lines upon his face betraying him.

"I am sorry to have been the cause of your disturbance," she said at last calmly, in a voice with the music of lulled little waves running on fairy isles in summer weather, almost without a trace that English was not her natural tongue, and that faint innuendo of the mountain melody but adding to the charm of her accent.

Count Victor ridiculously pulled at his moustache, troubled by this *sang froid* where he might naturally have looked for perturbation.

"Pardon, I demand your pardon!" was all that he could say, looking at the curl upon her shoulder that seemed uncommon white against the silk of her Indian shawl that veiled her form. She saw his gaze, instinctively drew closer her screen, then reddened at her error in so doing.

109

He had the woman there!

"Pardon," he repeated. "It is ridiculous of me, but I have heard the signals and the music more than once and wondered. I did not know"—he smiled the smile of the *flâneur*—"I did not know it was, let me say Orpheus and Eurydice, Orpheus with his lyre restored from among the constellations, and forgetting something of its old wonder. Madame, I hope Orpheus will not enrheum himself by his serenading."

Her lips parted slightly, her eyes chilled—an indescribable thing, but a plain lesson for a man who knew her sex, and Count Victor in that haughty instinct of her flesh and eye saw that here was not the place for the approach and opening of flippant parlours in the Rue Beautreillis.

"I fear I have not intruded for the first time," he went on, in a different tone. "It must have been your chamber I somewhat unceremoniously broke into last night. Till this moment the presence of a lady in Doom Castle had not occurred to me—at least I had come to consider the domestic was the only one of her sex we had here."

"It is easily explained," said the lady, losing some of her hauteur, and showing a touch of eagerness to be set right in the stranger's eye.

"There is positively not the necessity," protested Count Victor, realising a move gained, and delaying his withdrawal a moment longer.

"But you must understand that—" she went on.

Again he interrupted as courteously as he might. "The explanation is due from me, madame: I protest," said he, and she pouted. It gave her a look so bewitching, so much the aspect of a tempest bound in a cobweb, that he was compelled to smile, and for the life of her she could not but respond with a similar display. It seemed, when he saw her smile through her clouds, that he had wandered blindly through the world till now. France, far-off in sunshine, brimming with laughter and song, its thousand interests, its innumerable happy associations, were of little account to the fact that now he was in the castle of Doom, under the same roof with a woman who charmed magic flutes, who endowed the dusks with mystery and surprise. The night piped from the vaults, the crumbling walls hummed with the incessant wind and the vibration of the tempestuous sea; upon the outer stones the gargoyles poured their noisy waters—but this, but this was Paradise!

"The explanation must be mine," said he. "I was prying upon no amour, but seeking to confirm some vague alarms and suspicions."

"They were, perhaps, connected with my father," she said, with a divination that Count Victor had occasion to remember again.

"Your father!" he exclaimed, astonished that one more of his misconceptions should be thus dispelled. "Then I have been guilty of the unpardonable liberty of spying upon my hostess."

"A droll hostess, I must say, and I am the black-affronted woman," said she, "but through no fault of mine. I am in my own good father's house, and still, in a way, a stranger in it, and that is a hard thing. But you must not distrust my father: you will find, I think, before very long, that all the odd affairs in this house have less to do with him than with his daughter Olivia."

She blushed again as she introduced her name, but with a sensitiveness that Count Victor found perfectly entrancing.

"My dear mademoiselle," he said, wishing the while he had had a *friseur* at the making of his toilet that morning, as he ran his fingers over his beard and the thick brown hair that slightly curled above his brow,—"my dear mademoiselle, I feel pestilently like a fool and a knave to have placed myself in this position in any way to your annoyance. I hope I may have the opportunity before I leave Doom of proffering an adequate apology."

He expected her to leave him then, and he had a foot retired, preparing to re-enter his room, but there was a hesitancy in her manner that told him she had something more to say. She bit her nether lip—the orchards of Cammercy, he told himself, never bred a cherry a thousandth part so rich and so inviting

111

even to look at in candle-light; a shy dubiety hovered round her eyes. He waited her pleasure to speak.

"Perhaps," said she softly, relinquishing her brave demeanour—"perhaps it might be well that—that my father knew nothing of this meeting, or—or—or of what led to it."

"Mademoiselle Olivia," said Count Victor, "I am—what do you call it?—a somnambulist. In that condition it has sometimes been my so good fortune to wander into the most odd and ravishing situations. But as it happens, *helas*! I can never recall a single incident of them when I waken in the morning. *Ma foi!*" (he remembered that even yet his suspicions of the Baron were unsatisfied), "I would with some pleasure become a nocturnal conspirator myself, and I have all the necessary qualities—romance, enterprise, and sympathy."

"Mungo knows all," said the lady; "Mungo will explain."

"With infinite deference, mademoiselle, Mungo shall not be invited to do anything of the kind."

"But he must," said she firmly. "It is due to myself as well as to you, and I shall tell him to do so."

"Your good taste and judgment, mademoiselle, are your instructors. Permit me."

He took the candlestick from her hands, gravely led the way to her chamber door, and at the threshold restored the light with an excess of polite posturing not without its whimsicality. As she took the candlestick she looked in his face with a twinkle of amusement in her eyes, giving her a vivacity not hitherto betrayed.

Guessing but half the occasion of her smiles, he cried abruptly and not without confusion, "Ah! you were the amused observer of my farce in wading across from the shore. *Peste!*"

"Indeed and I was!" said she, smiling all the more brightly at the scene recalled. "Good night!"

And, more of a rogue than Count Victor had thought her, she disappeared into her chamber, leaving him to find his way back to his own.

XV

A Ray of Light

For the remainder of the night Count Victor's sleep was delicious or disturbed by dreams in which the gloomy habitation of that strange Highland country was lit with lamps—the brightest a woman's eyes. Sometimes she was Cécile, dancing—all abandoned, a child of dalliance, a nymph irresolute—to the music of a flageolet; sometimes another whose radiance fascinated, whose presence yet had terror, for (in the manner of dreams that at their maddest have some far-compassing and tremendous philosophy such as in the waking world is found in poems) she was more than herself, she was the other also, at least sharing the secrets of that great sisterhood of immaculate and despoiled, and, looking in his face, compelled to see his utter unworthiness.

He rose early and walked in the narrow garden, still sodden with rain though a bold warm sun shone high to the east. For ordinary he was not changeable, but an Olivia in Doom made a difference: those mouldering walls contained her; she looked out on the sea from those high peering windows; that bower would sometimes shelter her; those alien breezes flowing continually round Doom were privileged to kiss her hair. Positively there seems no great reason, after all, why he should be so precipitate in his removal to the town! Indeed (he told himself with a smile of his subconscious self at the subterfuge) there was a risk of miscarriage for his mission among tattling *aubergistes*, lawyers, and merchants. He was positively vexed when he encountered Mungo, and that functionary informed him that though he was early afoot the Baron was earlier still, and off to the burgh to arrange for his new lodgings. This precipitancy seemed unpleasantly like haste to be rid of him.

"Ah," said he to the little servant, "your master is so good,

113

so kind, so attentive. Yet I do not wonder, for your Highland hospitality is renowned. I have heard much of it from the dear exiles—Glengarry *par exemple*, when he desired to borrow the cost of a litre or the price of the diligence to Dunkerque in the season when new-come Scots were reaching there in a humour to be fleeced by a compatriot with three languages at command and the boast of connections with Versailles."

Mungo quite comprehended.

"Sir," said he with some feeling, "there was never bed nor board grudged at Doom. It's like father like son a' through them. The Baron's great-gutcher, auld Alan, ance thought the place no' braw enough for the eye o' a grand pairty o' Irish nobeelity that had bidden themsel's to see him, and the day they were to come he burned the place hauf doon. It was grand summer weather, and he camped them i' the park behin' there, sparing time nor money nor device in their entertainment. Ye see what might hae been a kin' o' penury in a castle was the very extravagance o' luxury in a camp. A hole in the hose is an accident nae gentleman need be ashamed o', but the same darned is a disgrace, bein' poverty confessed, as Annapla says."

It was a touchy servant this, Montaiglon told himself— somewhat sharper, too, than he had thought: he must hazard no unkind ironies upon the master.

"Charming, charming! good Mungo," said he. "The expedient might have been devised by my own great-grandfather—a gentleman of—of—of commercial pursuits in Lyons city. I am less fastidious perhaps than the Irish, being very glad to take Doom Castle as I have the honour to find it."

"But ye're thinkin' the Baron is in a hurry to billet ye elsewhere," said the servant bluntly.

In an ordinary lackey this boldness would have been too much for Count Victor; in this grotesque, so much in love, it seemed, with his employer, and so much his familiar and friend in a ridiculous Scots fashion, the impertinence appeared pardonable. Besides, he blamed himself for the ill-breeding of his own irony.

"That, if I may be permitted to point it out, is not for us to

114

consider, Monsieur Mungo," said he. "I have placed myself unreservedly in the Baron's hands, and if he considers it good for my indifferent health that I should change the air and take up my residence a little father along your delightful coast while my business as a wine merchant from Bordeaux is marching, I have no doubt he has reason."

A smile he made no effort to conceal stole over Mungo's visage.

"Wine merchant frae Bordeaux!" he cried. "I've seen a hantle o' them hereaboots at the fish-curin' season, but they cam' in gabbarts to French Foreland, and it wasnae usual for them to hae Coont to their names nor whingers to their hips. It was mair ordinar the ink-horn at their belts and the sporran at their groins."

"A malediction on the creature's shrewdness!" said Count Victor inwardly, while outwardly he simply smiled back.

"The red wine is my specialty," said he, patting his side where the hilt of his sword should be. "My whinger, as you call it, is an auger: who the devil ever broached a pipe of Scots spirits with a penknife? But I see you are too much in the confidence of the Baron for there to be any necessity of concealment between us."

"H'm!" exclaimed Mungo drily, as one who has a sense of being flattered too obviously. "The Baron's a bairn, like a' true gentlemen I've seen, and he kens me lang enough and likes me weel enough to mak' nae secret o' what it were to a'body's advantage should be nae secret to Mungo Byde. In this place I'm sentinel, spy, and garrison; it wad ill become the officer in command to let me be doin' my wark withoot some clue to the maist important pairt o't. Ye're here on a search for ane Drimdarroch."

"You are a wizard, Monsieur Mungo!" cried Montaiglon, not without chagrin at Doom's handing over so vast and vital a secret to a menial.

"Ay, and ye might think it droll that I should ken that; but I be't to ken it, for there's mony a plot against my maister, and nae foreigner comes inside thae wa's whase pedigree I canna hae an inklin' o'. Ye're here aifter Drimdarroch, and ye're no' very sure aboot your host, and that's the last thing I wad haggle wi' ye aboot, for your error'll come to ye by-and-by."

Count Victor waved a deprecating hand.

"Oh, I ken a' aboot what mak's ye sae suspicious," went on Mungo, undisturbed, "and it's a thing I could mak' clear to ye in a quarter-hoor's crack if I had his leave. Tak' my word for't, there's no' a better man wi' his feet in brogues this day than the Baron o' Doom. He should be searchin' the warld wi' the sword o' his faithers (and the same he can use), but the damned thing is the warld for him doesna gang by the snoot o' Cowal and the pass o' Glencroe. He had a wife ance; she's dead and buried in Kilmorich; noo he's doited on his hame and his dochter—"

"The charming Olivia!" cried Count Victor, thinking in one detail at all events to surprise this little custodian of all the secrets.

"Ye met her last night," said Mungo calmly, seeming to enjoy the rapidity with which his proofs of omniscience could be put forth. "That's half the secret. Ye were daunderin' aboot the lobby wi' thae fine French manners I hae heard o'—frae the French theirsels,—and wha' wad blame ye in a hoose like this? And ye're early up the day, but the lass was up earlier to tell me o' your meeting. She had to come to me before Annapla was aboot, for Annapla's no' in this part o' the ploy at all."

"I protest I have no head for charades?" said Count Victor, with a gesture of bewilderment. "I do not know what you mean."

Mungo chuckled with huge satisfaction.

"Man, it's as plain's parridge! There's a gentleman in the toon doon-by that's a hot wooer, and daddy's for nane o' his kind roon' Doom; dy'e tak' me?"

"But still—but still . . ."

"But still the trystin' gaes on, ye were aboot to say. That's very true, Coont, but it's only the like o' you and me that has nae dochters to plague oorsel's wi' that can guess the like o' that. Ay, it gaes on as ye say, and that's whaur me and Miss Olivia maun

116

put oor trust in you. In this affair I'll admit I'm a traitor in the camp—at least to the camp commander, but I think it's in a guid cause. The lassie's fair aff her heid, and nae wonder, for he's a fine mak' o' a man."

"And a good one, I hope?" interjected Count Victor.

"Humph!" said Mungo. "I thocht that wasna laid muckle stress on in France. He's a takin' deevil, and the kind's but middlin' morally, sae far as I hae had ony experience o' them. Guid or bad, Miss Olivia, nae further gane nor last Friday, refused to promise she wad gie up meetin' him,—though she's the gem o' dochters, God bless her bonny een! His lordship got up in a tirravee and ordered her to her room, wi' Annapla for warder, till he should mak' arrangements for sending her to his guid-sister's in the low country. Your comin' found us in a kin' o' confusion, but ye might hae spared yersel' my trepannin' in the tolbooth upstairs, and met her in a mair becomin' way at her faither's table if it hadna been for Annapla."

"For Annapla?" repeated Montaiglon.

"Oh, ay! Annapla has the Gift, ye ken. Dae ye think I wad hae been sae ceevil the ither nicht to her when she was yelping on the stair-heid if it hadna been her repute for the Evil E'e? Ye may lauch, but I could tell tales o' Annapla's capacity. The night afore ye cam' she yoked himsel' on his jyling the lassie, though she's the last that wad thraw him. 'Oh,' said he, 'ye're a' tarred wi' the ae stick: if ye connive at his comin' here without my kennin', I'll gie him death wi' his boots on!' It was in the Gaelic this, ye maun ken; Annapla gied me't efter. 'Boots here, boots there,' quo' she, 'love's the fine adventurer, and I see by the *griosach*' (that's the fire-embers, ye ken; between the ash o' a peat and the creesh o' a candle thae kin' o' witches can tell ye things frae noo to Hogmanay)—'I see by the *griosach*,' says she, 'that this ane'll come wi' his bare feet.' It staggered him; oh, ay! it staggered him a bit. 'Barefit or brogues,' said he, 'she'll see no man from this till the day she gaes.' And he's the man to keep his word; but it looks as though we might shuffle the pack noo and start a new game, for the plans o' flittin' her to Dunbarton hae fallen through, I hear, and he'll hae to produce her before ye leave."

"I'm in no hurry," said Count Victor, coolly twisting his moustache.

"What! To hae her produced?" said the little man slyly.

"*Farceur!* No, to leave."

'Indeed is that sae?" asked Mungo in a quite new tone, and reddening. "H'm! Ye may hae come barefit, but the ither ane has the preference."

"He has my sincere felicitations, I assure you," said Count Victor, "and I can only hope he is worthy of the honour of Master Mungo's connivance and the lady's devotion."

"Oh! *he's* a' richt! It's only a whim o' Doom's that mak's him discoontenance the fellow. I'll allow the gentleman has a name for gallantry and debt, and a wheen mair genteel vices that's neither here nor there, but he's a pretty lad. He's the man for my fancy—six feet tall, a back like a board, and an e'e like lightning. And he's nane the waur o' ha'in' a great interest in Mungo Byde's stories."

"Decidedly a diplomatist!" said Count Victor, laughing. "I always loved an enthusiast; go on—go on, good Mungo. And so he is my nocturnal owl, my flautist of the bower, my Orpheus of the mountains. Does the gifted Annapla also connive, and are hers the window signals?"

"Annapla ken's naething o' that. . . ."

"The—what do you call it?—the Second Sight appears to have its limitations."

"At least if it does she's nane the less willin' to be an unconscious help, and put a flag at the window at the biddin' o' Olivia to keep the witches awa'. The same flag that keeps aff a witch may easily fetch a bogle. There's but ae time noo and then when it's safe for the lad to venture frae the mainland, and for that there maun be a signal o' some kind, otherwise, if I ken his spirit, he wad never be aff this rock. I'm tellin' ye a' that by Mistress Olivia's command, and noo ye're in the plot like the lave o' us."

118

Mungo heaved a deep breath as if relieved of a burden.

"Still—still," said Count Victor, "one hesitates to mention it to so excellent a custodian of the family reputation—still there are other things to me somewhat—somewhat crepuscular."

His deprecatory smile and the gesture of his hands and shoulders conveyed his meaning.

"Ye're thinkin' o' the Baron in tartan," said Mungo bluntly. He smiled oddly. "That's the funniest bit of all. If ye're here a while langer that'll be plain to ye too. Between the darkest secrets and oor understanding o' them there's whiles but a rag, and that minds me that Mistress Olivia was behin' the arras tapestry chitterin' wi' fright when ye broke in by her window. Sirs! sirs! what times we're ha'in'; there's ploy in the warld yet, and me unable—tuts! I'm no' that auld either. And faith here's himsel'."

Mungo punctiliously saluted his master as that gentleman emerged beneath the frowning doorway and joined Count Victor in the dejected garden, lifted the faggot of firewood he had laid at his feet during his talk with the visitor, and sought his kitchen.

In Doom's aspect there was restraint: Count Victor shared the feeling, for now he realised that in some respects, at all events, he had been doing an injustice to his host.

"I find, M. le Count," said Doom, after some trivial introductories, "that you cannot be accommodated in the inn down-by for some days yet—possibly another week. The Circuit Court has left a pack of the legal gentlemen and jurymen there who will not be persuaded to return to Edinburgh so long as the cellar at the inn holds out, and my doer, Mr Petullo, expresses a difficulty in getting any other lodging."

"I regret exceedingly—"

"No regret at all, M. le Count," said Doom, "no regret at all, unless it be that you must put up with a while longer of a house that must be very dull to you. It is my privilege and pleasure to have you here—without prejudice to your mission—and the only difficulty there might be about it has been removed through—through—through your meeting with my daughter Olivia. I learn you met her on the stair last night. Well—it would look droll, I daresay, to have encountered that way and no word of her existence from me, but—but—but there has been a little disagreement between us. I hope I am a decently indulgent father, M. le Count, but . . ."

"You see before you one with great shame of his awkwardness, Baron," said Montaiglon. "Ordinarily I should respect a host's privacy to the extent that I should walk a hundred miles round rather than stumble upon it, but this time I do not know whether to blame myself for my gaucherie or feel pleased that for once it brought me into good company. Mungo has just hinted with his customary discretion at the cause of the mystery. I sympathise with the father; with the daughter *je suis ravi*, and—"

This hint of the gallant slightly ruffled Doom.

"Chut!" he cried. "The man with an only daughter had need be a man of patience. I have done my best with this Olivia of mine. She lost her mother when a child"—an accent of infinite tenderness here came to his voice. "These woods and this shore and this lonely barn of ours, all robbed of what once made it a palace to me and mine, were, I fancied, uncongenial to her spirit, and I sent her to the Lowlands. She came back educated as they call it—I think she brought back as good a heart as she took away, but singularly little tolerance sometimes for the life in the castle of Doom. It has been always the town for her these six months, always the town, for there she fell in with a fellow who is no fancy of mine."

Count Victor listened sympathetically, somewhat envying the lover, reviving in his mental vision the figure he had seen first twelve hours ago or less. He was brought to a more vivid interest in the story by the altered tone of Doom, who seemed to sour at the very mention of the unwelcome cavalier.

"Count," said he, "it's the failing of the sex—the very best of them, because the simplest and the sweetest—that they will prefer a fool to a wise man and a rogue to a gentleman. They're blind, because the rogue is for ever showing off his sham good qualities till they shine better than an ordinary decent man's may.

To my eyes, if not quite to my knowledge, this man is as great a scoundrel as was ever left unhung. It's in his look—well, scarcely so, to tell the truth, but something of it is in his mouth as well as in his history, and sooner than see my daughter take up for life with a creature of his stamp I would have her in her grave beside her mother. Unluckily, as I say, the man's a plausible rogue: that's the most dangerous rogue of all, and the girl's blind to all but the virtues and graces he makes a display of. I'll forgive Petullo his cheatry in the common way of his craft sooner than his introduction of such a man to my girl."

To all this Count Victor could no more than murmur his sympathy, but he had enough of the young gallant in him to make some mental reservations in favour of the persistent wooer. It was an alluring type this haunter of the midnight bower and melancholy sweet breather in the classic reed. All the wooers of only daughters, he reminded himself, as well as all the sweethearts of only sons, were unworthy in the eyes of parents, and probably Mungo's unprejudiced attitude towards the conspiring lovers was quite justified by the wooer's real character in spite of the ill repute of his history. He reflected that this confidence of Doom's left unexplained his own masquerade of the previous night, but he gave no whisper to the thought, and had indeed forgotten it by evening, when for the first time Olivia joined them at her father's table.

121

XVI

Olivia

It was a trying position in which Olivia found herself when first she sat at the same table with the stranger whose sense of humour, as she must always think, was bound to be vastly entertained by her ridiculous story. Yet she carried off the situation with that triumph that ever awaits on a frank eye, a good honest heart, and an unfailing trust in the ultimate sympathy of one's fellow-creatures. There was no *mauvaise honte* there, Count Victor saw, and more than ever he admired, if that were possible. It was the cruel father of the piece who was uneasy. He it was who must busy himself with the feeding of an appetite whose like he had not manifested before, either silent altogether or joining in the conversation with the briefest sentences.

There was never a Montaiglon who would lose such a good occasion, and Count Victor made the most of it. He was gentle, but not too gentle—for this was a lady to resent the easy self-effacement with which so many of her sex are deceived and flattered; he was not unmindful of the more honest compliments, yet he had the shrewdness to eschew the mere meaningless *blague* that no one could better employ with the creatures of Versailles, who liked their olives well oiled, or the Jeannetons and Mimis of the Italian comedy and the playhouse. Under his genial and shining influence Olivia soon forgot the ignominy of these recent days, and it was something gained in that direction that already she looked upon him as a confederate.

"I am so glad you like our country, Count Victor," she said, no way dubious about his praise of her home hills, those loud impetuous cataracts, and that alluring coast. "It rains—oh! it rains—"

"*Parfaitement*, mademoiselle, but when it shines!" and up went his hands in an admiration wherefor words were too little eloquent: at that moment he was convinced truly that the sun shone nowhere else than in the Scottish hills.

"Yes, yes, when it shines, as you say, it is the dear land! Then the woods—the woods gleam and tremble, I always think, like a girl who has tears in her eyes, the tears of gladness. The hills—let my father tell you of the hills, Count Victor; I think he must love them more than he loves his own Olivia—is that not cruel of a man with an only child? He would die, I am sure, if he could not be seeing them when he liked; but I cannot be considering the hills so beautiful as my own glens, my own little glens, that no one, I'll be fancying, is acquainted with to the heart but me and the red deer, and maybe a hunter or two. Of course we have the big glens too, and I would like if I could show you Shira Glen—"

"The best of it was once our own," said Doom, black at brow.

"—That once was ours, as father says, and is mine yet so long as I can walk there and be thinking my own thoughts in it when the wood is green, and the wild ducks are plashing in the lake."

Doom gave a significant exclamation: he was recalling that rumour had Shira Glen for his daughter's favourite trysting-place.

"Rain or shine," said Count Victor, delighting in such whole-souled rapture, delighting in that bright unwearied eye, that curious turn of phrase that made her in English half a foreigner like himself—"Rain or shine, it is a country of many charms."

"But now you are too large in your praise," she said, not quite so warmly. "I do not expect you to think it is a perfect countryside at any time and all times; and it is but natural that you should love the country of France, that I have been told is a brave and beautiful country, and a country I am sometimes loving myself because of its hospitality to folk that we know. I know it is a country of brave men, and sometimes I am wondering if it is the same for beautiful women. Tell me!" and

123

she leaned on an arm that shone warm, soft, and thrilling from the short sleeve of her gown, and put the sweetest of chins upon a hand for the wringing of hearts.

Montaiglon looked into those eyes so frank and yet profound, and straight became a rebel. "Mademoiselle Olivia," said he indifferently (oh, Cécile! oh, Cécile!), "they are considered not unpleasing; but for myself, perhaps acquaintance has spoiled the illusion."

She did not like that at all: her eyes grew proud and unbelieving.

"When I was speaking of the brave men of France," said she, "I fancied perhaps they would tell what they really thought— even to a woman." And he felt very much ashamed of himself.

"Ah! well, to tell the truth, mademoiselle," he confessed, "I have known very beautiful ones among them, and many that I liked, and still must think of with affection. *Mort de ma vie!* am I not the very slave of your sex, that for all the charms, the goodness, the kindnesses and purities is a continual reproach to mine? In the least perfect of them I have never failed to find something to remind me of my little mother."

"And now I think that is much better," said Olivia heartily, her eyes sparkling at that concluding filial note. "I would not care at all for a man to come from his own land and pretend to me that he had no mind for the beautiful women and the good women he had seen there. No; it would not deceive me, that: it would not give me any pleasure. We have a proverb in the Highlands, that Annapla will often be saying, that the rook thinks the pigeon hen would be bonny if her wings were black; and that is a *sean-fhacal*—that is an old-word that is true."

"If I seemed to forget France and what I have seen there of Youth and Beauty," said Count Victor, "it is, I swear it is—it is . . ."

"It is because you would be pleasant to a simple Highland girl," said Olivia, with just a hint of laughter in her eyes.

"No, no, *par ma foi!* not wholly that. But yes, I love my country—ah! the happy days I have known there, the sunny weather, the friends so good, the comradeship so true. Your

124

land is beautiful,—it is even more beautiful than the exiles in Paris told me; but I was not born here, and there are times when your mountains seem to crush my heart."

"Is it so indeed?" said Doom. "As for me, I would not change the bleakest of them for the province of Champagne." And he beat an impulsive hand upon the table.

"Yes, yes, I understand that," cried Olivia. "I understand it very well. It is the sorrow of the hills and woods you mean; ah! do I not know it too? It is only in my own little wee glens among the rowans that I can feel careless like the birds, and sing: when I walk the woods or stand upon the shore and see the hills without a tree or tenant, when the land is white with the snow and the mist is trailing, Olivia Lamond is not very cheery. What it is I do not know—that influence of my country; it is sad, but it is good and wholesome, I can tell you: it is then I think that the bards make songs, and those who are not bards, like poor myself, must just be feeling the songs there are no words for."

At this did Doom sit mighty pleased and humming to himself a bar of minstrelsy.

"Look at my father there!"said Olivia; "he would like you to be thinking that he does not care a great deal for the Highlands of Scotland."

"Indeed and that is not fair, Olivia; I never made pretence of that," said Doom. "Never to such as understand; Montaiglon knows the Highlands are at my heart, and that the look of the hills is my evening prayer."

"Isn't that a father, Count Victor!" cried Olivia, quite proud of the confession. "But he is the strange father, too, that will be pretending that he has forgotten the old times and the old customs of our dear people. We are the children of the hills and of the mists; the hills make no change, the mists are always coming back, and the deer is in the corrie yet, and when you will hear one that is of the Highland blood say he does not care any more for the old times, and preferring the English tongue to his own, and making a boast of his patience when the Government of England robs him of his plaid, you must be watchful of that man, Count Victor. For there is something wrong. Is it not true that I am saying, father?" She turned a questioning gaze to Doom, who had no answer but a sigh.

"You will have perhaps heard my father miscall the *breacan*, miscall the tartan and—"

"Not at all!" cried the Baron. "There is a great difference between condemning and showing an indifference."

"I think, father," said Olivia, "we are among friends. Count Victor, as you say, could understand about our fancies for the hills, and it would be droll indeed if he smiled at us for making a treasure of the tartan. Whatever my father, the stupid man, the darling, may be telling you of the tartan and the sword, Count Victor, do not believe that we are such poor souls as to forget them. Though we must be wearing the Saxon in our clothes and in our speech, there are many like me—and my dear father there—who will not forget."

It was a curious speech all that, not without a problem as well as the charm of the unexpected and the novel to Count Victor. For somehow or other there seemed to be an under-meaning in the words: Olivia was engaged upon the womanly task—he thought—of lecturing someone. If he had any doubt about that, there was Mungo behind the Baron's chair, his face just showing over his shoulder, seamed with smiles that spoke of some common understanding between him and the daughter of his master; and once, when she thrust more directly at her father, the little servitor deliberately winked to the back of his master's head—a very gnome of slyness.

"But you have not told me about the ladies of France," said she. "Stay! you will be telling me that again; it is not likely my father would be caring to hear about them so much as about the folk we know that have gone there from Scotland. They are telling me that many good brave men are there wearing their hearts out, and that is the sore enough trial."

Count Victor thought of Barisdale and his cousin-german, young Glengarry, gambling in that frouziest boozing-ken in the Rue Tarane—the Café de la Paix—without credit for a *louis d'or*;

126

he thought of James Mor Drummond and the day he came to him behind the Tuileries stable clad in rags of tartan to beg a loan: none of these was the picturesque figure of loyalty in exile that he should care to paint for this young woman.

But he remembered also Cameron, Macleod, Traquair, a score of gallant hearts, of handsome gentlemen, and Lochiel, true chevalier—perhaps a better than his king!

It was of these Count Victor spoke,—of their faith, their valiancies, their shifts of penury and pride. He had used often to consort with them at Cammercy, and later on in Paris. If the truth were to be told, they had made a man of him, and now he was generous enough to confess it.

"I owe them much, your exiles, Mademoiselle Olivia," said he. "When first I met with them I was a man without an ideal or an aim, without a scrap of faith or a cause to quarrel for. It is not good for the young, that, Baron, is it? To be passing the days in an *ennui* and the nights below the lamps. Well, I met your Scots after Dettingen, renewed the old acquaintance I had made at Cammercy, and found the later exiles better than the first— than the Balhaldies, the Glengarries, Murrays, and Sullivans. They were different, *ces gens-là*. Ordinarily they rendezvoused in the Taverne Tourtel of St Germains, and that gloomy palace shared their devotion with Scotland, whence they came and of which they were eternally talking like men in a nostalgia. James and his Jacquette were within these walls, often indifferent enough, I fear, about the cause our friends were exiled there for; and Charles, between Luneville and Liége or Poland and London, was not at the time an inspiring object of veneration, if you will permit me to say so, M. le Baron. But what does it matter? the cause was there, an image to keep the good hearts strong, unselfish, and expectant. Ah! the songs they sang, so full of that hopeful melancholy of the glens you speak of, mademoiselle; the stories they told of Tearlach's Year; the hopes that bound them in a brotherhood—and binds them yet, praise *le bon Dieu*! That was good for me. Yes; I like your exiled compatriots very much, Mademoiselle Olivia. And yet there was a *maraud* or two among them; no fate could be too hard for the spies who would betray them."

For the first time in many hours Count Victor remembered that he had an object in Scotland, but with it somehow Cécile was not associated.

"Mungo has been telling me about the spy, Count Victor. Oh, the wickedness of it! I feel black burning shame that one with a Highland name and a Highland mother would take a part like yon. I would not think there could be men in the world so bad. They must have wicked mothers to make such sons; the ghost of a good mother would cry from her grave to check her child in such a villainy." Olivia spoke with intense feeling, her eyes lambent and her lips quivering.

"Drimdarroch's mother must have been a rock," said Count Victor.

"And to take what was my father's name!"cried Olivia; "Mungo has been telling me that. Though I am a woman, I could be killing him myself."

"And here we're in our flights sure enough!" broke in the father, as he left them with a humorous pretence at terror.

"Now you must tell me about the women of France," said Olivia. "I have a friend who was there once and tells me, like you, he was indifferent; but I am doubting that he must have seen some there that were worth his fancy."

"Is it there sits the wind?" thought Montaiglon. "Our serene angel is not immune against the customary passions." An unreasonable envy of the diplomatist who had been indifferent to the ladies of France took possession of him: still, he might have gratified her curiosity about his fair compatriots had not Doom returned, and then Olivia's interest in the subject oddly ceased.

XVII

A Sentimental Secret

"Good night," said Olivia at last, and straightway Count Victor felt the glory of the evening eclipse. He opened the door to let her pass through.

"I go back to my cell quiet enough," she said in low tones, with a smiling frown upon her countenance.

"Happy prisoner!" said he, "to be condemned to no worse than your own company."

"Ah! it is often a very dull and pitiful company that, Count Victor," said Olivia, with a sigh.

It was not long till he, too, sought his couch, and the Baron of Doom was left alone.

Doom sat long looking at his crumbling walls, and the flaming fortunes, the blush, the heat-white and the dead grey ash of the peat-fire. He sighed now and then with infinite despondency; once or twice he pshawed his melancholy vapours, gave a pace back and forward on the oaken floor, with a bent head, a bereaved countenance, and sat down again, indulging the passionate void that comes to a bosom reft of its joys, its hopes, and loves, and only mournful recollection left. A done man! Not an old man; not even an elderly, but a done man none the less, with the heart out of him, and all the inspiration clean gone!

Count Victor's advent in the castle had brought its own bitterness, for it was not often now that Doom had the chance to see anything of the big brave outer world of heat and enterprise. This gallant revived ungovernably the remembrances he forever sought to stifle—all he had been and all he had seen, now past and gone for ever, as Annapla did not scruple to tell him when the demands of her Gift or a short temper compelled her.

His boyhood in the dear woods, by the reedy riverbanks, in the hill-clefts where stags harboured, on a shore for ever sounding with the enchanting sea—oh, sorrow! how these things came before him. The gentle mother with the wan beautiful face, the eager father looking ardent out to sea—they were plain to view. And then St Andrews, when he was a bejant of St Leonard's, roystering with his fellows, living the life of youth with gusto, but failing lamentably at the end; then the despondency of those scanty acres and decayed walls; his marriage with the dearest woman in the world, Death at the fireside, the bairn crying at night in the arms of her fosterer; his journeys abroad, the short hour of glory and forgetfulness with Saxe at Fontenoy and Laffeldt, to be followed only by these weary years of spoliation by law, of oppression by the usurping Hanoverian.

A done man! Only a poor done man of middle age, and the fact made all the plainer to himself by contrast with his guest, alert and even gay upon a fiery embassy of retribution.

It was exactly the hour of midnight by a clock upon the mantel; a single candle, by which he had made a show of reading, was guttering all to a side and an ungracious end in a draught that came from some cranny in the ill-seamed ingle-walls, for all that the night seemed windless. A profound stillness wrapped all; the night was huge outside, with the sea dead-flat to moon and pulsing star.

He shook off his vapours vexatiously, and, as he had done on the first night of Count Victor's coming, he went to his curious orisons at the door—the orisons of the sentimentalist, the home-lover. Back he drew the bars softly, and looked at the world that ever filled him with yearning and apprehension, at the draggled garden, at the sea with its roadway strewn with golden sand all shimmering, at the mounts—Ben Ime, Ardno, and Ben Artair, haughty in the night.

Then he shut the doors reluctantly, stood hesitating—more the done man than ever—in the darkness of the entrance, finally hurried to save the guttering candle. He lit a new one at its expiring flame and left the *salle*. He went, not to his bed-chamber but to the foot of the stair that led to the upper flats, to his daughter's room, to the room of his guest, and to the ancient chapel. With infinite caution he crept round and round on the narrow corkscrew stair, at any step it might have been a catacomb cell.

He listened at the narrow corridor leading to his Olivia's room; he paused, too, for a second, at Montaiglon's door. None gave sign of life. He went up higher.

A storey over the stage on which Count Victor slumbered, the stair ended abruptly at an oaken door, which he opened with a key. As he entered, a wild flurry of wings disturbed the interior, and by the light of the candle and some venturing rays of the moon a flock of bats or birds were to be seen in precipitous flight through unglazed windows and a broken roof.

Doom placed his candle in a niche of the wall and went over to an ancient *armoire* or chest, which seemed to be the only furniture of what had apparently once been the chapel of the castle, to judge from its size and the situation of an altar-like structure at the east end.

He unlocked the heavy lid, threw it open, looked down with a sigh at its contents, that seemed, in the light of the candle, nothing wonderful. But a suit of Highland clothes and some of the more martial appurtenances of the lost Highland state, including the dirk that had roused Montaiglon's suspicion!

He drew them out hurriedly upon the floor, but yet with an affectionate tenderness, as if they were the relics of a sacristy, and with eagerness substituted the gay tartan for his dull mulberry Saxon habiliments. It was like the creation of a man from a lay-figure. The jerk at the kilt-belt buckle somehow seemed to brace the sluggish spirit; his shoulders found their old square set above a well-curved back, his feet—his knees—by an instinct took a graceful poise they had never learned in the mean immersement of breeches and Linlithgow boots. As he fastened his buckled brogues, he hummed the words of MacMhaister Allaster's song:

"Oh! the black-cloth of the Saxon,
Dearer far's the Gaelic tartan!"

"Hugh Bethune's content with the waistcoat, is he?" he said
to himself. "He is no Gael to be so easily pleased, and him with
a freeman's liberty! And yet—and yet—I would be content
myself to have the old stuff only above my heart."

He assumed the doublet and plaid, drew down upon his brow
a bonnet with an eagle plume; turned him to the weapons. The
knife—the pistols—the dirk, went to their places, and last he put
his hand upon the hilt of a sword—not a claymore, but the
weapon he had worn in the foreign field. As foolish a piece of
masquerade as ever a child had found entertainment in, and yet,
if one could see it, with some great element of pathos and of
dignity. For with every item of the discarded and degraded
costume of his race he seemed to put on a grace not there before,
a manliness, a spirit that had lain in abeyance with the clothes
in that mothy chest. It was no done man who eagerly trod the
floor of the ruined chapel, no lack-lustre failure of life, but one
complete, commingling action with his sentiment. He felt the
world spacious about him again; a summons to ample fields
beyond the rotting woods and the sonorous shore of Doom. The
blood of his folk, that had somehow seemed to stay about his
heart in indolent clots, began to course to every extremity, and
gave his brain a tingling clarity, the wholesome intoxication of
the perfect man.

He drew the sword from its scabbard, joying hugely in the lisp
of the steel, at its gleam in the candle-light, and he felt anew the
wonder of one who had drunk the wine of life and venture to
its lees.

He made with the weapon an airy academic salute *à la Gerard*
and the new school of fence, thrust swift in tierce like a sun-flash
in forest after rain, followed with a parade, and felt an expert's
ecstasy. The blood tingled to his veins; his eyes grew large and
flashing; a flush came to that cheek, for ordinary so wan. Over
and over again he sheathed the sword, and as often withdrew

it from its scabbard. Then he handled the dirk with the pleasure of a child. But always back to the sword, handled with beauty and aplomb, always back to the sword, and he had it before him, a beam of fatal light, when something startled him as one struck unexpectedly by a whip.

There was a furious rapping at the outer door!

XVIII

"Loch Sloy!"

The rap that startled Doom in the midst of his masquerade in the chapel of his house, came like the morning beat of drums to his guest a storey lower. Count Victor sprang up with a certainty that trouble brewed, dressed with speed, and yet with the coolness of one who has heard alarums on menaced frontiers; took his sword in hand, hesitated, remembered Olivia, and laid it down again; then descended that dark stair that seemed the very pit of hazards.

A perturbing silence had succeeded the noisy summons on the oak, and Mungo, with a bold aspect well essayed, but in no accord with the tremor of his knees and the pallor of his countenance, stood, in dragging pantaloons and the gaudy Kilmarnock cap cocked upon his bald head, at the stair-foot with a flambeau in his hand. He seemed hugely relieved to have the company of Count Victor.

"Noo, wha the deevil can we hae here at sic an unearthly oor o' nicht," said he, trying a querulous tone befitting an irate sentinel; but the sentence trailed off unconvincingly, because his answer came too promptly in another peremptory summons from without.

"Lord keep 's!" whispered the little man, no longer studying to sustain his martial *rôle*. He looked nervously at Count Victor standing silently by, with some amusement at the perturbation of the garrison and a natural curiosity as to what so untimely a visit might portend. It was apparent that Mungo was for once willing to delegate his duty as keeper of the bartizan to the first substitute who offered, but here was no move to help him out of his quandary.

"It's gey gash this!" whispered the little man. "And the tide in, too! And the oor sae late!"

These sinister circumstances seemed to pile upon his brain till his knees bent below the weight of accumulated terror, and Montaiglon must smile at fears not all unreasonable, as he felt himself.

"Oh! better late than never—is not that the proverb, Master Mungo?" said he. "Though, indeed, it is not particularly consoling to a widow's husband."

"I'd gie a pound Scots to ken wha chaps," said Mungo, deaf to every humour.

"Might I suggest your asking? It is, I have heard, the customary proceeding," said Count Victor.

"Wha's there?" cried Mungo, with an ear to the wood that appeared to have nothing human outside, for now for a little there was absolute stillness. Then an answer as from a wraith— the humble request of someone for admission.

"Noo, that's michty droll," said Mungo, his face losing its alarm and taking on a look of some astonishment. "Haud that," and he thrust the torch in the Frenchman's hand. Without another word he drew back the bars, opened the door, and put out his head. He was caught by the throat and plucked forth into the darkness.

Count Victor could not have drawn a weapon had he had one ere the door fell in thundering on the walls. He got one glimpse of the *sans culottes*, appealed again to the De Chenier macer in his ancestry, and flung the flambeau at the first who entered.

The light went out; he dropped at a boy's intuition upon a knee and lowered his head. Over him in the darkness poured his assailants, too close upon each other in their eagerness, and while they struggled at the stair-foot he drew softly back. Out in the night Mungo wailed lugubrious in the hands of some of his captors; within there was a wonderful silence for a little, the baffled visitors recovering themselves with no waste of words, and mounting the stair in pursuit of the gentleman they presumed to have preceded them. When they were well up, he went to the

135

door and made it fast again, leaving Mungo to the fate his stupidity deserved.

Doom's sleeping-chamber lay behind: he passed along the corridor quickly, knocked at the door, got no answer, and entered.

It was as he had fancied—his host was gone, his couch had not been occupied. A storm of passion swept through him; he felt himself that contemptible thing, a man of the world betrayed by a wickedness that ought to be transparent. They were in the plot then, master and man, perhaps even—but no, that was a thought to quell on the moment of its waking; she at least was innocent of all these machinations, and upstairs now, she shared, without a doubt, the alarms of Annapla. That familiar of shades and witches, that student of the fates, was a noisy poltroon when it was the material world that threatened; she was shrieking again.

"Loch Sloy! Loch Sloy!" now rose the voices overhead, surely the maddest place in the world for a Gaelic slogan: it gave him a sense of unspeakable savagery and antique, for it was two hundred years since his own family had cried "Cammercy!" on stricken fields.

He paused a moment, irresolute.

A veritable farce! he thought. It would have been so much easier for his host to hand him over without these playhouse preliminaries.

But Olivia! but Olivia!

He felt the good impulse of love and anger, the old ichor of his folk surged through his veins, and without a weapon he went upstairs, trusting to his wits to deal best with whatever he would there encounter.

It seemed an hour since they had entered; in truth it was but a minute or two, and they were still in the bewildering blackness of the stair, one behind another in its narrow coils, and seemingly wisely dubious of too precipitate an advance. He estimated that they numbered less than half-a-dozen when he came upon the rearmost of the *queue*.

136

"Loch Sloy!" cried out the leader, somewhat too theatrically for illusion.

"Cammercy for me!" thought Montaiglon: he was upon the tail, and clutched to drag the last man down. Fate was kind, she gave the bare knees of the enemy to his hand, and behold! here was his instrument—in the customary knife stuck in the man's stocking. It was Count Victor's at a flash: he stood a step higher, threw his arm over the shoulder of the man, pulled him backward into the pit of the stair and stabbed at him as he fell.

"*Un!*" said he as the wretch collapsed upon himself, and the knife seemed now unnecessary. He clutched the second man, who could not guess the tragedy behind, for the night's business was all in front, and surely only friends were in the rear—he clutched the second lower, and threw him backward over his head.

"*Deux!*" said Count Victor, as the man fell limp behind him upon his unconscious confederate.

The third in front turned like a viper when Count Victor's clutch came on his waist, and drove out with his feet. The act was his own undoing. It met with no resistance, and the impetus of his kick carried him off the balance and threw him on the top of his confederates below.

"*Trois!*" said Montaiglon. "Pulling corks is the most excellent training for such a warfare," and he set himself almost cheerfully to number four.

But number four was not in the neck of the bottle: this ferment behind propelled him out upon the stairhead, and Montaiglon, who had thrown himself upon him, fell with him on the floor. Both men recovered their feet at a spring. A moment's pause was noisy with the cries of the domestic in her room, then the Frenchman felt a hand pass rapidly over his habiliments and seek hurriedly for his throat, as on a sudden inspiration. What that preluded was too obvious: he fancied he could feel the poignard already plunging in his ribs, and he swiftly tried a fall with his opponent.

It was a wrestler's grip he sought, but a wrestler he found, for

137

arms of a gigantic strength went round him, clasping his own to his side and rendering his knife futile; a Gaelic malediction hissed in his ear; he felt breath hot and panting; his own failed miserably, and his blood sang in his head with the pressure of those tremendous arms that caught him to a chest like a cuirass of steel. But if his hands were bound, his feet were free: he placed one behind his enemy and flung his weight upon him, so that they fell together. This time Count Victor was uppermost. His hands were free of a sudden; he raised the knife to stab at the breast heaving under him, but he heard as from another world—as from a world of calm and angels—the voice of Olivia in her room crying for her father, and a revulsion seized him, so that he hesitated at his ugly task. It was less than a second's slackness, yet it was enough, for his enemy rolled free and plunged for the stair. Montaiglon seized him as he fled; the skirt of his coat dragged through his hands, and left him with a button. He dropped it with a cry, and turned in the darkness to find himself more frightfully menaced than before.

This time the plunge of the dirk was actual; he felt it sear his side like a hot iron, and caught the wrist that held it, only in time to check a second blow. His fingers slipped, his head swam; a moment more, and a Montaiglon was dead very far from his pleasant land of France, in a phantom castle upon a shadowy sea among savage ghosts.

"Father! father!"

It was Olivia's voice; a light was thrown upon the scene, for she stood beside the combatants with a candle in her hand.

They drew back at a mutual spasm, and Montaiglon saw that his antagonist was the Baron of Doom!

XIX

Revelation

Doom, astounded, threw the dagger from him with an exclamation. His eyes, large and burning yet with passion, were wholly for Count Victor, though his daughter, Olivia, stood there at his side holding the light that had revealed the furies to each other, her hair in dark brown cataracts on her shoulders, and eddying in bewitching curls upon her ears and temples, that gleamed below like the foam of mountain pools.

"Father, father! what does this mean?" she cried. "There is some fearful mistake here."

"That is not to exaggerate the position at all events," thought Count Victor, breathing hard, putting the knife unobserved behind him. He smiled to this vision, and shrugged his shoulders. He left the elucidation of the mystery to the other gentleman, this counsellor of forgiveness and peace, clad head to foot in the garb he contemned, and capable of some excellent practice with daggers in the darkness.

"I'll never be able to say how much I regret this, Count Victor," said Doom. "Good God! your hands were going, and in a second or two more . . ."

"For so hurried a farce," said Count Victor, "the lowered light was something of a mistake, *n'est ce pas?* I—I—I just missed the point of the joke," and he glanced at the dagger glittering sinister in the corner of the stair.

"I have known your mistake all along," cried Olivia. "Oh, it is a stupid thing this. I will tell you! It is my father should have told you before."

The clangour of the outer door closing recalled that there was danger still below. Olivia put a frightened hand on her father's arm. "A thousand pardons, Montaiglon," cried he; "but here's

139

a task to finish." And without a word more of excuse or explanation he plunged downstairs.

Count Victor looked dubiously after him, and made no move to follow.

"Surely you will not be leaving him alone there?" said Olivia. "Oh! you have not your sword. I will get your sword." And before he could reply she had flown to his room. She returned with the weapon. Her hand was all trembling as she held it out to him. He took it slowly; there seemed no need for haste below now, for all was silent except the voices of Doom and Mungo.

"It is very good of you, Mademoiselle Olivia," said he. "I thank you, but—but—you find me in a quandary. Am I to consider M. le Baron as ally or—or—or . . ." He hesitated to put the brutal alternative to the daughter.

Olivia stamped her foot impetuously, her visage disturbed by emotions of anxiety, vexation, and shame.

"Oh, go! go!" she cried. "You will not, surely, be taking my father for a traitor to his own house—for a murderer."

"I desire to make the least of a pleasantry I am incapable of comprehending, yet his dagger was uncomfortably close to my ribs a minute or two ago," said Count Victor, reflectively.

"Oh!" she cried. "Is not this a coil? I must even go myself," and she made to descend.

"Nay, nay," said Count Victor softly, holding her back. "Nay, nay; I will go if your whole ancestry were ranked at the foot."

"It is the most stupid thing," she cried, as he left her; "I will explain when you come up. My father is a Highland gentleman."

"So, by the way, was Drimdarroch," said Montaiglon, but that was to himself. He smiled back into the illumination of the lady's candle, then descended into the darkness with a brow tense and frowning, and his weapon prepared for anything.

The stair was vacant, so was the corridor. The outer door was open; the sound of the sea came in faint murmurs, the mingled odours of pine and wrack borne with it. Out in the heavens a moon swung among her stars most queenly and sedate, careless altogether of this mortal world of strife and terrors; the sea had a golden roadway. A lantern light bobbed on the outer edge of the rock, shining through Olivia's bower like a will-o'-the-wisp, and he could hear in low tones the voices of Doom and his servant. Out at sea, but invisible, far beyond the moon's influence, a boat was being rowed fast: the beat of the oars on the thole-pins came distinctly. And in the wood behind, now cut off from them by the riding waves, owls called incessantly.

It was like a night in a dream, like some vast wheeling chimera of fever—that plangent sea before, those terrors fleeing, and behind, a maiden left with her duenna in a castle demoniac.

Doom and Mungo came back from the rock edge, silently almost, brooding over a mystery, and the three looked at each other.

"Well, they are gone," said the Baron at last, showing the way to his guest.

"What, gone!" said Montaiglon, incapable of restraining his irony. "Not all of them?"

"O Lord! but this is the nicht!"cried the little servant,who carried the lantern. "I micht hae bided a' my days in Fife and never kent what war was. The only thing that daunts me is that I should hae missed my chance o' a whup at them, for they had me trussed like a cock before I put my feet below me when they pu'd me oot."

He drew the bars with nervous fingers, and seemed to dread his master as much as he had done the enemy. Olivia had come down to the corridor; aloft Annapla had renewed her lamentations; the four of them stood clustered in the narrow passage at the stair-foot.

"What for did ye open the door, Mungo?" asked Doom,— not the Doom of doleful days, of melancholy evenings of study and of sour memories, not the done man, but one alert and eager, a soldier, in the poise of his body, the set of his limbs, the spirit of his eye.

"Here's a new man!" thought Montaiglon, silently regarding him. "Devilry appears to have a marvellous power of stimulation."

"I opened the door," said Mungo, much perturbed.

"For what?" said Doom shortly.

"There was a knock."

"I heard it. The knock was obvious; it dirled the very roof of the house. But it was not necessary to open at a knock at this time of morning; ye must have had a reason. Hospitality like that to half-a-dozen rogues from Arroquhar, who had already made a warm night for ye, was surely stretched a little too far. What did ye open for?"

Mungo seemed to range his mind for a reply. He looked to Montaiglon, but got no answer in the Frenchman's face; he looked over Montaiglon's shoulder at Olivia, standing yet in the tremor of her fears, and his eye lingered. It was no wonder, thought Count Victor, that it lingered there.

"Come, come, I'm waiting my answer!" cried Doom, in a voice that might have stirred a corps in the battlefield.

"I thought there wasna mair than ane," said Mungo.

"But even one! At this time of morning! And is it your custom to open to a summons of that kind without finding out who calls?"

"I thought I kent the voice," said Mungo, furtively looking again at Olivia.

"And whose was it, this voice that could command so ready and foolish an acquiescence on the part of my honest sentinel Mungo Boyd?" asked Doom incredulously.

"Ye can ask that!" replied the servant desperately; "it's mair than I can tell. All I ken is that I thought the voice fair-spoken, and I alloo it was a daft-like thing to do, but I pu'ed the bar. I had nae sooner dune't nor I was gripped by the thrapple and kep' doon by a couple o' the blackguards that held me a' the time the ither three or four were—"

Doom caught him by the collar and shook him angrily.

"Ye lie, ye Fife cat; I see't in your face!"

"I can speak as to the single voice and its humility and to the sudden plucking forth of this gentleman," said Count Victor quietly, at sea over this examination. But for the presence of the woman he would have cried out at the mockery of the thing.

142

"You must hear my explanation, Montaiglon," said Doom. "If you will come to the hall, I will give it. Olivia, you will come too. I should have taken your hints of yesterday morning, and the explanation of this might have been unnecessary."

Doom and his guest went to the *salle*; Olivia lingered a moment behind.

"Who was it, Mungo?" said she, whisperingly to the servant. "I know by the face of you that you are keeping something from my father."

"Am I?" said he. "Humph! It's Fife very soon for Mungo Byde, I'm tellin' ye."

"But who was it?" she persisted.

"The Arroquhar men," said he curtly; "and that's all I ken aboot it," and he turned to leave her.

"And that is not the truth, Mungo," said Olivia, with great dignity. "I think with my father that you are telling what is not the true word," and she said no more, but followed to the *salle*.

On the stairway Count Victor trod upon the button he had drawn from the skirts of his assailant; he picked it up without a word, to keep it as a souvenir. Doom preceded him into the room, lit some candles hurriedly at the smouldering fire, and turned to offer him a chair.

"Our—our friends are gone," said he. "You seem to have badly wounded one of them, for the others carried him bleeding to the waterside, as we have seen from his blood-marks on the rock: they have gone, as they apparently must have come, by boat. Sit down, Olivia."

His daughter had entered. She had hurriedly coiled her hair up, and the happy carelessness of it pleased Montaiglon's eye like a picture.

Still he said nothing; he could not trust himself to speak, facing, as he fancied yet he did, a traitor.

"I see from your face you must still be dubious of me," said Doom. He waited for no reply, but paced up and down the room excitedly, the pleats of his kilt and the thongs of his purse swinging to his movements: a handsome figure, as Montaiglon

143

could not but confess. "I am still shattered at the nerve to think that I had almost taken your life there in a fool's blunder. You must wonder to see me in this—in this costume."

He could not even yet come to his explanation, and Olivia must help him.

"What my father would tell you, if he was not in such a trouble, Count Victor, is what I did my best to let you know last night. It is just that he breaks the law of George the king in this small affair of our Highland tartan. It is a fancy of his to be wearing it in an evening, and the bats in the chapel upstairs are too blind to know what a rebel it is that must be play-acting old days and old styles among them."

A faint light came suddenly to Count Victor.

"Ah!" said he, "it is not, mademoiselle, that the bats alone are blind; here is a very blind Montaiglon. I implore your pardon, M. le Baron. It is good to be frank, though it is sometimes unpleasant, and I must plead guilty to an imbecile misapprehension."

Doom flushed, and took the proffered hand.

"My good Montaiglon," said he, "I'm the most shamefaced man this day in the shire of Argyll. Need I be telling you that I have all Olivia's sentiment and none of her honest courage?"

"My dear father!" cried Olivia fondly, looking with melting eyes at her parent; and Count Victor, too, thought this mummer no inadmirable figure.

"It is nothing more than my indulgence in the tartan that makes your host look sometimes scarcely trustworthy; and my secret got its right punishment this night. I will not be able to wear a kilt with an easy conscience for some time to come."

"My faith! Baron, that were a penance out of all proportion!" said Count Victor, laughing. "If you nearly gave me the key of the Olympian meadows there, 'tis I that have brought these outlaws about your ears."

"What beats me is that they should make so much ado about a trifle."

"A trifle!" said Count Victor. "True, in a sense. The wretch

144

but died. We must all die; we all know it, though none of us believe it."

"I am glad to say that after all you only wounded yon Macfarlane; so Petullo learned but yesterday, and I clean forgot to tell you sooner."

Montaiglon looked mightily relieved.

"So!" said he; "I shall give a score of the best candles to St Denys—if I remember when I get home again. You could not have told me such good tidings a moment too soon, dear M. le Baron, though of course a small affair like that would naturally escape one's memory."

"He was as good as dead, by all rumour; but being a thief and an Arroquhar man, he naturally recovered: and now it's the oddest thing in the world that an accident of the nature, that is all, as Black Andy well must know, in the ordinary way of business, should bring about so much *fracas*."

"It was part of my delusion," said Count Victor, "to fancy Mungo not entirely innocent. As you observed, he opened the door with an excess of hospitality."

"Yes, that was droll," confessed Doom, reflectively. "That was droll, indeed; but Mungo hates the very name of Arroquhar, and all that comes from it."

"Except our Annapla," suggested Olivia, smiling.

"Oh, except Annapla, of course!" said her father. "He's to marry her to avert her Evil Eye."

"And is she a Macfarlane?" asked Montaiglon, surprised.

"No less," replied Doom. "She's a cousin of Andy's; but there's little love lost between them."

"Speaking of bats!" thought Count Victor, but he did not hint at his new conclusions. "Well, I am glad," said he; "they left me but remorse last time; this time here's a souvenir," and he showed the button.

It was a silver chamfered lozenge, conspicuous and unforgettable.

"Stolen gear, doubtless," guessed the Baron, looking at it with indifference. "Silver buttons are not rife between here and the pass of Balmaha."

145

"Let me see it, please," said Olivia.

She took it in her hand but for a moment, turned slightly aside to look more closely at it in the sconce-light, paled with some emotion, and gave it back with slightly trembling fingers.

"I have a headache," she said suddenly. "I am not so brave as I thought I was; you will let me say Good night?"

She smiled to Count Victor with a face most wan.

"My dear, you are like a ghost," said her father, and as she left the room he looked after her affectionately.

XX

An Evening's Melody in the Boar's Head Inn

The Boar's Head Inn, for all its fine cognomen, was little better than any of the numerous taverns that kept discreet half-open doors to the wynds and closes of the Duke's burgh town, but custom made it a preserve of the upper class in the community. There it was the writers met their clients and cozened them into costly law pleas over the genial jug or chopine; the through-going stranger took his pack there and dwelt cheaply in the attics that looked upon the bay and on the little harbour where traffic dozed upon the swinging tide, waiting the goodwill of mariners in no hurry to leave a port so alluring; in its smoke-grimed public-room skippers frequented, full of loud tales of roving; and even the retinue of MacCailein was not averse from an evening's merriment in a company where no restraint of the castle was expected, and his Grace was mentioned but vaguely as a personal pronoun.

There was in the inn a *sanctum sanctorum* where only were allowed the bailies of the burgh, a tacksman of position, perhaps, from the landward part, or the like of the Duke's Chamberlain, who was no bacchanal, but loved the company of honest men in their hours of manumission. Here the bottle was of the best, and the conversation most genteel—otherwise there had been no Sim MacTaggart in the company where he reigned the king. It was a state that called for shrewd deportment. One must not be too free, for an excess of freedom cheapened the affability, and yet one must be hail fellow with magistrate—and even an odd master mariner—with no touch of condescension for the Highland among them who could scent the same like *aqua vitæ* and resent it like a push of the hand.

He came not often, but ever was he welcome, those nights the

147

more glorious for his qualities of humour and generosity, his tales that stirred like the brassy cry of trumpets, his tolerance of the fool and his folly, his fatalist excuse for any sin except the scurviest. And there was the flageolet! You will hear the echo of it yet in that burgh town where he performed; its charm lingers in melodies hummed or piped by old folks of winter nights, its magic has been made the stuff of myth, so that as children we have heard the sound of Simon's instrument in the spring woods when we went there white-hay-gathering, or for fagots for the school-house fire.

A few nights after that thundering canter from the spider's den where Kate Petullo sat amid her coils, the Chamberlain went to wander care among easy hearts. It was a season of mild weather though on the eve of winter; even yet the perfume of the stubble-field and of fruitage in forest and plantation breathed all about the country of MacCailein Mor. Before the windows of the inn the bay lay warm and placid, and Dunchuach, wood-mantled, and the hills beyond it vague, remote, and haunted all by story, seemed to swim in a benign air, and the outer world drew the souls of these men in a tavern into a brief acquaintanceship. The window of the large room they sat in looked out upon this world new lit by the tender moon that hung on Strone. A magistrate made to shutter it and bring the hour of Bacchus all the faster.

"Hold there, Bailie!" cried the Chamberlain. "Good God! let us have so long as we can of a night so clean and wholesome."

It needed but a hint of that nature from this creature of romance and curious destiny to silence their unprofitable discourse over herds and session discipline, and for a space they sat about the window, surrendered to the beauty of the night. So still that outer world, so vacant of living creature, that it might have been a picture! In the midst of their half circle the Chamberlain lay back in his chair and drank the vision in by gloating eyes.

"Upon my word," said he at last in a voice that had the rich profound of passion—"upon my word, we are the undeserving dogs!" and at an impulse he took his flageolet and played a

148

Highland air. It had the proper spirit of the hour—the rapturous evening pipe of birds in dewy thickets, serene yet someway touched by melancholy; there was no man there among them who did not in his breast repeat its words that have been heard for generations in hillside milking-folds where women put their ruddy cheeks against the kine and look along the valleys, singing softly to the accompaniment of the gushing pail.

He held his audience by a chain of gold: perhaps he knew it, perhaps he joyed in it, but his half-shut eyes revealed no more than that he still saw the beauty and peace of the night and thus rendered an oblation.

His melody ceased as abruptly as it began. Up he got hastily and stamped his foot and turned to the table where the bottle lay and cried loud out for lights, as one might do ashamed of a womanly weakness, and it is the Highland heart that his friends should like him all the more for that display of sentiment and shyness to confess it.

"By the Lord, Factor, and it's you have the skill of it!" said the Provost, in tones of lofty admiration.

"Is't the bit reed?" said the Chamberlain, indifferently. "Your boy Davie could learn to play better than I in a month's lessons."

"It's no' altogether the playing though," said the Provost slowly, ruminating as on a problem; "it's that too, but it's more than that; it's the seizing of the time and tune to play. I'm no great musicianer myself, though I have tried the trump; but there the now—with the night like that, and us like this, and all the rest of it—that lilt of yours—oh, damn! pass the bottle; what for should man be melancholy?" He poured some wine and gulped it hurriedly.

"Never heard the beat of it!" said the others. "Give us a rant, Factor," and round the table they gathered, the candles were being lit, the ambrosial night was to begin.

Simon MacTaggart looked round his company—at some with the maudlin tear of sentiment still on their cheeks, at others eager to escape this soft moment and make the beaker clink.

"My sorrow!" thought he, "what a corps to entertain! Is it

149

the same stuff as myself? Is this the best that Sim MacTaggart, that knows and feels things, can be doing? And still they're worthy fellows, still I must be liking them."

"Rants!" he cried, and stood among them tall and straight, and handsome, with lowering dark brows, and his face more pale than they had known it customarily,—"a little less rant would be the better for us. Take my word for it, the canty quiet lilt in the evening, and the lights low, and calm and honest thoughts with us, is better than all the rant and chorus, and I've tried them both. But Heaven forbid that Sim MacTaggart should turn to preaching in his middle age!"

"Faith! and it's very true what you say, Factor," acquiesced some sycophant.

The Chamberlain looked at him half in pity, half in amusement. "How do *you* ken, Bailie?" said he; "what are yearlings at Fa'kirk Tryst?" And then, waiting no answer to what indeed demanded none, he put the flageolet to his lips again and began to play a strathspey to which the company in the true bucolic style beat time with feet below the table. He changed to the tune of a minuet, then essayed at a melody more sweet and haunting than them all but broken ere its finish.

"A hole in the ballant," commented the Provost. "Have another skelp at it, Factor."

"Later on perhaps," said Sim MacTaggart. "The end of it aye escapes my memory. Rather a taking tune, I think,—don't you? Just a little—just a little too much of the psalm in it perhaps for common everyday use, but man! it grips me curiously;" and then on a hint from one at his shoulder he played "The Devil in the Kitchen," a dance that might have charmed the imps of Hallowe'en.

He was in the midst of it when the door of the room opened and a beggar looked in—a starven character of the neighbouring parish, all bedecked with cheap brooches and babs of ribbon, leading by the hand the little child of his daughter wronged and dead. He said never a word but stood just within the door expectant—a reproach to cleanliness, content, good clothes, the well fed, and all who make believe to love their fellows.

150

"Go away, Baldy!" cried the Bailies sharply, vexed by this intrusion on their moments of carouse: no one of them had a friendly eye for the old wanderer in his blue coat, and dumb but for his beggar's badge and the child that clung to his hand.

It was the child that Sim MacTaggart saw. He thought of many things as he looked at the little one, white-haired, bare-footed, and large-eyed.

"Come here, my dear!" said he, quite tenderly, smiling upon her.

She would have been afraid but for the manifest kindness of that dark commanding stranger; it was only shyness that kept her from obeying.

The Chamberlain rose and went over to the door and cried upon the landlord. "You will have a chopine of ale, Baldy," said he to the old wreck; "sometimes it's all the difference between hell-fire and content, and—for God's sake buy the bairn a pair of boots!" As he spoke he slipped, by a motion studiously concealed from the company, some silver into the beggar's poke.

The ale came in, the beggar drank for a moment, the Chamberlain took the child upon his knee, his face made fine and noble by some sweet human sentiment, and he kissed her, ere she went, upon the brow.

For a space the *sanctum sanctorum* of the Boar's Head Inn was ill at ease. This sort of thing—so common in Sim MacTaggart, who made friends with every gangrel he met—was like a week-day sermon, and they considered the Sunday homilies of Dr Macivor quite enough. They much preferred their Simon in his more common mood of wild devilry, and nobody knew it better than the gentleman himself.

"Oh, damn the lousy tribe of them!" cried he, beating his palm upon the table; "what's Long Davie the dempster thinking of to be letting such folk come sorning here?"

"I'll warrant they get more encouragement here than they do in Lorn," said the Provost, shrewdly, for he had seen the glint of coin and knew his man. "You beat all, Factor! If I lived a hundred years you would be more than I could fathom. Well,

151

well, pass the bottle, and ye might have another skelp at yon tune if it's your pleasure."

The Chamberlain most willingly complied: it was the easiest retort to the Provost's vague allusion.

He played the tune again, once more its conclusion baffled him, and as he tried a futile repetition Count Victor stood listening in the lobby of the Boar's Head Inn.

XXI

Count Victor Changes His Quarters

Count Victor had said *Au revoir* to Doom Castle that afternoon.

Mungo had rowed him down by boat to the harbour and left him with his valise at the inn, pleased mightily that his cares as garrison were to be relieved by the departure of one who so much attracted the unpleasant attentions of nocturnal foes, and returned home with the easiest mind he had enjoyed since the fateful day the Frenchman waded to the rock. As for Count Victor, his feelings were mingled. He had left Doom from a double sense of duty, and yet had he been another man he would have bided for love. After last evening's uproar, plain decency demanded that Jonah should obviate a repetition by removing himself elsewhere. There was also another consideration as pregnant, yet more delicate: the traditions of his class and family as well as his natural sense of honour compelled his separation from the fascinating influence of the ingenuous woman whose affections were pledged in another quarter. In a couple of days he had fallen desperately in love with Olivia—a precipitation that might seem ridiculous in any man of the world who was not a Montaiglon satiated by acquaintance with scores of Dame Stratagems, fair *intrigueuses* and puppets without hearts below their modish bodices. Olivia charmed by her freshness, and the simple frankness of her nature, with its deep emotions, gave him infinitely more surprise and thrill than any woman he had met before. "Wisdom wanting absolute honesty," he told himself, "is only craft: I discover that a monstrous deal of cleverness I have seen in her sex was only another kind of cosmetic daubed on with a sponge."

And then, too, Olivia that morning seemed to have become all of a sudden very cold to him. He was piqued at her silence,

153

he was more than piqued to discover that she too, like Mungo, obviously considered his removal a relief.

Behold him, then, with his quarters taken in the Boar's Head Inn, whence by good luck the legal gang of Edinburgh had some hours before departed, standing in the entrance feeling himself more the foreigner than ever, with the vexing reflection that he had not made any progress in the object of his embassy, but, on the contrary, had lost no little degree of his zest therein.

The sound of the flageolet was at once a blow and a salute. That unaccomplished air had helped to woo Olivia in her bower, but yet it gave a link with her, the solace of the thought that here was one she knew. Was it not something of good fortune that it should lead him to identify and meet one whose very name was still unknown to him, but with whom he was, in a faint measure, on slight terms of confederacy through the confession of Olivia and the confidence of Mungo Boyd?

"*Toujours l'audace!*" thought he, and he asked for the inn-keeper's introduction to the performer. "If it may be permitted, and the gentleman is not too pressingly engaged."

"Indeed," said the innkeeper—a jovial rosy gentleman, typical of his kind—"indeed, and it may very well be permitted, and it would not be altogether to my disadvantage that his lordship should be out of there, for the Bailies cannot very well be drinking deep and listening to Mr Simon MacTaggart's songs, as I have experienced afore. The name?"

"He never heard it," said Count Victor, "but it happens to be Montaiglon, and I was till this moment in the odd position of not knowing his, though we have a common friend."

A few minutes later the Chamberlain stood before him with the end of the flageolet protruding from the breast of his coat.

As they met in the narrow confine of the lobby—on either hand of them closed rooms noisy with clink of drinking-ware, with laugh and jest and all that rumour of carouse—Montaiglon's first impression was exceeding favourable. This Chamberlain pleased his eye to start with; his manner was fine-bred in spite of a second's confusion; his accent was cordial, and the flageolet,

154

displayed with no attempt at concealment, captured the heart of the Frenchman, who had been long enough in these isles to weary of a national character that dare not surrender itself to any unbusiness-like frisking in the meadows. And one thing more there was revealed—here was the kilted gallant of the miniature in Olivia's chamber, and here was the unfriendly horseman of the wood, here, in fine, was the lover of the story, and the jealousy (if it was a jealousy) he had felt in the wood, forgotten, for he smiled.

But now that he was face to face with Olivia's lover, Count Victor discovered that he had not the slightest excuse for refer-ring to her who was the only association between them! The lady herself and Mungo Boyd had conveyed a sense of very close conspiracy between all four, but from neither the lady nor any one else in Doom had he any passport to the friendship of this gentleman. It was only for a moment the difficulties of the situation mastered him.

"I have permitted myself, monsieur, to intrude upon you with an excuse that must seem scandalously inadequate," said he. "My name is Montaiglon. . . ."

"With the particle, I think?" said Sim MacTaggart.

Count Victor started slightly.

"But yes," said he, "it is so, though I never march with much baggage, and a De to a traveller is like a second hat. It is, then, that it is perhaps unnecessary to say more of myself?"

The Chamberlain with much *bonhomie* grasped his hand.

"M. Montaiglon," said he, "I am very proud to meet you. I fancy a certain lady and I owe something to your consideration, and Simon MacTaggart stands upon no ceremony."

Count Victor winced slightly at the conjunction, but otherwise he was delighted.

"I am ravished, monsieur!" said he. "Ceremony is like some people's assumption of dignity—the false bottoms they put in their boots to conceal the fact that they are under the average height, is it not?"

Arm in arm they went out in front of the inn and walked along the bay, and the Provost and the Bailies were left mourning for their king.

"You must not fancy the name and reputation of the gentlemen of Cammercy unknown in these parts," said the Chamberlain. "When the lady—who need not be more specifically mentioned—told me you had come to Doom, it was like the overcome of a song at first that I had heard of you before. And now that I see you, I mind the story went, when I was at Dunkerque some years ago, that Count Victor Jean, if all his other natural gifts had failed him, might have made a noble fortune as a *maître d'escrime*. Sir, I am an indifferent hand with the rapier myself, but I aye liked to see a man that was its master."

"You are very good," said Montaiglon; "and yet such a reputation, exaggerated as I fear it may be, is not, by my faith! the one I should desire under the circumstances that, as you have doubtless further heard, bring me here."

"About that, M. Montaiglon, it is perhaps as well that the Duke of Argyll's Chamberlain should know nothing at all. You are a wild lot, my gallant Jacobites"—he laughed softly as he spoke. "Between ourselves I have been more than bottle friends with some lovable persons on your side of the house, and you will be good enough to consider Simon MacTaggart no politician, though the Duke's Chamberlain *ex officio* is bound to be enemy to every man who will not swear King George the best of monarchs."

"From what I know of affairs in Europe now, and for all our heroics of invasion," said Count Victor, "his Majesty is like to remain in undisputed possession, and you may take my word for it, no affair of high politics is responsible for my being here. Monsieur himself has doubtless had affairs. I am seeking but for one man. . . . "

"Drimdarroch," said the Chamberlain. "So the lady told me. Our Drimdarroch will not provide very much interest for a *maître d'escrime*," and he laughed as he pictured Petullo the writer shivering before a flash of steel.

156

"Ah! you speak of the lawyer: Doom told me of him, and as he was good enough to interest himself in my lodging in this place, I must make him my compliments at the earliest and tell him I have settled down for myself in the *auberge*."

"To that much at least I can help you, though in the other affair I'm neutral in spite of my interest in any ploy of the kind. There's Petullo's house across the way; I'm on certain terms with him; if you care, we could see him now."

"*Le plus tôt sera le mieux!*" said Count Victor.

The Chamberlain led the way.

XXII

The Lonely Lady

When Petullo's work was done of an evening it was his practice to sit with his wife in their huge and draughty parlour, practising the good husband and the domestic virtues in an upright zealous manner, such as one may read of in the books. A noble thing to do, but what's the good of it when hearts are miles apart and the practitioner is a man of rags? Yet there he sat, strewing himself with snuff to keep himself awake, blinking with dim eyes at her, wondering for ever at her inscrutable nature, conversing improvingly upon his cases in the courts, or upon his growing fortune that he computed nightly like a miser. Sometimes, in spite of his drenchings of macabaw, sleep compelled him, and, humped in his lug-chair, he would forget his duty, yet waken at her every yawn. And she—she just looked at him as he slept! She looked— and loathed herself, that she—so clean, so graceful, so sweet in spite of all her sin—should be allied with a dead man. The evenings passed for her on fettered hours; but for the window she had died from her incubus, or at least stood up and shrieked and ran into the street.

But for the window! From there she saw the hill Dunchuach, so tranquil, and the bosky deeps of Shira Glen that she knew so well in dusky evenings and in moonlight, and must ever tenant, in her fancy, with the man she used to meet there. Often would she turn her back upon that wizened atomy of quirks and false ideals, and let her bosom pant to think tonight!—tonight!— tonight!

When the Chamberlain and Montaiglon were announced she could have cried aloud with joy. It was not hard in that moment of her elation to understand why once the Chamberlain had loved her: beside the man to whom her own mad young ambition manacled her, she seemed a vision of beauty, none the worse for being just a little ripened.

"Come awa' in!" cried the lawyer with effusion. "You'll find the mistress and me our lones, and nearly tiring o' each other's company."

The Chamberlain was disappointed. It was one of the evenings when Mrs Petullo was used to seek him in the woods, and he had thought to find her husband by himself.

"A perfect picture of a happy hearth, eh?" said he. "I'm sweer to spoil it, but I'm bound to lose no time in bringing to you my good friend M. Montaiglon, who has taken up his quarters at the Boar's Head. Madam, may I have the pleasure of introducing to you M. Montaiglon?" and Sim MacTaggart looked in her eyes with some impatience, for she hung just a second too long upon his fingers, and pinched ere she released them.

She was delighted to make monsieur's acquaintance. Her husband had told her that monsieur was staying farther up the coast and intended to come to town. Monsieur was in business; she feared times were not what they were for business in Argyll, but the air was bracing—and much to the same effect, which sent the pseudo wine merchant gladly into the hands of her less ceremonious husband.

As for Petullo, he was lukewarm. He saw no prospects of profit from this dubious foreigner thrust upon his attentions by his well-squeezed client the Baron of Doom. Yet something of style, some sign of race in the stranger, thawed him out of his suspicious reserve, and he was kind enough to be condescending to his visitor while cursing the man who sent him there and the man who guided him. They sat together at the window, and meanwhile in the inner end of the room a lonely lady made shameful love.

"Oh, Sim!" she whispered, sitting beside him on the couch and placing the candlestick on a table behind them; "this is just like old times—the dear darling old times, isn't it."

She referred to the first of their *liaison*, when they made their love in that same room under the very nose of a purblind husband.

The Chamberlain toyed with his silver box and found it easiest to get out of a response by a sigh that might mean anything.

"You have the loveliest hand," she went on, looking at his fingers, that certainly were shapely enough, as no one knew better than Simon MacTaggart. "I don't say you are in any way handsome,"—her eyes betrayed her real thought,—"but I'll admit to the hands,—they're dear pets, Sim."

He thrust them in his pockets.

"Heavens! Kate," he protested in a low tone, and assuming a quite unnecessary look of vacuity for the benefit of the husband, who gazed across the dim-lit room at them, "don't behave like an idiot; faithful wives never let their husbands see them looking like that at another man's fingers. What do you think of our monsher? He's a pretty enough fellow, if you'll not give me the credit."

"Oh, he's good enough, I daresay," she answered without looking aside a moment. "I would think him much better if he was an inch or two taller, a shade blacker, and Hielan' to boot. But tell me this, and tell me no more, Sim; where has your lordship been for three whole days? Three whole days, Simon MacTaggart, and not a word of explanation. Are you not ashamed of yourself, sir? Do you know that I was along the riverside every night this week? Can you fancy what I felt to hear your flageolet playing for tipsy fools in Ludovic's room? Very well, I said: let him! I have pride of my own, and I was so angry tonight that I said I would never go again to meet you. You cannot blame me if I was not there tonight, Sim. But there!—seeing you have rued your cruelty to me and made an excuse to see me even before him there, I'll forgive you."

"Oh! well!" drawled the Chamberlain ambiguously.

"But I can't make another excuse this week. He sits in here every night, and has a new daft notion for late suppers. Blame yourself for it, Sim, but there can be no trysts this week."

"I'm a most singularly unlucky person," said the Chamberlain, in a tone that deaf love alone could fail to take alarm at.

"I heard a story today that frightened me, Sim," she went on, taking up some fine knitting and bending over it while she spoke rapidly, always in tones too low to carry across the room. "It was that you have been hanging about that girl of Doom's you met here."

The Chamberlain damned internally.

"Don't believe all you hear, Kate," said he. "And even if it was the case,"—he broke off in a faint laugh.

"Even if what?" she repeated, looking up.

"Even if—even if there was anything in the story, who's to blame? Your goodman's not the ass he sometimes looks."

"You mean that he was the first to put her in your way, and that he had his own reasons?"

The Chamberlain nodded.

Mrs Petullo's fingers rushed the life out of her knitting. "If I thought—if I thought . . . !" she said, leaving the sentence unfinished. No more was necessary; Sim MacTaggart thanked Heaven he was not mated irrevocably.

"Is it true?" she asked. "Is it true of you, Sim, who did your best to make me push Petullo to Doom's ruin?"

"Now, my dear, you talk the damnedest nonsense!" said Simon MacTaggart firmly. "I pushed in no way; the fool dropped into your husband's hands like a ripe plum. I have plenty of shortcomings of my own to answer for without getting the blame of others."

"Don't lie like that, Sim, dear," said Mrs Petullo, decidedly. "My memory is not gone yet, though you seem to think me getting old. Oh yes! I have all my faculties about me still."

"I wish to the Lord you had prudence; old Vellum's cocking his lugs."

"Oh, I don't care if he is; you make me desperate, Sim." Her needles thrust like poignards, her bosom heaved. "You may deny it if you like, but who pressed me to urge him on to take Drimdarroch? Who said it might be so happy a home for us when—when—my goodman there—when I was free?"

161

"Heavens! what a hangman's notion!" thought the Chamberlain to himself, with a swift side-glance at this termagant, and a single thought of calm Olivia.

"You have nothing to say to that, Sim, I see. It's just too late in the day for you to be virtuous, laddie; your Kate knows you, and she likes you better as you are than as you think you would like to be. We were so happy, Sim, we were so happy!" A tear dropped on her lap.

"Now Heaven forgive me for my infernal folly!" cried out the soul of Sim MacTaggart; but never a word did he say aloud.

Count Victor, at the other end of the room, listening to Petullo upon wines he was supposed to sell and whereof Petullo was supposed to be a connoisseur, though as a fact his honest taste was buttermilk—Count Victor became interested in the other pair. He saw what it took younger eyes, and a different experience from those of the husband, to observe.

"Cognac"—this to M. le Connoisseur with the rheumy eye—"but yes, it is good; your taste in that must be a national affair, is it not? Our best, the La Rochelle, has the name of a Scot—I think of Fife—upon the cask;" but to himself, with a glance again at the tragic comedy in the corner of the couch, "*Fi donc!* Mungo had reason; my gentleman of the dark eye is suspiciously like *cavalière servante.*"

The Chamberlain began to speak fast upon topics of no moment, dreading the consequence of this surrender on the woman's part: she heard nothing as she thrust furiously and blindly with her needles, her eyes suffused with tears courageously restrained. At last she checked him.

"All that means, Sim, that it's true about the girl," said she. "I tried to think it was a lie when I heard it, but now you compel me to believe you are a brute. You are a brute, Sim, do you hear that? Oh God! oh God! that ever I saw you! That ever I believed you! What is wrong with me, Sim? tell me, Sim! What is wrong with me? Am I different in any way from what I was last spring? Surely I'm not so old as all that; not a grey hair in my head, not a wrinkle on my face. I could keep like that for twenty years yet, just for love of Sim MacTaggart. Sim, say something, for the love of Heaven! Say it's a lie. Laugh at the story, Sim! Oh Sim! Sim!"

The knitting-needles clicked upon each other in her trembling hands, like fairy castanets.

"Who will say that man's fate is in his own fingers?" the Chamberlain asked himself, at the very end of patience. "From the day I breathed I got no chance. A clean and decent road's before me and a comrade for it, and I'm in the mood to take it, and here's the glaur about my feet! I wonder what monsieur there would do in a plight like mine. Lord! I envy him to be sitting there, and never a skeleton tugging at his sleeve."

Mrs Petullo gulped a sob, and gave a single glance into his face as he stared across the room.

"Why do you hate that man?" she asked suddenly.

"Who?" said he smiling, and glad that the wild rush of reproach was checked. "Is it monsher? I hate nobody, my dear Kate, except sometimes myself for sin and folly."

"And still and on you hate that man," said she convinced. "Oh no! not with that face, with the face you had a second ago. I think—oh! I can guess the reason; he has been up in Doom Castle; has he been getting round Miss Milk-and-Water? If he has, he's far more like her than you are. You made me pauperise her father, Sim; I'm sorry it was not worse. I'll see that Petullo has them rouped from the door."

"Adorable Kate!" said the Chamberlain, ironically.

Her face flamed, she pressed her hand on her side.

"I'll not forget that, Sim," said she with a voice of marvellous calm, bracing herself to look indifferently across the room at her husband. "I'll not forget many things, Sim. I thought the man I was to raise from the lackey that you were ten years ago would have some gratitude. No, no, no, Sim; I do not mean that, forgive me. Don't look at me like that! Where are you to be tomorrow night, Sim? I could meet you at the bridge; I'll make some excuse, and I want you to see my new gown—such a gown, Sim! I know what you're thinking, it would be too dark to see it; but you could strike a light, sweetheart, and look. Do you mind when

163

you did that over and over again the first time, to see my eyes? I'm not going to say another word about—about Miss Milk-and-Water, if that's what angers you. She could never understand my Sim, or love the very worm he tramps on as I do. Now look at me smiling; amn't I brave? Would any one know to see me that my heart was sore? Be kind to me, Sim, oh! be kind to me; you should be kind to me, with all you promised!"

"Madame is smiling into a mist; alas! poor M. Petullo!" thought Count Victor, seeing the lady standing up and looking across the room.

"Kate," said the Chamberlain in a whisper, pulling unobserved at her gown, "I have something to say to you."

She sat down again in a transport, her cheeks reddening, her eyes dancing; poor soul! she was glad nowadays of the very crumbs of affection from Sim MacTaggart's table.

"I know you are going to say Yes for tomorrow night, Sim," said she triumphant. "Oh, you are my own darling! For that I'll forgive you everything."

"There's to be no more nonsense of this kind, Kate," said the Chamberlain. "We have been fools—I see that quite plainly—and I'm not going to carry it on any longer."

"That is very kind of you," said Mrs Petullo, with the ring of metal in her accent and her eyes on fire. "Do you feel a great deal of remorse about it?"

"I do," said he, wondering what she was to be at next.

"Poor man! I was aye sure your conscience would be the death of you some day. And it's to be the pretext for throwing over unhappy Kate Cameron, is it?"

"Not Kate Cameron—her I loved—but Mrs Petullo."

"Whom you only made-believe to? That is spoken like a true Highland gentleman, Sim. I'm to be dismissed with just that amount of politeness that will save my feelings. I thought you knew me better, Sim. I thought you could make a more plausible excuse than that for the dirty transaction when it had to be done, as they say it must be done some time with all who are in our position. As sure as death I prefer the old country style that's in

164

the songs, where he laughs and rides away. But I'm no fool, Sim; what about Miss Milk-and-Water? Has she been hearing about me, I wonder, and finding fault with her new jo? The Lord help her if she trusts him as I did!"

"I want you to give me a chance, Kate," said the Chamberlain desperately. Petullo and the Count were still intently talking; the tragedy was in the poor light of a guttering candle.

"A chance?" she repeated vaguely, her eyes in vacancy, a broken heart shown in the corners of her mouth, the sudden ageing of her countenance.

"That's it, Kate; you understand, don't you? A chance. I'm a boy no longer. I want to be a better man. . . ." The sentence trailed off, for the Chamberlain could not but see himself in the most contemptible of lights.

"A better man!" said she, her knitting and her hands drowned in her lap, her countenance hollow and wan. "Lord keep me, a better man! And am I to be any the better woman when my old lover is turned righteous? Have you no' a thought at all for me when I'm to be left with him that's not my actual husband, left without love, hope, or self-respect? God help poor women! It's Milk-and-Water then; that's settled, and I'm to see you at the kirk with her for a lifetime of Sundays after this, an honest woman, and me what I am for you that have forgotten me—forgotten me! I was as good as she when you knew me first, Sim; I was not bad, and oh, my God! but I loved you, Sim MacTaggart!"

"Of all that's damnable," said the Chamberlain to himself, "there's nothing beats a whining woman!" He was in a mortal terror that her transports could be heard across the room, and that would be to spoil all with a vengeance.

"God pity women!" she went on. "It's a lesson. I was so happy sometimes that it frightened me, and now I know I was right."

"What do you say, my dear?" cried out Petullo across the room, suspiciously. He fancied he had heard an overeager accent in her last words, that were louder spoken than all that had gone before. Fortunately he could not make out her face as he looked, otherwise he would have seen, as Montaiglon did with some surprise, a mask of Tragedy.

"I'm giving Mr MacTaggart my congratulations on his coming marriage," said she quickly, with a miraculous effort at a little laugh, and the Chamberlain cursed internally.

"Oh! it's that length, is it?" said Petullo with a tone of gratification. "Did I no' tell you, Kate? You would deny't, and now you have the best authority. Well, well, it's the way we a' maun gang, as the auld blin' woman said, and here's wishing you the best o' luck!"

He came across to shake hands, but the Chamberlain checked him hurriedly.

"Psha!" said he. "Madame's just a little premature, Mr Petullo; there must be no word o' this just now."

"Is it that way?" said Petullo. "Likely the Baron's thrawn. Man, he hasna a roost, and he should be glad . . ." He stopped on reflection that the Frenchman was an intimate of the family he spoke of, and hastily returned to his side without seeing the pallor of his wife.

"And so it was old Vellum who clyped to you," said the Chamberlain to the lady.

"I see it all plainly now," said she. "He brought her here just to put her in your way and punish me. Oh, heavens, I'll make him rue for that! And do you fancy I'm going to let you go so easily as all that, Sim? Will Miss Mim-mou' not be shocked if I tell her the truth about her sweetheart?"

"You would not dare!" said the Chamberlain.

"Oh! would I not?" Mrs Petullo smiled in a fashion that showed she appreciated the triumph of her argument. "What would I not do for my Sim?"

"Well, it's all by, anyway," said he shortly.

"What, with her?" said Mrs Petullo, but with no note of hope.

"No, with you," said he brutally. "Let us be friends, good friends, Kate," he went on, fearing this should too seriously arouse her. "I'll be the best friend you have in the world, my dear, if you'll let me, only—"

"Only you will never kiss me again," said she with a sob. "There can be no friendship after yon, Sim, and you know it. You are but lying again. Oh, God! oh, God! I wish I were dead! You have done your worst, Simon MacTaggart; and if all tales be true—"

"I'm saying not a word of what I might say in my own defence," he protested.

"What *could* you say in your own defence? There is not the ghost of an excuse for you. What *could* you say?"

"Oh! I could be pushed to an obvious enough retort," he said, losing patience, for now it was plain that they were outraging every etiquette by so long talking together while others were in the room. "I was to blame, Heaven knows! I'm not denying that, but you—but you . . ." And his fingers nervously sought in his coat for the flageolet.

Mrs Petullo's face flamed. "Oh, you hound!" she hissed, "you hound!" and then she laughed softly, hysterically. "That is the gentleman for you! The seed of kings, no less! What a brag it was! That is the gentleman for you!—to put the blame on me. No, Sim; no, Sim; I will not betray you to Miss Mim-mou', you need not be feared of that; I'll let her find you out for herself and then it will be too late. And, oh! I hate her! hate her! hate her!"

"Thank God for that!" said the Chamberlain with a sudden memory of the purity she envied, and at these words Mrs Petullo fell in a swound upon the floor.

"Lord, what's the matter?" cried her husband, running to her side, then crying for the maid.

"I haven't the slightest idea," said Sim MacTaggart. "But she looked ill from the first," and once more he inwardly cursed his fate that constantly embroiled him in such affairs.

Ten minutes later he and the Count were told the lady had come round, and with expressions of deep sympathy they left Petullo's dwelling.

XXIII

A Man of Noble Sentiment

There was a silence between the two for a little after they
came out from Petullo's distracted household. With a chilling
sentiment towards his new acquaintance, whom he judged the
cause of the unhappy woman's state, Count Victor waited for
the excuse he knew inevitable. He could not see the Chamberlain's face, for the night was dark now; the tide, unseen, was
running up on the beach of the bay, lights were burning in the
dwellings of the little town.

"M. Montaiglon," at last said the Chamberlain in a curious
voice where feelings the most deep appeared to strive together,
"yon's a tragedy, if you like."

"*Comment?*" said the Count. He was not prepared for an
opening quite like this.

"Well," said the Chamberlain, "you saw it for yourself; you
are not a mole like Petullo the husband. By God! I would be that
brute's death if he were thirty years younger, and made of
anything else than sawdust. It's a tragedy in there, and look at
this burgh!—like the grave but for the lights of it; rural, plodding,
unambitious, ignorant—and the last place on earth you might
seek in for a story so peetiful as that in there. My heart's wae,
wae for that woman; I saw her face was like a corp when we went
in first, though she put a fair front on to us. A woman in a
hundred, a brave woman, few like her, let me tell you, M.
Montaiglon, and heartbroken by that rat she's married on. I
could greet to think on all her trials. You saw she was raised
somewhat; you saw I have some influence in that quarter?"

For his life Count Victor could make no reply, so troubled was
his mind with warring thoughts of Olivia betrayed, perhaps, to
a debauchee *sans* heart and common pot-house decency; of

whether in truth this was the debauchee to such depths as he suggested, or a man in a false position through the stress of things around him.

The Chamberlain went on as in a meditation. "Poor Kate! poor Kate! We were bairns together, M. Montaiglon, innocent bairns, and happy, twenty years syne, and I will not say but what in her maidenhood there was some warmth between us, so that I know her well. She was compelled by her relatives to marriage with our parchment friend yonder, and there you have the start of what has been hell on earth for her. The man has not the soul of a louse, and as for her, she's the finest gold! You would see that I was the cause of her swound?"

"Unhappy creature!" said Montaiglon, beginning to fear he had wronged this good gentleman.

"You may well say it, M. Montaiglon. It is improper perhaps, that I should expose to a stranger the skeleton of that house, but I'm feeling what happened just now too much to heed a convention." He sighed profoundly. "I have had influence with the good woman, as you would see; for years I've had it, because I was her only link with the gay world she was born to be an ornament in, and the only one free to be trusted with the tale of her misery. Well, you know—you are a man of the world, M. Montaiglon— you know the dangers of such a correspondence between a person of my reputation, that is none of the best, because I have been less a hypocrite than most, and a lady in her position. It's a gossiping community this, long-lugged and scandal-loving like all communities of its size; it is not the Faubourg St Honoré, where intrigues go on behind fans and never an eye cocked or a word said about it; and I'll not deny but there have been scandalous and cruel things said about the lady and myself. Now, as God's my judge—"

"Pardon, monsieur," said the Count, eager to save this protesting gentleman another *bêtise*; "I quite understand, I think,— the lady finds you a discreet friend. Naturally her illness has unmanned you. The scandal of the world need never trouble a good man."

"But a merely middling-good man, M. Montaiglon," cried the Chamberlain; "you'll allow that's a difference. Lord knows I lay no claim to a crystal virtue! In this matter I have no regard for my own reputation, but just for that very reason I'm anxious about the lady's. What happened in that room there was that I've had to do an ill thing and make an end of an auld sang. I'm rarely discreet in my own interest, M. Montaiglon, but it had to be shown this time, and as sure as death I feel like a murderer at the havoc I have wrought with that good woman's mind!"

He stopped suddenly; a lump was in his throat. In the beam of light that came through the hole in a shutter of a house they passed, Montaiglon saw that his companion's face was all wrought with wretchedness, and a tear was on his cheek.

The discovery took him aback. He had ungenerously deemed the strained voice in the darkness beside him a mere piece of play-acting, but here was proof of genuine feeling, all the more convincing because the Chamberlain suddenly brisked up and coughed and assumed a new tone, as if ashamed of his surrender to a sentiment.

"I have been compelled to be cruel tonight to a woman, M. Montaiglon," said he, "and that is not my nature. And—to come to another consideration that weighed as much with me as any—this unpleasant duty of mine that still sticks in my throat like funeral-cake was partly forced by consideration for another lady—the sweetest and the best—who would be the last I should care to have hear any ill of me, even in a libel."

A protest rose to Montaiglon's throat; a fury stirred him at the gaucherie that should bring Olivia's name upon the top of such a subject. He could not trust himself to speak with calmness, and it was to his great relief the Chamberlain changed the topic—broadened it, at least, and spoke of women in the general, almost cheerfully, as if he delighted to put an unpleasant topic behind him. It was done so adroitly, too, that Count Victor was compelled to believe it prompted by a courteous desire on the part of the Chamberlain not too vividly to illuminate his happiness in the affection of Olivia.

"I'm an older man than you, M. Montaiglon," said the Chamberlain, "and I may be allowed to give some of my own conclusions upon the fair. I have known good, ill, and merely middling among them, the cunning and the simple, the learned and the utterly ignorant, and by the Holy Iron! honesty and faith are the best virtues in the lot of them. They all like flattery, I know. . . ."

"A dead man and a stupid woman are the only ones who do not. *Jamais beau parler n'écorcha la langue!*" said Montaiglon.

"Faith, and that's very true," consented the Chamberlain, laughing softly. "I take it not amiss myself if it's proffered in the right way—which is to say, for the qualities I know I have, and not for the imaginary ones. As I was saying, give me the simple heart and honesty; they're not very rife in our own sex, and—"

"Even there, monsieur, I can be generous enough," said Montaiglon. "I can always retain my regard for human nature, because I have learned never to expect too much from it."

"Well said!" cried the Chamberlain. "Do you know that in your manner of rejoinder you recall one Dumont I met once at the Jesuits' College when I was in France years ago?"

"Ah, you have passed some time in my country, then?" said the Count with awakened interest, a little glad of a topic scarce so abstruse as sex.

"I have been in every part of Europe," said the Chamberlain; "and it must have been by the oddest of mischances I have not been at Cammercy itself, for well I knew your uncle's friends, though, as it happened, we were of a different complexion of politics. I lived for months one time in the Hôtel de Transylvania, Rue Condé, and kept my *carosse de remise*, and gambled like every other ass of my kind in Paris till I had not a *louis* to my credit. Lord! the old days, the old days! I should be penitent I daresay, M. Montaiglon, but I'm putting that off till I find that a sober life has compensations for the entertainment of a life of liberty."

"Did you know Balhaldie?"

"Do I know the inside of my own pocket! I've played piquet

wi' the old rogue a score of times in the Sun tavern of Rotterdam. Pardon me speaking that way of one that may be an intimate of your own, but to be quite honest, the Scots gentlemen living on the Scots Fund in France in these days were what I call the scourings of the Hielan's. There were good and bad among them, of course, but I was there in the *entourage* of one who was no politician, which was just my own case, and I saw but the convivial of my exiled countrymen in their convivial hours. Politics! In these days I would scunner at the very word, if you know what that means, M. Montaiglon. I was too throng with gaiety to trouble my head about such trifles; my time was too much taken up in buckling my hair, in admiring the cut of my laced *jabot*, and the Mechlin of my wrist-bands."

They were walking close upon the sea-wall with leisurely steps, preoccupied, the head of the little town, it seemed, wholly surrendered to themselves alone. Into the Chamberlain's voice had come an accent of the utmost friendliness and flattering irrestraint; he seemed to be laying his heart bare to the Frenchman. Count Victor was by these last words transported to his native city, and his own far-off days of galliard. Why, in the name of Heaven! was he here listening to hackneyed tales of domestic tragedy and a stranger's reminiscences? Why did his mind continually linger round the rock of Doom, so noisy on its promontory, so sad, so stern, so like an ancient saga in its spirit? Cécile—he was amazed at it, but Cécile, and the Jacobite cause he had come here to avenge with a youth's ardour, had both fallen, as it were, into a dusk of memory!

"By the way, monsieur, you did not happen to have come upon any one remotely suggesting my Drimdarroch in the course of your travels?"

"Oh, come!" cried Sim MacTaggart; "if I did, was I like to mention it here and now?" He laughed at the idea. "You have not grasped the clannishness of us yet if you fancy—"

"But in an affair of strict honour, monsieur," broke in Count Victor eagerly. "Figure you a woman basely betrayed; your admirable sentiments regarding the sex must compel you to admit there is here something more than clannishness can condone. It is true there is the political element—but not much of it—in my quest, still—"

"Not a word of that, M. Montaiglon!" cried the Chamberlain: "there you address yourself to his Grace's faithful servant; but I cannot be denying some sympathy with the other half of your object. If I had known this by-named Drimdarroch you look for, I might have swithered to confess it, but as it is, I have never had the honour. I've seen scores of dubious cattle round the walls of Ludovico Rex, but which might be Drimdarroch and which might be decent honest men, I could not at this time guess. We have here among us others who had a closer touch with affairs in France than I."

"So?" said Count Victor. "Our friend the Baron of Doom suggested that for that very reason my search was for the proverbial needle in the haystack. I find myself in pressing need of a judicious friend at court, I see. Have you ever found your resolution quit you—not an oozing courage, I mean, but an indifference that comes purely by the lapse of time and the distractions on the way to its execution? It is my case at the moment. My thirst for the blood of this *inconnu* has modified considerably in the past few days. I begin to wish myself home again, and might set out incontinent if the object of my coming here at all had not been so well known to those I left behind. You would be doing a brilliant service—and perhaps but little harm to Drimdarroch after all—if you could arrange a meeting at the earliest."

He laughed as he said so.

"Man! I'm touched by the issue," said the Chamberlain; "I must cast an eye about. Drimdarroch, of course, is Doom, or was, if a lawyer's sheep-skins had not been more powerful nowadays than the sword; but"—he paused a moment as if reluctant to give words to the innuendo—"though Doom himself has been in France to some good purpose in his time, and though, for God knows what, he is no friend of mine, I would be the first to proclaim him free of any suspicion."

"That, monsieur, goes without saying! I was stupid enough to misunderstand some of his eccentricities myself but have learned in our brief acquaintanceship to respect in him the man of genuine heart."

"Just so, just so!" cried the Chamberlain, and cleared his throat. "I but mentioned his name to make it plain that his claim to the old title in no way implicated him. A man of great heart, as you say, though with a reputation for oddity. If I were not the well-wisher of his house, I could make some trouble about his devotion to the dress and arms forbidden here to all but those in the king's service, as I am myself, being major of the local Fencibles. And—by the Lord! here's MacCailein!"

They had by this time entered the policies of the Duke. A figure walked alone in the obscurity, with arms in a characteristic fashion behind its back, going in the direction they themselves were taking. For a second or two the Chamberlain hesitated, then formed his resolution.

"I shall introduce you," he said to Count Victor. "It may be of some service afterwards."

The Duke turned his face in the darkness, and, as they came alongside, recognised his Chamberlain.

"Good evening, good evening!" he cried cheerfully. " 'Art a late bird, as usual, and I am at that pestilent task the rehearsal of a speech."

"Your Grace's industry is a reproach to your Grace's Chamberlain," said the latter. "I have been at the speech-making myself, partly to a lady."

"Ah, Mr MacTaggart!" cried the Duke in a comical expostulation.

"And partly to this unfortunate friend of mine, who must fancy us a singularly garrulous race this side of the English Channel. May I introduce M. Montaiglon, who is at the inn below, and whom it has been my good fortune to meet for the first time tonight?"

Argyll was most cordial to the stranger, who, however, took the earliest opportunity to plead fatigue and return to his inn.

He had no sooner retired than the Duke expressed some natural curiosity.

"It cannot be the person you desired for the furnishing of our tolbooth the other day, Sim?" said he.

"No less," frankly responded the Chamberlain. "Your Grace saved me a *faux pas* there, for Montaiglon is not what I fancied at all."

"You were ever the dubious gentleman, Sim," laughed his Grace. "And what—if I may take the liberty—seeks our excellent and impeccable Gaul so far west."

"He's a wine merchant," said the Chamberlain, and at that the Duke laughed.

"What, man!" he cried at last, shaking with his merriment, "is our ancient Jules from Oporto to be ousted with the aid of Sim MacTaggart from the ducal cellars in favour of one Montaiglon?" He stopped, caught his Chamberlain by the arm, and stood close in an endeavour to perceive his countenance. "Sim," said he, "I wonder what Modene would say to find his cousin hawking vile claret round Argyll. Your friend's incognito is scarcely complete enough even in the dark. Why, the man's Born! I could tell it in his first sentence, and it's a swordsman's hand, not a cellarer's fingers, he gave me a moment ago. That itself would betray him even if I did not happen to know that the Montaiglons have the *particule*."

"It's quite as you say," confessed the Chamberlain with some chagrin at his position, "but I'm giving the man's tale as he desires to have it known here. He's no less than the Count de Montaiglon, and a rather decent specimen of the kind, so far as I can judge."

"But why the *alias*, good Sim?" asked the Duke. "I like not your *aliases*, though they have been, now and then—ahem!—useful."

"Your Grace has travelled before now as Baron Ilay," said the Chamberlain.

"True! true! and saved very little either in inn charges or in the pother of State by the device. And if I remember correctly,

I made no pretence at wine-selling on these occasions. Honestly now, what the devil does the Comte de Montaiglon do here—and with Sim MacTaggart?"

"The matter is capable of the easiest explanation. He's here on what he is pleased to call an affair of honour, in which there is implicated the usual girl and another gentleman, who, it appears, is someone, still unknown, about your Grace's castle." And the story in its entirety was speedily his Grace's.

"H'm," ejaculated Argyll at last when he had heard all. "And you fancy the quest as hopeless as it is quixotic? Now, mark me! Simon; I read our French friend, even in the dark, quite differently. He had little to say there, but little as it was 'twas enough to show by its manner that he's just the one who will find his man even in my crowded corridors."

XXIV

A Broken Tryst

The Chamberlain's quarters were in the eastern turret, and there he went so soon as he could leave his Grace, who quickly forgot the Frenchman and his story, practising upon Simon the speech he had prepared in his evening walk, alternated with praise extravagant—youthfully rapturous almost—of his duchess, who might, from all his chafing at her absence, have been that night at the other end of the world, instead of merely in the next county on a few days' visit.

"Ah! you are smiling, Sim!" said he. "Old whinstone! You fancy Argyll an imbecile of uxoriousness. Well, well, my friend, you are at liberty; Lord knows, it's not a common disease among dukes! Eh, Sim? But then women like my Jean are not common either or marriages were less fashious. Upon my word, I could saddle Jock and ride this very night to Luss, just to have the fun of throwing pebbles at her window in the morning, and see her wonder and pleasure at finding me there. Do you know what, cousin? I am going to give a ball when she comes home. We'll have just the neighbours, and I'll ask M. Soi-disant, who'll give us the very latest step. I like the fellow's voice, it rings the sterling metal. . . . And now, my lords, this action on the part of the Government. . . . Oh, the devil fly away with politics! I must go to a lonely bed!" and off set MacCailein Mor, the noble, the august, the man of silk and steel, whom 'twas Sim MacTaggart's one steadfast ambition in life to resemble even in a remote degree.

And then we have the Chamberlain in his turret room, envious of that blissful married man, and warmed to a sympathetic glow with Olivia floating through the images that rose before him.

He drew the curtains of his window and looked in that

direction where Doom, of course, was not for material eyes, finding a vague pleasure in building up the picture of the recluse tower, dark upon its promontory. It was ten o'clock. It had been arranged at their last meeting that without the usual signal he should go to her tonight before twelve. Already his heart beat quickly; his face was warm and tingling with pleasant excitation, he felt a good man.

"By God!" he cried. "If it was not for the old glaur! What for does Heaven—or hell—send the worst of its temptations to the young and ignorant? If I had met her twenty years ago! Twenty years ago! H'm! 'Clack!' goes the weaver's shuttle! Twenty years ago it was her mother, and Sim MacTaggart without a hair on his face trying to kiss the good lady of Doom, and her, perhaps no' half unwilling. I'm glad—I'm glad."

He put on a pair of spurs, his fingers trembling as those of a lad dressing for his first ball, and the girl a fairy in white, with her neck pink and soft and her eyes shy like little fawns in the wood.

"And how near I was to missing it!" he thought. "But for the scheming of a fool I would never have seen her. It's not too late, thank the Lord for that! No more of yon for Sim MacTaggart, I've cut with the last of it, and now my face is to the stars."

His hands were spotless white, but he poured some water in a basin and washed them carefully, shrugging his shoulders with a momentary comprehension of how laughable must that sacrament be in the eyes of the worldly Sim MacTaggart. He splashed the water on his lips, drew on a cloak, blew out the light, and went softly downstairs and out at a side-door for which he had a pass-key. The night was still, except for the melancholy sound of the river running over its cascades and echoing under the two bridges; odours of decaying leaves surrounded him, and the air of the night touched him on his hot face like a benediction. A heavy dew clogged the grass of Cairnbaan as he made for the stables, where a man stood out in the yard waiting with a black horse saddled. Without a word he mounted and rode, the hoofs thudding dull on the grass. He left behind him the castle, quite

178

dark and looming in its nest below the sentinel hill; he turned the bay; the town revealed a light or two; a bird screamed on the ebb shore. Something of all he saw and heard touched a fine man in his cloak, touched a decent love in him; his heart was full with wholesome joyous ichor; and he sang softly to the creaking saddle, sang an air of good and clean old Gaelic sentiment that haunted his lips until he came opposite the very walls of Doom.

He fastened his horse to a young hazel and crossed the sandy interval between the mainland and the rock, seawrack bladders bursting under his feet, and the smells of seaweed dominant over the odours of the winter wood. The tower was pitch dark. He went into the bower, sat on the rotten seat among the damp bedraggled strands of climbing flowers, and took his flageolet from his pocket.

He played softly, breathing in his instrument the very pang of love. It might have been a psalm and this forsaken dew-drenched bower a great cathedral, so rapt, so devoted, his spirit as he sought to utter the very deepest ecstasy. Into the reed he poured remembrance and regret; the gathered nights of riot and folly lived and sorrowed for; the ideals cherished and surrendered; the remorseful sinner, the awakened soul.

No one paid any heed in Castle Doom.

That struck him suddenly with wonder, as he ceased his playing for a moment and looked through the broken trellis to see the building black below the starry sky. There ought, at least, to be a light in the window of Olivia's room. She had made the tryst herself, and never before had she failed to keep it. Perhaps she had not heard him. And so to his flageolet again, finding a consolation in the sweetness of his own performance.

"Ah!" said he to himself, pausing to admire—"Ah! there's no doubt I finger it decently well—better than most—better than any I've heard, and what's the wonder at that? for it's all in what you feel, and the most of people are made of green wood. There's no green timber here; I'm cursed if I'm not the very ancient stuff of fiddles!"

He had never felt happier in all his life. The past?—he wiped

179

that off his recollection as with a sponge; now he was a new man with his feet out of the mire and a clean road all the rest of the way, with a clean sweet soul for his companion. He loved her to his very heart of hearts; he had, honestly, for her but the rendered passion of passion—why! what kept her?

He rammed the flageolet impatiently into his waistcoat, threw back his cloak, and stepped out into the garden. Doom Castle rose over him black, high and low, without a glimmer. A terrific apprehension took possession of him. He raised his head and gave the signal call, so natural that it drew an answer almost like an echo from an actual bird far off in some thicket at Achnatra. And oh! felicity; here she was at last!

The bolts of the door slid back softly; the door opened; a little figure came out. Forward swept the lover all impatient fires—to find himself before Mungo Boyd!

He caught him by the collar of his coat as if he would shake him.

"What game is this? what game is this?" he furiously demanded. "Where is she?"

"Canny, man, canny!" said the little servitor, releasing himself with difficulty from the grasp of this impetuous lover. "Faith! it's anither warnin' this no' to parley at nicht wi' onything less than twa or three inch o' oak dale atween ye and herm."

"Cut clavers and tell me what ails your mistress!"

"Oh, weel; she hisna come oot the nicht," said Mungo, waving his arms to bring the whole neighbourhood as witness of the obvious fact.

The Chamberlain thrust at his chest and nearly threw him over.

"Ye dull-witted Lowland brock!" said he; "have I no' the use of my own eyes? Give me another word but what I want and I'll slash ye smaller than ye are already with my Ferrara."

"Oh, I'm no' that wee!" said Mungo. "If ye wad jist bide cool—"

" 'Cool,' quo' he! Man! I'm up to the neck in fire. Where is she?"

"Whaur ony decent lass should be at this 'oor o' the nicht—in her naked bed."

"Say that again, you foul-mouthed hog o' Fife, and I'll gralloch you like a deer!" cried the Chamberlain, his face tingling.

"Losh! the body's cracked," said Mungo Boyd, astounded at this nicety.

"I was to meet her tonight; does she know I'm here?"

"I rapped at her door mysel' to mak' sure she did."

"And what said she?"

"She tauld me to gae awa'. I said it was you, and she said it didna maitter."

"Didna maitter!" repeated the Chamberlain, viciously, mimicking the eastland accent. "What ails her?"

"Ye ought to ken that best yoursel'. It was the last thing I daur ask her," said Mungo Boyd, preparing to retreat, but his precaution was not called for; he had stunned his man.

The Chamberlain drew his cloak about him, cold with a contemptuous rebuff. His mouth parched; violent emotions wrought in him, but he recovered in a moment, and did his best to hide his sense of ignominy.

"Oh, well!" said he, "it's a woman's way, Mungo."

"You'll likely ken," said Mungo; "I've had sma' troke wi' them mysel'."

"Lucky man! And now that I mind right, I think it was not tonight I was to come, after all; I must have made a mistake. If you have a chance in the morn's morning you can tell her I wasted a tune or two o' the flageolet on a wheen stars. It is a pleasant thing in stars, Mungo, that ye aye ken where to find them when ye want them!"

He left the rock, and took to horse again, and home. All through the dark ride he fervently cursed Count Victor, a prey of an idiotic jealousy.

XXV

Reconciliation

Mungo stood in the dark till the last beat of the horse-hoofs could be heard, and then went in disconsolate and perplexed. He drew the bars as it were upon a dear friend out in the night, and felt as there had gone the final hope for Doom and its inhabitants.

"An auld done rickle o' a place!" he soliloquised, lifting a candle high that it might show the shame of the denuded and crumbling walls. "An auld done rickle: I've seen a better barn i' the Lothians, and fancy me tryin' to let on that it's a kind o' Edinbro'! Sirs! sirs! 'If ye canna' hae the puddin' be contented wi' the bree,' Annapla's aye sayin', but here there's neither bree nor puddin'. To think that a' my traison against the maister i' the interest o' his dochter and himsel' should come to naethin', and that Sim MacTaggart should be sent awa' wi' a flea in his lug, a' for the tirravee o' a lassie that canna' value a guid chance when it offers! I wonder what ails her, if it's no' that monsher's ta'en her fancy! Women are a' like weans; they never see the crack in an auld toy till some ane shows them a new ane. Weel! as sure as death I wash my haun's o' the hale affair. She's daft; clean daft, puir dear! If she kent whit I ken, she micht hae some excuse, but I took guid care o' that. I doot yon's the end o' a very promisin' match, and the man, though he mayna' think it, has his merchin' orders."

The brief bow-legged figure rolled along the lobby, pshawing with vexation, and in a little, Doom, to all appearance, was a castle dark and desolate.

Yet not wholly asleep, however dark and silent; for Olivia, too, had heard the last of the thundering hoofs, had suffered the agony that comes from the wrench of a false ideal from the place of its long cherishing.

She came down in the morning a mere wraith of beauty, as it seemed to the little servitor, shutting her lips hard, but ready to burst into a shower.

"Guid Lord!" thought Mungo, setting the scanty table. "It's clear she hasna' steeked an e'e a' nicht, and me sleepin' like a peerie. That's ane o' the advantages o' being ower the uneasy age o' love—and still I'm no' that auld. I wonder if she's rued it the day already."

She smiled upon him bravely, but woe-begone, and could not check a quivering lip, and then she essayed at a song hummed with no bad pretence as she cast from the window a glance along the wintry coast, that never changed its aspect though hearts broke. But, as ill-luck had it, the air was the unfinished melody of Sim's bewitching flageolet. She stopped it ere she had gone farther than a bar or two, and turned to find Mungo irresolute and disturbed.

"He ga'ed awa'—" began the little man, with the whisper of the conspirator.

"Mungo!" she cried, "you will not say a word of it. It is all bye with me, and what for not with you? I command you to say no more about it, do you hear?" And her foot beat with an imperiousness almost comical from one with such a broken countenance.

"It's a gey droll thing—"

"It is a gey hard thing, that is what it is," she interrupted him, "that you will not do what I tell you, and say nothing of what I have no relish to hear, and must have black shame to think of. Must I go over all that I have said to you already? It is finished, Mungo; are you listening? Did he—did he—look vexed? But it does not matter, it is finished, and I have been a very foolish girl."

"But that needna' prevent me tellin' ye that the puir man's awa' clean gyte."

She smiled just the ghost of a smile at that, then put her hands upon her ears.

"Oh!" she cried despairingly, "have I not a friend left?"

Mungo sighed and said no more then, but went to Annapla

and sought relief for his feelings in bilingual wrangling with that dark abigail. At low tide beggars from Glencroe came to his door with yawning pokes and all their old effrontery: he astounded them by the fiercest of receptions, condemned them all eternally for limmers and sorners, lusty rogues and vagabonds.

"Awa'! awa'!" he cried, an implacable face against their whining protestations—"Awa', or I'll gie ye the gairde! If I was my uncle Erchie, I wad pit an end to your argy-bargying wi' hail frae a gun!" But to Annapla it was, "Puir deevils, it's gey hard to gie them the back o' the haun' and them sae used to rougher times in Doom. What'll they think o' us? It's sic a doon-come, but we maun be hainin' seein' Leevie's lost her jo, and no' ither way clear oot o' the bit. I'm seein' a toom girnel and done beef here lang afore next Martinmas."

These plaints were to a woman blissfully beyond comprehending the full import of them, for so much was Annapla taken up with her Gift, so misty and remote the realms of Gaelic dream wherein she moved, that the little Lowland oddity's perturbation was beneath her serious attention.

Olivia had that day perhaps the bitterest of her life. With love outside—calling in the evening and fluting in the bower, and ever (as she thought) occupied with her image even when farther apart—she had little fault to find with the shabby interior of her home. Now that love was lost, she sat with her father, oppressed and cold as it had been a vault. Even in his preoccupation he could not fail to see how ill she seemed that morning: it appeared to him that she had the look of a mountain birch stricken by the first of winter weather.

"My dear," he said, with a tenderness that had been some time absent from their relations, "you must be taking a change of air. I'm a poor parent not to have seen before how much you need it." He hastened to correct what he fancied from her face was a misapprehension. "I am speaking for your red cheeks, my dear, believe me; I'm wae to see you like that."

"I will do whatever you wish, father," said Olivia in much agitation. Coerced she was iron, coaxed she was clay. "I have not been a very good daughter to you, father; after this I will be trying to be better."

His face reddened; his heart beat at this capitulation of his rebel: he rose from his chair and took her into his arms—an odd display for a man so long stone-cold but to his dreams.

"My dear, my dear!" said he, "but in one detail that need never again be named between us two, you have been the best of girls, and, God knows, I am not the pattern parent!"

Her arm went round his neck, and she wept on his breast.

"Sour and dour . . . " said he.

"No, no!" she cried.

"And poor to penury."

"All the more need for a loving child. There are only the two of us."

He held her at arm's-length and looked her wistfully in the wet wan face and saw his wife Christina there. "By Heaven!" he thought, "it is no wonder that this man should hunt her."

"You have made me happy this day, Olivia," said he; "at least half happy. I dare not mention what more was needed to make me quite content."

"You need not," said she. "I know, and that—and that—is over too. I am just your own Olivia."

"What!" he cried elate; "no more?"

"No more at all."

"Now praise God!" said he. "I have been robbed of credit and estate, and even of my name; I have seen king and country foully done by, and black affront brought on our people, and still there's something left to live for."

XXVI

The Duke's Ball

For some days Count Victor chafed at the dull and somewhat squalid life of the inn. He found himself regarded coldly among strangers; the flageolet sounded no longer in the private parlour; the Chamberlain stayed away. And if Drimdarroch had seemed ill to find from Doom, he was absolutely undiscoverable here. Perhaps there was less eagerness in the search because other affairs would for ever intrude—not the Cause (that now, to tell the truth, he somehow regarded moribund; little wonder after eight years' inaction!) nor the poignant home-thoughts that made his ride through Scotland melancholy, but affairs more recent, and Olivia's eyes possessed him.

A morning had come of terrific snow, and made all the colder, too, his sojourn in the country of MacCailein Mor. Now he looked upon mountains white and far, phantom valleys gulping chilly winds, the sea alone with some of its familiar aspect, yet it, too, leaden to eye and heart as it lay in a perpetual haze between the headlands and lazily rose and fell in the bays.

The night of the ball was to him like a reprieve. From the darkness of those woody deeps below Dunchuach the castle gleamed with fires, and a Highland welcome illumined the greater part of the avenue from the town with flambeaux, in whose radiance the black pines, the huge beeches, the waxen shrubbery round the lawns all shrouded, seemed to creep closer round the edifice to hear the sounds of revelry and learn what charms the human world when the melodious winds are still and the weather is cold and out of doors poor thickets must shiver in appalling darkness.

A gush of music met Count Victor at the threshold; dresses were rustling, a caressing warmth sighed round him, and his host was very genial.

"M. Montaiglon," said his Grace in French, "you will pardon our short notice; my good friend, M. Montaiglon, my dear; my wife, M. Montaiglon—"

"But M. Montaiglon merely in the inns, my lord," corrected the Frenchman, smiling. "I should be the last to accept the honour of your hospitality under a *nom de guerre*."

The Duke bowed. "M. le Comte," he said, "to be quite as candid as yourself, I pierced your incognito even in the dark. My dear sir, a Scots traveller named for the time being the Baron Ilay once had the privilege of sharing a glass coach with your uncle between Paris and Dunkerque; 'tis a story that will keep. Meanwhile, as I say, M. Montaiglon will pardon the shortness of our notice; in these wilds one's dancing-shoes are presumed to be ever airing at the fire. You must consider these doors as open as the woods so long as you are in this neighbourhood. I have some things I should like to show you that you might find not wholly uninteresting—a Raphael, a Rembrandt (so reputed), and several Venetians—not much, in faith, but regarding which I should value your criticism. . . ."

Some other guests arrived, his Grace's speech was broken, and Count Victor passed on, skirting the dancers, who to his unaccustomed eyes presented features strange yet picturesque as they moved in the puzzling involutions of a country dance. It was a noble hall hung round with tapestry and bossed with Highland targets, trophies of arms and the mountain chase; from the gallery round it drooped little banners with the devices of all those generations of great families that mingled in the blood of MacCailein Mor.

The Frenchman looked round him for a familiar face, and saw the Chamberlain in Highland dress in the midst of a little group of dames.

Mrs Petullo was not one of them. She was dancing with her husband—a pitiful spectacle, for the lawyer must be pushed through the dance as he were a doll, with monstrous ungracefulness, and no sense of the time of the music, his thin legs quarrelling with each other, his neighbours all confused by his inexpert gyrations, and yet himself with a smirk of satisfaction on his sweating countenance.

"Madame is not happy," thought Count Victor, watching the lady who was compelled to be a partner in these ungainly gambols.

And indeed Mrs Petullo was far from happy, if her face betrayed her real feelings, as she shared the ignominy of the false position into which Petullo had compelled her. When the dance was ended she did not take her husband's proffered arm, but walked before him to her seat, utterly ignoring his pathetic courtesies.

This little domestic comedy only engaged Count Victor for a moment, he felt vexed for the woman in a position for which there seemed no remedy, and he sought distraction from his uneasy feeling by passing every man in the room under review, and guessing which of them, if any, could be the Drimdarroch who had brought him there from France. It was a baffling task. For many were there with faces wholly inscrutable who might very well have among them the secret he cherished, and yet nothing about them to advertise the scamp who had figured so effectively in other scenes than these. The Duke, their chief, moved now among them—suave, graceful, affectionate, his lady on his arm, sometimes squeezing her hand, a very boy in love!

"That's a grand picture of matrimonial felicity, Count," said a voice at Count Victor's ear, and he turned to find the Chamberlain beside him.

"Positively it makes me half envious, monsieur," said Count Victor. "A following influenced by the old feudal affections and wellnigh worshipping; health and wealth, ambitions gratified, a name that has sounded in camp and Court, yet a heart that has stayed at home; the fever of youth abated, and wedded to a beautiful woman who does not weary one, *pardieu!* his Grace has nothing more in this world to wish for."

"Ay! he has most that's needed to make it a very comfortable world. Providence is good. . . ."

"But sometimes grudging . . ."

"But sometimes grudging, as you say; yet MacCailein has got everything. When I see him and her there so content I'm wondering at my own wasted years of bachelordom. As sure as you're there, I think the sooner I draw in at a fire and play my flageolet to the guidwife the better for me."

"It is a gift, this domesticity," said Count Victor, not without an inward twinge at the picture. "Some of us have it, some of us have not, and no trying hard for content with one's own wife and early suppers will avail unless one is born to it like the trick of the sonnet. I have been watching our good friend, your lawyer's wife, distracted over the—over the—*balourdise* of her husband as a dancer: he dances like a bootmaker's sign, if you can imagine that, and I dare not approach them till her very natural indignation has simmered down."

The Chamberlain looked across the hall distastefully and found Mrs Petullo's eyes on him. She shrugged, for his perception alone, a white shoulder in a manner that was eloquent of many things.

"To the devil!" he muttered, yet essayed at the smile of good friendship which was now to be their currency, and a poor exchange for the old gold.

"Surely Monsieur MacTaggart dances?" said the Count; "I see a score of ladies here who would give their garters for the privilege."

"My dancing days are over," said Sim MacTaggart, but merely as one who repeats a formula; his eyes were roving among the women. The dark green-and-blue tartan of the house well became him: he wore diced hose of silk and a knife on the calf of his leg; his plaid swung from a stud at the shoulder, and fell in voluminous and graceful folds behind him. His eyes roved among the women, and now and then he lifted the whitest of hands and rubbed his shaven chin.

Count Victor was a little amused at the vanity of this village hero. And then there happened what more deeply impressed him with wonder at the contrarieties of character here represented, for the hero brimmed with sentimental tears!

189

They were caused by so simple a thing as a savage strain of music from the Duke's piper, who strutted in the gallery fingering a melody in an interval of the dance—a melody full of wearisome iterations in the ears of the foreigner, who could gain nothing of fancy from the same save that the low notes sobbed. When the piece was calling in the hall, ringing stormily to the roof, shaking the banners, silencing the guests, the Duke's Chamberlain laughed with some confusion in a pretence that he was undisturbed.

"An air with a story, perhaps?" asked Count Victor.

"They are all stories," answered this odd person, so responsive to the yell of guttural reeds. "In that they're like our old friend Balhaldie, whose tales, as you may remember,—the old rogue!—would fill many pages."

"Many leaves, indeed," said Count Victor—"preferably fig-leaves."

"The bagpipe moves me like a weeping woman, and here, for all that, is the most indifferent of musicians."

"*Tenez!* monsieur; I present my homages to the best of flageolet-players," said Count Victor, smiling.

"The flageolet! a poor instrument, and still—and still not without its qualities. Here's one at least who finds it the very salve for weariness. Playing it, I often feel in the trance of rapture. I wish to God I could live my life upon the flute, for there I'm on the best and cleanest terms with myself, and no backwash of penitence. Eh! listen to me preaching!"

"There is one air I have heard of yours—so!—that somehow haunts me," said Count Victor; "its conclusion seemed to baffle you."

"So it does, man, so it does! If I found the end of that, I fancy I would find a new MacTaggart. It's—it's—it's not a run of notes I want—indeed the air's my own, and I might make it what I chose—but an experience or something of that sort outside my opportunities, or my recollection."

Count Victor's glance fell on Mrs Petullo, but hers was not on him; she sought the eyes of the Chamberlain.

"Madame looks your way," he indicated, and at once the Chamberlain's visage changed.

"She'd be better to look to her man," he said, so roughly that the Count once more had all his misgivings revived.

"We may not guess how bitter a prospect that may be," said he with pity for the creature, and he moved towards her, with the Chamberlain, of necessity, but with some reluctance, at his heel.

Mrs Petullo saw the lagging nature of her old love's advance; it was all that was needed now to make her evening horrible.

"Oh!" said she, smiling, but still with other emotions than amusement or goodwill struggling in her countenance, "I was just fancying you would be none the waur o' a wife to look to your buttons."

"Buttons!" repeated the Chamberlain.

"See," she said, and lightly turned him round so that his back was shown, with his plaid no longer concealing the absence of a button from a skirt of his Highland jacket.

Count Victor looked, and a rush of emotions fairly overwhelmed him, for he knew he had the missing button in his pocket.

Here was the nocturnal marauder of Doom, or the very devil was in it!

The Chamberlain laughed, but still betrayed a little confusion: Mrs Petullo wondered at the anger of his eyes, and a moment later launched upon an abstracted minuet with Montaiglon.

XXVII

The Duel on the Sands

The Chamberlain stood near the door with his hand in the bosom of his coat, fingering the flageolet that was his constant companion even in the oddest circumstances, and Count Victor went up to him, the button concealed in his palm.

"Well, you are for going?" said Simon, more like one who puts a question than states a position, for some hours of Count Victor's studied contempt created misgivings.

"*Il y a terme à tout!* And possibly monsieur will do me the honour to accompany me so far as the avenue?"

"Sir!" said the Chamberlain.

"I have known men whose reputations were mainly a matter of clothes. Monsieur is the first I have met whose character hung upon a single button. Permit me to return your button with a million regards."

He held the silver lozenge out upon his open hand.

"There are many buttons alike," said the Chamberlain. Then he checked himself abruptly, and—"Well, damn it! I'll allow it's mine," said he.

"I should expect just this charming degree of manly frankness from monsieur. A button is a button, too, and a devilish serious thing when, say, off a foil."

He still held out the accusation on his open hand, and bowed with his eyes on those of the other man.

At that MacTaggart lightly struck up the hand, and the button rolled tinkling along the floor.

Count Victor glanced quickly round him to see that no one noticed. The hall, but for some domestics, was left wholly to themselves. The ball was over, the company had long gone, and he had managed to stay his own departure by an interest feigned

192

in the old armour that hung, with all its gallant use accomplished, on the walls, followed by a game at cards with three of the ducal *entourage*, two of whom had just departed. The melancholy of early morning in a banquet-room had settled down, and all the candles guttered in the draught of doors.

"I fancy monsieur will agree that this is a business calling for the open air," said Count Victor, no way disturbed by the rudeness. "I abhor the stench of hot grease."

"Tomorrow—" began the Chamberlain, and Count Victor interrupted.

"Tomorrow," said he, "is for reflection; today is for deeds. Look! it will be totally clear in a little."

"I'm the last man who would spoil the prospect of a ploy," said the Chamberlain, changing his Highland sword for one of the rapiers on the wall that was in more conformity with the Frenchman's weapon; "and yet this is scarcely the way to find your Drimdarroch."

"*Mais oui!* Our Drimdarroch can afford to wait his turn. Drimdarroch is wholly my affair; this is partly Doom's, though I, it seems, was made the poor excuse for your inexplicable insolence."

The Chamberlain slightly started, turned away, and smiled. "I was right," thought he. "Here's a fellow credits himself with being the cause of jealousy."

"Very well!" he said aloud at last, "this way," and with the sword tucked under his arm he led, by a side-door in the turret-angle, into the garden.

Count Victor followed, stepping gingerly, for the snow was ankle-deep upon the lawn, and his red-heeled dancing-shoes were thin.

"We know we must all die," said he in a little, pausing with a shiver of cold, and a glance about that bleak grey garden—"We know we must all die, but I have a preference for dying in dry hose, if die I must. Cannot monsieur suggest a more comfortable quarter for our little affair?"

"Monsieur is not so dirty particular," said the Chamberlain.

"If I sink my own rheumatism, it is not too much for you to risk your hose."

"The main avenue . . . " suggested Count Victor.

"Is seen from every window of the ballroom, and the servants are still there. Here is a great to-do about nothing!"

"But still, monsieur, I must protest on behalf of my poor hose," said Count Victor, always smiling.

"By God! I could fight on my bare feet," cried the Chamberlain.

"Doubtless, monsieur; but there is so much in custom, *n'est ce pas?* and my ancestors have always been used with boots."

The Chamberlain overlooked the irony and glanced perplexed about him. There was, obviously, no place near that was not open to the objection urged. Everywhere the snow lay deep on grass and pathway; the trees were sheeted ghosts, the chill struck through his own Highland brogues.

"Come!" said he at last, with a sudden thought; "the sand's the place, though it's a bit to go," and he led the way hurriedly towards the riverside.

"One of us may go farther today and possibly fare worse," said Montaiglon with unwearied good-humour, stepping in his rear.

It was the beginning of the dawn. Already there was enough of it to show the world of hill and wood in vast, vague, silent masses, to render wan the flaming windows of the castle towers behind them. In the east a sullen sky was all blotched with crimson, some pine-trees on the heights were struck against it, intensely black, intensely melancholy, perhaps because they led the mind to dwell on wild, remote, and solitary places, the savagery of old forests, the cruel destiny of man, who has come after and must go before the dead things of the wood. There was no wind; the landscape swooned in frost.

"My faith! 'tis an odd and dolorous world at six o'clock in the morning," thought Count Victor; "I wish I were asleep in Cammercy and all well."

A young fallow-deer stood under an oak-tree, lifting its head to gaze without dismay, almost a phantom; every moment the dawn spread wider; at last the sea showed, leaden in the bay, mists revealed themselves upon Ben Ime. Of sound there was only the wearying plunge of the cascades and the roll of the shallows like tumbril-wheels on causeway as the river ran below the arches.

"Far yet, monsieur?" cried Count Victor to the figure striding ahead, and his answer came in curt accents.

"We'll be there in ten minutes. You want a little patience."

"We shall be there, *pardieu!* in time enough," cried out Count Victor. " 'Tis all one to me, but the march is pestilent dull."

"What! would ye have fiddlin' at a funeral?" asked the Chamberlain, still without turning or slowing his step; and then, as though he had been inspired, he drew out the flageolet that was ever his bosom friend, and the astounded Frenchman heard the strains of a bagpipe march. It was so incongruous in the circumstances that he must laugh.

"It were a thousand pities to kill so rare a personage," thought he, "and yet—and yet—'tis a villainous early morning."

They passed along the riverbank; they came upon the sea-beach; the Chamberlain put his instrument into his pocket and still led the way upon the sand that lay exposed far out by the low tide. He stopped at a spot clear of weed, flat and dry and firm almost as a table. It was the ideal floor for an engagement, but for the uncomfortable sense of espionage from the neighbourhood of a town that looked with all its windows upon the place as it were upon a scene in a playhouse. The whole front of the town was not two hundred yards away!

"We shall be disturbed here, monsieur," said Count Victor, hesitating as the other put off his plaid and coat.

"No!" said Sim MacTaggart shortly, tugging at a belt, and yet Count Victor had his doubts. He made his preparations, it is true, but always with an apprehensive look at that long line of sleeping houses, whose shutters—with a hole in the centre of each—seemed to stare down upon the sand. No smoke, no flame, no sign of human occupance was there: the seagull and the pigeon pecked together upon the doorsteps or the windowsills, or perched upon the ridges of the high-pitched roofs, and a heron stalked at the outlet of a gutter that ran down the street. The sea, quiet and dull, the east turned from crimson to grey; the mountains streaming with mist . . .

"Cammercy after all!" said Count Victor to himself; "I shall wake in a moment, but yet for a nightmare 'tis the most extraordinary I have ever experienced."

"I hope you are a good Christian," said the Chamberlain, ready first and waiting, bending his borrowed weapon in malignant arcs above his head.

"Three-fourths of one at least," said Montaiglon; "for I try my best to be a decent man," and he daintily and deliberately turned up his sleeve upon an arm as white as milk.

"I'm waiting," said the Chamberlain.

"So! *en garde!*" said his antagonist, throwing off his hat and putting up his weapon.

There was a tinkle of steel like the sound of ice afloat in a glass.

The town but seemed to sleep wholly; as it happened, there was one awake in it who had, of all its inhabitants, the most vital interest in this stern business out upon the sands. She had gone home from the ball rent with vexation and disappointment; her husband snored, a mannikin of parchment, jaundice-cheeked, scorched at the nose with snuff; and, shuddering with distaste of her cage and her companion, she sat long at the window, all her finery on, chasing dream with dream, and every dream, as she knew, alas! with the inevitable poignancy of waking to the truth. For her the flaming east was hell's own vestibule, for her the greying dawn was a pallor of the heart, the death of hope. She sat turning and turning the marriage-ring upon her finger, sometimes all unconsciously essaying to slip it off, and tugging viciously at the knuckle-joint that prevented its removal, and her eyes, heavy for sleep and moist with sorrow, still could pierce the woods of Shira Glen to their deepmost recesses and see her lover there. They roamed so eagerly, so hungrily into that far distance, that for a while she failed to see the figures on the nearer sand. They swam into her recognition like wraiths up-sprung, as it were, from the sand itself or exhaled upon a breath from the sea: at first she could not credit her vision.

It was not with her eyes—those tear-blurred eyes—she knew him; it was by the inner sense, the nameless one that lovers know; she felt the tale in a thud of the heart, and ran out with "Sim!" shrieked on her dumb lips. Her gown trailed in the pools and flicked up the ooze of weed and sand; a shoulder bared itself; some of her hair took shame and covered it with a veil of dull gold.

XXVIII

The Duel on the Sands (continued)

And now it was clear day. The lime-washed walls of the town gleamed in sunshine, and the shadows of the men at war upon the sand stretched far back from their feet toward the white land. Birds twittered, and shook the snow from the shrubbery of the Duke's garden; the river cried below the arches, but not loud enough to drown the sound of stumbling steps, and Montaiglon threw a glance in the direction whence they came, even at the risk of being spitted on his opponent's weapon.

He parried a thrust in quarte and cried, "Stop! stop! *remettez-vous, monsieur!* Here comes a woman."

The Chamberlain looked at the dishevelled figure running awkwardly over the rough stones and slimy weeds, muttered an oath, and put his point up again.

"Come on," said he; "we'll have the whole town about our lugs in ten minutes."

"But the lady?" said Count Victor, guarding under protest.

"It's only Kate," said the Chamberlain, and aimed a furious thrust in tierce. Montaiglon parried by a beat of the edge of his forte, and forced the blade upwards. He could have disarmed by the simplest trick of Girard, but missed the opportunity from an insane desire to save his opponent's feelings in the presence of a spectator. Yet the leniency cost them dear.

"Sim! Sim!" cried out the woman in a voice full of horror and entreaty, panting towards the combatants. Her call confused her lover: in a mingling of anger and impatience he lunged wildly, and Count Victor's weapon took him in the chest.

"*Zut!*" cried the Frenchman, withdrawing the sword and flicking the blood from the point with a ludicrous movement.

The Chamberlain writhed at his feet, muttering something

198

fierce in Gaelic, and a great repugnance took possession of the other. He looked at his work; he quite forgot the hurrying woman until she ran past him and threw herself beside the wounded man.

"Oh, Sim! Sim!" she wailed, in an utterance the most distressing. Her lover turned upon his back and smiled sardonically at her out of a face of paper. "I wish ye had been a little later, Kate," he said, "or that I had begun with a hale arm. Good God! I've swallowed a hot cinder. I love you, my dear; I love you, my dear. Oh, where the de'il's my flageolet?" And then his head fell back.

With frantic hands she unloosed his cravat, sought and staunched the wound with her handkerchief, and wept the while with no sound, though her bosom, white like the spray of seas, seemed bound to burst above her corsage.

Count Victor sheathed his weapon, and "Madame," said he with preposterous inadequacy, "this—this—is distressing; this—this . . ." he desired to offer some assistance, but baulked at the fury of the eyes she turned on him.

"Oh, you!—you!—you!" she gasped, choking to say even so little. "It is enough, is it not, that you have murdered him, without staying to see me tortured?"

To this he could, of course, make no reply. His quandary was immense. Two hundred yards away was that white phantom town shining in the morning sun that rose enormous over the eastern hills beyond the little lapping silver waves. A phantom town, with phantom citizens doubtless prying through the staring eyes of those closed shutters. A phantom town—town of fairy tale, with grotesque roofs, odd *corbeau*-stepped gables, smokeless chimneys, all white with snow, and wild birds on its terrace, preening in the blessed light of the sun. He stood with his back to the pair upon the sand. "My God! 'tis a dream," said he, "I shall laugh in a moment." He seemed to himself to stand thus an age, and yet in truth it was only a pause of minutes when the Chamberlain spoke with the tone of sleep and insensibility as from another world.

"I love you, my dear; I love you, my dear—Olivia."

199

Mrs Petullo gave a cry of pain and staggered to her feet. She turned upon Count Victor a face distraught and eyes that were wild with the wretchedness of the disillusioned. Her fingers were playing nervously at her lips; her shoulders were roughened and discoloured by the cold; her hair falling round her neck gave her the aspect of a slattern. She, too, looked at the façade of the town and saw her husband's windows shuttered and indifferent to her grief.

"I do not know whether you have killed him or not," she said at last. "It does not matter—oh! it matters all—no, no, it does not matter—Oh! could you not—could you not kill me too?"

For his life he could not have answered: he but looked at her in mortal pity, and at that she ground her teeth and struck him on the lips.

"Awake, decidedly awake!" he said, and shrugged is shoulders; and then for the first time he saw that she was shivering.

"Madame," he said, "you will die of cold: permit me," and he stooped and picked up his coat from the sand and placed it without resistance on her shoulders like a cloak. She drew it, indeed, about her with trembling fingers as if her senses craved the comfort though her detestation of the man who gave it was great. But in truth she was demented now, forgetting even the bleeding lover. She gave little paces on the sand, with one of her shoes gone from her feet, and wrung her hands and sobbed miserably.

Count Victor bent to the wounded man and found him regaining consciousness. He did what he could, though that of necessity was little, to hasten his restoration, and relinquished the office only when approaching footsteps on the shore made him look up to see a group of workmen hastening to the spot where the Chamberlain lay on the edge of the tide, and the lady and the foreigner beside him.

"This man killed him," cried Mrs Petullo, pointing an accusing finger.

"I hope I have not killed him," said he, "and in any case it was an honourable engagement; but that matters little at this moment when the first thing to do is to have him removed home. So far as I am concerned, I promise you I shall be quite ready to go with you and see him safely lodged."

As the wounded man was borne through the lodge gate with Count Victor, coatless, in attendance, the latter looked back and saw Mrs Petullo, again bare-shouldered, standing before her husband's door and gazing after them.

Her temper had come back; she had thrown his laced coat into the approaching sea!

XXIX

The Cell in the Fosse

By this time the morning was well gone; the town had wakened to the day's affairs—a pleasant light grey reek with the acrid odour of burning wood soaring from chimneys into a sky intensely blue; and the roads that lay interlaced and spacious around the castle of Argyll were—not thronged, but busy at least with labouring folk setting out upon their duties. To them, meeting the wounded form of the Chamberlain, the hour was tragic, and figured long at fireside stories after, acutely memorable for years. They passed astounded or turned to follow him, making their own affairs secondary to their interest in the state of one who, it was obvious even to Montaiglon, was deep in their affections. He realised that a few leagues farther away from the seat of a Justiciary-General it might have gone ill with the man who had brought Simon MacTaggart to this condition, for menacing looks were thrown at him, and more than once there was a significant gesture that made plain the animosity with which he was regarded. An attempt to escape—if such had occurred to him—would doubtless have been attended by the most serious consequences.

Argyll met his Chamberlain with the signs of genuine distress: it was touching, indeed, to see his surrender to the most fraternal feeling, and though for a while the Duke's interest in his Chamberlain left him indifferent to him who was the cause of it, Count Victor could not but perceive that he was himself in a position of exceeding peril. He remembered the sinister comments of the Baron of Doom upon the hazards of an outsider's entrance to the boar's cave, and realised for the first time what that might mean in this country, where the unhappy wretch from Appin, whose case had some resemblance to his

202

own, had been remorselessly made the victim (as the tale went) to world-old tribal jealousies whose existence was incredible to all outside the Highland line. In the chill morning air he stood, coatless and shivering, the high embrasured walls lifting above him, the jabbering menials of the castle grouped a little apart, much of the language heard savage and incomprehensible in his ears, himself, as it were, of no significance to any one except the law that was to manifest itself at any moment. Last night it had been very gay in this castle, the Duke was the most gracious of hosts; here, faith! was a vast difference.

"May I have a coat?" he asked a bystander, taking advantage of a bustle in the midst of which the wounded man was taken into the castle. He got the answer of a scullion.

"A coat!" exclaimed the man he addressed. "A rope's more like it." And so, Count Victor, shrugging his shoulders at this impertinence, was left to suffer the air that bit him to the marrow.

The Chamberlain disposed of, and in the leech's hands, Argyll had the Frenchman brought to his rooms, still in his shirt-sleeves. The weapon of his offence was yet in his hand for evidence, had that been wanting, of an act he was prepared to admit with frankness.

"Well, M. le Comte," said his Grace, pacing nervously up and down the room before him, "this is a pretty matter. You have returned to see my pictures somewhat sooner than I had looked for, and in no very ceremonious circumstances."

"Truly," said the Count, with a difficult essay at meeting the man in his own humour—"Truly, but your Grace's invitation was so pressing—*ah! c'est grand dommage! mais—mais*—I am not, with every consideration, in the key for badinage. M. le Duc, you behold me exceedingly distressed at the discommoding of your household. At your age this—"

He pulled himself up confused a little, aware that his customary politeness had somehow for once shamefully deserted him with no intention on his part.

"That is to put the case with exceeding delicacy," said the Duke. "At my age, as you have said, my personal inconvenience

203

is of little importance in face of the fact that a dear friend of mine may be at death's door. At all events there is a man, if signs mislead me not, monstrously near death under this roof, a man well liked by all that know him, a strong man and a brave man, and a man, in his way, of genius. He goes out, as I say, hale and hearty, and comes back bloody in your company. You came to this part of the world, monsieur, with the deliberate intention of killing my Chamberlain!"

"That's as Heaven, which arranges these things without consulting us, may have decided, my lord; on my honour, I had much preferred never to have set eyes on your Chamberlain."

"Come, come!" said the Duke with a high head and slapping with open hand the table beside him—"Come, come! I am not a fool, Montaiglon—even at my age. You deliberately sought this unfortunate man."

"Monsieur the Duke of Argyll has my word that it was not so," said the Count softly.

"I fancy in that case, then, you had found him easy to avoid," said the Duke, who was in an irrestrainable heat. "From the first—oh come! sir, let us not be beating about the bush, and let us sink all these evasions—from the first you have designed a meeting with MacTaggart, and your every act since you came to this country has led up to this damned business that is likely to rob me of the bravest of servants. It was not the winds of Heaven that blew you against your will into this part of Scotland, and brought you in contact with my friend on the very first night of your coming here."

"And still, M. le Duc, with infinite deference, and a coolness that is partly due to the unpleasant fact (as you may perceive) that I have no coat on, 'twas quite the other way, and your bravest of servants thrust himself upon my attention that had otherwise been directed to the real object of my being in Scotland at all."

The Duke gave a gesture of impatience. "I am not at the heart of these mysteries," said he, "but—even at my age—I know a great deal more about this than you give me credit for. If it is your whim to affect that this wretched business was no more than a passage between gentlemen, the result of a quarrel over cards or the like in my house—"

"Ah!" cried the Count, "there I am all to blame. Our affair ought more properly to have opened elsewhere. In that detail your Grace has every ground for complaint."

"That is a mere side affair," said the Duke, "and something else more closely affects me. I am expected to accept it, then, that the Comte de Montaiglon, travelling incognito in the unassuming *rôle* of a wine merchant, came here at this season simply from a passion for our Highland scenery. I had not thought the taste for dreary mountains and black glens had extended to the Continent."

"At least 'twas not to quarrel with a servant I came here," retorted Count Victor.

"That is ill said, sir," said his Grace. "My kinsman has ten generations of ancestry of the best blood of Scotland and the Isles underground."

"To that, M. le Duc, there is an obvious and ancient retort—that therein he is like a potato plant; the best of him is buried."

Argyll stood before the Frenchman dubious and embarrassed; vexed at the tone of the encounter, and convinced, for reasons of his own, that in one particular at least the foreigner prevaricated, yet impressed by the manly front of the gentleman whose affair had brought a morning's tragedy so close upon the heels of an evening's mirth. Here was the sort of quandary in which he would naturally have consulted with his Duchess, but it was no matter to wake a woman to, and she was still in her bed-chamber.

"I assume you look for this unhappy business to be treated as an affair of honour?" he asked at last.

"So to call it," replied Count Victor, "though in truth, the honour, on my word, was all on one side."

"You are in doubtful taste to put it quite in these terms," said the Duke more sternly, "particularly as you are the one to come out of it so far scathless."

205

"Would M. le Duc know how his servant compelled my— my attentions?"

"Compelled your attentions! I do not like the tone of your speeches, monsieur. Dignity—"

"*Pardieu!* M. le Duc, would you expect a surfeit of dignity from a man without a jacket?" said the Count, looking pathetically at his arms.

"Dignity—I mean the sense of it—would dictate a more sober carriage in face of the terrible act you have committed. I am doing my best to find the slightest excuse for you, because you are a stranger here, a man of good family though engaged upon a stupendous folly, and I have before now been in the reverence of your people. You ask me if I know what compelled your attention (as you say) to my Chamberlain, and I will answer you frankly that I know all that is necessary."

At that the Count was visibly amazed. This was, indeed, to put a new face on matters and make more regrettable his complacent surrender after his affair on the sands.

"In that case, M. le Duc," said he, "there is no more to be said. I protest I am unable to comprehend your Grace's complacence towards a rogue—even of your own household."

Argyll rung a bell and concluded the interview.

"There has been enough of this," he said. "I fear you do not clearly realise all the perils of your situation. You came here— you will pardon a man at my age insisting upon it, for I know the facts—with the set design of challenging one who properly or improperly has aroused your passion; you have accomplished your task, and must not consider yourself harshly treated if you have to pay the possible penalty."

"Pardon, M. le Duc, it is not so, always with infinite deference, and without a coat as I have had the boldness to remark before: my task had gone on gaily enough had your Monsieur MacTaggart not been the victim of some inexplicable fever—unless as I sometimes suspect it were a preposterous jealousy that made me the victim of his somewhat stupid folly play."

"You have accomplished your task, as I say," proceeded Argyll, heedless of the interruption, "and to tell the truth, the thing has been done with an unpardonably primitive absence of form. I am perhaps an indifferent judge of such ceremonies; at my age—as you did me the honour to put it—that is only to be expected, but we used, when I was younger, to follow a certain formula in inviting our friend the enemy out to be killed. What is this hasty and clandestine encounter before the law of the land but a deliberate attempt at murder? It would be so even in your own country under the circumstances. M. le Comte, where were your seconds? Your wine-selling has opened in villainously bad circumstances, and you are in error to assume that the details of the code may be waived even among the Highland hills."

A servant entered.

"Take this gentleman to the fosse," said the Duke, with the ring of steel in his voice and his eyes snapping.

"At least there is as little form about my incarceration as about my poor duel," said Count Victor.

"My father would have been somewhat more summary in circumstances like these," said the Duke, "and, by Heaven! the old style had its merits too; but these are different days, though, if I were you, I fancy I'd prefer the short shrift of Long David the dempster to the felon's cell. Be good enough to leave your sword."

Count Victor said never a word, but placed the weapon in a corner of the room, made a deep *congé*, and went forth a prisoner.

In the last few minutes of the interview he had forgotten the cold, but now when he was led into the open air he felt it in his coatless condition more poignant than his apprehension at his position otherwise. He shivered as he walked along the fosse, through which blew a shrewd north wind, driving the first flakes of an approaching snowstorm. The fosse was wide and deep, girding the four-square castle, mantled on its outer walls by dense ivy, where a few birds twittered. The wall was broken at intervals by the doors of what might very well serve as cells if cells were wanted, and it was to one of these that Count Victor found himself consigned.

"My faith, Victor, thou art a fool of the first water!" he said to himself as he realised the ignominy of his situation. For he was in the most dismal of dungeons, furnished as scantily as a cellar, fireless, damp, and almost in sepulchral darkness, for what light might have entered by a little window over the door was obscured by drifted snow.

By-and-by his eyes became accustomed to the obscurity, and he concluded that he was in what had at one time been a wine-cellar, as bottles were racked against the back wall of his arched apartment. They were empty—he confirmed his instinct on that point quickly enough, for the events of the morning left him in the mood for refreshment. It was uncomfortable all this; there was always the possibility of justice miscarried; but at no time had he any fear of savage reprisals such as had alarmed him when Mungo Boyd locked him up in Doom and the fictitious broken clan cried "Loch Sloy!" in darkness. For this was not wholly the wilds, and Argyll's manner, though stern, was that of one who desired in all circumstances to be just.

So Count Victor sat on a box and shivered in his shirt-sleeves and fervently wished for breakfast. The snow fell heavily now, and drifted in the fosse and whitened the world; outside, there-fore, all was silent; there must be bustle and footsteps, but here they were unheard: it seemed in a while that he was buried in catacombs, an illusion so vexatious that he felt he must dispel it at all hazards.

There was but one way to do so. He stood on his box and tried to reach the window over his door. To break the glass was easy, but when that was done and the snow was cleared away by his hand, he could see out only by pulling himself up with an awkward and exhausting grasp on the narrow ledge. Thus he secured but the briefest of visions of what was outside, and that was not a reassuring one.

Had he meditated escape from the window, he must now abandon it; for on the other side of the ditch, cowering in the shelter of one of the castle doors, was standing one of the two men who had placed him in the cell, there apparently for no other purpose than to keep an eye on the only possible means of exit from the discarded wine-cellar.

The breaking glass was unheard by the watcher; at all events he made no movement to suggest that he had observed it, and he said nothing about it when some time later in the forenoon he came with Count Victor's breakfast, which was generous enough to confirm his belief that in Argyll's hands he was at least assured of the forms of justice, though that, in truth, was not the most consoling of prospects.

His warder was a dumb dog, a squint-eyed Cerberus with what Count Victor for once condemned as a tribal gibberish for his language, so that he was incapable of understanding what was said to him even if he had been willing to converse.

"It is little good to play the guitar to an ass," said the Frenchman, and fell to his viands.

XXX

A Ducal Disputation

If Count Victor, buried among cobwebs in the fosse, stung by cold till he shivered as in a quartan ague, suffering alternately the chagrin of the bungler self-discovered and the apprehension of a looming fate whose nature could only be guessed at, was in a state unenviable, Argyll himself was scarcely less unhappy. It was not only that his Chamberlain's condition grieved him, but that the whole affair put him in a quandary, where the good citizen quarrelled in him with another old Highland gentleman whose code of morals was not in strict accord with written statutes. He had studied the Pandects at Utrecht, but also he had been young there, and there was a place (if all tales be true) on the banks of the Yssel river where among silent polders a young Scot had twice at least fought with the sword upon some trivial matter of debate with Netherlanders of his college. And then he knew his Chamberlain. About Simon MacTaggart Argyll had few illusions, though they perhaps made all the difference in his conduct to the gentleman in question. That MacTaggart should have brought upon himself a tardy retribution for acts more bold than scrupulous was not to be wondered at, that the meeting with Count Victor was honourably conducted, although defective in its form, was almost certain; but here the assailant was in his custody, and whether he liked it or not he must hand him over to the law.

His first impulse had been to wash his hands of all complicity in the Frenchman's fate by sending him straightway to the common town tolbooth, pending his trial in the ordinary course; but he hesitated from an intuition that the step would find no favour in the eyes of his Duchess, who had her own odd prejudices regarding Sim MacTaggart, and an interest in

Count Victor none the less ardent because it was but a day or two old.

"A man! Archie, every bit of him!" she had said at the conclusion of last evening's entertainment; and though without depreciating his visitor he had attempted to convince her that her estimate ran the risk of being prejudiced by her knowledge of the quixotic mission the foreigner was embarked on, she had refused to see in Count Victor's accent, face, and carriage anything but the most adorable character. She ever claimed a child's attribute of attraction or repulsion on mere instinct to and from men's mere exteriors, and her husband knew it was useless to expect any approval from her for any action that might savour of the slightest harshness to the foreigner.

But above all he feared—he dreaded—something else. Simon MacTaggart was to him more than a servant; he knew many of his failings, but seemed to tolerate them because he also, like Count Victor, had learned not to expect too much from human nature. But it was ever his fear that his lenience for the sins and follies of his Chamberlain would some day suffer too hard a strain, and lead to that severance that in the case of old friends and familiars was his Grace's singular terror in life.

The day passed heavily for Argyll. Many a time he looked out of his window into the fosse slow drifting full of snow; and though he could not from that point see the cell-door of his prisoner, his fancy did enough to feed his unhappiness. Vainly he paced his library, vainly sought the old anodyne—the blessed anodyne of books; he was consumed with impatience to consult with his wife, and she, fragile always, and fatigued by last evening's gaieties, was still asleep.

He went for the twentieth time into the room where the Chamberlain was lying. The doctor, a lank pock-pitted embodiment of mad chirurgy from books and antique herbal delusions inherited from generations of simple-healers, mixed noxious stuff in a gallipot and plumed himself upon some ounces of gore drawn from his victim. Clysters he prated on; electuaries; troches; the weed that the Gael of him called *slanlus* or "heal-all";

211

of unguents loathsomely compounded, but at greatest length and with fullest rapture of his vile phlebotomy.

"Six ounces, your Grace!" he cried gleefully, in a laughable high falsetto, holding up the bowl with trembling fingers as if he proffered for the ducal cheer the very flagon of Hebe.

Argyll shuddered.

"I wish to God, Dr MacIver," said he, "your practice in this matter of blood-letting may not be so much infernal folly. Why! the man lost all he could spare before he reached you."

And there, unconscious, Simon MacTaggart slept, pale as parchment, fallen in at the jaw, twitching a little now and then at the corners of the mouth, otherwise inert and dead. Never before had his master seen him off his guard—never, that is to say, without the knowledge that he was being looked at, and if his Grace had expected that he should find any grosser man than he knew revealed, he was mistaken. 'Twas a child that slept—a child not unhappy, at most only indifferent to everything with that tremendous naïveté of the dead and of the soundly sleeping—that great carelessness that comes upon the carcass when the soul's from home. If he had sinned a million times;—let the physiognomists say what they will!—not a line upon his face betrayed him, for there the ideals only leave their mark, and his were for ever impeccable.

His coat hung upon the back of a chair, and his darling flageolet had fallen out of the pocket and lay upon the floor. Argyll picked it up and held it in his hand a while, looking upon it with a little contempt, and yet with some kindness.

"Fancy that!" he said more to himself than to the apothecary; "the poor fellow must have his flageolet with him even upon an affair of this kind. It beats all! My dear man of moods! my good vagabond! my windlestraw of circumstance! constant only to one ideal—the unattainable perfection in a kind of roguish art. To play a perfect tune in the right spirit he would sacrifice everything, and yet drift carelessly into innumerable disgraces for mere lack of will to lift a hand. I daresay sometimes Jean is in the rights of it after all—his gifts have been his curse: wanting his skill of this simple instrument that was for ever to himself and others an intoxication, and wanting his outward pleasing form, he had been a good man to the very marrow. A good man! H'm! Ay! and doubtless an uninteresting one. Doctor! doctor! have you any herb for the eyesight?"

"Does your Grace have a dimness? I know a lotion—"

"Dimness! faith! it is the common disease, and I suffer it with the rest. Sometimes I cannot see the length of my nose."

"The stomach, your Grace; just the stomach," cried the poor leech. "My own secret preparation—"

"Your own secret preparation, doctor, will not, I am sure, touch the root of this complaint or the devil himself is in it. I can still see—even at my age—the deer on Tom-a-chrochair, and read the scurviest letters my enemies send me, but my trouble is that I cannot understand the flageolet."

"The flageolet, your Grace," said MacIver bewildered. "I thought you spoke of your eyesight."

"And so I did. I cannot see through the mysteries of things; I cannot understand why man should come into the world with fingers so apt to fankle that he cannot play the finest tunes all the time and in the best of manners. These, however, are but idle speculations, beyond the noble jurisdiction of the chymist. And so you think our patient will make a good recovery?"

"With care, your Grace; and the constant use of my styptic, a most elegant nostrum, your Grace, that has done wonders in the case of a widow up the glen."

"This folly of a thing they call one's honour," said the Duke, "has made a great deal of profitable trade for your profession?"

"I have no cause of complaint, your Grace," said the doctor complacently, "except that nowadays honour nor nothing else rarely sends so nice a case of haemorrhage my way. An inch or two to the left and Mr MacTaggart would have lifted his last rents."

Argyll grimaced with distaste at the idea.

"Poor Sim!" said he. "And my tenants would have lost a tolerant agent, though I might easily find one to get more money

213

out of them. Condemn that Frenchman! I wish the whole race of them were at the devil."

"It could never have been a fair fight this," said the doctor, spreading a plaster.

"There never *was* a fair fight," said Argyll, "or but rarely, and then neither of the men was left to tell the tale. The man with most advantages must ever win."

"The other had them all here," said the doctor, "for the Chamberlain was fighting with an unhealed wound in his right arm."

"A wounded arm!" cried Argyll. "I never heard of that."

It was a wound so recent, the doctor pointed out, that it made the duel madness. He turned over the neck of his patient's shirt and showed the cicatrice, angry and ugly. "A stab, too!" said he.

"A stab?" said the Duke.

"A stab with a knife or a thrust with a sword," said the doctor. "It has gone clean through the arm and come out at the back."

"Gad! this is news indeed! What does it mean? It's the reason for the pallor and the abstraction of some days back, for which I put the blame upon some love-affair of his. He never breathed a word of it to me, nor I suppose to you?"

"It has had no attention from me or any one else," said the doctor; "but the wound seems to have healed of itself so far without anything being done for it."

"So that a styptic—even the famous styptic—can do no more wonders than a good constitution after all. Poor Sim, I wonder what folly this came of. And yet—to look at him there—his face so gentle, his brow so calm, his mouth—ah, poor Sim!"

From a distant part of the house a woman's voice arose, crying, "Archie, Archi-e-e!" in a lingering crescendo: it was the Duchess, and as yet she had not heard of the day's untoward happenings. He went out and told her gently. "And now," he went on when her agitation had abated, "what of our Chevalier?"

"Well!" said she, "what of him? I hope he is not to suffer for this, seeing MacTaggart is going to get better, for I should dearly like to have him get some return for his quest."

214

"Would you, indeed?" said the Duke. "H'm," and stared at her. "The Count is at this moment cooling his heels in the fosse cell."

"That is hard!" said she, reddening.

"But what would you, my dear? I am still as much the representative of the law as ever, and am I to connive at such outrages under my own windows because the chief offender is something of a handsome young gentleman who has the tact to apologise for a disturbance in my domestic affairs that must, as he puts it, be disconcerting to a man at my age? A man of my age—there's France!—*toujours la politesse*, if you please! At my age! Confound his impudence!"

The Duchess could not suppress a smile.

"At his age, my dear," said she, "you had the tact to put so obvious a thing differently or leave it alone."

"Not that I heed his impudence," said the Duke hastily; "that a man is no longer young at sixty is the most transparent of facts."

"Only he does not care to have it mentioned too unexpectedly. Oh, you goose!" And she laughed outright, then checked herself at the recollection of the ailing Chamberlain.

"If I would believe myself as young as ever I was, my dear lass," said he, "credit me it is that it is more to seem so in the eyes of yourself," and he put his arm around her waist.

"But still," said she after a little—"still the unlucky Frenchman is in the fosse more for his want of tact, I fear, than for his crime against the law of the land. Who pinked—if that's the nasty word—who pinked the Dutchman in Utrecht?—that's what I should like to know, my dear Justice-General."

"This is different, though; he came here for the express purpose—"

"Of quarrelling with the Chamberlain!"

"Well, of quarrelling with somebody, as you know," said the nobleman hesitatingly.

"I am sorry for MacTaggart," said the Duchess, "really sorry, but I cannot pretend to believe he has been very ill done by—

215

I mean unjustly done by. I'm sure my Frenchman must have had some provocation, and is really the victim."

"You—that is we—know nothing about that, my dear," said Argyll.

"I cannot be mistaken; you would be the first at any other time to admit that I could tell whether a man was good or evil on a very brief acquaintance. With every regard for your favour to the Chamberlain, I cannot stand the man. If my instinct did not tell me he was vicious, my ears would, for I hear many stories little to his credit."

"And yet a brave man, goodwife, a faithful servant and an interesting fellow. Come now! Jean, is it not so?"

She merely smiled, patting his ruffles with delicate fondling fingers. It was never her habit to argue with her Duke.

"What!" he cried smilingly, "none of that, but contradict me if you dare."

"I never contradict his Grace the Duke of Argyll," said she, stepping back and sweeping the floor with her gown in a stately courtesy; "it is not right, and it is not good for him—at his age."

"Ah, you rogue!" he cried, laughing. "But soberly now, you are too hard on poor Sim. It is the worst—the only vice of good women that they have no charity left for the imperfect either of their own sex or of mine. Let us think what an atom of wind-blown dust is every human being at the best, bad or good in his blood as his ancestry may have been, kind or cruel, straight or crooked, pious or pagan, admirable or evil, as the accidents of his training or experience shall determine. As I grow older I grow more tolerant, for I have learned that my own scanty virtues and graces are no more my own creation than the dukedom I came into from my father—or my red hair."

"Not red, Archie," said the Duchess, "not red, but reddish fair; in fact, a golden;" and she gently pulled a curl upon his temple. "What about our Frenchman? Is he to lie in the fosse till the Sheriff sends for him or till the great MacCailein Mor has forgiven him for telling him he was a little over the age of thirty?"

"For once, my dear, you cannot have your way," said the

Duke firmly. "Be reasonable! We could not tolerate so scandalous an affair without some show of law and—"

"Tolerate!" said the Duchess. "You are very hard on poor Montaiglon, Archie, and all because he fought a duel with a doubtful gentleman who will be little the worse for it in a week or two. Let us think," she went on banteringly—"let us think what an atom of windblown dust is every human being at the best, admirable or evil as his training—"

Her husband stopped her with a kiss.

"No more of that, Jean; the man must thole his trial, for I have gone too far to draw back even if I had the will to humour you."

There was one tone of her husband's his wife knew too decisive for her contending with, and now she heard it. Like a wise woman, she made up her mind to say no more, and she was saved an awkward pause by an uproar in the fosse. Up to the window where those two elderly lovers had their kindly disputation came the sound of cries. Out into the dusk of the evening Argyll thrust his head and asked an explanation.

"The Frenchman's gone!" cried somebody.

He drew in his head, with a smile struggling on his countenance.

"You witch!" said he, "you must have your own way with me, even if it takes a spell!"

XXXI

Flight

Long after, when Count Victor Jean de Montaiglon was come into great good fortune, and sat snug by charcoal-fires in the chateau that bears his name, and stands, an edifice even the Du Barry had the taste to envy, upon the gusset of the roads which break apart a league to the south of the forest of Saint Germain-en-Laye, he would recount, with oddly inconsistent humours of mirth and tense dramatics, the manner of his escape from the cell in the fosse of the great MacCailein. And always his acutest memory was of the whipping rigour of the evening air, his temporary sense of utter helplessness upon the verge of the fantastic wood. "Figure you! Charles," would he say, "the thin-blooded wand of forty years ago in a brocaded waistcoat and a pair of dancing-shoes seeking his way through a labyrinth of demoniac trees, shivering half with cold and half with terror like a *forçat* from the *bagne* of Toulouse, only that he knew not particularly from what he fled nor whereto his unlucky footsteps should be turned. I have seen it often since—the same place— have we not, *mignonne?*—and I avow 'tis as sweet and friendly a spot as any in our own neighbourhood; but then in that pestilent night of black and grey I was like a child, tenanting every tiny thicket with the were-wolf and the sheeted spectre. There is a stupid feeling comes to people sometimes in the like circumstances, that they are dead, that they have turned the key in the lock of life, as we say, and gone in some abstraction into the territory of shades. 'Twas so I felt, messieurs, and if in truth the ultimate place of spirits is so mortal chilly, I shall ask Père Antoine to let me have a greatcoat as well as the viaticum ere setting out upon the journey."

It had been an insufferably cruel day, indeed, for Count

Victor in his cell had he not one solace, so purely self-wrought, so utterly fanciful, that it may seem laughable. It was that the face of Olivia came before him at his most doleful moments—sometimes unsought by his imagination, though always welcome; with its general aspect of vague sweet sadness played upon by fleeting smiles, her lips desirable to that degree he could die upon them in one wild ecstasy, her eyes for depth and purity the very mountain wells. She lived, breathed, moved, smiled, sighed in this same austere atmosphere under the same grey sky that hung low outside his cell; the same snowfall that he could catch a glimpse of through the tiny space above his door was seen by her that moment in Doom; she must be taking the flavour of the sea as he could sometimes do in blessed moments even in this musty *oubliette*.

The day passed, a short day with the dusk coming on as suddenly as if someone had drawn a curtain hurriedly over the tiny aperture above the door. And all the world outside seemed wrapped in silence. Twice again his warder came dumbly serving a meal, otherwise the prisoner might have been immeasurably remote from any life and wholly forgotten. There was, besides his visions of Olivia, one other thing to comfort him; it was when he heard briefly from some distant part of the castle the ululation of a bagpipe playing an air so jocund that it assured him at all events the Chamberlain was not dead, and was more probably out of danger. And then the cold grew intense beyond his bearance, and he reflected upon some method of escape if it were to secure him no more than exercise for warmth.

The window was out of the question, for in all probability the watch was still on the other side of the fosse—a tombstone for steadfastness and constancy. Count Victor could not see him now even by standing on his box and looking through the aperture, yet he gained something, he gained all, indeed, so pregnant a thing is accident—even the cosy charcoal-fires and the friends about him in the chateau near Saint Germain-en-Laye—by his effort to pierce the dusk and see across the ditch.

For as he was standing on the box, widening softly the

aperture in the drifted snow upon the little window-ledge, he became conscious of cold air in a current beating upon the back of his head. The draught, that should surely be entering, was blowing out!

At once he thought of a chimney, but there was no fireplace in his cell. Yet the air must be finding entrance elsewhere more freely than from the window. Perplexity mastered him for a little, and then he concluded that the current could come from nowhere else than behind the array of marshalled empty bottles.

"*Tonnerre!*" said he to himself, "I have begun my career as wine merchant rather late in life or I had taken more interest in these dead gentlemen. *Avancez, donc, mes princes!* your ancient spirit once made plain the vacancies in the heads of his Grace's guests; let us see if now you do not conceal some holes that were for poor Montaiglon's profit."

One by one he pulled them out of their positions until he could intrude a sensitive hand behind the shelves where they had been racked.

There was an airy space.

"*Très bon! merci, messieurs les cadavres*, perhaps I may forgive you even yet for being empty."

Hope surged, he wrought eagerly; before long he had cleared away a passage—that ended in a dead wall!

It was perhaps the most poignant moment of his experience. He had, then, been the fool of an illusion! Only a blank wall! His fingers searched every inch of it within reach, but came upon nothing but masonry, cold, clammy, substantial.

"A delusion after all!" he said, bitterly disappointed. "A delusion, and not the first that has been at the bottom of a bottle of wine." He had almost resigned himself again to his imprisonment when the puffing current of colder air than that stagnant within the cell struck him for the second time, more keenly felt than before, because he was warm with his exertions. This time he felt that it had come from somewhere over the level of his head. Back he dragged his box and stood upon it behind the bottle-bin, and felt higher upon the wall than he could do standing, to discover that it stopped short about nine feet from the floor, and was apparently an incompleted curtain partitioning his cell from some space farther in.

Not with any vaulting hopes, for an egress from this inner space seemed no less unlikely than from the one he occupied, he pulled himself on the top of the intervening wall and lowered himself over the other side. At the full stretch of his arms he failed to touch anything with his feet. An alarming thought came to him: he would have pulled himself back, but the top of the wall was crumbling to his fingers, a mass of rotten mortar threatening each moment to break below his grasp, and he realised with a spasm of the diaphragm that now there was no retreat. What—this was his thought—what if this were the mouth of a well? Or a medieval trap for fools? He had seen such things in French castles. In the pitch darkness he could not guess whether he hung above an abyss or had the ground within an inch of his straining toes.

To die in a pit!

To die in a pit! good God!—was this the appropriate conclusion to a life with so much of open-air adventure, sunshine, gaiety, and charm in it? The sweat streamed upon his face as he strove vainly to hang by one of his arms and search the cope of the crumbling wall for a surer hold with the other; he stretched his toes till his muscles cramped, his eyes in the darkness filled with a red cloud, his breath choked him, a vision of his body thrashing through space overcame him, and his slipping fingers would be loose from the mortar in another minute!

To one last struggle for a decent mastery his natural manhood rose, and cleared his brain and made him loosen his grip.

He fell less than a yard!

For a moment he stopped to laugh at his foolish terror, and then set busily to explore this new place in which he found himself. The air was fresher; the walls on either hand contracted into the space of a lobby; he felt his way along for twenty paces before he could be convinced that he was in a sort of tunnel. But figure a so-convenient tunnel in connection with a prison cell!

221

It was too good to be true.

With no great surrender to hope even yet, he boldly plunged into the darkness, reason assuring him that the *cul-de-sac* would come sooner or later. But for once reason was wrong: the passage opened ever before him, more airy than ever, always dank and odorous, but with never a barrier—a passage the builders of the castle had executed for an age of sudden sieges and alarms, but now archaic and useless, and finally forgotten altogether.

He had walked, he knew not how long, when he was brought up by a curious sound—a prolonged, continuous, hollow roar as of wind in a wood or a sea that rolled on a distant beach. Vainly he sought to identify it, but finally shook aside his wonder and pushed on again till he came to the apparent end of the passage, where a wooden door barred his progress farther. He stopped as much in amazement as in dubiety about the door, for the noise that had baffled him farther back in the tunnel was now close at hand, and he might have been in a ship's hold and the ship all blown about by tempest, to judge from the inexplicable thunder that shook the darkness. A score of surmises came quickly, only to be dismissed as quickly as they came; that extraordinary tumult was beyond his understanding, and so he applied himself to his release. Still his lucky fortune remained with him; the door was merely on a latch. He plucked it open eagerly, keen to solve the puzzle of the noise, emerging on a night now glittering with stars, and clamant with the roar of tumbling waters.

A simple explanation!—he had come out beside the river. The passage came to its conclusion under the dumb arch of a bridge whose concaves echoed back in infinite exaggeration every sound of the river as it gulped in rocky pools below.

The landscape round about him in the starshine had a most bewitching influence. Steep banks rose from the riverside and lost themselves in a haze of frost, through which, more eminent, stood the boles and giant members of vast gaunt trees, their upper branches fretting the starry sky. No snow was on the spot where he emerged, for the wind, blowing huge wreaths against

222

the buttresses of the bridge a little higher on the bank, had left some vacant spaces, but the rest of the world was blanched well-nigh to the complexion of linen. Where he was to turn to first puzzled Count Victor. He was free in a whimsical fashion, indeed, for he was scarcely more than half-clad, and he wore a pair of dancing-shoes, ludicrously inappropriate for walking in such weather through the country. He was free, but he could not be very far yet from his cell; the discovery of his escape might be made at any moment; and even now while he lingered here he might have followers in the tunnel.

Taking advantage of the uncovered grass, he climbed the bank and sought the shelter of a thicket where the young trees grew too dense to permit the snow to enter. From here another hazard of flight was manifest, for he could see now that the face of the country outside on the level was spread as with a tablecloth, its white surface undisturbed, ready for the impress of so light an object as a hopping wren. To make his way across it would be to drag his bonds behind him, plainly asking the world to pull him back. Obviously there must be a more tactical retreat, and without more ado he followed the river's course, keeping ever, as he could, in the shelter of the younger woods, where the snow did not lie, or was gathered by the wind in alleys and walls. Forgotten was the cold in his hurried flight through the trees; but by-and-by it compelled his attention, and he fell to beating his arms in the shelter of a plantation of yews.

"*Mort de ma vie!*" he thought while in this occupation, "why should I not have a roquelaire? If his very ungracious Grace refuses to see when a man is dying of cold for want of a coat, shall the man not help himself to a loan? M. le Duc owes Cammercy something for that ride in a glass coach, and for a night of a greatcoat I shall be pleased to discharge the family obligation."

Count Victor there and then came to a bold decision. He would, perhaps, not only borrow a coat and cover his nakedness, but furthermore cover his flight by the same strategy. The only place in the neighbourhood where he could obscure his footsteps in

223

that white night of stars was in the castle itself—perhaps in the very fosse whence he had made his escape. There the traffic of the day was bound to have left a myriad tracks, amongst which the imprint of a red-heeled Rouen shoe would never advertise itself. But it was too soon yet to risk so bold a venture, for his absence might be at this moment the cause of search round all the castle, and ordinary prudence suggested that he should permit some time to pass before venturing near the dwelling that now was in his view, its lights blurred by haze, no sign apparent that they missed or searched for him.

For an hour or more, therefore, he kept his blood from congelation by walking back and forward in the thicket into which the softly breathing but shrewish night wind penetrated less cruelly than elsewhere, and at last judged the interval enough to warrant his advance upon the enterprise.

Behold then Count Victor running hard across the white level waste of the park into the very boar's den—a comic spectacle, had there been any one to see it, in a dancer's shoes and hose, coatless and excited. He looked over the railing of the fosse to find the old silence undisturbed.

Was his flight discovered yet? If not, it was something of a madness, after all, to come back to the jaws of the trap.

"Here's a pretty problem!" he told himself, hesitating upon the brink of the ditch into which dipped a massive stair—"Here's a pretty problem! to have the roquelaire or to fly without it and perish of cold, because there is one chance in twenty that monsieur the warder opposite my chamber may not be wholly a fool and may have looked into his mouse-trap. I do not think he has: at all events, here are the alternatives, and the wiser is invariably the more unpleasant. *Allons! Victor, advienne que pourra*, and Heaven help us!"

He ran quickly down the stair into the fosse, crept along in the shelter of the ivy for a little, saw that no one was visible, and darted across and up to a postern in the eastern turret. The door creaked noisily as he entered, and a flight of stairs, dimly lit by candles, presented itself, up which he ventured with his heart in

224

his mouth. On the first landing were two doors, one of them ajar; for a second or two he hesitated with every nerve in his flesh pulsating and his heart tumultuous in his breast, then hearing nothing, took his courage in his hands and blandly entered, with his feet at a fencer's balance for the security of his retreat if that were necessary. There was a fire glowing in the apartment—a tempting spectacle for the shivering refugee—a dim light burned within a glass shade upon the mantel, and a table laden with drug-vials was drawn up to the side of a heavily curtained bed.

Count Victor compassed the whole at a glance, and not the least pleasant part of the spectacle was the sight of a coat—not a greatcoat, but still a coat—upon the back of a chair that stood between the bed and the fire.

"With a thousand apologies to his Grace," he whispered to himself, and tiptoed in his soaking shoes across the floor without reflecting for a second that the bed might have an occupant. He examined the coat: it had a familiar look that might have indicated its owner even if there had not been the flageolet lying beside it. Instinctively Count Victor turned about and went up to the bed, where, silently peeping between the curtains, he saw his enemy of the morning so much in a natural slumber as it seemed that he was heartened exceedingly. Only for a moment he looked; there was the certainty of someone returning soon to the room, and accordingly he rapidly thrust himself into the coat and stepped back upon the stair.

There was but one thing wanting—a sword. Why should he not have his own back again? As he remembered the interview of the morning, the chamber in which he had left his weapon at the bidding of the Duke was close at hand, and probably it was still there. Each successive hazard audaciously faced emboldened him the more; and so he ventured along, searching amid a multitude of doors in dim rush-light till he came upon one that was different from its neighbours only inasmuch as it had a French motto painted across the panels. The motto read "*Revenez bientôt*," and smiling at the omen, Count Victor once more took his valour in his fingers and turned the handle. "*Revenez*

225

bientôt," he was whispering softly to himself as he noiselessly pushed in the door. The sentence froze on his lips when he saw the Duchess seated in a chair, and turned half round to look at him.

XXXII

Her Grace the Duchess

There was no drawing back; the circumstances positively forbade it, even if a certain smile following fast upon the momentary embarrassment of the Duchess had not prompted him to put himself at her mercy.

"A thousand pardons, Madame la Duchesse," he said, standing in the doorway. "*Je vous dérange.*"

She rose from her chair composedly, a figure of matured grace and practised courtliness, and above all with an air of what he flattered himself was friendliness. She directed him to a seat.

"The pleasure is unexpected, monsieur," she said; "but it is a moment for quick decision, I suppose. What is the cue? To be desperate?"—here she laughed softly,—"or to take a chair? Monsieur has called to see his Grace. I regret exceedingly that a pressing business has called my husband to the town, and he is unlikely to be back for another hour at least. If monsieur—assuming desperation is not the cue—will please to be seated . . ."

Count Victor was puzzled for a second or two, but came farther into the room, and, seeing the lady resume her seat, he availed himself of her invitation and took the chair she offered.

"Madame la Duchesse," he went on to say with some evidence of confusion that prejudiced her the more in his favour, "I am, as you see, in the drollest circumstances, and—pardon the *bétise*—time is at the moment the most valuable of my assets."

"Oh!" she cried with a low laugh that gave evidence of the sunniest disposition in the world—"Oh! that is not a pretty speech, monsieur! But there! you cannot, of course, know my powers of entertainment. Positively there need be no hurry. On my honour, as the true friend of a gentleman who looked very

227

like monsieur, and was, by the way, a compatriot, I repeat there is no occasion for haste. I presume monsieur found no servants—those stupid servants!—to let him into the house, and wisely found an entrance for himself? How droll! It is our way in these barbaric places; people just come and go as they please; we waive ceremony. By the way, monsieur has not done me the honour to confide to me his name."

"Upon my word, Madame la Duchesse, I—I forget it myself at the moment," said Count Victor, divining her strategy, but too much embarrassed to play up to her lead. "Perhaps madame may remember."

She drew down her brows in a comical frown, and then rippled into low laughter. "Now, how in the world should I know if monsieur does not? I, that have never"—here she stared in his face with a solemnity in which her amusement struggled—"never, to my knowledge, seen him before. I have heard the Duke speak of a certain Monsieur Soi-disant; perhaps monsieur is Monsieur Soi-disant?"

"*Sans doute*, Madame la Duchesse, and madame's very humble servant," acquiesced Count Victor, relieved to have his first impression of strategy confirmed, and inclining his head.

She looked at him archly and laughed again. "I have a great admiration for your sex, M. Soi-disant," she said; "my dear Duke compels it, but now and then—now and then—I think it a little stupid. Not to know your own name! I hope monsieur does not hope to go through life depending upon women all the time to set him at ease in his chair. You are obviously not at ease in your chair, Monsieur Soi-disant."

"It is this coat, Madame la Duchesse," Count Victor replied, looking down at the somewhat too ample sleeves and skirt. "I fell into it—"

"That is very obvious," she interrupted, with no effort to conceal her amusement.

"I fell into it by sheer accident, and it fits me like an evil habit, and under the circumstances is as inconvenient to get rid of."

"And still an excellent coat, monsieur. Let me see; has it not

228

a familiar look? Oh! I remember; it is very like one I have seen with the Duke's Chamberlain—poor fellow! Monsieur has doubtless heard of his accident, and will be glad to learn that he is out of danger, and like to be abroad in a very short time."

This was a humour touching him too closely; he replied in a monosyllable.

"Perhaps it was the coat gave me the impression that I had seen monsieur somewhere before. He reminds me, as I have said, of a compatriot who was the cause of the Chamberlain's injury."

"And is now, doubtless, in prison," added the Count, bent on giving evidence of some inventiveness of his own.

"Nay! by no means," cried the Duchess. "He was in a cell, but escaped two or three hours ago, as our watchman discovered, and is now probably far away from here."

"Ah, then," said Count Victor with nonchalance, "I daresay they will speedily recapture him. If they only knew the way with any of my compatriots it is to put a woman in his path, only she must be a woman of *esprit* and charm, and she shall engage him, I'll warrant, till the pursuit come up, even if it takes a century and the axe is at the end of it."

The Duchess coughed.

The Count hemmed.

They both broke into laughter.

"Luckily, then," said she, "he need have no anxiety on that score, should he meet the lady, for the pursuit is neither hot nor hearty. Between ourselves, monsieur, it is non-existent. If I were to meet this person we speak of, I should—but for the terror I know I should feel in his society—tell him that so long as he did not venture within a couple of miles of this castle he was perfectly safe from interference."

"And yet a dangerous man, Madame la Duchesse," said Count Victor; "and I have heard the Duke is determined on his punishment, which is of course proper—from his Grace's point of view."

"Yes, yes! I am told he is a dangerous man, a very monster. The Duke assured me of that, though, if I were to tell the truth,

Monsieur Soi-disant, I saw no evidence of it in the young gentleman when I met him last night. A most harmless fellow, I assure you. Are monsieur's feet not cold?"

She was staring at his red-heeled dancing-shoes.

"*Pas du tout!*" he replied promptly, tucking them under his chair. "These experiments in costume are a foible with me."

There was a step along the corridor outside, which made him snap off his sentence hurriedly and turn listening and apprehensive. Again the Duchess was amused.

"No, monsieur, it is not his Grace yet: you are all impatience to meet him, I see, and my poor company makes little amends for his absence; but it is as I say, he will not be back for another hour. You are interested, doubtless, in the oddities of human nature: for me, I am continually laughing at the transparency of the stratagems whereby men like my husband try to lock their hearts up like a garden and throw away the key before they come into the company of their wives. I'm *sure* your poor feet must be cold. You did not drive? Such a night of snow too! I cannot approve of your foible for dancing-shoes to wade through snow in such weather. As I was saying, you are not only the stupid sex sometimes, but a most transparent one. I will let you into a little secret that may convince you that what I say of our Count What's-his-name not being hunted is true. I see quite clearly that the Duke is delighted to have this scandal of a duel—oh! the shocking things duels, Monsieur Soi-disant!—shut up. In the forenoon he was mightily vexed with that poor Count What-do-you-call-him for a purely personal reason that I may tell you of later, but mainly because his duty compelled him to secure the other party to the—let us say, outrage. You follow, Monsieur Soi-disant?"

"*Parfaitement*, Madame la Duchesse," said Count Victor, wondering where all this led to.

"I am a foolish sentimentalist, I daresay you may think—for a person of my age (are you quite comfortable, monsieur? I fear that chair does not suit you)—I am a foolish sentimentalist, as I have said, and I may tell you I pleaded very hard for the release

230

of this luckless compatriot of yours who was then in the fosse. But, oh dear! his Grace was adamant, as is the way with dukes, at least in this country, and I pleaded in vain."

"Naturally, madame; his Grace had his duty as a good subject."

"Doubtless," said the Duchess; "but there have been occasions in history, they assure me, when good subjects have been none the less nice husbands. Monsieur can still follow me?"

Count Victor smiled and bowed again, and wished to Heaven her Grace the Duchess had a little more of the gift of expedition. He had come looking for a sword and found a sermon.

"I know I weary you," she went on complacently. "I was about to say that while the Duke desires to do his duty, even at the risk of breaking his wife's heart, it was obvious to me he was all the time sorry to have to do it, and when we heard that our Frenchman had escaped I, take my word for it, was not the only one relieved."

"I do not wonder, madame," said Montaiglon, "that the subject in this case should capitulate to—to—to the . . ."

"To the loving husband, you were about to say. La! you are too gallant, monsieur, I declare. And as a matter of fact the true explanation is less to my husband's credit and less flattering to me, for he had his own reasons."

"One generally has," reflected the Count aloud.

"Quite! and in his case they are very often mine. Dear Archie! Though he did not think I knew it, I saw clearly that he had his own reasons, as I say, to wish the Frenchman well out of the country. Now could you guess what these reasons were?"

Count Victor confessed with shame that it was beyond him.

"I will tell you. They were not his own interests, and they were not mine, that influenced him: I had not to think very hard to discover that they were the interests of the Chamberlain. I fancy his Grace knows that the less inquiry there is into this encounter the better for all concerned."

"I daresay, Madame la Duchesse," agreed Count Victor; "and yet the world speaks well of the Chamberlain, one hears."

231

" 'Woe unto you when all men speak well of you!' " quoted the Duchess sententiously.

"It only happens when the turf is in our teeth," said the Count, "and then *De mortuis* is a motto our dear friends use more as an excuse than as a moral."

"I do not like our Chamberlain, monsieur; I may frankly tell you so. I should not be surprised to learn that my husband knows a little more about him than I do, and I give you my word I know enough to consider him hateful."

"These are most delicate considerations, Madame la Duchesse," said the Count, vastly charmed by her manner but naturally desirous of the open air. Every step he heard in neighbouring lobbies, every slammed door, spoiled his attention to the lady's confidences, and he had an uneasy sense that she was not wholly unamused at his predicament, however much his friend.

"Delicate considerations, true, but I fear they do not interest Monsieur Soi-disant. How should they indeed? Gossip, monsieur, gossip! At our age, as you might say, we must be chattering. I *know* you are uncomfortable on that chair. Do, monsieur, please take another."

This time he was convinced of his first suspicion that she was having her revenge for his tactless remark to her husband, for he had not stirred at all in his chair, but had only reddened, and she had a smile at the corners of her mouth.

"At my age, Madame la Duchesse, we are quite often impertinent fools. There is, however, but one age—the truly golden. We reach it when we fall first in love, and there love keeps us. His Grace, Madame la Duchesse, is, I am sure, the happiest of men."

She was seated opposite him. Leaning forward a little, she put forth her hand in a motherly unembarrassed way, and placed it for a moment on his knee, looking into his face, smiling.

"Good boy! good boy!" she said.

And then she rose as if to hint that it was time for him to go.

"I see you are impatient; perhaps you may meet the Duke on his way back."

"Charmed, Madame la Duchesse, I assure you," said the Count with a grimace, and they both fell into laughing.

She recovered herself first to scan the shoes and coat again. "How droll!" said she. "Ah, monsieur, you are delightful in your foibles, but I wish it had looked like any other coat than Simon MacTaggart's. I have never seen his without wondering how many dark secrets were underneath the velvet. Had this coat of yours been a perfect fit, believe me I had not expected much from you of honour or of decency. Oh! there I go on chattering again, and you have said scarcely twenty words."

"Believe me, Madame la Duchesse, it is because I can find none good enough to express my gratitude," said Count Victor, making for the door.

"Pooh! Monsieur Soi-disant, a fig for your gratitude! Would you have me inhospitable to a guest who would save me even the trouble of opening my door? And that, by the way, reminds me, monsieur, that you have not even hinted at what you might be seeking his Grace for? Could it be—could it be for a better fit in coats?"

"For a mere trifle, madame, no more than my sword."

"Your sword, monsieur? I know nothing of Monsieur Soi-disant's sword, but I think I know where is one might serve his purpose."

With these words she went out of the room, hurried along the corridor, and returned in a moment or two with Count Victor's weapon, which she dragged back by its belt as if she loathed an actual contact with the thing itself.

"There!" she said, affecting a shudder. "A mouse and a rapier, they are my bitterest horrors. If you could only guess what a coward I am! Good night, monsieur, and I hope—I hope"—she laughed as she hung on the wish a moment—"I hope you will meet his Grace on the way. If so, you may tell him 'tis rather inclement weather for the night air—at his age," and she laughed again. "If you do not see him—as is possible—come back soon; look! my door bids you in your own language— *Revenez bientôt*. I am sure he will be charmed to see you; and

233

to make his delight the more, I shall never mention you were here tonight."

She went along the lobby and looked down the stair to see that the way was clear; came back and offered her hand.

"Madame la Duchesse, you are very magnanimous," he said, exceedingly grateful.

"Imprudent, rather," she corrected him.

"Magnanimity and Prudence are cousins who, praise *le bon Dieu*! never speak to each other, and the world is very much better for it." He pointed to the motto on the panel. "I may never come back, madame," said he, "but at least I shall never forget."

"*Au plaisir de vous revoir*, Monsieur Soi-disant," she said in conclusion, and went into her room and closed the door.

"Now there's a darling!" said the Duchess as she heard his footsteps softly departing. "Archie was just such another—at his age."

XXXIII

Back in Doom

The night brooded on the Highlands when Count Victor reached
the shore. Snow and darkness clotted in the clefts of the valleys
opening innumerably on the sea, but the hills held up their heads
and thought among the stars—unbending and august and pure,
knowing nothing at all of the glens and shadows. It was like a
convocation of spirits. The peaks rose everywhere white to the
brows and vastly ruminating. An ebbing tide too, so that the
strand was bare. Up on the sands where there had been that folly
of the morning the waves rolled in an ascending lisp, spilled upon
at times with gold when the decaying moon—a halbert-head
thrown angrily among Ossian's flying ghosts, the warrior clouds—
cut through them sometimes and was so reflected in the sea. The
sea was good—good to hear and smell; the flying clouds were
grateful to the eye; the stars—he praised God for the delicious
stars not in words but in an exultation of gratitude and affection,
yet the mountain-peaks were most of all his comforters.

He had run from the castle as if the devil had been at his red
heels, with that ridiculous coat flapping its heavily braided skirts
about his calves; passed through snow-smothered gardens, bor-
dered boding dark plantations of firs, leaped opposing fell-dykes
whence sheltering animals ran terrified at the apparition, and he
came out upon the seaside at the bay as one who has overcome
a nightmare and wakens to see the familiar friendly glimmer of
the bedroom fire.

A miracle! and mainly worked by a glimpse of these blanched
hills. For he knew now they were an inseparable part of his
memory of Olivia, *her* hills, *her* sheltering sentinels, the mere
sight of them Doom's orisons. Though he had thought of her so
much when he shivered in the fosse, it had too often been as

something unattainable, never to be seen again perhaps, a part of his life past and done with. An incubus rode his chest, though he never knew till now when it fled at the sight of Olivia's constant friends the mountains. Why, the girl lived! her home was round the corner there dark-jutting in the sea! He could, with some activity, be rapping at her father's door in a couple of hours!

"*Grâce de Dieu!*" said he, "let us leave trifles and go home."

It was a curious sign of his preoccupation, ever since he had escaped from his imprisonment, that he should not once have thought on where he was to fly to till this moment when the hills inspired. "Silence, thought, calm, and purity, here they are!" they seemed to tell him, and by no means unattainable. Where (now that he had time to think of it) could he possibly go tonight but to the shelter of Doom? Let the morrow decide for itself. *À demain les affaires sérieuses!* Doom and—Olivia. What eyes she had, that girl! They might look upon the assailant of her wretched lover with anything but favour; yet even in anger they were more to him than those of all the world else in love.

Be sure Count Victor was not standing all the time of these reflections shivering in the snow. He had not indulged a moment's hesitation since ever he had come out upon the bay, and he walked through the night as fast as his miserable shoes would let him.

The miles passed, he crossed the rivers that mourned through hollow arches and spread out in brackish pools along the shore. Curlews piped dolorously the very psalm of solitude, and when he passed among the hazel-woods of Strone and Achnatra, their dark recesses belled continually with owls. It was the very pick of a lover's road: no outward vision but the sombre masses of the night, the valleys of snow, and the serene majestic hills to accompany that inner sight of the woman; no sounds but that of solemn waters and the forest creatures to make the memory of her words the sweeter. A road for lovers, and he was the second of the week, though he did not know it. Only, Simon MacTaggart had come up hotfoot on his horse, a trampling conqueror (as he fancied); the Count trudged shamefully undignified through snow that came high upon the silken stockings, and long ago had made his dancing-shoes shapeless and sodden. But he did not mind that: he had a goal to make for, an ideal to cherish timidly. Once or twice he found himself with some surprise humming Gringoire's song, that surely should never go but with a light heart.

And in the fulness of time he approached the point of land from which he knew he could first see Doom's dark promontory if it were day. There his steps slowed. Somehow it seemed as if all his future fortune depended upon whether or not a light shone through the dark to greet him. Between him and the sea rolling in upon a spit of the land there was—of all things!—a herd of deer dimly to be witnessed running back and forward on the sand as in some confusion at his approach: at another time the thing should have struck him with amazement, but now he was too busy with his speculation whether Doom should gleam on him or not to study this phenomenon of the frosty wilds. He made a bargain with himself: if the isle was black, that must mean his future fortune; if a light was there, however tiny, it was the star of happy omen, it was—it was—it was several things he dared not let himself think upon for fear of immediate disappointment.

For a minute he paused as if to gather his courage and then make a dash round the point.

Ventre Dieu! Blackness! His heart ached.

And then, as most men do in similar circumstances, he decided that the test was a preposterous one. Why, faith! should he relinquish hope of everything because—

What! the light was there. Like a fool he had misjudged the distance in the darkness, and had been searching for it in the wrong place. It was so bright that it might be a star estrayed, a tiny star and venturesome, gone from the keeping of the maternal moon and wandered into the wood behind Doom to tangle in the hazel boughs. A dear star! a very gem of stars! a star more precious than all the others in that clustered sky, because it was the light of Olivia's window. A plague on all the others with their

237

twinkling search among the clouds for the little one lost! he wished it had been a darker night that he might have only this one visible.

By rights he should be weary and cold, and the day's events should trouble him; but, to tell the truth, he was in a happy exaltation all the rest of the way. Sometimes the star of hope evaded him as he followed the bending path, trees interposing: he only ran the faster to get it into his vision again, and it was his beacon up to the very walls of Doom.

The castle took possession of the night.

How odd that he should have fancied that brave tower arrogant: it was tranced in the very air of friendliness and love—the fairy residence, the moated keep of all the sweet old tales his nurse was used to tell him when he was a child in Cammercy.

And there he had a grateful memory of the ringleted middle-aged lady who had alternately whipped and kissed him, and in his night's terrors soothed him with tales. "My faith!" said he, "thou didst not think thy Perrault's 'Contes des Fées' might, twenty years after, have so close an application to a woman and a tower in misty Albion."

He walked deliberately across to the rock, went round the tower, stood a moment in the draggled arbour—the poor arbour of dead ideals. Doom, that once was child of the noisy wars, was dead as the Château d'Arques save for the light in its mistress's window. Poor old shell! and yet somehow he would not have had it otherwise.

He advanced and rapped at the door. The sound rang in the interior, and presently Mungo's shuffling steps were heard and his voice behind the door inquiring who was there.

"A friend," answered Count Victor, humouring the little old man's fancy for affairs of arms.

"A friend!" repeated Mungo with contempt. "A man on a horse has aye hunders o' frien's in the gutter, as Annapla says, and it wad need to be somethin' rarer to get into Doom i' the mirk o' nicht. I opened the door to a frien' the ither nicht, and he gripped me by the craig and fair choked me afore I could cry a barley."

"*Peste!* Do not flatter my English so much as to tell me you do not recognise Count Victor's accent through a door."

"Lord keep 's!" cried Mungo, hastily drawing his bolts. "Hae ye changed ye'r mind already and left the inns? It's a guid thing for your wife ye're no marrit, or she wad be the sorry woman wi' sic a shiftin' man."

His astonishment was even greater when Count Victor stood before him a ludicrous figure with his too ample coat.

"Dinna tell me ye hae come through the snaw this nicht like that!" he cried incredulous, holding up his candle the better to examine the figure.

Count Victor laughed, and for an answer simply thrust forth a sopping foot to his examination.

"Man, ye must hae been hot on't!" said the servant, shaking his cowled head till the tassel danced above his temple. "Ye'r shoon's fair steeped wi' water. Water's an awfu' thing to rot ye'r boots: I aye said if it rotted ane's boots that way, whit wad it no' dae to ane's stamach? Oh, sirs! sirs! this is becomin' the throng hoose, wi' comin's and goin's and raps and roars and collieshangies o' a' kin's. If it wasna me was the canny gaird o't it's Himsel' wad hae to flit for the sake o' his nicht's sleep."

"You behold, Mungo, the daw in borrowed plumes," said Count Victor as the door was being barred again. "I hope the daw felt more comfortable than I do in mine," and he ruefully surveyed his apparel. "Does Master Mungo recognise these peacock feathers?"

Mungo scanned the garment curiously.

"It's gey like ane I've seen on a bigger man," he answered.

"And a better, perhaps, thought my worthy Mungo. I remember me that our peacock was a diplomatist and had a huge interest in your delightful stories."

A movement of Mungo's made him turn to see the Baron standing behind him a little bewildered at this apparition.

"*Failte!*" said the Baron, "and I fancy you would be none the waur, as we say, of the fireside."

He went before him into the *salle*, taking Mungo's candle.

239

Mungo was despatched for Annapla, and speedily the silent abigail of visions was engaged upon that truly Gaelic courtesy, the bathing of the traveller's feet. The Baron considerately made no inquiries: if it was a caprice of Count Victor's to venture in dancing-shoes and a borrowed jacket through dark snow-swept roads, it was his own affair. And the Count was so much interested in the new cheerfulness of his host (once so saturnine and melancholy) that he left his own affairs unmentioned for a while as the woman worked. It was quite a light-hearted recluse this, compared with that he had left a week ago.

"I am not surprised you found yon place dull," at the last hazarded the Baron.

"*Comment?*"

"Down-by, I mean. I'm glad myself always to get home out of it at this season. When the fishers are there it's all my fancy, but when it does not smell of herring, the stench of lawyers' sheepskins gets on the top and is mighty offensive to any man that has had muckle to do with them."

"Dull!" repeated Count Victor, now comprehending; "I have crowded more experience into the past four-and-twenty hours than I might meet in a month anywhere east of Calais. I have danced with a duchess, fought a stupid duel, with a town looking on for all the world as if it were a performance in a circus with lathen weapons, moped in a dungeon, broken through the same, stolen a coat, tramped through miles of snow in a pair of pantoufles, forgotten to pay the bill at the inn, and lost my baggage and my reputation—which latter I swear no one in these parts will be glad to pick up for his own use. Baron, I'll be shot if your country is not bewitched. My faith! what happenings since I came here expecting to be killed with *ennui*! I protest I shall buy a Scots estate and ask all my friends over here to see real life. Only they must have good constitutions; I shall insist on them having good constitutions. And there's another thing—it necessitates that they must have so kind a friend as Monsieur le Baron and so hospitable a house as Doom to fall back on when their sport comes to a laughable termination, as mine has done tonight."

"Ah! then you have found your needle in the haystack after all?" cried Doom, vastly interested.

"Found the devil!" cried Montaiglon, a shade of vexation in his countenance, for he had not once that day had a thought of all that had brought him into Scotland. "The haystack must be stuck full of needles like the bran of a pin-cushion."

"And this one, who is not the particular needle named Drimdarroch?"

"I shall give you three guesses, M. le Baron."

Doom reflected, pulled out his nether lip with his fingers, looking hard at his guest.

"It is not the Chamberlain?"

"*Peste!*" thought the Count, "can the stern unbending parent have relented? You are quite right," he said; "no other. But it is not a matter of the most serious importance. I lost my coat and the gentleman lost a little blood. I have the best assurances that he will be on foot again in a week or two, by which time I hope— at all events I expect—to be out of all danger of being invited to resume the entertainment."

"In the meantime here's Doom, yours—so long as it is mine— while it's your pleasure to bide in it if you fancy yourself safe from molestation," said the Baron.

"As to that I think I may be tranquil. I have, there too, the best assurances that the business will be hushed up."

"So much the better, though in any case this seems to have marred your real engagements here in the matter of Drimdarroch."

Count Victor's turn it was to feel vexation now. He pulled his moustache and reddened. "As to that, Baron," said he, "I pray you not to despise me, for I have to confess that my warmth in the mission that brought me here has abated sadly. You need not ask me why. I cannot tell you. As for me and my affair, I have not forgotten, nor am I likely wholly to forget; but your haystack is as *difficile* as you promised it should be, and—there are divers other considerations. It necessitates that I go home. There shall be some raillery at my expense, doubtless—*Ciel!*

how Louis my cousin will laugh!—but no matter."

He spoke a little abstractedly, for he saw a delicate situation approaching. He was sure to be asked—once Annapla's service was over—what led to the encounter, and to give the whole story frankly involved Olivia's name unpleasantly in a vulgar squabble. He saw for the first time that he had been wholly unwarranted in taking the defence of the Baron's interests into his own hands. Could he boldly intimate that in his opinion jealousy of himself had been the spring of the Chamberlain's midnight attacks on the castle of Doom? That were preposterous! And yet that seemed the only grounds that would justify his challenging the Chamberlain.

When Annapla was gone then Doom got the baldest of histories. He was encouraged to believe that all this busy day of adventure had been due to a simple quarrel after a game of cards, and where he should have preferred a little more detail he had to content himself with a humorous narrative of the escape, the borrowing of the coat, and the interview with the Duchess.

"And now with your permission, Baron, I shall go to bed?" at last said Count Victor. "I shall sleep tonight like a *sabot*. I am, I know, the boldest of beggars for your grace and kindness. It seems I am fated in this country to make free, not only with my enemy's coat, but with my dear friend's domicile as if it were an inn. Tomorrow, Baron, I shall make my dispositions. The coat can be returned to its owner none the worse for my use of it, but I shall not so easily be able to square accounts with you."

XXXIV

In Days of Storm

In a rigorous privacy of storm that lasted many days after his return, and cut Doom wholly off from the world at large, Count Victor spent what but for several considerations would have been—perhaps indeed they really were—among the happiest moments of his life. It was good in that tumultuous weather, when tempests snarled and frosts fettered the countryside, and the sea continually wrangled round the rock of Doom, to look out on the inclemency from windows where Olivia looked out too. She used to come and stand beside him, timidly perhaps at first, but by-and-by with no self-consciousness. Her sleeve would touch his, sometimes indeed her shoulder must press against his arm and little strands of her hair almost blow against his lips, as in the narrow apertures of the tower they watched the wheeling birds from the outer ocean. For these birds she had what was little less than a passion. To her they represented the unlimited world of liberty and endeavour; at sight of them something stirred in her that was the gift of all the wandering years of that old Ulysses, her grandfather, to whom the beckoning lights of ships at sea were irresistible; and though she doted on the glens of her nativity, she had the spirit that invests every hint of distant places and far-off happenings with magic parts.

She seemed content, and yet not wholly happy: he could hear her sometimes sigh, as he thought, from a mere wistfulness that had the illimitable spaces of the sea, the peopled isles and all their mystery, for background. To many of the birds that beat and cried about the place she gave names, investing them with histories, recounting humorously their careers. And it was odd that however far she sent them in her fancy—to the distant Ind, to the vexed Pole itself—with joy in their travelling, she assumed that their greatest joy was when they found themselves at Doom. The world was a place to fare forth in as far as you could, only to give you the better zest for Doom on your return.

This pleased her father hugely, but it scarcely tallied with the views of one who had fond memories of a land where sang the nightingale in its season, and roads were traversable in the wildest winter weather: still Count Victor was in no mood to question it.

He was, save in rare moments of unpleasant reflection, supremely happy, thrilling to that accidental contact, paling at the narrow margins whereby her hair escaped conferring on him a delirium. He could stand at a window all day pretending interest in the monotonous hills and empty sea, only that he might keep her there too and indulge himself upon her eyes. They—so eager, deep, or busied with the matters of her thoughts—were enough for a common happiness; a debauch of it was in the contact of her arm.

And yet something in this complacence of hers bewildered him. Here, if you please, was a woman who but the other night (as it were) was holding clandestine meetings with Simon MacTaggart, and loving him to that extent that she defied her father. She could not but know that this foreigner had done his worst to injure her in the inner place of her affections, and yet she was to him more friendly than she had been before. Several times he was on the point of speaking on the subject. Once, indeed, he made a playful allusion to the flautist of the bower that was provocative of no more than a reddened cheek and an interlude of silence. But tacitly the lover was a theme for strict avoidance. Not even the Baron had a word to say on that, and they were numberless the topics they discussed in this enforced sweet domesticity.

A curious household! How it found provisions in these days Mungo alone could tell. The little man had his fishing-lines out continually, his gun was to be heard in neighbouring thickets that seemed from the island inaccessible, and when gun and line failed him it was perhaps not wholly wanting his persuasion that kain fowls came from the hamlet expressly for "her ladyship" Olivia. In pauses of the wind he and Annapla were to be heard in other quarters of the house in clamant conversation—otherwise it had seemed to Count Victor that Doom was left, an enchanted castle, to him and Olivia alone. For the father relapsed anew into his old strange melancholies, dozing over his books, indulging feint and riposte in the chapel overhead, or gazing moodily along the imprisoned coast. That he was free to dress now as he chose in his beloved tartan entertained him only briefly; obviously half the joy of his former recreations in the chapel had been due to the fact that they were clandestine: now that he could wear what he chose indoors, he pined that he could not go into the deer-haunted woods and the snowy highways in the *breacan* as of old. But that was not his only distress, Count Victor was sure.

"What accounts for your father's melancholy?" he had the boldness one day to ask Olivia.

They were at the window together, amused at the figure Mungo presented, as, with an odd travesty of the soldier's strategy, and all unseen as he fancied, he chased a fowl round the narrow confines of the garden bent upon its slaughter.

"And you do not know the reason for that?" she asked, with her humour promptly clouded, and a loving and pathetic glance over her shoulder at the figure bent beside the fire. "What is the dearest thing to you?"

She could have put no more embarrassing question to Count Victor, and it was no wonder he stammered in his reply.

"The dearest," he repeated. "Ah! well—well—the dearest, Mademoiselle Olivia; *ma foi!* there are so many things."

"Yes, yes," she said impatiently, "but only one or two are at the heart's core." She saw him smile at this, and reddened. "Oh, how stupid I am to ask that of a stranger! I did not mean a lady—if there is a lady."

"There *is* a lady," said Count Victor, twisting the fringe of her shawl that had come of itself into his fingers as she turned.

A silence followed: not even he, so versed in all the evidence

245

of love or coquetry, could have seen a quiver to betray her even if he had thought to look for it.

"I am the one," said she at length, "who will wish you well in that; but after her—after this—this lady—what is it that comes closest?"

"What but my country!" cried he, with a surging sudden memory of France.

"To be sure!" she acquiesced, "your country! I am not wondering at that. And ours is the closest to the core of cores in us that have not perhaps so kind a country as yours, but still must love it when it is most cruel. We are like the folks I have read of—they were the Greeks who travelled so far among other clans upon the trade of war, and bound to burst in tears when they came after strange hills and glens to the sight of the same sea that washed the country of their infancy. 'Thalatta!'—was it not that they cried? When I read the story first in school in Edinburgh, I cried, myself, 'Lochfinne!' and thought I heard the tide rumbling upon this same rock. It is for that; it is because we must be leaving here my father is sad."

Here indeed was news!

"Leaving!" said Count Victor in astonishment.

"It is so. My father has been robbed; his people have been foolish; it is not a new thing in the Highlands of Scotland, Count Victor. You must not be thinking him a churl to be moping and leaving you to my poor entertainment, for it is ill to keep the pipes in tune when one is drying tears."

"Where will you go?" asked Count Victor, disturbed at the tidings and the distress she so bravely struggled to conceal.

"Where? indeed!" said Olivia. "That I cannot tell you yet. But the world is wide, and it is strange if there is any spot of it where we cannot find some of our own Gaelic people who have been flitting for a generation, taking the world for their pillow. What is it that will not come to an end? My sorrow! the story on our door down there has been preparing me for this since ever I was a bairn. My great-great-grandfather was the wise man and the far-seeing when he carved it there—'Man, Behauld the

End of All. Be Nocht Wiser than the Hiest. Hope in God!'" She struggled courageously with her tears that could not wholly be restrained, and there and then he could have gathered her into his arms. But he must keep himself in bounds and twist the fringes of her shawl.

"Ah, Olivia," said he, "you will die for the sight of home."

At that she dashed her hand across her eyes and boldly faced him, smiling.

"That would be a shameful thing in a Baron's daughter," said she. "No, indeed! when we must rise and go away, here is the woman who will go bravely! We live not in glens, in this house nor in that, but in the hearts that love us, and where my father is and friends are to be made, I think I can be happy yet. Look at the waves there, and the snow and the seabirds! All these are in other places as well as here."

"But not the same, but not the same! Here I swear I could live content myself."

"What!" said she, smiling, and the rogue a moment dancing in her eyes. "No, no, Count Victor; to this you must be born like the stag in the corrie and the seal on the rock. We are a simple people, and a poor people—worse fortune!—poor and proud. Your world is different from ours, and there you will have friends that think of you."

"And you," said he, all aglow in passion but with a face of flint, "you are leaving those behind that love you too."

This time he watched her narrowly: she gave no sign.

"There are the poor people in the clachan there," said she; "some of them will not forget me, I am hoping, but that is all. We go. It is good for us, perhaps. Something has been long troubling my father more than the degradation of the clans and all these law pleas that Petullo has now brought to the bitter end. He is proud, and he is what is common in the Highlands when the heart is sore—he is silent. You must not think it is for myself I am vexing to leave Doom Castle; it is for him. Look! do you see the dark spot on the side of the hill yonder up at Ardno? That is the yew-tree in the churchyard where my mother,

247

his wife, lies: it is no wonder that at night sometimes he goes out to look at the hills, for the hills are over her there and over the generations of his people in the same place. I never knew my mother, *mothruaigh*! but he remembers, and it is the hundred dolours (as we say) for him to part. For me I have something of the grandfather in me, and would take the seven bens for it, and the seven glens, and the seven mountain moors, if it was only for the sake of the adventure, though I should always like to think that I would come again to these places of heredity."

And through all this never a hint of Simon MacTaggart! Could there be any other conclusion than the joyous one—it made his heart bound!—that that affair was at an end? And yet how should he ascertain the truth about a matter so close upon his heart? He put his pride in his pocket and went down that afternoon with the Chamberlain's coat in his hands. There was a lull in the wind, and the servitor was out of doors caulking the little boat, the argosy of poor fortunes, which had been drawn up from the menacing tides so that its prow obtruded on the half-hearted privacy of the lady's bower. Deer were on the shore, one sail was on the blue of the sea, a long way off, a triumphant flash of sun lit up the innumerable glens. A pleasant interlude of weather, and yet Mungo was in what he called, himself, a tirravee. He was honestly becoming impatient with this undeparting foreigner, mainly because Annapla was day by day the more insistent that he had not come wading into Doom without boots entirely in vain, and that her prediction was to be fulfilled.

"See! Mungo," said the Count; "the daw, if my memory fails not, had his plumes pecked off him, but I seem fated to retain my borrowed feathers until I pluck myself. Is it that you can have them at the first opportunity restored to our connoisseur in *contes*—your friend the Chamberlain? It comes to occur to me that the gentleman's wardrobe may be as scanty as my own, and the absence of his coat may be the reason, more than my unfortunate pricking with a bodkin, for his inexplicable absence from—from—the lady's side."

Mungo had heard of the duel, of course; it was the under-

248

standing in Doom that all news was common property inasmuch as it was sometimes almost the only thing to pass round.

"Humph!" said he. "It wasna' sae ill to jag a man that had a wound already."

"Expiscate, good Master Mungo," said Count Victor, wondering. "What wound already? You speak of the gentleman's susceptible heart perhaps?"

"I speak o' naethin' o' the kind, but o' the man's airm. Ye ken fine ye gied him a push wi' your whinger that first night he cam' here wi' his fencible gang frae the Maltland and play-acted Black Andy o' Arroquhar."

"The devil!" cried Count Victor. "I wounded somebody, certainly, but till now I had no notion it might be the gentleman himself. Well, let me do him the justice to say he made rather pretty play with his weapon on the sands, considering he was wounded. And so, honest Mungo, the garrison was not really taken by surprise that night you found yourself plucked out like a periwinkle from your wicket? As frankness is in fashion, I may say that for a while I gave you credit for treason to the house, and treason now it seems to have been, though not so black as I thought. It was MacTaggart who asked you to open the door?"

"Wha else? A bonny-like cantrip! Nae doot it was because I tauld him Annapla's prophecy aboot a man wi' the bare feet. The deil's buckie! Ye kent yersel' brawly wha it was."

"I, Master Mungo! Faith, not I!"

Mungo looked incredulous.

"And what ails her ladyship, for she kent? I'll swear she kent the next day, though I took guid care no' to say cheep."

"I daresay you are mistaken there, my good Mungo."

"Mistaken! No me! It wasna' a'thegither in a tantrum o' an ordinar' kind she broke her tryst wi' him the very nicht efter ye left for the inns doon-by. At onyrate, if she didna' ken then she kens noo, I'll warrant."

"Not so far as I am concerned, certainly."

Mungo looked incredulous. That any one should let go the chance of conveying so rare a piece of gossip to persons so immediately concerned was impossible of belief. "Na, na," said he, shaking his head; "she has every word o't, or her faither at least, and that's the same thing. But shoon or nae shoon, yon's the man for my money!"

"Again he has my felicitations," said Count Victor, with a good-humour unfailing. Indeed he could afford to be good-humoured if this were true. So here was the explanation of Olivia's condescension, her indifference to her lover's injury, of which her father could not fail to have apprised her even if Mungo had been capable of a miracle and held his tongue. The Chamberlain, then, was no longer in favour! Here was joy! Count Victor could scarce contain himself. How many women would have been flattered at the fierceness of devotion implied in a lover's readiness to commit assassination out of sheer jealousy of a supposititious rival in her affections? But Olivia—praise *le bon Dieu*!—was not like that.

He thrust the coat into Mungo's hands and went hurriedly up to his room to be alone with his thoughts, that he feared might show themselves plainly in his face if he met either the lady or her father, and there for the first time had a memory of Cécile—some odd irrelevance of a memory—in which she figured in a masque in a Paris garden. Good God! that he should have failed to see it before: this Cécile had been an actress, as, he told himself, were most of her sex he had hitherto encountered, and 'twas doubtful if he once had touched her soul. Olivia had shown him now, in silences, in sighs, in some unusual *aura* of sincerity that was round her like the innocence of infancy, that what he thought was love a year ago was but its drossy elements. Seeking the first woman in the eyes of the second, he had found the perfect lover there!

XXXV

A *Damnatory Document*

Mungo took the coat into the castle kitchen, the true arcanum of Doom, where he and Annapla solved the domestic problems that in later years had not been permitted to disturb the mind of the master or his daughter. An enormous fireplace, arched like a bridge, and poorly enough fed nowadays compared with its gluttony in those happier years of his continual bemoaning, when plenty kept the spit perpetually at work, if it were only for the good of the beggars who blackened the road from the Lowlands, had a handful of peat in its centre to make the yawning orifice the more pathetic to eyes that had seen the flames leap there. Everywhere the evidence of the old abundant days—the rusting spit itself, the idle battery of cuisine, long rows of shining covers. Annapla, who was assumed to be true tutelary genius of these things, but in fact was beholden to the martial mannikin of Fife for inspiration and aid with the simplest of ragouts, though he would have died sooner than be suspected of the unsoldierly art of cookery,—Annapla was in one of her trances. Her head was swathed mountainously in shawls; her wild, black, lambent eyes had the look of distant contemplation.

"Lord keep's!" said Mungo, entering, "what are ye doverin' on noo? Wauken up, ye auld bitch, and gie this coat a dicht. D'ye ken wha's ocht it? It belangs to a gentleman that's no' like noo to get but this same and the back-o'-my-haun'-to-ye oot o' Doom Castle."

She took the coat and brushed it in a lethargy, with odd, unintelligible chanting.

"Nane o' your warlock canticles!" cried Mungo. "Ye gied the lassie to the man that cam' withouten boots—sorrow be on the bargain! And if it's castin' a spell on the coat ye are, I'll raither clean't mysel'."

251

With that he seized the garment from her and lustily applied himself.

"A bonny-like hostler-wife ye'll mak'," said he. "And few'll come to Mungo Byde's hostelry if his wife's to be eternally in a deevilish dwaam, concocting Hielan' spells when she should be stirring at the broth. No' that I can blame ye muckle for a want o' the uptak' in what pertains to culinairy airts; for what hae ye seen here since ye cam' awa' frae the rest o' the drove in Arroquhar but lang kail, and oaten brose, and mashlum bannocks? Oh! sirs, sirs!—I've seen the day!"

Annapla emerged from her trance, and ogled him with an amusing admiration.

"And noo it's a' by wi't; it's the end o' the auld ballant," went on the little man. "I've kent auld Doom in times o' rowth and splendour, and noo I'm spared to see't rouped, the laird a dyvour and a hameless wanderer ower the face o' the earth. He's gaun abroad, he tells me, and ettles to sit doon aboot Dunkerque in France. It's but fair, maybe, that whaur his forbears squandered he should gang wi' the little that's to the fore. I mind o' his faither gaun awa' at the last hoved up, a fair Jeshurun, his een like to loup oot o' his heid wi' fat, and comin' back a pooked craw frae the dicing and the drink, nae doot among the scatter-brained white cockades. Whatna shilpit man's this that Leevie's gotten for her new jo? As if I dinna see through them! The tawpie's ta'en the gee at the Factor because he played yon ploy wi' his lads frae the Maltland barracks, and this Frenchy's ower the lugs in love wi' her, I can see as plain as Cowal, though it's a shameless thing to say't. He's gotten gey far ben in a michty short time. Ye're aye saying them that come unsent for should sit unserved; but wha sent for this billy oot o' France? and wha has been sae coothered up as he has since he cam' here? The Baron doesnae ken the shifts that you and me's been put to for to save his repitation. Mony a lee I tauld doon there i' the clachan to soother them oot o' butter and milk and eggs, and a bit hen at times; mony a time I hae gi'en my ain denner to thae gangrel bodies frae Glencroe sooner nor hae them think there was nae rowth o' vivers whaur they never were sent awa' empty-haunded afore. I aye keepit my he'rt up wi' the notion that him doon-by the coat belangs to wad hae made a match o't, and saved us a' frae beggary. But there's an end o' that, sorry am I. And sorry may you be, ye auld runt, to hear't, for he's been the guid enough friend to me; and there wad never hae been the Red Sodger Tavern for us if it wasnae for his interest in a man that has aye kep' up the airmy."

Annapla seemed to find the dialect of Fife most pleasing and melodious. She listened to his monologue with approving smiles, and, sitting on a stool, cowered within the arch, warming her hands at the apology for a flame.

"Wha the deevil could hae tauld her it was the lad himsel' was here that nicht wi' his desperate chiels frae the barracks? It couldna' be you, for I didna' tell ye mysel' for fear ye wad bluitter it oot and spoil his chances. She kent onyway, and it was for no ither reason she gie'd him the route, unless—unless she had a notion o' the Frenchman frae the first glisk o' him. There's no accoontin' for tastes: clap a bunnet on a tawtie-bogle, wi' a cock to the ae side that's kin' o' knowin', and ony woman'll jump at his neck, though ye micht pap peas through the place whaur his wame should be. The Frenchy's no' my taste onyway; and noo, there's Sim! Just think o' Sim gettin' the dirty gae-bye frae a glaikit lassie hauf his age; and no' his equal in the three parishes, wi' a leg to tak' the ee o' a hale dancin'-school, and auld Knapdale's money comin' till him whenever Knapdale's gane, and I'm hearin' he's in the deid-thraws already. Ill fa' the day fotch the Frenchy! The race o' them never brocht ocht in my generation to puir Scotland worth a bodle, unless it micht be a new fricassee to fyle a stamach wi'. I'm fair bate to ken what this Coont wants here. 'Drimdarroch,' says he, but that's fair rideeculous, unless it was the real auld bauld Drimdarroch, and that's nae ither than Doom. I winna wonder if he heard o' Leevie ere ever he left the France."

Annapla began to drowse at the fire. He saw her head nod, and came round with the coat in his hand to confirm his suspicion that she was about to fall asleep. Her eyes were shut.

"Wauken up, Luckie!" he cried, disgusted at this absence of appreciation. "What ails the body? Ye're into your damnable dwaam again. There's them that's gowks enough to think ye're seein' Sichts, when it's neither mair nor less than he'rt-sick laziness, and I was ance ane o' them mysel'. Ye hinnae as muckle o' the Sicht as wad let ye see when Leevie was makin' a gowk o' ye to gar ye hang oot signals for her auld jo. A bonny-like brewster-wife ye'll mak', I warrant!" He tapped her, not unkindly, on the head with the back of his brush, and brought her to earth again.

"Are ye listenin', ye auld runt?" said he. "I'm goin' doon to the toon i' the aifternoon wi' this braw coat and money for Monsher's inn accoont, and if ye're no' mair wide-awake by that time, there's de'il the cries'll gae in wi' auld MacNair."

The woman laughed, not at all displeased with herself nor with her rough admirer, and set to some trivial office. Mungo was finished with the coat; he held it out at arm's-length, admiring its plenitude of lace, and finally put off his own hodden garment that he might try on the Chamberlain's.

"God!" said he, "it fits me like an empty ale-cask. I thocht the Coont looked gey like a galoshan in't, but I maun be the bonny doo mysel'. And I'm no' that wee neither, for it's ticht aboot the back."

Annapla thought her diminutive admirer adorable; she stood raptly gazing on him, with her dish-clout dripping on the floor.

"I wonder if there's no' a note or twa o' the New Bank i' the pouches," said Mungo, and began to search. Something in one of the pockets rustled to the touch, and with a face of great expectancy he drew forth what proved to be a letter. The seal was broken, there was neither an address nor the superscription of the writer; the handwriting was a faint Italian, betokening a lady,—there was no delicate scrupulosity about the domestic, and the good Mungo unhesitatingly indulged himself.

"It's no' exactly a note," said he, contracting his brows above the document. Not for the first time Annapla regretted her inability to read, as she craned over his shoulder to see what

254

evidently created much astonishment in her future lord.

"Weel, that bates a'!" he cried when he had finished, and he turned, visibly flushing, even through his apple-red complexion, to see Annapla at his shoulder.

"It's a guid thing the Sicht's nae use for English write," said he, replacing the letter carefully in the pocket whence it had come. "This'll gae back to himsel', and naebody be nane the wiser o't for Mungo Byde."

For half an hour he busied himself with aiding Annapla at the preparation of dinner, suddenly become silent as a consequence of what the letter had revealed to him, and then he went out to prepare his boat for his trip to town.

Annapla did not hesitate a moment: she fished out the letter and hurried with it to her master, less, it must be owned, from a desire to inform him, than from a womanly wish to share a secret that had apparently been of the greatest interest to Mungo.

Doom took it from her hands in an abstraction, for he was whelmed with the bitter prospect of imminent farewells: he carelessly scanned the sheet with half-closed eyes, and was well through perusing it before he realised that it had any interest. He began at the beginning again, caught the meaning of a sentence, sat bolt upright in the chair where Annapla had found him lolling, and finished with eagerness and astonishment.

Where had she got this? She hesitated to tell him that it had been pilfered from the owner's pocket, and intimated that she had picked it up outside.

"Good woman," said he in Gaelic, "you have picked up a fortune. It would have saved me much tribulation, and yourself some extra work, if you had happened to pick it up a month ago!"

He hurried to Olivia.

"My dear," he said, "I have come upon the oddest secret."

His daughter reddened to the roots of her hair, and fell to trembling with inexplicable shame. He did not observe it.

"It is that you have got out of the grip of the gled. Yon person was an even blacker villain than I guessed."

"Oh!" she said, apparently much relieved, "and is that your secret? I have no wonder left in me for any new display of wickedness from Simon MacTaggart."

"Listen," he said, and read her the damnatory document. She flushed, she trembled, she wellnigh wept with shame; but "Oh!" she cried at the end, "is he not the noble man?"

"The noble man!" cried Doom at such an irrelevant conclusion. "Are you out of your wits, Olivia?"

She stammered an explanation. "I do not mean—I do not mean—this—wretch that is exposed there, but Count Victor. He has known it all along."

"H'm," said Doom. "I fancy he has. That was, like enough, the cause of the duel. But I do not think it was noble at all that he should keep silent upon a matter so closely affecting the happiness of your whole life."

Olivia saw this too, when helped to it, and bit her lip. It was, assuredly, not right that Count Victor, in the possession of such secrets as this letter revealed, should allow her to throw herself away on the villain there portrayed.

"He may have some reason we cannot guess," she said, and thought of one that made her heart beat wildly.

"No reason but a Frenchman's would let me lose my daughter to a scamp out of a pure punctilio. I can scarcely believe that he knew all that is in this letter. And you, my dear, you never guessed any more than I that these attacks under cover of night were the work of Simon MacTaggart."

"I must tell you the truth, father," said Olivia. "I have known it since the second, and that it was that turned me. I learned from the button that Count Victor picked up on the stair, for I recognised it as his. I knew—I knew—and yet I wished to keep a doubt of it; I felt it so, and still would not confess it to myself that the man I loved—the man I thought I loved—was no better than a robber."

"A robber indeed! I thought the man bad; I never liked his eye, and less his tongue, that was ever too plausible. Praise God, my dear! that he's found out."

XXXVI

Love

It was hours before Count Victor could trust himself and his tell-tale countenance before Olivia, and as he remained in an unaccustomed seclusion for the remainder of the day, she naturally believed him cold, though a woman with a fuller experience of his sex might have come to a different conclusion. Her misconception, so far from being dispelled when he joined her and her father in the evening, was confirmed, for his natural gaiety was gone, and an emotional constraint, made up of love, dubiety, and hope, kept him silent even in the precious moments when Doom retired to his reflections and his book, leaving them at the other end of the room alone. Nothing had been said about the letter; the Baron kept his counsel on it for a more fitting occasion, and though Olivia, who had taken its possession, turned it over many times in her pocket, its presentation involved too much boldness on her part to be undertaken in an impulse. The evening passed with inconceivable dulness; the gentleman was taciturn to clownishness; Mungo, who had come in once or twice to replenish fires and snuff candles, could not but look at them with wonder, for he plainly saw two foolish folks in a common misunderstanding.

He went back to the kitchen crying out his contempt for them.

"If yon's coortin'," he said, "it's the drollest I ever clapt een on! The man micht be a carven image, and Leevie no better nor a shilfy in the pook. I hope she disnae rue her change o' mind alreadys, for I'll warrant there was nane o' yon blateness aboot Sim MacTaggart, and it's no' what the puir lassie's been used to."

But these were speculations beyond the sibyl of his odd adoration: Annapla was too intent upon her own elderly love-affairs to be interested in those upstairs.

And upstairs, by now, a topic had at last come on between the silent pair that did not make for love or cheerfulness. The Baron had retired to his own room in the rear of the castle, and they had begun to talk of the departure that was now fixed for a date made imminent through the pressure of Petullo. Where were they bound for but France? Doom had decided upon Dunkerque because he had a half-brother there in a retirement compelled partly for political reasons Count Victor could appreciate.

"France!" he cried, delighted. "This is ravishing news indeed, Mademoiselle Olivia!"

"Yes?" she answered dubiously, reddening a little, and wondering why he should particularly think it so.

"*Ma foi!* it is," he insisted heartily. "I had the most disturbing visions of your wandering elsewhere. I declare I saw my dear Baron and his daughter immured in some pestilent Lowland burgh town, moping mountain creatures among narrow streets, in dreary tenements, with glimpse of neither sea nor tree to compensate them for pleasures lost. But France!—Mademsoielle has given me an exquisite delight. For, figure you! France is not so vast that friends may not meet there often—if one were so greatly privileged—and every roadway in it leads to Dunkerque— and—I should dearly love to think of you as, so to speak, in my neighbourhood, among the people I esteem. It is not your devoted Highlands, this France, Mademoiselle Olivia, but, believe me, it has its charms. You shall not have the mountains— there I am distressed for you—nor yet the rivulets; and you must dispense with the mists; but there is ever the consolation of an air that is like wine in the head, and a frequent sun. France, indeed! *Je suis ravi!* I little thought when I heard of this end to the old home of you that you were to make the new one in my country: how could I guess, when anticipating my farewell to the Highlands of Scotland, that I should have such good company to the shore of France?"

"Then you are returning now?" asked Olivia, her affectation of indifference just a little overdone.

In very truth he had not, as yet, so determined; but he boldly lied like a lover.

" 'Twas my intention to return at once. I cannot forgive myself for being so long away from my friends there."

Olivia had a bodice of paduasoy that came low upon her shoulders and showed a spray of jasmine in the cleft of her rounded breasts, which heaved with what Count Victor could not but perceive was some emotion. Her eyes were like a stag's, and they evaded him; she trifled with the pocket of her gown.

"Ah," she said, "it is natural that you should weary here in this sorry place and wish to get back to the people you know. There will be many that have missed you."

He laughed at that.

"A few—a few, perhaps," he said. "Clancarty has doubtless often sought me vainly for the trivial coin: some butterflies in the *coulisse* of the playhouse will have missed my pouncet-box; but I swear there are few in Paris who would be inconsolable if Victor de Montaiglon never set foot on the *trottoir* again. It is my misfortune, mademoiselle, to have a multitude of friends so busy with content and pleasure—who will blame them?—that an absentee makes little difference; and as for relatives, not a single one except the Baroness de Chenier, who is large enough to count as double."

"And there will be—there will be the lady," said Olivia, with a poor attempt at raillery.

For a moment he failed to grasp her allusion.

"Of course, of course," said he hastily; "I hope, indeed, to see *her* there." He felt an exaltation simply at the prospect. To see her there! To have a host's right to bid welcome to his land this fair wild-flower that had blossomed on rocks of the sea, un-spoiled and unsophisticated!

The jasmine stirred more obviously: it was fastened with a topaz brooch that had been her mother's, and had known of old a similar commotion; she became diligent with a book.

It was then there happened the thing that momentarily seemed a blow of fate to both of them. But for Mungo's voice at intervals in the kitchen, the house was wholly still, and through the calm winter night there came the opening bars of a melody, played very softly by Sim MacTaggart's flageolet. At first it seemed incredible—a caprice of imagination—and they listened for some moments speechless. Count Victor was naturally the least disturbed: this unlooked-for entertainment meant the pleasant fact that the Duchess had been nowise over-sanguine in her estimate of the Chamberlain's condition. Here was another possible homicide off his mind: the Gaelic frame was capable, obviously, of miraculous recuperation. That was but his first and momentary thought; the next was less pleasing, for it seemed not wholly unlikely now that after all Olivia and this man were still on an unchanged footing, and Mungo's sowing of false hopes was like to bring a bitter reaping of regretful disillusions. As for Olivia, she was first a flame and then an icicle. Her face scorched; her whole being seemed to take a sudden wild alarm. Count Victor dared scarcely look at her, fearing to learn his doom or spy on her embarrassment until her first alarm was over, when she drew her lips together tightly and assumed a frigid resolution. She made no other movement.

A most bewitching flageolet! It languished on the night with an o'ermastering appeal, sweet inexpressibly and melting, the air unknown to one listener at least, but by him enviously confessed a very siren spell. He looked at Olivia, and saw that she intended to ignore it.

"Orpheus has recovered," he ventured with a smile.

She stared in front of her with no response; but the jasmine rose and fell, and her nostrils were dilated. Her face had turned from the red of her first surprise to the white of suppressed indignation. The situation was inconceivably embarrassing for both: now his bolt was shot, and unless she cared to express herself, he could not venture to allude to it again, though a whole orchestra augmented the efforts of the artist in the bower.

By-and-by there came a pause in the music, and she spoke.

"It is the blackest of affronts, this," was her comment, that seemed at once singular and sweet to her hearer.

"*D'accord,*" said Count Victor, but that was to himself. He was quite agreed that the Chamberlain's attentions, though well meant, were not for a good woman to plume herself on.

The flageolet spoke again—that curious unfinished air. Never before had it seemed so haunting and mysterious—a mingling of reproaches and command. It barely reached them where they sat together listening, a fairy thing and fascinating, yet it left the woman cold. And soon the serenade entirely ceased. Olivia recovered herself; Count Victor was greatly pleased.

"I hope that is the end of it," she said with a sigh of relief.

"Alas, poor Orpheus! he returns to Thrace, where perhaps Madame Petullo may lead the ladies in tearing him to pieces!"

"Once that hollow reed bewitched me, I fancy," said she with a shy air of confession; "now I cannot but wonder and think shame at my blindness, for yon Orpheus has little beyond his music that is any way admirable."

"And that the gift of nature, a thing without his own deserving, like his—like his regard for you, which was inevitable, Mademoiselle Olivia."

"And that the hollowest of all," she said, turning the evidence of it in her pocket again. "He will as readily get over that as over his injury from you."

"Perhaps 'tis so. The most sensitive man, they say, does not place all his existence on love; 'tis woman alone who can live and die in the heart."

"There I daresay you speak from experience," said Olivia, smiling, but impatient that he should find a single plea in favour of a wretch he must know so well.

"Consider me the exception," he hurried to explain. "I never loved but once, and then would die for it." The jasmine trembled in its chaste white nunnery, and her lips were temptingly apart. He bent forward boldly, searching her provoking eyes.

"She is the lucky lady!" said Olivia in a low voice, and then a pause. She trifled with her book. "What I wonder is that you could have a word to say of plea for this that surely is the blackest of his kind."

"Not admirable, by my faith! no, not admirable," he confessed; "but I would be the last to blame him for intemperately loving you. There, I think his honesty was beyond dispute; there he might have found salvation. That he should have done me the honour to desire my removal from your presence was flattering to my vanity, and a savage tribute to your power, Mademoiselle Olivia."

"Oh!" cried Olivia, "you cannot deceive me, Count Victor. It is odd that all your sex must stick up for each other in the greatest villainies."

"Not the greatest, Mademoiselle Olivia," said Count Victor with an inclination; "he might have been indifferent to your charms, and that were the one thing unforgivable. But soberly, I consider his folly scarce bad enough for the punishment of your eternal condemnation."

"This man thinks lightly indeed of me," thought Olivia. "Drimdarroch has a good advocate," said she shortly, "and the last I would have looked for in his defence was just yourself."

"Drimdarroch?" he repeated, in a puzzled tone.

"Will you be telling me that you do not know?" she said. "For what did Simon MacTaggart harass our household?"

"I have been bold enough to flatter myself; I had dared to think—"

She stopped him quickly, blushing. "You know he was Drimdarroch, Count Victor," said she, with some conviction.

He jumped to his feet and bent to stare at her, his face all wrought with astonishment.

"*Mon Dieu!* Mademoiselle, you do not say the two were one? And yet—and yet—yes, *pardieu!* how blind I have been; there is every possibility."

"I thought you knew it," said Olivia, much relieved, "and felt anything but pleased at your seeming readiness in the circumstances to let me be the victim of my ignorance. I had too much of trust in the wretch."

"Women distrust men too much in the general and too little in particular. And you knew?" asked Count Victor.

262

"I learned today," said Olivia, "and this was my bitter schooling."

She passed him the letter. He took it and read aloud:

"I have learned now," said the writer, "the reason for your black looks at Monsher the wine merchant that has a Nobleman's Crest upon his belongings. It is because he has come to look for Drimdarroch. And the stupid body cannot find him! *We* know who Drimdarroch is, do we not, Sim? Monsher may have sharp eyes, but they do not see much further than a woman's face if the same comes in his way. And Simon MacTaggart (they're telling me) has been paying late visits to Doom Castle that were not for the love of Miss Milk-and-Water. Sim! Sim! I gave you credit for being less o' a Gomeral. To fetch the Frenchman to my house of all places! You might be sure he would not be long among our Indwellers here without his true business being discovered. Drimdarroch, indeed! Now I will hate the name, though I looked with a difference on it when I wrote it scores of times to your direction in the Rue Dauphine of Paris, and loved to dwell upon a picture of the place there that I had never seen, because my Sim (just fancy it!) was there. You were just a Wee Soon with the title, my dear Traitor, my bonny Spy. It might have been yours indeed, and more if you had patience, yes perhaps and Doom forby, as that is like to be my goodman's very speedily. What if I make trouble, Sim, and open the eyes of Monsher and the mim-mou'ed Madame at the same moment by telling them who is really Drimdarroch? Will it no' gar them Grue, think ye?"

Count Victor stood amazed when he had read this. A confusion of feelings were in his breast. He had blundered blindly into his long-studied reprisals whose inadequate execution he was now scarce willing to regret, and Olivia had thought him capable of throwing her to this colossal rogue! The document shook in his hand.

"Well?" said Olivia at last. "Is it a much blacker man that is there than the one you thought? I can tell you I will count it a disgrace to my father's daughter that she ever looked twice the road he was on."

"And yet I can find it in me to forgive him the balance of his punishment," cried the Count.

"And what for might that be?" said she.

"Because, Mademoiselle Olivia, he led me to Scotland and to your father's door."

She saw a rapture in his manner, a kindling in his eye, and drew herself together with some pride.

"You were welcome to my father's door—I am sure of that of it, whatever," said she; "but it was a poor reward for so long a travelling. And now, my grief! We must steep the withies and go ourselves to the start of fortune like any beggars."

"No! no!" said he, and caught her hand that trembled in his like a bird. "Olivia!—oh, God, the name is like a song—*je t'aime! je t'aime!* Olivia, I love you!"

She plucked her hand away and threw her shoulders back, haughty, yet trembling and on the brink of tears.

"It is not kind—it is not kind," she stammered, almost sobbing. "The lady that is in France—"

"*Petite imbecile!*" he cried, "there is no lady in France worthy to hold thy scarf. 'Twas thyself, *mignonne*, I spoke of all the time; only, the more I love the less I can express."

He drew her to him, crushing the jasmine till it breathed in a fragrant dissolution, bruising her breast with the topaz.

XXXVII

The Futile Flageolet

But Simon MacTaggart did not pipe wholly in vain. If Olivia was unresponsive, there was one at least in Doom who was his, whole-heartedly, and Mungo, when the flageolet made its vain appeal, felt a personal injury that the girl should subject his esteemed impersonation of all the manly graces and virtues—so to call them—to the insult of indifference.

As the melodies succeeded each other without a sign of response from overhead, he groaned, and swore with vexation and anger.

"Ye can be bummin' awa' wi' your chanter," he said as he stood listening in the kitchen. "Her leddyship wadnae hae ye playin' there lang your lane a saison syne, but thae days is done wi'; there's nae lugs for a tirlin' at the winnock whaur there's nae love—at least wi' Mistress Leevie."

Annapla heard the music with a superstitious terror: her eyes threatened to leap out of her head, and she clutched the arm of her adorer.

"Gae 'wa'!" he told her, shaking her off with a contempt for her fears. "Are ye still i' the daft Hielan' notion that it's a ghaist that's playin' there? That was a story he made up himsel', and the need for 't 's done. There's naethin' waur nor Sim MacTaggart oot there i' the gairden, wastin' his wund on a wumman that's owre muckle ta'en up i' the noo wi' the whillywhaes o' a French sneckdrawer that haesnae the smeddum to gi'e her a toozlin' at the 'oor she needs it maist. Ay, ay! caw awa' wi' yer chanter, Sim, ye'll play hooly and fairly ere ever ye play 't i' the lug o' Leevie Lamond, and her heid against your shouther again."

When it seemed at last the player's patience was at an end, the little servitor took a lamp and went to the door. He drew the bolts softly, prepared to make a cautious emergence, with a recollection of his warm reception before. He was to have a great surprise, for there stood Simon MacTaggart leaning against the jamb—a figure of dejection!

"Dod!" cried Mungo, "ye fair started me there, wi' your chafts like clay and yer een luntin'. If I hadnae been tauld when I was doon wi' yer coat the day that ye was oot and aboot again, I wad hae taen 't for your wraith."

The Chamberlain said nothing. There was something inexpressibly solemn in his aspect as he leaned wearily against the side of the door, his face like clay, as Mungo had truly said, and his eyes flaming in the light of the lantern. The flageolet was in his hand: he was shivering with cold. And he was silent. The silence of him was the most staggering fact for the little domestic, who would have been relieved to hear an oath, or even have given his coat-collar to a vigorous shaking, rather than be compelled to look on misery inarticulate. Simon looked past him into the shadows of the hall as a beggar looks into a garden where is no admission for him or his kind. A fancy seized Mungo that perhaps this dumb man had been drinking. "He's gey like a man on the ran-dan," he said to himself, peering curiously, "but he never had a name for the glass though namely for the lass."

"Is she in?" said the Chamberlain suddenly, without changing his attitude, and with scanty interest in his eyes.

"Oh ay! She's in, sure enough," said Mungo. "Whaur else wad she be but in?"

"And she'll have heard me?" continued the Chamberlain.

"I'll warrant ye!" said Mungo.

"What's wrong?"

Mungo pursed out his lips and shook his lantern. "Ye can be askin' that," says he. "Gude kens!"

The Chamberlain still leaned wearily against the door-jamb, mentally whelmed by dejection, bodily weak as water. His ride on a horse along the coast had manifestly not been the most fitting exercise for a man new out of bed and the hands of his physician.

266

"What about the foreigner?" said he at length, and glowered the more into the interior as if he might espy him.

Mungo was cautious. This was the sort of person who on an impulse would rush the guard and create a commotion in the garrison: he temporised.

"The foreigner?" said he, as if there were so many in his experience that some discrimination was called for. "Oh ay, the Coont. A gey queer birkie yon! He's no awa' yet. He's sittin' on his dowp yet, waitin' a dispensation o' Providence that'll gie him a heeze somewhere else."

"Is—he—is he with her?" said Simon.

"Oh thereaboots, thereaboots," admitted Mungo, cautiously. "There's nae doot they're gey and chief got sin' he cam' back, and she foun' oot wha created the collieshangie."

"Ay, man, and she kens that?" said the Chamberlain with unnatural calm.

" 'Deed does she, brawly! though hoo she kens is mair nor I can guess. Monsher thrieps it wasnae him, and I'll gie my oath it wasnae me."

"Women are kittle cattle, Mungo. There's whiles I think it a peety the old law against witchcraft was not still to the fore. And so she kent, did she? and nobody tell't her. Well, well!" He laughed softly, with great bitterness.

Mungo turned the lantern about in his hand and had nothing to say.

"What's this I'm hearing about the Baron—the Baron and her—and her, leaving?" said the Chamberlain.

"It's the gude's truth that," said the little man; "and for the oots and ins o't ye'll hae to ask Petullo doon-by, for he's at the root o't. Doom's done wi'; it's his decreet, and I'm no' a day ower soon wi' the promise o' the Red Sodger—for the which I'm muckle obleeged to you, Factor. Doom's done; they're gaun awa' in a week or twa, and me and Annapla's to be left ahint to steek the yetts."

"So they tell me, Mungo; so they tell me," said the Chamberlain, neither up nor down at this corroboration. "In a week or twa! ay! ay! It'll be the bower nae langer then," he went on, unconsciously mimicking the Lowland Scots of the domestic. "Do ye ken the auld sang?—

> 'O Bessie Bell and Mary Gray,
> They were twa bonnie lassies!
> They bigged a bower on yon burn-brae,
> And theekit it o'er wi' rashes.' "

He lilted the air with indiscreet indifference to being heard within; and "Wheesh! man, wheesh!" expostulated Mungo. "If himsel' was to ken o' me colloguing wi' ye at the door at this 'oor o' the nicht, there wad be Auld Hornie to pay."

"Oh! there's like to be that the ways it is," said the Chamberlain, never lifting his shoulder from the door-post, beating his leg with the flageolet, and in all with the appearance of a casual gossip reluctant to be going. "Indeed, and by my troth! there's like to be that!" he repeated. "Do ye think, by the look of me, Mungo, I'm in a pleasant condition of mind?"

"Faith and ye look gey gash, sir," said Mungo; "there's no denyin' that of it."

The Chamberlain gave a little crackling laugh, and held the flageolet like a dirk, flat along the inside of his arm and his fingers straining round the thick of it.

"Gash!" said he. "That's the way I feel. By God! Ye fetched down my coat today. It was the first hint I had that this damned dancing-master was here, for he broke jyle: who would have guessed he was fool enough to come here, where—if we were in the key for it—we could easily set hands on him? He must have stolen the coat out of my own room; but that's no' all of it, for there was a letter in the pocket of it when it disappeared. What was in the letter I am fair beat to remember, but I know that it was of some importance to myself, and of a solemn secrecy, and it has not come back with the coat."

Mungo was taken aback at this, but to acknowledge he had seen the letter at all would be to blunder.

268

"A letter!" said he; "there was nae letter that I saw:" and he concluded that he must have let it slip out of the pocket.

The Chamberlain for the first time relinquished the support of the doorway, and stood upon his legs, but his face was more dejected than ever.

"That settles it," said he, filling his chest with air. "I had a small hope that maybe it might have come into your hands without the others seeing it, but that was expecting too much of a Frenchman. And the letter's away with it! My God! Away with it!

'. . . Bigged a bower on yon burn-brae,
And theekit it o'er wi' rashes!' "

"For gudesake!" said Mungo, terrified again at this mad lilting from a man who had anything but song upon his countenance.

"You're sure ye didnae see the letter?" asked the Chamberlain again.

"Amn't I tellin' ye?" said Mungo.

"It's a pity," said the Chamberlain, staring at the lantern, with eyes that saw nothing. "In that case ye need not wonder that her ladyship in-by should ken all, for I'm thinking it was a very informing bit letter, though the exact wording of it has slipped my recollection. It would be expecting over much of human nature to think that the foreigner would keep his hands out of the pouch of a coat he stole, and keep any secret he found there to himself. I'm saying, Mungo!"

"Yes, sir?"

"Somebody's got to sweat for this!"

There was so much venom in the utterance and such a frenzy in the eye that Mungo started: before he could find a comment the Chamberlain was gone.

His horse was tethered to a thorn; he climbed wearily into the saddle and swept along the coast. At the hour of midnight his horse was stabled, and he himself was whistling in the rear of Petullo's house, a signal the woman there had thought never to hear again.

269

She responded in a joyful whisper from a window, and came down a few minutes later with her head in a capuchin hood.

"Oh, Sim! dear, is it you indeed? I could hardly believe my ears."

He put down the arms she would throw about his neck and held her wrists, squeezing them till she almost screamed with pain. He bent his face down to stare into her hood; even in the darkness she saw a plain fury in his eyes: if there was a doubt about his state of mind, the oath he uttered removed it.

"What do you want with me?" she gasped, struggling to free her hands.

"You sent me a letter on the morning of the ball?" said he, a little relaxing his grasp, yet not altogether releasing her prisoned hands.

"Well, if I did!" said she.

"What was in it?" he asked.

"Was it not delivered to you? I did not address it nor did I sign it, but I was assured you got it."

"That I got it has nothing to do with the matter, woman. What I want to know is what was in it?"

"Surely you read it?" said she.

"I read it a score of times——"

"My dear Sim!"

"——And cursed two score of times, as far as I remember; but what I am asking now is what was in it?"

Mrs Petullo began to weep softly, partly from the pain of the man's unconsciously cruel grasp, partly from disillusion, partly from a fear that she had to do with a mind deranged.

"Oh, Sim, have you forgotten already? It did not use to be that with a letter of mine!"

He flung away her hands and swore again.

"Oh, Kate Cameron," he cried, "damned black was the day I first clapt eyes on you! Tell me this, did your letter, that was through all my dreams when I was in the fever of my wound, and yet that I cannot recall a sentence of, say you knew I was Drimdarroch? It is in my mind that it did so."

"Black the day you saw me, Sim!" said she. "I'm thinking it is just the other way about, my honest man. Drimdarroch! And spy, it seems, and something worse! And are you feared that I have clyped it all to Madame Milk-and-Water? No, Simon, I have not done that; I have gone about the thing another way."

"Another way," said he. "I think I mind you threatened it before myself, and Doom is to be rouped at last to pleasure a wanton woman."

"A wanton woman! Oh, my excellent tutor! My best respects to my old dominie! I'll see day about with you for this!"

"Day about!" said he. "My good sweet-tempered Kate! You need not fash—your hand is played; your letter trumped the trick, and I am done. If that does not please your ladyship, you are ill to serve. And I would not just be saying that the game is finished altogether even yet, so long as I know where to lay my fingers on the Frenchman."

She plucked her hands free, and ran from him without another word, glad for once of the sanctuary of a husband's door.

271

XXXVIII

A Warning

Petullo was from home. It was in such circumstances she found her bondage least intolerable. Now she was to find his absence more than a pleasant respite—it gave her an opportunity of warning Doom. She had scarce made up her mind how he should be informed of the jeopardies that menaced his guest, whose skaithless departure with Olivia was even, from her point of view, a thing wholly desirable, when the Baron appeared himself. It was not on the happiest of errands he came down on the first day of favouring weather; it was to surrender the last remnant of his right to the home of his ancestors. With the flourish of a quill he brought three centuries of notable history to a close.

"Here's a lesson in humility, Mr Campbell," said he to Petullo's clerk. "We builded with the sword, and fell upon the sheepskin. Who would think that so foolish a bird as the grey goose would have Doom and its generations in its wing?"

He had about his shoulders a plaid that had once been of his tartan, but had undergone the degradation of the dye-pot for a foolish and tyrannical law: he threw it round him with a dignity that was half defiance, and cast his last glance round the scene of his sorriest experiences—the dusty writing-desks, the confusion of old letters, the taped and dog-eared, fouled, and forgotten records of pithy causes; and, finally, at the rampart of deed-chests, one of which had the name "Drimdarroch" blazoned on it for remembrance if he had been in danger of forgetting.

"And is it yourself, Baron?" cried a woman's voice as he turned to go. "I am so sorry my husband is from home."

He turned again with his hat off for the lady who had an influence on his fate that he could never guess of.

"It is what is left of me, ma'am," said he. "And it is more than is like to be seen of me in these parts for many a day to come," but with no complaint in his expression.

"Ah," said she, "I know; I know! and I am so sorry. You cannot leave today of any day without a glass of wine for *deoch-an-doruis.*"

"I thank you, ma'am," said Doom, "but my boat is at the quay, and Mungo waits for me."

"But, indeed, you must come in, Baron," she insisted. "There is something of the greatest importance I have to say to you, and it need not detain you ten minutes."

He followed her upstairs to her parlour. It was still early in the day and there was something of the slattern in her dragging gown. As he walked behind her, the remembrance would intrude of that betraying letter, and he had the notion that perhaps she somehow knew he shared her shameful secret. Nor was the idea dispelled when she stopped and faced him in the privacy of her room with her eyes swollen and a trembling under-lip.

"And it has come to this of it, Baron?" said she.

"It has come to this," said Doom simply.

"I cannot tell you how vexed I am. But you know my husband. . . ."

"I have the honour, ma'am," said he, bowing with an old-fashioned inclination.

". . . You know my husband, a hard man, Baron, though I perhaps should be the last to say it, and I have no say in his business affairs."

"Which is doubtless proper enough," said Doom, and thought of an irony breeding forbade him to give utterance to.

"But I must tell you I think it is a scandal you should have to go from the place of your inheritance; and your sweet girl too! I hope and trust she is in good health and spirits?"

"My good girl is very well," said he, "and with some reason for cheerfulness in spite of our misfortunes. As for them, ma'am, I am old enough to have seen and known a sufficiency of ups and downs, of flux and change, to wonder at none of them.

I am not going to say that what has come to me is the most joco of happenings for a person like myself that has more than ordinary of the sentimentalist in me, and is bound to be wrapped up in the countryside hereabouts. But the tail may go with the hide, as the saying runs. Doom, that's no more than a heartbreak of memories and an empty shell, may very well join Duntorvil and Drimdarroch and the Islands of Lochow, that have dribbled through the courts of what they call the law and left me scarcely enough to bury myself in another country than my own."

Mrs Petullo was not, in truth, wholly unmoved, but it was the actress in her wrung her hands.

"I hear you are going abroad," she cried. "That must be the hardest thing of all."

"I am not complaining, ma'am," said Doom.

"No, no; but oh! it is so sad, Baron—and your dear girl too, so sweet and nice—"

The Baron grew impatient; the "something of importance" was rather long of finding an expression, and he took the liberty of interrupting.

"Quite so, ma'am," said he, "but there was something in particular you had to tell me. Mungo, as I mentioned, is waiting me at the quay, and time presses, for we have much to do before we leave next week."

A look of relief came to Mrs Petullo's face.

"Next week!" she cried. "Oh then, that goes far to set my mind at ease." Some colour came to her cheeks; she trifled with a handkerchief. "What I wished to say, Baron, was that your daughter and—and—and the French gentleman, with whom we are glad to hear she is like to make a match of it, could not be away from this part of the country a day too soon. I overheard a curious thing the other day, it is only fair I should tell you, for it concerns your friend the French gentleman, and it was that Simon MacTaggart knew the Frenchman was back in your house and threatened trouble. There may be nothing in it, but I would not put it past the same person, who is capable of any wickedness."

"It is not the general belief, ma'am," said the Baron, "but I'll take your word for it, and, indeed, I have long had my own suspicions. Still, I think the same gentleman has had his wings so recently clipped that we need not be much put about at his threats."

"I have it on the best authority that he broods mischief," said she.

"The best authority," repeated Doom, with never a doubt as to what that was. "Well, it may be, but I have no fear of him. Once, I'll confess, he troubled me, but the man is now no more than a rotten kail-stock so far as my household is concerned. I thank God that Olivia is happy!"

"And so do I, I'm sure, with all my heart," chimed in the lady. "And that is all the more reason why the Count—you see we know his station—should be speedily out of the way of molestation, either from the law or Simon MacTaggart."

Doom made to bring the interview to a conclusion. "As to the Count," said he, "you can take my word for it, he is very well able to look after himself, as Drimdarroch, or MacTaggart, or whatever is the Chamberlain's whim to call himself, knows very well by now. Drimdarroch, indeed! I could be kicking him myself for his fouling of an honest old name."

"Kicking!" said she; "I wonder at your leniency. I cannot but think you are far from knowing the worst of Simon MacTaggart."

"The worst!" said Doom. "That's between himself and Hell, but I know as much as most, and it's enough to make me sure the man's as boss as an empty barrel. He was once a sort of friend of mine, till twenty years ago my wife grew to hate the very mention of his name. Since then I've seen enough of him at a distance to read the plausible rogue in his very step. The man wears every bawbee virtue he has like a brooch in his bonnet; and now when I think of it, I would not dirty my boots with him."

Mrs Petullo's lips parted. She hovered a second or two on a disclosure that explained the wife's antipathy of twenty years ago, but it involved confession of too intimate a footing on her own part with the Chamberlain, and she said no more.

275

XXXIX

Betrayed by a Ballad

Some days passed and a rumour went about the town, in its
origin as undiscoverable as the birthplace of the winds. It
engaged the seamen on the tiny trading vessels at the quay, and
excited the eagerest speculation in Ludovic's inn. Women put
down their water-stoups at the wells and shook mysterious
heads over hints of Sim MacTaggart's history. No one for a
while had a definite story, but in all the innuendoes the Chamberlain figured vaguely as an evil influence. That he had slain a
man in some parts abroad was the first and the least astonishing
of the crimes laid to his charge, though the fact that he had never
made a brag of it was counted sinister; but, by-and-by, surmise
and sheer imagination gave place to a commonly accepted tale
that Simon had figured in divers escapades in France with the
name Drimdarroch; that he had betrayed men and women there,
and that the Frenchman had come purposely to Scotland seeking
for him. It is the most common of experiences that the world
will look for years upon a man admiringly and still be able to
recall a million things to his discredit when he is impeached with
some authority. It was so in this case. The very folks who had
loved best to hear the engaging flageolet, feeling the springs of
some nobility bubble up in them at the bidding of its player, and
drunk with him and laughed with him and ever esteemed his
free gentility, were the readiest to recall features of his character
and incidents of his life that—as they put it—ought to have set
honest men upon their guard. The tale went seaward on the
gabbarts, and landward, even to Lorn itself, upon carriers' carts
and as the richest part of the packman's budget. Furthermore,
a song or two were made upon the thing, that even yet old
women can recall in broken stanzas, and of one of these, by far

276

the best informed, Petullo's clerk was the reputed author.

As usual, the object of the scandal was for a while uncon-scious. He went about experiencing a new aloofness in his umquhile friends, and finally concluded that it was due to his poor performance in front of the foreigner on the morning of the ball, and that but made him the more venomously ruminant upon revenge. In these days he haunted the avenues like a spirit, brooding on his injuries, pondering the means of a retaliation: there were no hours of manumission in the inn; the reed was still. And yet, to do him justice, there was even then the frank and suave exterior; no boorish awkward silence in his ancient gossips made him lose his jocularity; he continued to embellish his conversation with morals based on universal kindness and goodwill.

At last the thunder broke, for the scandal reached the castle, and was there overheard by the Duchess in a verse of the ballad sung under her window by a gardener's boy. She made some inquiries, and thereafter went straight to her husband.

"What is this I hear about your Chamberlain?" she asked.

Argyll drew down his brows and sighed. "My Chamberlain?" said he. "It must be something dreadful by the look of her Grace the Duchess. What is it this time? High treason, or marriage, or the need of it? Or has old Knapdale died by a blessed disposition and left him a fortune? That would save me the performance of a very unpleasant duty."

"It has gone the length of scurrilous songs about our worthy gentleman. The town has been ringing with scandals about him for a week, and I never heard a word about it till half an hour ago."

"And so you feel defrauded, my dear, which is natural enough, being a woman as well as a duchess. I am glad to know that so squalid a story should be so long of reaching your ears: had it been anything to anybody's credit you would have been the first to learn of it. To tell the truth, I've heard the song myself, and if I have seemed unnaturally engaged for a day or two it is because I have been in a quandary as to what I should do. Now

277

that you know the story, what do you advise, my dear?"

"A mere woman must leave that to the Lord Justice General," she replied. "And now that your Chamberlain turns out a greater scamp than I thought him, I'm foolish enough to be sorry for him."

"And so am I," said the Duke, and looked about the shelves of books lining the room. "Here's a multitude of counsellors; a great deal of the world's wisdom so far as it has been reduced to print, and I'll swear I could go through it from end to end without learning how I should judge a problem like Sim MacTaggart."

She would have left him then, but he stopped her with a smiling interrogation. "Well?" he said.

She waited.

"What about the customary privilege?" he went on.

"What is that?"

"Why, you have not said 'I told you so.'"

She smiled at that. "How stupid of me!" said she. "Oh! but you forgave my Frenchman, and for that I owe you some consideration."

"Did I, faith?" said he. "'Twas mighty near the compounding of a felony, a shocking lapse in a Justice General. To tell the truth, I was only too glad, in MacTaggart's interest, while he was ill, to postpone disclosures so unpleasant as are now the talk of the country; and, like you, I find him infinitely worse in these disclosures than I guessed."

The Duchess went away; the Duke grew grave, reflecting on his duty. What it clearly was he had not decided until it was late in the evening, and then he sent for his Charmberlain.

XL

The Day of Judgment

Simon went to the library and saw plainly that the storm was come.

"Sit down, Simon, sit down," said his Grace, and carefully sharpened a pen.

The Chamberlain subsided in a chair; crossed his legs; made a mouth as if to whistle. There was a vexatious silence in the room till the Duke got up and stood against the chimney-piece and spoke.

"Well," said he, "I could be taking a liberty with the old song and singing 'Roguery Parts Good Company' if I were not, so far as music goes, as timber as the table there and in anything but a key for music even if I had the faculty. Talking about music, you have doubtless not heard the ingenious ballant connected with your name and your exploits. It has been the means of informing her Grace upon matters I had preferred she knew nothing about, because I like to have the women I regard believe the world much better than it is. And it follows that you and I must bring our long connection to an end. When will it be most convenient for my Chamberlain to send me his resignation after 'twelve years of painstaking and intelligent service to the Estate,' as we might be saying on the customary silver salver?"

Simon cursed within but outwardly never quailed.

"I know nothing about a ballant," said he coolly, "but as for the rest of it, I thank God I can be taking a hint as ready as the quickest. Your Grace no doubt has reasons. And I'll make bold to say the inscription it is your humour to suggest would not be anyway extravagant, for the twelve years have been painstaking enough, whatever about their intelligence, of which I must not be the judge myself."

"So far as that goes, sir," said the Duke, "you have been a pattern. And it is your gifts that make your sins the more heinous: a man of a more sluggish intelligence might have had the ghost of an excuse for failing to appreciate the utmost loathsomeness of his sins."

"Oh! by the Lord Harry, if it is to be a sermon—!" cried Simon, jumping to his feet.

"Keep your chair, sir! keep your chair like a man!" said the Duke. "I am thinking you know me well enough to believe there is none of the common moralist about me. I leave the preaching to those with a better conceit of themselves than I could afford to have of my indifferent self. No preaching, cousin, no preaching, but just a word among friends, even if it were only to explain the reason for our separation."

The Chamberlain resumed his chair defiantly and folded his arms.

"I'll be cursed if I see the need for all this preamble," said he; "but your Grace can fire away. It need never be said that Simon MacTaggart was feared to account for himself when the need happened."

"Within certain limitations, I daresay that is true," said the Duke.

"I aye liked a tale to come to a brisk conclusion," said the Chamberlain, with no effort to conceal his impatience.

"This one will be as brisk as I can make it," said his Grace. "Up till the other day I gave you credit for the virtue you claim—the readiness to answer for yourself when the need happened. I was under the delusion that your duel with the Frenchman was the proof of it."

"Oh, damn the Frenchman!" cried the Chamberlain with contempt and irritation. "I am ready to meet the man again with any arm he chooses."

"With any arm!" said the Duke drily. " 'Tis always well to have a whole one, and not one with a festering sore, as on the last occasion. Oh yes," he went on, seeing Simon change colour, "you observe I have learned about the old wound, and, what is more, I know exactly where you got it."

"Your Grace seems to have trustworthy informants," said the Chamberlain less boldly, but in no measure abashed. "I got that wound through your own hand as surely as if you had held the foil that gave it, for the whole of this has risen, as you ought to know, from your sending me to France."

"And that is true, in a sense, my good sophist. But I was, in that, the unconscious and blameless link in your accursed destiny. I had you sent to France on a plain mission. It was not, I make bold to say, a mission on which the Government would have sent any man but a shrewd one and a gentleman, and I was mad enough to think Simon MacTaggart was both. When you were in Paris as our agent—"

"Fah!" cried Simon, snapping his fingers and drawing his face in a grimace. "Agent, quo' he! for God's sake take your share of it and say spy and be done with it!"

The Duke shrugged his shoulders, listening patiently to the interruption. "As you like," said he. "Let us say spy, then. You were to learn what you could of the Pretender's movements, and incidentally you were to intromit with certain of our settled agents at Versailles. Doubtless a sort of espionage was necessary to the same. But I make bold to say the duty was no ignoble one so long as it was done with some sincerity and courage, for I count the spy in an enemy's country as engaged upon the gallantest enterprise of war, using the shrewdness that alone differs the quarrel of the man from the fury of the beast, and himself the more admirable because his task is a thousand times more dangerous than if he fought with the claymore in the field."

"Doubtless! doubtless!" said the Chamberlain. "That's an old tale between the two of us, but you should hear the other side upon it."

"No matter; we gave you the credit and the reward of doing your duty as you engaged, and yet you mixed the business up with some extremely dirty work no sophistry of yours or mine will dare defend. You took our money, MacTaggart—and you sold us! Sit down, sit down and listen like a man! You sold us—

there's the long and the short of it; and you sold our friends at Versailles to the very people you were sent yourself to act against. Countersap with a vengeance! We know now where Bertin got his information. You betrayed us and the woman Cécile Favart in the one filthy transaction."

The Chamberlain showed in his face that the blow was home. His mouth broke, and he grew as grey as a rag.

"And that's the way of it?" he said, after a moment's silence.

"That's the way of it," said the Duke. "She was as much the agent—let us say the spy, then—as you were yourself, and seems to have brought more cunning to the trade than did our simple Simon himself. If her friend Montaiglon had not come here to look for you, and thereby put us on an old trail we had abandoned, we would never have guessed the source of her information."

"I'll be cursed if I have a dog's luck!" cried Simon.

Argyll looked pityingly at him. "So!" said he. "You mind our old country saying, *Ni droch dhuine dàn da féin*—a bad man makes his own fate?"

"Do you say so?" cried MacTaggart, with his first sign of actual insolence, and the Duke sighed.

"My good Simon," said he, "I do not require to tell you so, for you know it very well. What I would add is that all I have said is, so far as I am concerned, between ourselves: that's my only tribute to our old acquaintanceship. Only I can afford to have no more night escapades at Doom or anywhere else with my fencibles, and so, Simon, the resignation cannot be a day too soon."

"Heaven forbid that I should delay it a second longer than is desirable, and your Grace has it here and now! A fine *fracas* all this about a puddock-eating Frenchman! I do not value him nor his race to the extent of a pin. And as for your Grace's Chamberlain—well, Simon MacTaggart has done very well hitherto on his own works and merits."

"You may find, for all that," said his Grace, "that they were all summed up in a few words—'he was a far-out cousin to the Duke.' *Sic itur ad astra.*"

At that Simon put on his hat and laughed with an eerie and unpleasant stridency. He never said another word, but left the room. The sound of his unnatural merriment rang on the stair as he descended.

"The man is fey," said the Duke to himself, listening with a startled gravity.

XLI

Dawn

Simon MacTaggart went out possessed by the devils of hatred and chagrin. He saw himself plainly for what he was in truth— a pricked bladder, his career come to an ignoble conclusion, the single honest scheme he had ever set his heart on brought to nought, and his vanity already wounded sorely at the prospect of a contemptuous world to be faced for the remainder of his days. All this from the romantics of a Frenchman who walked through life in the step of a polonaise, and a short season ago was utterly unaware that such a man as Simon MacTaggart existed, or that a woman named Olivia bloomed, a very flower, among the wilds! At whatever angle he viewed the congregated disasters of the past few weeks he saw Count Victor in their background—a sardonic, smiling, light-hearted Nemesis; and if he detested him previously as a merely possible danger, he hated him now with every fibre of his being as the cause of this upheaval.

And then, in his way, that is not uncommon with the sinner, he must pity himself because circumstances had so consistently conspired against him.

He had come into the garden after the interview with Argyll had made it plain that the darkest passages in his servant's history were known to him, and had taken off his hat to get the night breeze on his brow which was wet with perspiration. The snow was still on the ground; among the laden bushes, the silent soaring trees of fir and ash, it seemed as if this was no other than the land of outer darkness whereto the lost are driven at the end. It maddened him to think of what he had been brought to: he shook his fist in a childish and impotent petulance at the spacious unregarding east where Doom lay—the scene of all his passions.

"God's curse on the breed of meddlers!" he said. "Another month and I was out of these gutters, and Hell no more to tempt me. To be the douce goodman, and all the tales of storm forgotten by the neighbours that may have kent them; to sit perhaps with bairns—her bairns and mine—about my knee, and never a twinge of the old damnable inclinations, and the flageolet going to the honestest tunes. All lost! All lost for a rat that takes to the hold of an infernal ship, and comes here to chew at the ropes that dragged me to salvation. This is where it ends! It's the judgment come a day ower soon for Sim MacTaggart. But Sim MacTaggart will make the rat rue his meddling."

He had come out with no fixed idea of what he next should do, but one step seemed now imperative—he must go to Doom, otherwise his blood would burst every vein in his body. He set forth with the stimulus of fury for the barracks where his men lay, of whom half-a-dozen at least were his to the gate of the Pit itself, less scrupulous even than himself because more ignorant, possessed of but one or two impulses—a foolish affection for him and an inherited regard for rapine too rarely to be indulged in these tame latter days. To call them out, to find them armed and ready for any enterprise of his, was a matter of brief time. They set out knowing nothing at all of his object, and indifferent so long as this adorable gentleman was to lead them.

When they came to Doom the tide was full and round about it, so they retired upon the hillside, sheltering in a little plantation of fir through which they could see the stars, and Doom dense black against them without a sign of habitation.

And yet Doom, upon the side that faced the sea, was not asleep. Mungo was busy upon the preparations for departure, performing them in a funereal spirit, whimpering about the vacant rooms with a grief that was trivial compared with that of Doom himself, who waited for the dawn as if it were to bring him to the block, or of Olivia, whose pillow was wet with unavailing tears. It was their last night in Doom. At daybreak Mungo was to convey them to the harbour, where they should embark upon the vessel that was to bear them to the Lowlands.

It seemed as if the seagulls came earlier than usual to wheel and cry about the rock, half-guessing that it was so soon to be untenanted, and finally, as it is today, the grass-grown mound of memories. Olivia rose and went to her window to look out at them, and saw them as yet but vague, grey, floating shapes slanting against the paling stars.

And then the household rose; the boat nodded to the leeward of the rock, with its mast stepped, its sail billowing with a rustle in the faint air, and Mungo at the sheet. The dawn came slowly, but fast enough for the departing, and the landward portion of the rock was still in shadow when Olivia stepped forth with a tear-stained face, and a trembling hand on Victor's arm. He shared her sorrow, but was proud and happy too that her trials, as he hoped, were over. They took their seat in the boat and waited for the Baron. Now the tide was down, the last of it running in tiny rivulets upon the sand between the mainland and the rock, and Simon and his gang came over silently. Simon led, and turned the corner of the tower hastily with his sword in his hand to find the Baron emerging. He had not seen the boat and its occupants, but the situation seemed to flash upon him, and he uttered a cry of rage.

Doom drew back under the frowning eyebrow of what had been his home, tugged the weapon from his scabbard, and threw himself on guard.

"This is kind, indeed," he said in a pause of his assailant's confusion at finding this was not the man he sought. "You have come to say 'Goodbye.' On guard, black dog, on guard!"

"*So dhuit mata!*—here then is for you," cried Sim, and waving back his followers, engaged with a rasp of steel. It lasted but a moment: Doom crouched a little upon bending knees, with a straight arm, parrying the assault of a point that flew in wild disorder. He broke ground for a few yards with feints in quarte. He followed on a riposte with a lunge—short, sharp, conclusive, for it took his victim in the chest and passed through at the other side with a thud of the hilt against his body. Sim fell with a groan, his company clustering round him, not wholly forgetful of retaliation, but influenced by his hand that forbade their interference with his enemy.

"Clean up your filth!" said Doom in the Gaelic, sheathing his sword and turning to join his daughter. "He took Drimdarroch from me, and now, by God! he's welcome to Doom."

"Not our old friends, surely?" said Count Victor, looking backward at the cluster of men.

"The same," said Doom, and kept his counsel further.

Count Victor put his arm round Olivia's waist. The boat's prow fell off; the sail filled; she ran with a pleasant ripple through the waves, and there followed her a cry that only Doom of all the company knew was a coronach, followed by the music of Sim MacTaggart's flageolet.

It rose above the ripple of the waves, above the screaming of the birds, finally stilling the coronach, and the air it gave an utterance to was the same that had often charmed the midnight bower, failing at the last abruptly as it had always done before.

"By heavens! it is my Mary's favourite air, and that was all she knew of it," said Doom, and his face grew white with memory and a speculation.

"Had he found the end of that air," said Count Victor, "he had found, as he said himself, another man. But I, perhaps, had never found Olivia!"